STILLNESS OF TIME

Stillness of Time

J.M. Buckler

Stillness of Time

First Edition: March 2018
Revised Edition: March 2019

Published by: Sojourn Publishing, LLC
Published for: Gratus Publishing, LLC

Visit my website at www.jmbuckler.com
Instagram: author_j.m.buckler

Printed in the United States of America

Paperback ISBN: 978-1-62747-234-0
E-Book ISBN: 978-1-62747-217-3

Edited by: Tiffany White Writers Untapped
Cover Art and Interior Art Illustrated by: Adam Rabalais
Interior Design: Ghislain Viau

To the ones worth fighting for . . .
the ones who aren't afraid to live.

RATINGS ARE NOT REQUIRED FOR BOOKS

Out of respect for my younger and more sensitive readers, please be advised that this book contains the following: adult language, violence, and graphic scenes that some may find disturbing.

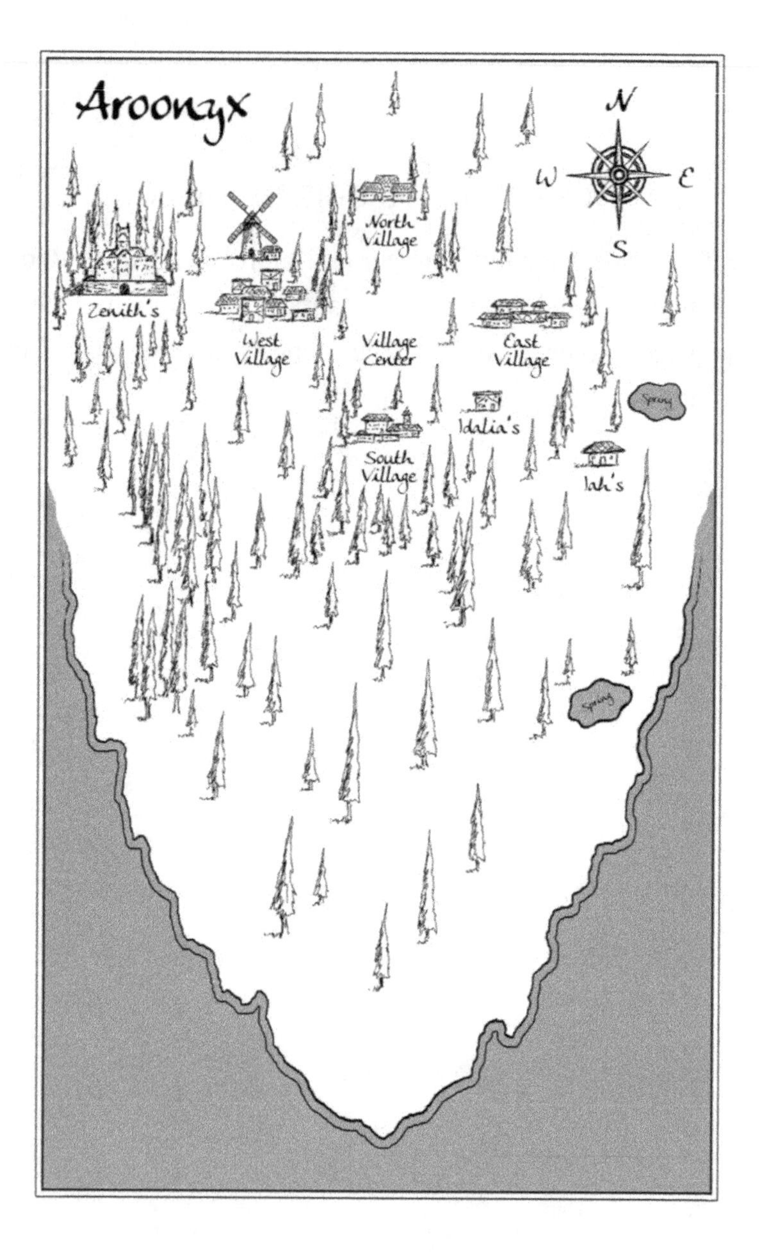
Aroonyx
N
W
E
S
Zenith's
West Village
North Village
Village Center
East Village
Idalia's
South Village
Iah's
Spring
Spring

ONE

Unexpected Visitors

The quiet peacefulness between consciousness and sleep was the last thing I felt before my eyes found Jax. I gasped, inhaling the dry air. My heart pounded in my ears as I stood immobile, unable to release the tight grip I had around the Lunin's rough hand. *We're here—we actually made it to Aroonyx.* My brother let go within an instant, his expression stuck somewhere between wonder and bewilderment.

The three of us remained silent, staring at one another as if seeing each other for the first time. Cyrus stood tall and confident, his Solin courage shining forth. He rolled his broad shoulders and his amber eyes flickered between me and Jax. His short blond hair barely moved in the warm breeze as he let out a small breath.

I glanced at Jax, surprised to find the muscles in his jaw twitching with a look of uncertainty. His usual unfazed demeanor shifted to a more focused, rigid one. The wind blew his jet-black hair into his blue eyes. Carelessly, he brushed it away. I reached with my free hand for the straps of my backpack but frowned when my fingers touched only the narrow sleeves of my shirt.

"I can't believe it worked." Jax sighed as he dropped my hand. "Honestly, I wasn't sure if we'd all make it back."

"What in the hell is that supposed to mean?" Cyrus asked, his amber eyes narrowing on the Lunin. "You told us it would work."

I squeezed my vibrating hands into fists, the heat surging through me.

"Cyrus," Jax said, an irritation lingering in his voice. "Nothing is certain until you experience it to be true. I had a strong intuition that I could return to Aroonyx with you both." He motioned to me and my brother. "But I never tried. It was only natural I had my reservations."

The intense buzzing sensation faded from my palms as I looked at my brother. I nodded my approval of Jax's explanation. He huffed a breath and used the back of his hand to wipe the beads of sweat that formed on his brow.

Jax walked between the two of us, then turned and gestured to the breathtaking landscape that filled our vision.

Our jaws dropped. We stood only feet away from the edge of a tall cliff that overlooked a vast body of water. Its gray waves crashed against the white jagged rocks that decorated the shoreline with determined force. Emerald-green grass covered the top of the cliff like a delicate blanket.

A strong breeze whirled around us, cooling my warm skin. I breathed deeply, filling my lungs with the purest air I had ever inhaled. My head snapped to the opposite end of the steep cliffside, and I was surprised to have only then noticed the enormous trees gathered together, creating a dense forest. The rich, ebony-colored bark was like nothing found on Earth. Sharing Cyrus's powerful Solin eyesight, I observed how it resembled the stem of the Moon Drop: soft and smooth. The bright green leaves, larger than my two hands put together, cast an ominous shadow over the unfamiliar space.

I glanced at my feet, pleased to see my body still intact after our journey while Cyrus spun in circles with his mouth hanging open.

"Jax," I said, whipping around to face him. "During all our conversations about Aroonyx, you never thought it appropriate to mention the beauty of the planet?"

My brother stepped closer to the edge of the cliff. "Seriously. This place doesn't even look real."

A tiny grin crossed the Lunin's face as he walked to where Cyrus stood on the white rock's smooth ledge. He pointed over the water toward the horizon. "I wanted the two of you to see it for yourselves."

With great caution, I scooted closer to the edge. My head spun and vision blurred—my fear of heights taking over. "That's a long way down."

The calluses on Jax's rough palm brushed against my skin when he rested a hand on my shoulder, and in a calm and silky voice, he said, "If you keep your focus on the beauty of everything, the fear will dissolve."

I nodded, absorbing the underlying meaning behind his words. When Jax removed his hand, I stammered, noting the uniquely colored green sky. "It's . . . not blue."

"I mentioned there were a few differences," Jax murmured, hiding his amusement.

Cyrus pointed to the surf. "And the water—it's gray."

"Yes, and it's not an ocean."

Slack jawed, we looked at the Lunin.

"There's no saltwater on Aroonyx." Our eyes widened. Jax waved a hand at the massive body of water. "It only resembles an ocean by its size and movement."

I blinked. "Wait, so it's fresh water, like a giant lake?"

"Yes, and unlike Earth, the water is pure. You need not boil or treat it before drinking."

"Amazing," I said, inching my foot closer to the cliff's edge.

A strong gust of wind rustled the tree branches in the near distance. Inhaling the fresh air once more, I squinted at the persimmon-colored sun that rested high in the cloudless sky.

"What kind of rock is this?" Cyrus asked, jumping up and down on the stone ledge.

My tongue hissed against my teeth, watching chunks fall into the water.

"Sorry, sis."

I flashed him a stern glance. Ignoring me, he bent down and investigated the white stone by rubbing his fingers over the smooth surface.

"It's called Clear Stone."

My brother stretched his neck to look at Jax. "But it's white."

"It only appears that way."

"How so?" I asked, folding my arms across my chest.

Jax reached into his back pocket and retrieved his gray knife. With a flick of his wrist, he exposed the sharp blade.

Cyrus flinched, still sore from their altercation that day at the beach. I giggled at his nervous reaction while Jax scraped the blood-stained blade against the stone. It wasn't long before a pile of white, chalk-like substance appeared. He brushed the dust into one of his hands and brought it closer for Cyrus to inspect.

"It's called Clear Stone because of its unique properties." Jax poured the small heap into my brother's open palm. "Rub your hands together."

"What's going to happen?" Cyrus asked, agreeing to his request.

Jax gave me a smug grin before turning his attention back to the Solin. "Now, open your hands."

Cyrus hesitated, his palms still glued together.

"It won't bite." Jax chuckled.

I laughed, remembering my brother's fear of snakes.

He glared at me and Jax. "Ya'll aren't funny."

"Just open your damn hands," the Lunin demanded.

Cyrus sucked in a sharp breath, and in slow motion exposed his empty palms. "Where did the dust go?" he asked, rotating his wrist.

Bewildered by the disappearing act, I took a knee beside the two men and touched Cyrus's open-faced palm.

Sensing our shared confusion, Jax said, "If you break apart Clear Stone and compact it"—he pinched a bit of the remaining dust that he scraped with his knife—"it disappears." He demonstrated. "You could crush this entire cliffside." Jax motioned to the steep drop. "And it would be like it never existed."

Struggling to digest this interesting fact, Cyrus continued to inspect his hands for traces of the white residue.

"You're not going to find anything," Jax whispered, folding the knife blade back into the handle. "It's gone."

My brother's lips vibrated with a mixture of awe and surrender. Tossing in the towel, he stood and stretched his muscular arms overhead.

A random thought flew into my mind as I reached for Jax's outstretched hand. "Are there any magical creatures on Aroonyx?"

He arched a brow. "Magical?"

"Yeah." I tucked a stray hair behind my ear. "You know like dragons . . . or uni—" I stopped, embarrassed that the inner child had spoken.

Jax shook his head as if I had asked for the impossible, and in a firm tone said, "No. This isn't a fairytale."

I frowned, then snorted when my brother added some flair to the conversation. "No dragons? That's lame. I would have tamed one and flew into the sunset."

Jax rolled his eyes, unamused with Cyrus's witty comment.

"I thought it was funny," I mouthed.

Cyrus winked, offering me a fist bump.

The Lunin let out a long breath as he widened his stance and crossed his toned arms. His blue eyes drifted between me and my brother while he spoke. "I could spend all day, every day, explaining the differences between Earth and Aroonyx. Unfortunately, I don't have the time because the clock started ticking when your feet hit Aroonyx's soil."

His words hit the pit of my stomach like a heavy weight. My parents' faces flashed in my mind. Though minutes had passed since I'd seen them last, already I felt a lifetime away. I tried to swallow, but a giant ball of anxiety formed in my throat when I caught my brother's eye.

Acknowledging my inner turmoil, he looked at Jax. "We need to know if you can take us back to Earth."

The Lunin sighed, running his fingers through his dark hair. "You're right." He reached for our hands. "Now is as good a time as any."

Like he did on the trail, Cyrus grabbed Jax's hand without hesitation. Lacking his Solin courage, I kept my arm glued to my side. *Is this a good idea?* Doubt and uncertainty tapped on the quiet door of my mind.

I directed my attention to the Lunin who offered me his hand. "If you can take us back, do you think it's possible to jump to Aroonyx with us once more?"

"Elara, I can't answer that question. If for some reason, I'm able to take you back to Earth"—my heart sank at the lack of confidence in his voice—"then hopefully, I can repeat the process."

Sucking in a sharp breath, I shut my eyes and reached for his hand. *What the hell?* Only empty space surrounded me. My eyes shot open and my pulse quickened when I saw Jax holding a finger to his mouth—a silent gesture for us to remain quiet.

Looking equally concerned, Cyrus stared at Jax with wide eyes. I strained my ears, listening for sounds other than rustling tree branches and crashing waves.

My lips moved to question the Lunin's behavior but stopped when he jerked his chin at the forest. I stilled. Out of the dense brush walked four men.

Sharing Cyrus's detailed eyesight, I studied their familiar features: tall, white-blond hair, orange eyes, bronze skin—Solins. Even their muscular builds mirrored my brother's physique. The young men moved as one, talking amongst each other while keeping their focus on the ground in front of them.

Without saying a word, Jax crouched down and pointed to a white boulder that rested near the cliff's edge. Before I could blink, he vanished behind the rock.

My brother and I stood with our feet planted in the grass. Jax cursed under his breath at our deer-in-the-headlight expressions, then waved a hand for us to join him. We dashed to his side right before one of the Solins lifted his gaze.

"Jax," I stammered, curious why we hid from strangers.

His quick tongue cut me off. "The two of you are to stay hidden no matter what."

"Why?" I eyed Cyrus, my heart hammering in my chest.

Backing me up, he asked, "What the hell is going on?"

Ignoring our questions, Jax kept his eyes focused on the four men. "I'll use myself as a distraction. Let them chase me into the woods." I shook my head in disagreement, but he went on, "Do not leave this spot until I return. Do I make myself clear?"

Panic consumed me. Jax had never spoken with such authority or severity. I swore. Every muscle in his body tensed. His left hand gripped the rock, his knuckles white. My heart pounded even harder when he reached for the knife in his back pocket.

"I need to hear your compliance," he said, exposing the blade with a flick of his wrist.

I gulped, my mouth drier than the surrounding air.

"We got it," my brother answered for the both of us. "We'll stay put."

"Jax," I managed through half breaths. "Why are we hiding?"

Making his presence known, he stood from behind the rock.

Desperate for an answer, I tugged at his patched pant leg and whispered, "Just tell us. Who are they?"

His blue eyes narrowed at the four Solins, and before he dashed into the unknown, a simple word rolled off his tongue—a word I never wanted to hear. "Collectors."

TWO

Trapped in Time

Instinctively I tried chasing after Jax, but Cyrus's strong grip thwarted my efforts.

"Get down!" he demanded, pulling me behind the large boulder.

I groaned while yanking my arm away from his firm grasp. "Cyrus, we need to go after him."

"No." His fingers tightened around my bicep when I lifted my gaze over the rock. "Stop that. Jax told us to stay here."

"I know what he said," I whispered, brushing away his hand. "But those were four Collectors." I craned my neck once more.

"Elara, get down."

Frustrated, I whipped around and leaned my back against the white stone. Noting my proximity to the cliff's edge, I tucked my knees into my chest and stared at the horizon instead of the vertical drop.

Only a moment passed before I asked, "Can you hear anything?"

Cyrus closed his eyes. The low sound of muffled voices blurred together somewhere in the distance. He shook his head. "I can't make out what they're saying."

A drop of sweat trickled down the side of my face when my lips pressed together. *This is insanity. We're not back for ten minutes and something bad happens.*

My pulse raced as I recalled my conversation with Jax about the Collectors and their advanced combative skills. I looked at my brother. "We need to help him."

"No."

"We can't let him fight off four Collectors."

"He's Jax." Cyrus scoffed at my concerns. "He'll be fine. This is his home turf. He knows how to survive on Aroonyx. We need to listen and . . ."

His words trailed off at the sound of voices yelling and feet moving. Ignoring his request to stay hidden, I spun around and peered over the white stone.

My hand shot to my mouth. *Damn it.* The four Solins sprinted into the dark forest after Jax.

Watching my posture tense, Cyrus grabbed my wrist. "Don't even think about it."

My hands buzzed with heat, the sensation overwhelming me.

"Elara, you've got to calm down. Keep it up and you'll blow our cover."

"I'm sorry." I sighed, turning back around. "It's just—"

"I know." His amber eyes filled with compassion and understanding. "It's a lot to digest, but we're here now." He motioned to the surrounding space. "We haven't a clue how this world works, so we need to stay together."

My shoulders sagged as the air rushed out of my lungs. *Breathe. Just breathe.*

"Hey," Cyrus soothed, squeezing my hand. "Everything is going to be okay. *We* are going to be okay."

"How can you be so sure?"

"I don't know, sis. I'm not intuitive like Jax, but for some reason, being back on Aroonyx feels . . . right." I nodded. "Like we chose the best path, and deep inside, I know that in the end everything will work out."

I wanted to disagree, but how could I? He was right. We made a commitment: return to Aroonyx—our place of birth—and defeat Zenith.

My anxiety lessened while the appreciation for my brother's level-headed approach grew. Cyrus had the unique ability to calm my nerves and open my eyes to the obvious path.

I wiped the sweat from the back of my neck. "Why is it so hot here?"

"It is much warmer than I expected." He pointed at the sun in the emerald sky. "Do you think it's closer or just bigger?"

I squinted, observing the red glowing orb. "Who knows? We could be in another galaxy."

"Damn. You're right."

We sat in silence for long minutes. The two of us shifted our weight, bothered by the extreme heat. I grimaced, watching my pale skin turn a bright shade of pink. *Where is a cloud when I need one?*

The saliva in my mouth thickened. "I'm so thirsty," I said, scraping my tongue against my teeth.

"I'd pay good money for a Gatorade right now."

I stifled a pleasurable moan. "That sounds amazing." My taste buds danced at the thought of a cool beverage. "But not the gross yellow one."

Cyrus's jaw fell open. "What? Lemon-lime is the best flavor." I made a sour face. He shook his head in disappointment. "Don't knock a classic."

"It doesn't hide the fact that it still tastes like shit."

He glared, but a tiny smirk tugged at the corner of his mouth. "Thanks for ruining my favorite beverage. You're such a dream crusher."

I flashed him a smug grin.

My brother rotated his muscular body around to face the forest. Following his lead, I rolled onto my knees and peeked over the rock.

"Can you see anything?"

"No." His eyes darted back and forth. "Just trees."

"What do you think we should do?"

He turned and ran a hand through his blond hair. "We wait."

Of course we do. I groaned and used the sweat on my forehead to slick back the stray hairs that fell into my face while Cyrus leaned against the rock.

"I can't believe Jax left us on the edge of a cliff."

"He'll be back," Cyrus said, wiping the moisture off his brow.

"When?"

"Chill. Getting this worked up won't bring him back any sooner."

"Then distract me with something."

His cheeks puffed. "Fine. Let's guess what sorority Hillary will join at the University of Texas. I'm thinking Zeta."

I laughed at the absurdity of his comment. "You're ridiculous, you know that?"

"Maybe." His pearly teeth glowed in the sunlight. "But you asked for a distraction."

"Thanks. Now I'm envisioning Hillary doing keg stands at frat parties."

"You're welcome." He winked.

Switching gears, I added, "Isn't it weird that everyone thinks we're on our way to boot camp?"

"Or that we're already there. Don't forget about the time difference."

A knot formed in my stomach when my parents' faces popped in my mind.

Watching the color drain from my rosy cheeks, Cyrus said, "We'll ask Jax to try again when he gets back."

"What if it doesn't work? Don't forget about that night on the beach. Remember his strong feeling?" My brother shut his eyes. "Jax thinks he can't jump to Earth until we've defeated Zenith."

"Regardless, let's stay positive."

Right, because that's so easy. I focused my gaze over the cliff's edge.

Long minutes passed before Cyrus spoke once more. "It was strange seeing other Solins."

"Yeah, they looked just like you. Tall, muscular—"

His face beamed. "So you think I have large muscles?"

Sharing his Solin strength, I punched him in the bicep. "You're impossible."

Cyrus winced but laughed at his own joke. "You know"—he nudged me in the arm—"Jax is pretty muscular too."

Blood rushed to my cheeks. "Shut your mouth."

Ignoring me, he went on, "The guy's definitely into you." He paused. "In a weird, detached sort of way."

"You're delusional. The heat is affecting your sanity."

"Just calling it like I see it, sis."

"Well, you see it wrong."

I leaned forward to adjust my shirt, and when I scooted closer to the rock, something shifted in my back pocket. *The picture.* I smiled, relieved it made the journey. Carefully, I removed the tattered photo and handed it to Cyrus.

Guilt showed its ugly face. "I'm sorry I never showed you this."

His brows raised as he saw our biological parents for the first time. "Wow." He brushed a thumb over their faces. "You were right."

"Doesn't our father look exactly like you—only older?"

"Yeah, but you look just like our mother."

I moved closer. "Strange, huh? The life that never was."

Cyrus let out a deep sigh. "Yeah, you can say that again. I wish we could have spent more time with them."

"Me too," I murmured, staring at the vast body of water. "Jax said he would show us their gravesite."

"I'd like to pay my respects."

"Then we'll go," I said, placing the photo back into my pocket.

We sat with our eyes closed, accepting our place in the new world. Sweat beaded the back of my neck while I listened to the tree branches battle the strong winds.

I dropped my chin to my chest. "This is taking forever."

"He'll come back for us."

"I hope you're right."

"He is."

My head whipped around at the sound of Jax's silky voice. Cyrus flinched at his stealthy return.

"You're back," I said, scrambling to my feet.

"And just in time." My brother climbed off the ground. "Elara was about to go AWOL."

I scanned Jax for injuries. No blood, no bruising—nothing. His jet-black hair hung into his piercing blue eyes, his striking face untouched by the Collectors' hands.

"I'm sorry to have left you for so long, but I needed to make sure the Solins wouldn't return to the cliffside."

A smug grin crossed Cyrus's face. "Elara tried to run after you." He tapped his chest. "But I told her to stay put."

Daggers shot out of my eyes. *Bastard. He just threw me under the bus.*

Jax's head snapped in my direction. "I told you to stay hidden."

"I'm aware of this, I just thought—"

"You thought what?" he asked, folding his arms across his chest.

"I thought you might need help. There were four Collectors, Jax—"

"Thank you for stating the obvious." I rolled my eyes, but he went on. "I can take care of myself." He inclined his head at me and my brother. "It's the two of you I worry about."

I flashed Cyrus a vulgar gesture when he mouthed, "Sorry," in my direction.

Jax widened his stance. I hung my head, preparing for the inevitable lecture.

"I understand this is a new experience for you both and can only imagine how strange and surreal this world appears. Typically, Collectors stay near the villages. Today they ventured farther than usual. The four Solins were not a threat." He shifted his weight. "If they were members of Zenith's Inner Circle, I would have informed you to run."

I gulped and eyed the forest while Cyrus stood tall, his eyes never leaving Jax.

"We must keep your identities a secret. All hell will break loose if Zenith hears of your return."

"What will he do?" Cyrus asked.

"He'll dispatch the Inner Circle to hunt you down."

My mouth went dry. *This is bad—really bad.*

Jax found my worried eyes. "But this won't happen if you listen and do as I say. The two of you must stay together at all times. You can share each other's traits, which gives you the upper hand. We need time to defeat Zenith. If your cover is blown, that time will diminish."

Cyrus and I exchanged anxious glances.

"From this moment on there will be *zero* hesitation from either of you. If I tell you to do something, don't think about it, just do it. I've lived on Aroonyx for my entire life and understand how things work." He waved a hand at the forest. "These woods are my home. This will never work unless the two of you trust me."

"We do," I said, fanning my damp shirt.

Jax looked at my brother. "Cyrus?"

He nodded, wiping the sweat off his brow.

"Come on." Jax motioned for us to follow. "Let's get you a drink of water. It will take time for your bodies to adjust to the heat."

"How hot does it get on Aroonyx?" Cyrus asked, as we made our way toward the shade of the forest.

"Hot. Very hot. There are only two seasons, and they rotate every few weeks. Summer is brutal, and winter is . . . well, it's colder than anything you've ever experienced."

Awesome. I can't wait.

"You never wanted to hear about the weather patterns," Jax muttered, reminding me of our initial conversation about Aroonyx.

I remained silent, refusing to argue.

Short minutes passed before Cyrus nudged my arm. Like dogs pulled on a tight leash, we halted our pace.

"We need to see if you can take us back to Earth," Cyrus said to Jax.

He turned and offered us his hands. I hesitated, glancing at the forest.

"They're gone," Jax reassured me.

I sighed, then held his warm palm while Cyrus grabbed his other.

"Like I mentioned before, I doubt this will work."

Cyrus popped his neck. "Just do it."

My stomach churned with anxiety and my mind raced with thoughts of uncertainty. Drops of sweat dripped down the side of my brother's face when he closed his eyes. I looked at Jax. He gave my hand a gentle squeeze.

I sucked in a sharp breath and held it, preparing for the strange sensation of jumping between worlds. I shut my eyes and counted. *One, two, three.* Nothing happened.

The strong winds circulated around our motionless bodies. My eyes opened when Jax released my hand.

"It . . . didn't work," I stammered, watching my parents' faces dissolve from my mind's eye.

"No shit." Cyrus pointed at Jax. "Maybe you should try jumping alone."

The Lunin shook his head.

"Dude. Just give it a shot."

"Trust me, it won't work."

The reality of our situation grabbed hold of me. *Breathe. Just breathe.* My chest ached as if a vice grip had clamped around my heart.

Cyrus curled his hands into fists. "How can you say that? You haven't tried."

"I have tried." Jax's voice raised as he took a step closer to my brother. "I can't get back to Earth. End of story."

My mind flashed to the image of my parents checking the mailbox for letters—the letters I wrote—letters filled with lies about my pretend life at boot camp. Trying to catch my breath, I rested a hand on my hip. My vision blurred. *What if we don't defeat Zenith? What if we're stuck on Aroonyx forever? We gave Coach Burnell a year's worth of letters. That's it. Our parents will never know what happened to us.*

I swayed side to side while focusing on Jax and Cyrus. The spite-filled words that left their mouths sounded as if they were speaking under water. *It's too hot.* My knees wobbled. *I'm going to pass out.* I reached out a hand, desperate for someone to catch my falling body.

THREE

Welcome Home

My eyes shot open when hushed voices filled the quiet space. Long black branches swayed back and forth in a hypnotic rhythm, their leaves brushing against one another in a violent dance. Darkness surrounded me. Not from the absence of daylight but from the shade of the massive trees. I lay motionless, mesmerized by their beauty.

"She's awake."

I flinched at the sound of my brother's voice. Quick to act, I sat up, then groaned at the pounding in my head.

"Take it easy," Jax said, kneeling beside me.

"What happened?"

"You passed out," Cyrus answered.

Jax handed me a unique drinking vessel that resembled a leather canteen. "Here, drink this."

Parched, I grabbed it from his hand and drained every last drop of the cool water.

He smiled, finding my eyes. "Better?"

I nodded. "How long was I out?"

"A little while," he said, taking a seat. "From now on, I don't want you going anywhere without water."

"Copy that, boss." I ran a finger over the pouch. "Is it made out of leather? I thought Aroonyx didn't have cows or large mammals."

"We don't. It's not leather, but it's equally durable and also water repellent. It comes from a common animal found on Aroonyx. We eat the meat and use the hide for water pouches, bags, belts, shoes." He lifted his boot. "The animal's hair resembles sheep's wool and we use it like cotton found on Earth."

"Damn." Cyrus arched a brow. "That's one useful animal."

The Lunin shrugged, indifferent to my brother's comment.

When I pushed myself off the soft grass, Jax hopped to his feet and wrapped one hand around my waist while the other held my arm. He didn't let go until I assured him I was steady on my feet.

"Where are we?" I asked, my head turning every which way.

"Camp Jax." Cyrus jerked his chin at a small shelter made from the branches of the black trees that sat camouflaged between two trunks. A gray bag with shoulder straps leaned against it, and remnants of an extinguished fire decorated the area in front of the makeshift dwelling.

My brows furrowed. "Is this a temporary living space?"

Jax cocked his head to one side as he observed the shelter. "Temporary, as it's here for now."

Cyrus eyed the Lunin. "So you do live here? In the woods."

"Yes, and I change locations every few days."

"Why?" I asked, glancing over my shoulder.

He rubbed a thumb over the scar on his palm. "It's best that I keep moving."

"Does this have something to do with the person who gave you that scar?" I pointed to his face. "The acquaintance you ran into before we drove to Crystal Beach?"

Jax brushed me off by murmuring, "Something like that," while walking toward his gray bag.

Right. I'll drop it. I knew better than to pry about Jax's personal life on Aroonyx. If he wanted to share something, he did, and this was not one of those times.

Cyrus strolled toward the shelter and shook one of the branches, causing the others to fall to the ground. Jax shut his eyes.

"So you rebuild this thing in a new spot every few days?"

"Yes." A muscle feathered in the Lunin's jaw as he searched for something in the bag. He spoke to Cyrus in a tone sharper than the blade in his pocket. "I understand you're having a difficult time processing it all, but I've lived like this for nine years." Jax closed the bag. "I have few needs: shelter, food—"

"Where do you sleep?" Cyrus asked, searching for a cot.

"On the ground."

My brother squished up his face with displeasure. "Aren't you worried about ants or scorpions crawling on you at night?"

I shuddered at the thought of a giant alien bug burrowing in my hair while I slept.

"That's not a concern."

"Why? Aroonyx doesn't have ants or scorpions?" I asked.

"Insects don't exist on Aroonyx."

Our mouths gaped. I crouched to the ground, searching for signs of life. My fingers separated the silky blades of grass. Nothing. Just black soil that felt like fine grains of sand. I looked at Jax. "How is that possible?"

He shrugged. "One of the many differences."

"Jax, you can't say something that crazy without giving us an explanation."

He chuckled under his breath as he walked toward me and my brother. On hands and knees, we continued our investigation.

Jax lowered himself onto the ground beside us. "It's obvious the differences between the two worlds have you both"—he paused, noting our shocked expressions—"perplexed."

I shot him a sarcastic glance.

He returned my gesture with a smirk. "Moving forward, we can't afford any distractions, so let's have a little Q&A session, shall we?"

We stopped our search and sat in front of Jax like pre-school children eager for story time. I admired the vast forest, observing the pristine vegetation. Similar in height, the long branches of the black trees reached to touch the green sky.

Their leaves blocked most of the sunlight, casting a cool shade around us. The short blades of grass looked as though a groundskeeper had finished a long day of work; the green river flowed between the trees. I turned my head. Massive stepping stones made of white Clear Stone decorated the forest floor every so often. I cupped a hand to my ear, listening for sounds of life.

"It looks like a movie set," I said, gesturing to the surrounding space. "Why is everything so . . . perfect?"

My brother rubbed a hand over the fine blades of grass. "Seriously, it reminds me of a fairway on a golf course."

"It is quite the contrast, isn't it?" Jax leaned back on his hands. "The first time I jumped to Earth, I wondered why everything was in such disarray."

"Wait. It just grows like this?"

Jax laughed at my observation. "Elara, it's not like Zenith pays someone to keep it looking this way."

"Fine. Then explain why there are no weeds or brown spots in the grass?"

"I can't." He tossed up his hands. "It's just one of those unexplained things in life."

"And no bugs?" I pressed.

Cyrus's back straightened. "What about snakes?"

Jax dragged a hand down his face before speaking. "I'm sure it's confusing, wondering how things grow and decay without the help of insects, but things work differently here."

"It's so quiet." My brother looked up at the trees. "Where are all the animals?"

Curious, I followed his gaze. Thanks to my brother's proximity, I used his powerful Solin eyesight to scan the top branches. Nothing. No birds and no squirrels.

"There are a few animals on Aroonyx," Jax said. "Not nearly the number of species you find on Earth. Birds are rare. They're silent and fly through the woods before the seasons change. Like I mentioned before, large mammals don't exist. Aroonyx has a few herbivores." He watched us carefully before the next sentence rolled off his tongue. "Predators don't exist."

I coughed, choking on my spit while Cyrus stumbled over his words.

"No carnivores?" he stammered.

Quiet laughter rumbled in Jax's chest as he tossed his hair out of his eyes. "That's right. Only plant eaters."

"No wolves, dogs, or cats?"

"Nope." He winked at Cyrus. "And no snakes."

My brother celebrated by pumping his fist in the air. Wondering if it were all a dream, I collapsed onto my back. Cyrus followed my lead, surrendering to the overflow of information.

"It's like the perfect planet," I said, staring at the swaying branches.

"Except for the fact that it's ruled by a murdering dictator."

I jabbed my brother in the ribs. "Thanks for the reality check."

"You're welcome."

Jax moved beside me and rested his hands underneath his head. My face flushed when his elbow brushed against me. "Cyrus brings up a good point, Elara. Aroonyx is far from perfect." He huffed a breath. "That's the irony of it all, isn't it?"

I thought of our time on the cliffside before I fainted. "Hey Jax?"

"Mm-hmm."

"Are you sure you can't get back to Earth?"

"That's correct."

I swallowed before asking my next question. "Did you try jumping by yourself?"

"Yes. I already told you this." He inhaled a long breath. "After the Collectors left. When I was alone in the woods."

An unspoken awareness passed between us. *We're stuck on Aroonyx unless we find a way to defeat Zenith. Damn. If something happens to Jax, we're screwed. He's our one-way ticket home.*

"I can't predict the future," the Lunin said, "but I have a strong intuition that when this is over, I'll have the power to take you back to Earth."

My brother's lips pressed together. "Anything's possible. This morning I was in my house brushing my teeth and now—"

I waved a hand at the trees. "We're living on another planet."

"I was going to say lying in the grass together, but that works too."

I chuckled, amused with Cyrus's endless humor. The Lunin shifted his weight.

I turned my head to face him. "Anytime you spoke about Aroonyx, you made it sound like this hostile world."

"I didn't want to risk swaying your decision. Had I told you about the wonderful gifts Aroonyx has to offer, your minds would have wandered and possibly obscured the purpose of your return." Jax pushed himself to the seated position. "Also, I thought the beauty would be a positive distraction from the negativity you'll soon face."

I cursed under my breath.

"About that," Cyrus said, sitting up. "What's the plan?" Jax's expression remained unreadable. "The plan, Jax. How are we defeating Zenith?"

"I'm not sure," he mumbled, climbing to his feet. "It'll come to me."

Heat surged through my body as my brother hurried to stand. His eyes narrowed and his voice raised when he asked, "You don't have a plan?"

I shook my warming hands and stood, ready to play mediator.

"Maybe you should have asked about the details before you left Earth," Jax countered.

Cyrus glared, every muscle in his body tense.

"Jax, that's not fair," I said. "We left everything behind because you told us to."

"Don't give me that shit. You made this decision on your own. I never said I had a plan. I only said we needed to defeat Zenith."

"Screw you," Cyrus snapped. "I hate being blindsided. You pulled a smooth one on us."

"How did I blindside you?" My brother's lips moved to answer, but Jax's quick tongue interrupted his efforts. "You assumed I had a plan. That's where you went wrong. Your mistake, not mine."

Anger pulsated through my veins. "Why are you being such an asshole?"

Jax swore, scrubbing his face with his hands. "I'm not. I'm being honest."

"That's a fine line with you, Jax." I glared.

"Listen, both of you." His frustrated tone shifted to a more severe one. "No, I don't have a detailed plan of how to defeat Zenith, but there is a ripple effect in everything we do. A change is coming. I can feel it."

"Why are you always so cryptic?" Cyrus barked. "It's like you're speaking another language half the time."

Jax mumbled inaudible words as he stepped closer to my brother. "Then let me spell it out for you." The line between his eyebrows deepened. "We need more time. There is no way in hell you're ready to tackle a Collector." He reached into his back pocket. Cyrus flinched when Jax offered him his knife. "Open it," he instructed.

"What?"

"Arm yourself."

Cyrus tried using his thumb and index finger to pull the blade from the handle. Before I could blink, Jax grabbed the knife, flicked his wrist, and pretended to stab Cyrus in the neck.

"And just like that—you're dead."

My brother shut his eyes.

Jax lowered his hand and folded the blade back into the handle before slipping it in his pocket. “You haven’t trained with weapons. We need more time.”

Cyrus stared at the Lunin.

I touched my brother’s arm. “He’s right. We’re not ready.”

“Fair enough.” His defensive posture relaxed.

I shook my hands, the heated sensation fading.

Jax looked through the gaps in the canopy above, and after a long pause, he said, “I want to show you something, but we need to hurry.”

I eyed Cyrus who motioned for Jax to lead the way.

We walked in silence for long minutes before my brother asked me, “Is he taking us back to the cliffside?”

“Who knows? This is all new to me. I was passed out the last time we took a walk, remember?”

His eyes widened. “Oh, I remember. I had to carry your ass the entire way. Good thing it was daylight and I had my Solin strength.” He knocked my shoulder with his arm. “You aren’t the lightest thing to lug around.”

Jax paused his quick pace as we approached the edge of the woods, then scanned the vast area before moving forward once more.

After a short walk, the three of us stood on the cliffside. The setting sun rested a touch above the horizon, a glowing orb of red and orange hues. *It is beautiful.* The jade-colored sky merged with the sunset, casting caramel tones over the gray water.

Cyrus slid his feet dangerously close to the edge of the vertical drop and rotated his head back and forth as he admired the stunning sight. I kept my distance and focused my attention on the setting sun.

"Watch closely," Jax whispered, resting his hand on my lower back.

"Where?"

He lifted his free hand. "There."

In an instant, the sun vanished beneath the horizon. I gasped, watching the sky transform into a kaleidoscope of colors. The brownish hue faded to pink before settling on the most beautiful shade of purple I had ever seen.

Twinkling stars filled the atmosphere as though an invisible painter had added them one brush stroke at a time. Cyrus sucked in a sharp breath while pointing at the two crescent moons that hung side by side. Letting his hand fall from my back, Jax walked between where Cyrus and I stood with our mouths still gaped.

"I've waited almost ten years to say this." He smiled, gesturing to the vast space before our eyes. "Welcome home."

FOUR

Valid Concerns

I groaned, rolling onto my side. My stiff muscles hadn't adjusted to sleeping on the hard ground every night. I used my arm as a pillow, tucking it under the side of my face, and watched Jax and Cyrus sleep. I chuckled, noting their different postures. Cyrus lay sprawled on his back, far away in dreamland. His chest rose and fell with slow, deep breaths and a subtle smile crossed his relaxed face.

Then there was Jax, who looked serious even while sleeping. His pale body, as if prepared for a burial, lay motionless on the emerald grass with his hands glued to his sides. I focused my attention on his chest; it barely moved with each breath. His dark hair fell out of his eyes, exposing the striking features of his pale face.

Flipping onto my back, I searched for the sky between the gaps in the canopy above. The early mornings were the most peaceful time of day. I inhaled a long breath of the humid air and stared at the tree branches. They didn't budge. The stillness and perfection sent a chill up my spine. *Maybe this is the calm before the storm.* My night vision faded as the forest glowed a copper hue, signaling the start of a new day.

Without making a sound, I sat up and eyed Jax. *Today is the day.* Over the past week, the two of us had started an unspoken game. Each morning I tried standing without waking him. I always lost because every time his eyes would shoot open at the quietest sound or smallest movement.

I eased myself onto my knees, then placed a hand on the cool grass. Holding my breath, I stretched my bent legs, victory within reach. *Only a few more inches to go.* I neared the standing position.

"Maybe tomorrow."

I cursed at the sound of his silky voice. "Damn it, Jax. How do you always know?"

His eyes remained closed, but a tiny smirk tugged at the corner of his mouth. "It's a talent I've picked up over the years."

"I'm going to win this little game one day."

He yawned, stretching his toned arms. "I'm looking forward to it."

My heart skipped a beat. Jax snuck a hidden message in his words, a metaphor that had nothing to do with our daily game of catch Elara standing.

I cleared my throat while reaching for a change of clothes in the gray bag. "I'm going to freshen up."

He leaned on his elbows. "Just don't be—"

"I won't," I said, strolling toward the secluded spring.

My absence always made Jax uneasy. He wanted me to stay close but loosened the reigns when I reminded him that as a woman, I needed time alone for basic hygiene needs. He agreed and allowed me and Cyrus a small amount of uninterrupted time in the mornings and evenings at the spring. The only drawback was that if we were gone too long, he'd send the other one searching.

I strolled through the woods, reflecting on the previous week, still amazed that we were living on another planet. Every day, I worried that Coach Burnell would forget to mail our letters, or that they would get lost and never make it to my parents' waiting hands.

Cyrus reassured me that my fears were irrational and asserted that I needed to stay positive. Jax, sensing my need for a distraction, filled our days with combative training and lectures on the differences between the two worlds. We spent the late evenings around a crackling fire, discussing Zenith and his Collectors. Yes, the busyness of the day numbed my fearful thoughts—but it didn't resolve my concerns. It only masked them.

Tiny beads of sweat formed on the back of my neck; the air was thick with humidity. I quickened my pace, longing to feel clean from the previous day. I hopped over a piece of Clear Stone while dodging a low-lying tree branch as I approached the small body of water. The spring, ten feet in diameter, gurgled—an audible invitation to submerge into its depths. I shed my grass-stained clothes, then lowered my body into the gray water.

Exhaling, I sank deeper into the spring, my hearing muffled by the loud bubbles. I longed for a moment's peace, desperate to process the emotions that surfaced when I envisioned my future.

I groaned. *If I don't hurry, Jax will send Cyrus to fetch me.*

The thought of my brother seeing me naked was all the motivation I needed to quicken my routine.

Within minutes, I had bathed and exited the spring. Without a towel, I fanned my wet body before pulling the crème-colored shirt over my long torso. I shook my head, baffled that Jax had guessed our correct sizes. He mentioned we needed to blend in with our Solin and Lunin counterparts. Apparently, our Earth clothes were too colorful and modern; they'd put us at risk if seen by anyone. We tossed them into the fire by our campsite on the first night of our return. The act itself felt symbolic of leaving our old lives behind.

I gathered my hair over one shoulder and twisted the long locks to remove the excess water. My fingers acted as a comb, sliding through the silky strands with minimal effort. *I'd make millions if I could bottle this water and bring it to Earth. My hair has never looked this healthy or shiny.*

I kneeled beside the spring and submerged the previous day's clothes underneath the gurgling bubbles. I chuckled, remembering Jax's expression when I asked for soap. He informed us that the water had a special quality. It could clean and sanitize any article of clothing, including the human body.

My hands buzzed with heat as I wrung water from the shirt and shorts. "I wasn't even gone that long."

"You know how he worries," Cyrus said, moving closer to the spring.

I squeezed the clothes one last time before looking at my brother. "Glad I'm dressed."

"It's not a big deal." He tossed his shirt to the ground and winked. "We're family, remember?"

I spun around when he unbuttoned his pants. Cyrus let out a hearty laugh and sprayed me with water when he did a cannon ball into the spring. *Why is he so annoying?*

Our relationship had gone full swing into brother-sister mode. Half the time, we drove each other crazy, but Cyrus always had my back and I had his. During our daily combative training, we worked as a team and used every opportunity to try and overtake Jax. Unfortunately, our failed attempts left us covered in scrapes and bruises.

Signaling my departure, I waved a hand over my shoulder before heading back toward the campsite. The air temperature dropped as the forest grew darker around me. I inhaled a long breath. *Smells like rain.*

I slowed my casual pace to a crawl when I noticed Jax standing like a statue, his eyes focused on the ashes of the previous night's fire. Lost deep in thought, he rubbed the scar on the palm of his hand. I tiptoed toward the shelter, not wanting to interrupt his inner dialogue.

"The rain will be here soon," he said, his voice barely above a whisper.

I glanced up at the darkening sky before looking at the somber Lunin. "Is everything okay?"

"Mm-hmm."

"Right," I said, dragging out each letter.

I flinched when his head snapped in my direction.

"Elara, are you happy?"

I stammered, caught off guard by his question.

"Here, on Aroonyx?" he clarified.

My pulse raced. I didn't have a clue how to answer his question. *Happy here alone? Or happy here with Jax?*

I tossed my damp hair behind my back. "That's a multifaceted question." He nodded. "And a hard one to answer." I sighed and let a half-truth roll off my tongue. "If I didn't leave my parents the way I did, and if Zenith and the Collectors were nonexistent, then . . . yeah, I guess I could be happy living here."

He forced a smile and locked his piercing blue eyes onto mine before saying, "Good, because your happiness means everything to me."

I looked away and shifted my weight, but Jax's eyes never left me. Any romantic feelings I had toward the Lunin were kept hidden in a private room of my mind. I couldn't let those emotions show. He was Jax: mature, serious, skilled in more ways than I liked to imagine, and then there was me. The awkward, unexperienced girl who stumbled through the motions.

I sighed, twisting my hair into a bun. The small but intense moments we shared satisfied my desire to be with him on a more intimate level. Jax was always ten steps ahead of my every move. In no way could I speculate his feelings for me.

If he has any at all. Don't let your mind wander. It would never work.

Our heads turned at the sound of Cyrus's voice.

"No one ever comes looking for me."

Grateful for his timing, I faced my brother. "That's because we don't worry about you."

A huge grin crossed his face as he pointed to his flexed shirtless torso. "Is it because of my large muscles?"

I laughed hard, pleased with his ability to lighten the mood. Cyrus winked as he approached the campsite. Jax, the only one unamused by my brother's behavior, motioned for us to join him under the shelter. Cyrus jogged the remaining steps and slipped on his shirt once inside the dwelling.

Huge raindrops fell from the sky after a loud boom of thunder. My brother and I flinched at the sound, but Jax remained unfazed.

We stood in silence, observing the downpour. Within minutes, puddles formed on the lush grass and drops of rain splattered against the Clear Stone that decorated the forest floor.

I crossed my arms, watching Jax out of the corner of my eye. *Something's different. He's quieter than usual.* Every muscle in his body tensed, and the vein on his neck pulsated like a ticking time bomb ready to detonate at any second. I glanced at Cyrus, relieved to see him calm, relaxed.

"I need to visit one of the villages," Jax said, breaking the silence. "We're getting low on supplies."

My brother flashed me a curious glance. I shrugged. We spent our first week isolated from the people living on Aroonyx.

Cyrus and I longed to see the other inhabitants, and we wanted to explore the villages that Jax spoke of during our daily lectures. Cabin fever had set in. We needed a change of scenery.

I bit my lip, trying to hide my excitement. "Do we get to go?"

Jax scratched the short hairs of his beard while he watched the falling rain. "I can't risk leaving you here alone—so yes."

Our faces beamed, then fell at the severity of his tone.

"You must stay together at all times." Jax's eyes drifted between me and my brother. "And do not speak to anyone, under any circumstance." We nodded. "I want you practicing the art of blending in with other Solins and Lunins. I'll get what I need and that's it. We won't linger or enjoy the sights."

"What about the Collectors?" Cyrus asked. "You said they don't wear uniforms. How will we recognize them?"

Jax paused, watching the rain subside, then cleared his throat before speaking. "The Collectors are only a threat if a citizen has caused a disruption or if their leader has sent them on a mission." He touched the scar on his hand. "Zenith isn't aware of your return, and I don't expect either of you to steal anything from a vendor, so the Collectors shouldn't be a problem."

I swallowed. The word *shouldn't* made me uneasy.

"The quickest way to spot a Collector is to watch the eyes," Jax said.

"What do you mean?" I asked.

"They won't make eye contact."

My brother crossed his arms. "Why not?"

"Because they've lived a life full of dishonesty. It's written all over their damned faces."

Cyrus's head bobbed up and down as if making a mental checklist. "Noted. We'll watch the eyes."

I blew out a long breath and the palms of my hands were damp with moisture. "Hey Jax?" He met my gaze. "I know the Collectors aren't aware of our identities." I waved a hand at myself and my brother. "But considering how often you move campsites, and that altercation you had with the person who gave you that scar. Makes me wonder—"

"I understand your concerns," he interrupted. "And they're valid."

Well, that doesn't make me feel any better.

Jax tossed the hair out of his eyes. "Zenith has many Collectors. I don't know the exact number, but I do know that nine members, five Solins and four Lunins, create the Inner Circle. This elite group stays close to Zenith at all times unless a specific situation requires their attention. They rarely make appearances in the villages, but when they do, everyone takes note and gets out of their way. Of all the Collectors, only the identities of these nine men are known. The acquaintance I ran into last year"—he traced the scar on his face—"is the unspoken leader of the Inner Circle."

My eyes grew.

Cyrus's words caught in his throat when he asked, "Dude. Are you—like a—wanted criminal or something?"

The Lunin snickered and returned his gaze to the damp forest.

"It's a legitimate question, Jax," I snapped, annoyed by his smug expression.

"We don't have to worry about the Inner Circle unless your cover is blown. This is why you must stay close and do as I say."

My hands buzzed with heat as Cyrus took a step closer. "What if the Inner Circle makes an appearance today and recognizes your face?"

"That's unlikely. They usually stick to the West Village."

Cyrus cursed and tossed up his hands. "Is this just a game to you? Our lives are on the line and you want to play Russian roulette."

"You're right," Jax countered. "Life is just a game of chance, so you better listen up. Both of you." I gulped. "Elara, I told you this months ago, and Cyrus, you're only now hearing it for the first time. If I am ever apprehended, run. Don't try to help." He looked at Cyrus. "*Don't* be the hero. I don't care what happens to me. This endeavor is bigger than one person—it's bigger than all of us. You must defeat Zenith, even if that means doing it without me by your side."

I forced a lump of grief down my throat while my brother murmured, "We understand."

"Good. Then let's go."

I stood motionless with my feet glued to the grass. A gut-wrenching uneasiness washed over me as I watched Cyrus follow Jax out of the shelter. The unsettling shift rattled me to my core. I let the air rush out of my lungs and released on the emotions that surfaced before hurrying to catch up with the two men.

Beads of sweat decorated my brow. It was hot, but the thought of the unknown sent an icy chill up my spine. We were living on Aroonyx, and regardless of what Zenith and his Collectors threw at us, escaping to the safety of Earth wasn't an option.

A wicked laugh echoed in my ears. I stilled when a masked figure appeared behind a hidden door in my mind, and my heart nearly leapt out of my chest when it whispered, *Don't worry, Elara. Your fate has been sealed. In time everything will be revealed.*

FIVE

A Fool's Mistake

After the emotionally jarring moment with the visitor in my mind, I found myself grateful for the easy-going journey to the village. Intense heat surrounded us, but the shade from the canopy of leaves cooled our warm skin.

I rolled my neck. The tension in my shoulders dissolved as I strolled behind Jax. He turned his head every so often, his eyes peeled for other inhabitants. I kept my attention focused on the trail while I braided my long hair over one shoulder. *I wonder how the other girls dress? Do they wear makeup? Is there makeup on Aroonyx? Not like it matters. I never wear it anyway.* I touched my eyelashes. *Though some mascara would be nice.*

Cyrus walked beside me and whispered random thoughts near my ear while Jax remained silent. The enormous trees crowded closer together as we approached the edge of the forest. My brother tapped my shoulder and pointed to the wide trail that snaked its way between the black trunks: the first sign of civilization we'd seen since our return.

"It's not much farther," Jax said, ducking under a low-lying branch.

After a few minutes of silence, noisy chatter filled our ears. The Lunin's posture shifted as we approached the end of the path. "Remember everything I told you."

We nodded, stretching our necks to get a better look.

"And stay close," he added.

It took every ounce of restraint to stifle the loud gasp that escaped my mouth. A clearing, the size of a football field, was jam-packed with hand-built stands that sold food, clothing, tools, and other assorted items. *It's like an old farmer's market.*

"Wow," Cyrus whispered, pointing to a blacksmith. "It's like we've gone back in time."

Jax's lips barely moved when he said, "That's great, now tone down the excitement." We wiped the elated expressions from our faces. "Follow me and stay together," he instructed, heading into the bustling market.

My eyes grew as I trailed behind our guide. Solins and Lunins chatted amongst themselves while others bartered with vendors. *It's like I'm staring in a distorted mirror.*

More than half the crowd shared my physical features: pale skin, black hair, and blue eyes. A sense of oneness washed over me as we weaved through the crowd. Instinctively, I smiled at the other Lunins.

I eyed Cyrus, reading his inner thoughts. Every Solin we passed looked related to him by blood. Their white-blond hair glowed under the sun that peeked through the residual rain clouds. I blinked, fascinated with the varying shades of orange-colored eyes that glanced in our direction. Physically, we matched our Lunin and Solin counterparts—but mentally, we were worlds away.

I raised my brows with curiosity, watching Jax stroll through the crowd. Men and women stepped aside, their heads lowered and eyes averted. No smiles, no head nods—nothing.

Jax always exuded confidence when he walked, but the way the others parted like the Red Sea before him was nothing short of alarming. His posture changed the deeper we went into the market. He held his head high, but his arms stayed glued to his sides, hands clenched into fists.

The Lunin paused his quick pace, allowing a Solin to pass. The man didn't struggle while carrying five sacks of what looked like grain in his muscular arms.

Jax turned to face me and my brother. "I need to speak with a vendor about some supplies." His eyes narrowed on us. "Stay together and don't leave this area. I won't be gone long."

I nodded and Cyrus murmured, "Sure thing," though he hadn't listened to Jax's instructions.

He was too busy watching an attractive Solin amble through the crowd; his eyes glazed over with lust. The young woman's platinum-blonde hair swayed back and forth, mirroring the movement of her hips. Her shapely breasts bounced up and down with each step and her golden eyes shimmered in the bright sunlight.

Cyrus wiped the drool off his chin. *Oh geez.*

The woman flashed my brother a seductive grin and brushed her arm against his when she passed. His entire body shuddered.

Sharing his Solin strength, I elbowed him in the ribs. Though snapped out of his trance, he couldn't hide the smile that grew across his handsome face.

Jax squeezed the bridge of his nose.

"We're fine," I pressed, shooing him away with my hand. He hesitated. "Just go."

The Lunin looked at Cyrus one last time, then said, "Okay, but don't talk to anyone."

I touched his arm. "We won't."

Jax pivoted and headed in the opposite direction, leaving me and my brother alone in the crowded space.

Cyrus craned his neck, searching for the mysterious young woman while my eyes stayed focused on Jax.

"What booth should we check out first?"

I lowered my gaze. "I think you've checked out plenty."

Cyrus tossed his head back to the overcast sky and laughed. "I can't help it if I appreciate the beauty of the female figure." I pinned him with a long stare. "You're forgetting that I've been stuck in the woods with you and Jax for days. I'm the third wheel."

"Really? You're going to play that card."

"It's true. All day I'm forced to watch the awkward sexual tension between you two." My cheeks reddened. "The guy better man up and make a move before you—"

"Cyrus," I scolded, hiding my face in my hands. "Stop."

"Only if you stop giving me shit for checking out a girl."

"Fine," I grumbled, dropping my hands.

Switching the subject, he asked, "So what booth do you want to check out?"

"We only have two options." I pointed to the surrounding vendors.

My brother eyed the booths: a man selling gray parchment and a woman selling rooted vegetables. "As exciting as that sounds, I'll pass." He gestured to the other vendors. "Come on, let's go find something else to look at."

"No, Jax told us to stay here."

"We won't go far."

"We're supposed to stay together."

He rested a hand on my shoulder. "I won't let you out of my sight."

I groaned his name while glancing at the rustic shops in the near distance, my curiosity getting the best of me. I found Jax at the far end of the market, speaking animatedly with a middle-aged Lunin.

My shoulders sagged with a long exhale. "Okay, but don't go far and stay where I can see you."

"There's the adventurous sister I love."

"Well, don't get used to it."

Cyrus chuckled under his breath while heading in the opposite direction.

Short minutes passed before I found a vendor selling jewelry. A Solin sat on a black wooden chair, hunched over a pile of stunning gemstones. Her tan fingers moved with ease as she transformed the glittering rocks into a gorgeous necklace.

"Would you like to try it on?" she asked, offering me the delicate item.

Recalling Jax's stern orders, I shook my head and held up a hand, motioning my intention to pass. She smiled and focused on the pile of gemstones once more.

I touched the intricate designs displayed on her table, impressed with the woman's attention to detail. I stopped my inspection when a dazzling ring caught my eye. Holding it with my thumb and index finger, I rotated it from side to side. Depending on how the light reflected, the unique center stone changed colors from pink to clear. The surrounding gems resembled white diamonds and glittered in the shining sun. I slipped it onto my ring finger. It was the perfect fit.

"It suits you," she said, glancing up from her work.

I mouthed, "Thank you," before resting it on the wooden table.

Not wanting to overstay my welcome, I headed back to the spot where Jax had left us.

I saw my brother inspecting a booth that sold dried meats. My face squished up in disgust when the owner of the shop offered him a piece of withered gray jerky. Cyrus shrugged, then tossed it into his mouth. I giggled, watching his face turn sickly.

The vendor's brows furrowed at his reaction. Trying to recover, Cyrus swallowed the foreign substance, though he looked like he wanted to vomit. The elderly man leaned forward to speak with my brother. Cyrus whispered near the Solin's ear, then pointed to where I stood and flashed me his pearly grin.

I gave him a stern look with a small wave. *Great job following the rules, bro.* The vendor scanned me up and down, his orange eyes settling on my face. Bothered by his intense stare, I looked away.

The touch of a calloused hand caused my head to turn.

"That was fast," I said, surprised to find Jax standing beside me. "Did you get everything you needed?"

His pale fingers dug into my arm. "What is your brother doing?"

I stammered, "Um . . . eating samples."

Cyrus's face fell when he looked in our direction.

"Get over here," I mouthed, motioning for him to hurry.

He said goodbye to the man before jogging toward us. His amber eyes filled with concern as he approached Jax. "What's wrong?"

The Lunin stared at the vendor as he asked, "What did you say to that man?"

"Not . . . much."

Jax locked his eyes onto Cyrus. "I need to know exactly what you said."

Cyrus sighed, glancing at the owner of the shop. A wicked smirk crossed the man's face as he looked at Jax.

"He just asked me what village I lived in—"

"And?" Jax interrupted, his tone sharper than before.

Bewildered by his interrogation, Cyrus tossed up his hands. "I told him I was just visiting . . . with my sister."

Jax closed his eyes and gritted his teeth, every fiber in his body on high alert. I glanced at my brother, panic washing over me.

Cyrus stepped closer and whispered, "Jax, what's wrong?"

His blue eyes shot open. "We need to get out of here—now."

I shifted my weight, suddenly uneasy in the crowded market.

Blue and orange eyes scanned us with curiosity, and a woman pointed at Jax, then averted her eyes as she passed.

I breathed hard. "Jax, what's going on?"

He jerked his chin toward the opposite end of the market. "Keep your heads down and stay close."

We hurried after Jax. He moved with a purpose, each step more determined than the last.

"What did I say wrong?" Cyrus asked me, his lips barely moving.

"I don't know, but we weren't supposed to talk to anyone."

He dragged a hand down his face as we headed away from the market.

Jax's posture didn't relax once we stepped onto the manmade path. The whites of his knuckles showed as he stormed through the forest. We jogged to keep up, and after long minutes of awkward silence, the secluded area we called home appeared before our eyes.

The momentary comfort of the familiar space dissolved in a heartbeat. In one violent motion, Jax kicked the small shelter, sending branches flying in every direction. My brother used his body as a shield to protect me from the projectile pieces of wood while I stood frozen with shock.

"Do you realize what you've done?" Jax yelled, whipping around to face us.

Fear rippled through me; I had never seen Jax lose control. My hands buzzed with heat as Cyrus pushed me farther behind him.

"This is all your fault," Jax said, glaring at my brother. He marched over to where we stood.

My heart hammered in my chest. Feeling threatened, I grabbed Cyrus's arm.

The Lunin's fierce eyes filled with rage as he stepped closer. "Did you not hear my orders?" He went on before Cyrus could answer. "Or were you too distracted by that girl?"

My brother tensed.

"I told you not to speak to anyone." Jax closed the gap between them. "But you didn't listen because your head was too far up your ass."

Cyrus scoffed at the verbal jab. "I barely said anything to the man."

"Oh, you said plenty," Jax countered, the pupils of his eyes constricting.

I kept my fingers wrapped around my brother's arm as I moved beside him. "Jax, now is not the time to be cryptic. Why are you so upset?"

"Upset?" His brows raised. "I'm not upset, I'm pissed."

"Why?" I gulped, tightening my grip around Cyrus.

"Because your brother has put our lives in grave danger!"

My face fell. "I don't understand. How?"

"He told the man that he was visiting . . . with his sister." Jax paused, waiting for our reaction.

Confused, we remained silent.

The Lunin focused his attention on Cyrus, and through gritted teeth he said, "Aroonyx doesn't have visitors. Everyone lives in one of the four villages: North, South, East, or West." His voice raised, spit spraying in my brother's face. "Seekers are the only people who use the term 'visit.'"

My heart sank into the pit of my stomach. *Shit. I see where he's going with this.*

"And to make matters worse, you pointed at Elara in the crowd." Cyrus let out a pained breath as Jax got in his face. "Don't you get it? Two visitors, brother and sister, close in age, one Solin and one Lunin."

Short breaths entered my lungs, my mind racing with fearful thoughts. "Maybe he won't—"

"Of course he will. Zenith will reward anyone who tells him the whereabouts of a Seeker, and when he hears the part about the Solin Seeker having a Lunin sister close in age, he'll know you've returned."

Cyrus swore.

"Yeah, that's right," Jax added. "And you know what Zenith will do?" I shut my eyes, not wanting to hear the answer. "He'll dispatch the Inner Circle to capture you so he can slice your necks and let you bleed out one painful drop at a time."

My hand shot to my mouth.

"Okay, so I *fucked* up!" Cyrus yelled.

I squeezed his arm, begging him to stand down.

Jax moved his face only inches away from my brother's. "Over the past nine years, I've done everything in my power to keep you both safe." He snapped his fingers. "And just like that, you ruin it all."

The intense heat radiated throughout my body. It needed to escape. I shook my free hand, willing it away.

"Jax," I begged. "It was an honest mistake."

"A mistake we'll pay for with our lives."

At this comment, Cyrus stood tall and rolled his shoulders. I glanced at my free hand. Like a mirage in the desert, the heat extended from my vibrating palm. Baffled by the strange phenomenon, I let go of Cyrus and clasped my hands together.

My brother's voice lowered to a growl. "You're no saint, Jax." He held up his index finger. "I've made one mistake. You, on the other hand, seemed to have made plenty."

Before I could blink, Jax pulled back his arm and moved to strike. His knuckles stopped a hair away from my brother's jawline. After sucking in a sharp breath, Jax turned and headed toward the spring.

I rested my warm hands on my trembling knees and steadied my breathing. The heat that flowed through my veins cooled when Cyrus stormed off into the forest.

I called his name.

"Not now, Elara."

I dashed after him but skidded to a stop when he spun around to face me.

"I'm so sorry," he whispered.

"Stop that. You didn't do it on purpose."

Guilt clouded his amber eyes.

"Hey," I said, placing my hands on the sides of his face. "Everything is going to be okay. Remember? *We* are going to be okay. Everyone makes mistakes."

"Yeah, well apparently, I made a grave one."

"Listen." I tossed my braided hair behind my back. "Jax is always telling us that everything happens for a reason. Maybe you were supposed to talk to that man."

"And get us all killed?"

"Don't be dramatic. That's my job."

He forced a smile.

"Look at it this way," I said. "We have a short amount of time to defeat Zenith. I don't know about you, but I'm tired of sitting on my ass all day. Aroonyx is great and all—but I'm ready to go home." He nodded. "If the 'mistake' you made today accelerates our mission, then so be it."

"When did you become the optimist?"

"I guess your Solin attitude is rubbing off on me."

Cyrus glanced over my shoulder. "Jax is so pissed."

"It'll pass. Just give him some time to cool off."

"I thought he was going to hit me."

"I did too," I said, muffling my laughter.

"Why is that funny?"

"I'm sorry. It's not."

"Then why are you laughing?"

"I don't know." I tossed up my hands. "I think the fact that we're living on another planet has me—"

"Disturbed?"

The two of us expressed our amusement in the shade of the forest, our postures relaxing with each passing minute.

Cyrus rested a hand on my shoulder. "Thanks, sis."

"For what?"

"For not yelling at me."

"I think Jax did enough yelling for everyone."

"I bet he would have kept his cool if you were the one who spoke to the man."

My cheeks puffed with disagreement. "Doubtful."

"Elara, in Jax's eyes, you can do no wrong."

"Agree to disagree," I murmured as we headed back toward the collapsed shelter.

Cyrus squatted to inspect the fallen branches. "Should we try to rebuild it?"

I sighed, using the toe of my shoe to move a piece aside.

"No, we move campsites tonight."

Our chins lifted at the sound of Jax's voice. I did a double take, noting his shirtless torso. Yes, he had visited the spring. *Good Lord. I don't remember him looking that good.*

Jax strolled toward the dismantled structure. His jet-black hair was slicked out of his striking face, and the damp shirt that hung over his toned shoulder swayed back and forth with each step.

The last time I saw him without his shirt was the night at the beach. I had forgotten about the numerous scars that lined his chest and abdomen. They varied in shape and size, ranging in colors from light pink to flesh tone.

My mouth hung open; desire surged through me. *Get it together.* I forced my eyes away from his attractive body and back to the pile of debris, hoping the redness in my face would lessen.

Refusing to look at Jax, Cyrus pushed a fallen branch with the toe of his boot. "Do you want us to carry this to a new location?"

The Lunin shook his head. "There's no point in rebuilding it. From this point on, we'll be on the move—daily."

I mumbled my agreement, eyes fixed on the ground. *I wish he'd put on his damn shirt so I could focus.*

Still sore from the argument, Cyrus shoved his hands into his pockets.

"We'll sleep at the other end of the forest tonight," Jax added.

I looked up, watching him reach for his shirt. He gave it a quick shake to remove the excess water before pulling it over his head. The slightest movement caused every muscle on his chiseled abdomen to contract. I shifted my weight. *Stay focused. Don't wander. Too late.* My eyes drifted to the sharp V lines on his lower stomach.

Cyrus snickered at my girlish behavior. I knew better than to pay him any mind.

Jax adjusted the gray shirt and ran a hand through his hair before taking the final steps to where Cyrus and I stood, both equally uncomfortable, but for different reasons.

I held my breath when Jax moved his body in front of my brother. "We can only move forward from here," he said, extending his hand.

The air rushed out of Cyrus's lungs in a loud whoosh as he shook Jax's hand. I smiled, relieved they had made amends.

"So now what?" I asked.

Jax pulled the knife from his back pocket and exposed the blade, slower than usual. He tossed it from one hand to the next, then circled his right arm. Before we could blink, he hurled the knife, sending it flying blade over handle. It plunged into the bark of a massive tree over fifty feet from where we stood.

I stilled, awestruck by the impressive feat.

"Damn," Cyrus whispered, touching the scar on his neck.

"You can say that again."

Jax chuckled, observing our expressions.

"Are you trying to tell us something?" I asked, meeting his gaze.

A smug grin spread across his face. "Yeah. Your weapons training begins now."

SIX

A Little Trick

Cyrus rubbed his hands together, eager to get started while the Lunin jogged toward the tree to retrieve the embedded blade. I gulped, remembering how I cut myself with Jax's knife the day I found it on the trail.

My brother laughed under his breath as he found my eyes. "Are you going to be okay there, sis, or do you need to take five and go cool off at the spring?"

"Are you done?"

"Do you think Jax kept his shirt off so it could dry, or so you could drool?" He touched his chin. "I think you missed a spot."

I flashed him a one-fingered gesture. "Keep it up, Cyrus. I'll tell him it was your idea to separate at the village."

The smug grin on his unshaven face dissolved. "Truce?" His hand shot out.

"Depends on how you behave," I said, slapping it away.

Cyrus's lips moved in protest but paused when Jax appeared, the sharp blade at his side.

"Knives on Aroonyx are rare and hard to come by unless you're a Collector or have connections with the black market."

"Wait," I interrupted, recalling my history lesson on Aroonyx. "I thought a Seeker brought plans from Earth, showing Arun how to make knives more efficient for hunting?"

"He did, but they were never implemented for anyone other than Arun and his Collectors."

"If there are no knives, then how do people hunt or prepare food?" Cyrus asked.

"Dull knives that you butter bread with in your kitchens back home are approved, but anything like this"—Jax dangled the blade before our eyes—"is strictly forbidden."

My face squished up with confusion. "Why?"

"After Arun's death, the disbanded group of Collectors ransacked his dwelling. They stole the original plans, and within months, the number of knives on Aroonyx grew to an all-time high. Robberies were common, and the price of meat went down after hunting became easier, boosting the supply." Jax shifted his weight. "Once Zenith took control, he sent his Collectors into the villages to remove these knives from people's possessions. He passed an ordinance forbidding anyone to own a knife other than the dull ones found in kitchens. The people were angry because their leader made life difficult once more. It took longer to prepare food, and it made hunting nearly impossible. Even the sharp tools you find on Earth that Arun developed with the help of the Seekers were modified."

"Why don't the people sharpen their own tools?" Cyrus asked. "It's not like Zenith would know."

"That's a fair question—coming from Earth. But you're forgetting that Aroonyx has a small population." Cyrus crossed his arms while Jax went on. "The Collectors are Zenith's eyes and ears. They keep a close watch on everything and everyone. They'd know if people were modifying tools into weapons. Zenith is not a forgiving man. If he passes an ordinance, he expects compliance."

"What happens if someone breaks the law?" I asked. "Is there a jail?"

Jax stared at his armed hand. "Aroonyx doesn't have jails like the ones found on Earth. If a citizen doesn't comply with an ordinance, they're executed by Zenith."

A low whistle left my brother's pursed lips.

Jax added, "If he wants to get through to them on a deeper level, he takes the guilty party to a designated area in his dwelling. I'll spare you the disturbing details of what happens down there." He tossed a piece of hair out of his eyes. "As you can see, the need for a 'jail' is superfluous."

My jaw fell open. Jax spoke about Zenith and his twisted ideals of punishment like he was talking about the weather.

"Jax." I eyed my brother for backup. "That's horrible. No wonder the people are scared shitless of Zenith and his Collectors. I'm surprised they haven't run off."

"Seriously dude," Cyrus said. "That's messed up."

Jax shrugged. "It's been like this for over sixteen years. The people who lived during Arun's reign are the only ones who know any different."

I thought of the time I spent under the bridge with Jax. He mentioned that Arun had pure intentions until Saros, the first Seeker, disappeared and never returned.

"Zenith is a conniving master at manipulation," Jax said. "When he first passed the ordinance about the knives, he lied, saying it was for everyone's safety. Zenith told the people they should thank him for ridding the planet of such destructive and dangerous weapons." He shifted his weight. "You know what's crazy?" We shook our heads. "Everyone believed him. They actually bought his bullshit."

Cyrus stole a glance in my direction. *I know, bro. This gets crazier by the minute.*

Jax ran his finger along the smooth side of the blade.

"What happened to the knives the Collectors confiscated?" my brother asked.

"They were added to Zenith's arsenal. When the ordinance passed, word spread like wildfire to the men running the black market. They got their hands on a few before the Collectors snatched up the rest."

Cyrus pointed to Jax's armed hand. "So how did you get yours?"

"I have my ways," he said, folding the blade back into the handle.

I bet you do.

Jax cleared his throat. "That's enough chatting about Aroonyx's troubled history for one day. We have a lot of ground to cover, so let's begin with the basics. Like how to deflect an attack." I gulped. "Elara, you're up first." He looked at my brother. "You better pay attention because I don't like repeating myself."

Snapped out of his trance, Cyrus focused on me and Jax.

"The most important thing to remember when fighting a Collector is this: don't let him take you to Zenith. I'm not trying to frighten you"—Jax looked only at me while he spoke—"I'm preparing you for what lies ahead."

I blew out a nervous breath; sweat dotted the back of my neck.

"Zenith takes great pleasure in watching others suffer. He's tortured people to the brink of insanity. If any discomfort arises when fighting a Collector—which we'll soon be doing." He glared at Cyrus. "Remember, it's nothing compared to what you will feel around Zenith."

The saliva evaporated from my mouth. *I'd like to go home now.*

My brother stood tall with his shoulders rolled back, his Solin courage shining forth. "Don't let them take you. Got it."

"An attack with a knife can look like this."

Within an instant, Jax flicked his wrist, exposed the blade and raised it to the side of my neck. I stumbled backward. Cyrus's hand shot out, catching my fall.

"It's natural to react the way you did when threatened."

Obviously. I rolled my eyes and moved in front of Jax once more.

"My job is to train you to do the opposite. I'll teach you how to anticipate an attack and use it to your advantage. Every Collector is well-trained in the art of combat. If provoked, they'll come at you full force. Nine times out of ten, a knife is used, and blood is always spilled. I need to make sure this blood is not your own."

I mouthed, "What is happening right now?" to Cyrus.

Jax chuckled and said, "I'm teaching you how to defend yourself."

"Fine, then please elaborate, Master Yoda."

Cyrus snorted at my Earthly reference while Jax stared at me with blank eyes.

Ignoring the comparison, he said, "I want you to anticipate their every move. Instead of taking a step backward, I want you to move forward. Here." Jax offered me the sharp blade. "Try to attack me. Aim for the side of my neck or my lower back, near the kidneys."

"Why not your chest?"

Jax tapped his sternum. "It takes a lot of force to get through the bones that protect the heart." He ran a finger down his ribs. "And you must perfect your aim if you want to slide a blade through these."

"Okay." I gripped the handle. "I'll go for the neck."

"Good choice. That's a kill shot. Just make sure you bring the knife forward once inserted so you cut the trachea."

I swore, wiping the sweat off my neck with my free hand. *Like I could ever do that to anyone.*

"Go on," he encouraged.

Without giving it much thought, I swung my arm and aimed for the side of Jax's neck. Like an elegant dance, he stepped forward and rotated his left arm in a circular motion around my armed hand, locking it between his bicep and forearm. I winced when he twisted it higher, forcing me to bend in a dramatic bow. He then used his right forearm to push my neck down to hip level.

"You see how that worked in my favor?" Jax said, holding me in place. "I used your attack to my advantage. The knife is a safe distance away from my body, and you can't stab anyone other than yourself." He wiggled my wrist to show me how close the blade was to my back. "From here, I can knee you in the face." He lifted his leg, stopping inches from my nose. "Or force your arm higher so you drop the knife."

I groaned, my muscles protesting the unnatural position.

Jax released his tight grip and took the knife from my hand. "Your turn."

I laughed at his ridiculous request. "There's no way I can do that."

"You must and you will. It takes practice."

"He's right, Elara," my brother added. "Give it a shot."

I inhaled a long breath and cracked my joints, preparing for our role reversal.

Jax rotated the knife in his hand. "I'll go slow so you can learn the proper technique."

I nodded, unsure of what to do with my hands.

Jax raised the sharp blade and lunged. I stepped with my left foot and moved forward, then circled my arm around his.

He scowled and shook his head in disapproval. "Cyrus, what did your sister do wrong?"

"Uh . . . I'm not sure."

"She exposed the underside of her arm. I could have easily cut the tendon"—he ran a finger over the crease between his bicep and forearm—"or the arteries in her wrist. Never expose a critical part of the body to your attacker. The Collectors are aware of the vital tendons and arteries and know which ones to cut."

I tucked a stray hair behind my ear. "When did you become an anatomy expert?"

"Inventions weren't the only thing Seekers brought back from Earth." Jax winked.

"I almost failed Biology," Cyrus said.

I laughed at my brother. "What does that have to do with anatomy?"

"I don't know. That's probably why I almost bombed the class. I never understood a word that left the teacher's mouth."

"Moving on," Jax said, motioning for us to repeat the lesson.

The two of us practiced the maneuver for long minutes. Jax displayed great patience while teaching me the proper steps while Cyrus watched from the sidelines, mirroring our every move.

"That's better," Jax said as I pretended to knee him in the face. "Now, let's try it for real."

I released my grip and adjusted the sweat-soaked shirt over my torso.

"I'm going to attack you like a Collector would in this situation. Use Cyrus's shared Solin strength to assist in apprehending me, all right?"

"I'll try," I murmured.

The Lunin shifted his posture to a more upright one. My pulse quickened and mind raced as I tried to recall the numerous steps. He charged, aiming for the side of my neck. I moved forward, and without thinking, exposed the palm of my hand.

I screamed when it connected with the sharp blade. Blood gushed from the wound. Cyrus cringed, watching me fall to my knees; the intense pain overwhelmed me.

Jax dropped the knife and knelt beside me. Colorful words left my mouth when he grabbed my injured hand and forced it open to examine the wound. I shut my eyes, unable to look at the torn flesh. Jax ripped off the sleeve of his shirt and wrapped it around my palm. My eyes watered as he applied pressure.

"Keep your hand closed in a fist," he instructed. "It's a deep cut, but stitches aren't required."

I gritted my teeth. "If you say so."

He jerked his chin at the gray bag near the fallen shelter. "I have something that will help the blood clot."

I waved him away. Jax hopped to his feet and urged Cyrus to take his place.

Unsure of how to help, my brother rested a hand on my shoulder and squatted beside me. "Do you want me to cut your other hand?"

"That's not funny."

"I'm trying to help you out, sis. If you have another injury, Jax might rip off his entire shirt and use it as a bandage."

I glared, knocking his hand off my shoulder.

"Does it hurt?" he asked, grimacing at the blood-soaked cloth.

"No, Cyrus. These are tears of joy."

He frowned, wiping the stream of blood that dripped down my wrist. "Sorry. That was a stupid question."

"Here, this will help," Jax said, lowering himself to the ground once more.

He reached for my hand and peeled the wet fabric from the wound. I stifled my complaints, fighting back tears.

"This will sting a bit," he said, after opening the small jar.

My entire body recoiled when he pressed a powdered substance into the wound.

"Sting?" I snapped. "Jax, that felt like you poured acid onto my skin."

"You're being dramatic again."

"Screw you."

He looked at my brother. "Hold your sister. I can't restrain her with one arm while I'm trying to do this. She's too strong while sharing your Solin strength."

Cyrus moved behind me, then held me in a bear hug.

"Nope. I don't like this."

Jax poured the powder into his palm. "The more you struggle, the longer this will take."

I whimpered, offering him my trembling hand.

His eyes found mine. "Ready?"

"Just do it."

Profanity escaped my mouth. The intense heat I felt around Cyrus surged through me faster than ever before. Overwhelmed by the searing pain, I grabbed Jax's wrist with my uninjured hand. The heat pulsated in waves and concentrated in my fingers. I closed my eyes and allowed it to escape. Jax gasped and fell backward.

"What the hell?" Cyrus released his tight grip.

Jax touched the large burn on his skin. A red handprint, my handprint wrapped around his wrist. He grimaced, pressing his finger near the bubbling flesh.

"What just happened?" I asked, my voice trembling. "How did I do that?"

Jax looked at Cyrus, assembling the missing puzzle piece, and a tiny grin crossed his handsome face when he said, "I don't know. But that's one hell of a trick." His smile grew from ear to ear. "A trick that Zenith and his Collectors won't see coming."

SEVEN

Intimidation Game

My eyes darted back and forth between Jax's injured hand and my own.

The words tripped over my tongue when I said, "I don't . . . understand what happened."

Jax helped me to my feet. "I don't either. I've never seen anything like it."

"That's a serious burn," Cyrus added.

The Lunin touched his blistered skin. "I'll deal with it later. Right now, I need to see if your sister can repeat this new talent of hers."

"No way," I said, hiding my uninjured hand behind my back. "I'm not doing that again."

Jax's eyes narrowed and his voice lowered. "Elara, this will give you a huge advantage over the Collectors." He reached behind my back and grabbed my wrist. "This little trick could save your life."

"He's right, sis. You need to try."

Why am I always outnumbered? I shut my eyes and allowed the gentle breeze to cool my flushed skin before looking at Jax. "I don't even know how it happened."

"What were you feeling right before you grabbed my wrist?"

"Pain."

He rotated my hand back and forth, searching for answers on my pale skin. "Can you elaborate?"

"It hurt like hell once you started pushing that powdered stuff into my cut. The familiar warming sensation moved through my body, the same way it does every time I'm around Cyrus. Then it got stronger, like when he gets angry." Cyrus cocked his head to one side. I paused, chewing on my lip. "But—something felt different."

"How so?" Jax asked.

"The intensity."

"Go on."

I slicked back a flyaway hair. "I always feel it in my hands, like that afternoon on the beach when you held the knife to his throat. That time, the heat wanted to escape"—I struggled to find the right words—"but this time it felt like it *needed* to. Like it was trapped or something."

"Cyrus, did you feel anything when you had Elara restrained?"

"Nothing like she described. It made me uncomfortable to see her in so much pain, though."

"Anything else?"

My brother scratched the stubble on his chin. "The warming sensation moved through me like it always does but—"

"But what?" I asked, noting his wide-eyed expression.

His mouth gaped. "It's like the heat drained from my body and passed to you."

A huge grin crossed Jax's face. "Elara, not only do you share your brother's Solin traits when in proximity, but you can absorb his power when physically connected."

"Okay," I stammered, unsure what to say. "So—"

"So?" Jax laughed hard. "Do you realize that together, the two of you could take down any Collector—and maybe even Zenith."

Relief washed over me as I glanced at Cyrus. He gave me a warm smile followed by a wink.

"Don't get too excited," Jax said. "Let's see if you can repeat the process."

The elated expression on my brother's face fell. Without speaking, he stepped behind me and wrapped his arms around me once more.

"Oh, hell no." I twisted in his tight grip and curled my injured hand into a fist. "I don't want you digging in my wound to see if you can get the same response."

Jax held up his hands in an unthreatening stance. "Fair enough, I won't intervene. Try it on your own."

Cyrus released me from the bear hug.

"Go on, take her hand," Jax encouraged him.

Cyrus flung the sweat off his brow before wrapping his fingers around my uninjured hand.

"Do you feel the warming sensation you spoke of?" Jax asked, as he circled us.

"I always feel warm around Cyrus."

My brother shook his head. "I don't feel anything unusual."

"Elara, why don't you focus on the sensation and see if you can locate its point of origin."

I shut my eyes and surrendered to the gentle waves of heat. I couldn't pinpoint an exact location because it pulsated throughout my entire body.

Jax stopped his circling and stood in front of my brother. "Is the heat leaving your hand?"

"Nope."

"I'm sorry, Elara. I have to try" were the last words I heard before Jax grabbed my wounded hand and squeezed it harder than I could bear.

I hollered at the top of my lungs. The comfortable warming sensation ignited into a raging fire. It zipped from one side of my body to the other. Like before, the heat concentrated in my hand, then released onto Jax's flesh.

His tongue hissed against his teeth as he let me go. Cyrus dropped my hand and searched his skin for hidden evidence.

"Damn it, Jax!" I yelled, adjusting the blood-soaked bandage. "Why did you do that?"

"You know the reason," he answered, showing me his scorched palm.

I cringed at the burn and hid my hands behind my back. "I'm sorry."

"Don't apologize. I did it to myself. Cyrus, did you feel the heat leave your body?"

"It happened so fast," he murmured, staring at his hand. "But yeah, I did. Like a quick jolt or something."

I winced, my injury throbbing in pain once more.

Jax pressed the heels of his palms into his eyes. "This trick won't help us if you can only repeat it when experiencing pain. We can't waste time trying to replicate it. I need to focus on your weapons training." He sighed, looking at the burn marks. "I won't let you risk your lives with uncertainty."

I eyed my brother. "We'll work on it in our free time."

He agreed.

The Lunin glanced at the swaying tree branches. "I'm sure the answer will reveal itself at the most opportune time."

I shuddered a breath, thinking of Zenith and the Collectors. *Let's hope so.*

I followed Jax's gaze and focused my attention on the bright green leaves that brushed against one another in a violent yet elegant dance. I frowned when a leaf lost its partner. It spun in endless circles, drifting farther away, leaving the other one alone, attached to a branch—stuck. It couldn't help its partner if it tried. No, it was gone.

My eyes stung with tears.

"Elara, why don't you take a break?" Jax suggested, inclining his head toward the spring. "Go cool off for a bit."

"I'll go with her," Cyrus said.

Jax nodded, his eyes never leaving me.

My brother and I walked side by side through the sweltering forest. The late afternoons were the warmest time of day. I fanned my shirt while Cyrus wiped his forehead with the back of his hand.

"Well, this has been quite the eventful day," he said, keeping his focus ahead.

"You can say that again."

He turned his head to find my eyes. "We have to find a way for you to absorb my power."

Uncertainty lingered in my voice when I said, "We will—eventually."

Cyrus's jaw cracked open. "What if I can absorb your power?" I arched a brow as he said, "We should try it—tonight. Hold hands and see what happens. Maybe we can run at the speed of sound or jump like Spiderman."

I snorted. The hilarious image of us racing through the woods flashed in my mind.

"I wasn't even trying to be funny."

"I know." I chuckled. "I just got this visual of us chasing after each other in a giant blur."

"Like vampires?"

"Exactly."

My brother rotated his tan arm in the sun. "Too bad we don't sparkle."

"I do." Cyrus shot me an incredulous look. "In here," I said, touching my heart.

The Solin roared with laughter. "We could write a comedy."

I waved my hand like a banner through the air. "Conversations with Elara and Cyrus."

We continued our mindless banter until we approached the spring.

"Want to go for a swim?" he asked.

"Yes, I'm literally sticking to my shirt."

Cyrus dashed forward and jumped fully clothed into the pool of water. Quick to follow, I tossed the bloodied bandage to the ground, kicked off my shoes, and leapt into the spring.

My body temperature dropped to a comfortable level as I submerged my head under the gurgling bubbles. I inhaled a deep breath when I surfaced. The large gash across my palm fizzed as if I had poured hydrogen peroxide into the wound. The throbbing pain subsided, allowing me to open and close my hand without discomfort.

"Better?" Cyrus asked.

"Much," I said, flipping onto my back.

My brother treaded water beside me. "I wish we could stay here at the spring and forget about Zenith and his Collectors."

"You have no idea."

"Can you imagine living on Aroonyx? Like—forever."

Jax's face appeared in my mind. I turned right side up and shook water from my ears. "It might not be so bad."

"What? You'd volunteer to go back in time?"

"It would take some adjusting, but I'd get used to it."

"I guess." He found my eyes. "It's weird, huh? For some reason, being back on Aroonyx feels right." He paused to dip his head in the water. "But at the same time, it feels like we don't belong."

"I hear ya. It's hard not comparing everything to Earth."

My brother pointed to the surrounding space. "But it is beautiful, isn't it?"

I smiled, acknowledging the lush grounds. Flat pieces of Clear Stone decorated the area around the spring, giving it a zen-like quality. The fine blades of the emerald-green grass flowed through the space like a fleece blanket. I looked up. The trees created a circle around the body of water, allowing us an unrestricted view of the cloudless sky.

"We better head back or Jax will start to worry," Cyrus said, swimming to the edge of the pool.

I sighed, unwilling to leave the serene space. Cyrus lifted himself out of the water, reached out a hand, and pulled me from the depths.

The corner of his mouth turned up into a smirk. "Uh . . . sis?"

"What's up?" I asked, wringing out my hair.

"Your shirt's a little see through."

I looked down and gasped.

Cyrus laughed at my misfortune as he removed his wet shirt. "Don't be embarrassed. It looks like you're wearing a swimsuit."

I cursed. The thin fabric exposed my entire bra.

"Try wringing out the water," he suggested, twisting his shirt with his hands.

I hesitated, considering my options.

"I'll turn around if it makes you feel better."

I nodded and pulled the wet shirt from my body after his back faced me. *Damn it. I can't wring it out.*

"You'll have to do it." I threw my brother the shirt, hitting him between his shoulder blades. "My hand's too sore."

Cyrus turned and picked it up off the ground. Embarrassed, I crossed my arms over my chest.

"Elara, you're my sister. I don't look at you like other girls. Plus, Hillary's swimsuits were way more revealing than your boring bra, so calm the hell down."

I envisioned Hillary's shapely figure. "Thanks for the mental picture."

He grinned before tossing me the still-wet shirt. I spun around and pulled it over my head. *Great.*

I looked at Cyrus and gestured to our failed attempt. "You have to go back to the campsite and bring me some dry clothes."

"Hell no."

"Why not?"

"I'm already in enough trouble with Jax. Can you imagine what he'd do if I strolled back to camp without you by my side?" He pulled the damp shirt over his head. "He would definitely punch me in the face this time."

"Please," I begged, bobbing up and down.

"Sorry, sis. That's a hard no. Get your own clothes."

I muttered, "I want a new brother," over my shoulder as I hurried toward the campsite.

Cyrus snickered, following close behind.

Hearing our footsteps, Jax turned. He did a double take, noting my appearance.

My brother murmured, "This will be fun to watch," as I dashed toward the gray bag.

I dropped the F-bomb in my mind at the sight of the fallen shelter. *Perfect. Let's make things even more awkward.* I turned my back on the two men and changed out of the wet shirt faster than one could blink, then whipped around only to find my brother laughing hysterically and Jax's head turned in the opposite direction. I glared at Cyrus while shaking my head in disapproval, then mouthed, "Bastard," which caused him to laugh even harder.

Jax pulled the knife from his back pocket. "Okay, Cyrus, you're up." The humor dissolved from my brother's expression when Jax flicked his wrist, the blade still wet with my blood. "I hope you paid attention earlier."

Cyrus gulped, the color draining from his tan face. Jax flashed me a tiny smirk. I winked, pleased with his intimidation game.

I looked at my brother. *Serves you right. You're not the only one who has my back.*

I plopped onto the soft grass and giggled at Cyrus's nervous expression when Jax resumed the attack position.

EIGHT

Forgiveness & a Kiss

The late-afternoon sun cast a copper hue across the vast forest, giving a majestic quality to the already stunning landscape. I sat across from Jax, discussing the logistics of how to escape a knife attack from behind while we waited for Cyrus to return from the spring. My fingers grazed the pale scar that ran across the palm of my hand—a reminder that more than two weeks had passed since the injury.

After Cyrus's mistake in the South Village, Jax accelerated our weapons training. We worked from sun up to sun down, stopping only for meals and bathroom breaks. My muscles, sore and fatigued, begged me to stop, but time was of the essence, so Jax pushed us harder with each passing day.

Cyrus and I learned how to escape several life-threatening situations. After my injury, Jax replaced his knife with a stick while training me. My brother didn't receive this special treatment. Thanks to our teacher's quick reaction time, knife marks decorated his hands and forearms.

Cyrus excelled in combative training. His Solin courage propelled him forward, and he never hesitated. Fluid and calculated, his movements reminded me of a well-trained stuntman on a movie set. Unlike my brother, I struggled with every step and always flinched when Jax attacked. I couldn't open the knife with one hand, hit a target, or disarm my training partners. Concerned with my learning curve, Jax instructed me in the late evenings after Cyrus fell asleep—but my progress still lagged, even with his private lessons.

We moved campsites daily. Fortunately, the Collectors didn't venture into the woods. If they did, we never saw them.

Jax visited the South Village every few days to restock our supplies. He mentioned talk of a male Seeker but assured us that few believed the rumor.

My brother and I longed to escape the secluded forest, but we knew better than to ask Jax to accompany him on his outings. When alone, we tried repeating the strange anomaly of absorbing my brother's Solin power. I summoned every negative emotion: anger, fear, sadness. Nothing happened. We even explored the option of him absorbing my Lunin power. Yes, we did run together at night through the woods, looking like a couple of idiots. Unfortunately, our little trick didn't work the other way around. Cyrus assured me we still had time—but if so, how much?

I sighed, looking up at Jax.

"Stop worrying, Elara. You'll get it."

"You say that, but it's been weeks. Cyrus—"

He held up his hand. "Yes, your brother is excelling in his training." My face fell. "But don't forget, he's played sports his entire life. His body is conditioned, and he's a Solin. This gives him the upper hand." I dropped my chin to my chest. Jax lowered his head to meet my gaze. "Trust me, one day everything will click, and these maneuvers will become second nature. Your body will react without thinking."

"If you say so."

"I do." He tossed the hair out of his eyes. "I try to avoid talking out of my ass."

I giggled and twisted my braid into a high bun, then slid the tie off my wrist. *Maybe I should cut my hair? It's hot enough without it sticking to me all day.*

"Hey, Jax?"

"No, I don't have any scissors."

I laughed hard, amazed with his ability to guess my thoughts.

"What's up?" he asked, hiding the smirk that tugged at the corner of his mouth.

"I never said thank you."

"For what?"

"Forgiving Cyrus."

"I didn't forgive your brother."

I frowned. "But you shook hands that day."

"That wasn't an act of forgiveness. That was me moving on."

I scoffed, crossing my legs in front of me. "Jax, it's not like Cyrus did it on purpose. How was he supposed to know that the word 'visitor' could cause so much trouble?"

"No, it wasn't his intention to put our lives at risk, but he disobeyed my orders and . . ." His voice trailed off.

"And what?"

Jax rubbed the back of his neck while saying, "I struggle with forgiveness. In my opinion, the mistake your brother made is unforgivable."

I rolled my eyes. "And you say I'm dramatic?" He mirrored my previous gesture. "That's a little harsh, don't you think?"

"No, it's not."

Frustrated with his limited view, I sat taller and said, "One doesn't search for forgiveness. It's always there. Waiting for you to use it."

"It's not that easy."

"Yes, it is. I did it with my adoptive parents. Do you think I wanted to forgive them? They lied to me for eighteen years."

"That's different. They never put you in danger. They kept your adoption a secret out of love."

I gritted my teeth. "You're wrong. Forgiveness is one in the same, regardless of the situation. A wise man once said, 'There are no justified resentments.'"

Jax tossed his head back to the late-afternoon sky.

"It's not funny," I scolded. "It's true. Forgiving Cyrus doesn't mean you approve his mistake. It means you accept his naiveté to the situation. It's your choice: condemn or forgive.

If Cyrus had known better, he would have never spoken to that man. Mistakes are due to ignorance, and in my eyes—that's easy to forgive." I rolled onto my knees. "Do you want to know what this last year has taught me?"

"Sure. Enlighten me."

"Forgiveness is a gift to yourself. It only takes a moment, then you're free of the weight of resentment."

Jax scanned my face, his eyes searching the depths of my soul. After a long pause, he said, "Your maturity and wisdom surprise me. I'm impressed."

My face warmed; compliments always made me uncomfortable.

A gentle heat flowed through my veins. *Cyrus must be near.* Jax hopped to his feet and pulled me off the ground, his pale hand lingering longer than necessary.

"I miss the first campsite," Cyrus said, walking toward us. "It was closer to the spring."

"Did you want to borrow the car next time?"

He glared and shook his head, sending water flying into my face. I stuck out my tongue. Jax chuckled at our sibling behavior.

"What combative skills are we learning this afternoon?" Cyrus asked.

"We're done for today," Jax answered, reaching for his gray bag.

I stole a glance at my brother. Speaking as one, we asked, "Why?"

"We need to visit the outskirts of a village."

"We?" Cyrus stammered.

"Yes." Jax tossed the bag over his shoulder. "The journey is far. I'm not comfortable leaving the two of you alone overnight." He looked at Cyrus. "You're excelling in your weapons training. You need your own knife. I want more than one of us armed at all times."

Cyrus's head nodded with great enthusiasm.

"What about me?" I asked.

"Elara, I'm not comfortable giving you a knife—not yet at least."

Cyrus tucked his hands into his pockets and stared at the ground.

"Then how am I supposed to protect myself?"

"You've learned the proper steps of how to escape a hold and how to deflect an attack."

Barely.

Jax adjusted the worn straps of his bag. "I can't give you a knife if it can be used against you in an altercation. It's too dangerous. You're not ready."

I sighed. *He's right. I'd end up stabbing myself with the damned thing.*

"How are you going to get your hands on another one?" my brother asked. "I thought they were only available to Collectors or on the black market?"

"I have a close friend who owns a public house." Our heads cocked to one side, unfamiliar with the word. "A pub," Jax clarified. "You know like a bar on Earth."

Cyrus's eyelids moved in slow motion. "You have a friend?"

"I do." Jax smirked, bending down to re-tie the lace of his boot. "And I'm sure you find that surprising." My brother mumbled his agreement. "But I've known this trustworthy person for many years, so we're in good hands."

"How long does it take to get there?" I asked.

"A few hours," Jax said, facing us once more. "I don't want us traveling after dark, so we'll stay the night. Even if you could repeat your little trick, it won't do us any good because Cyrus can't use his Solin traits once the sun goes down. If Collectors are on the prowl, Lunins will be waiting to pounce."

My heart hammered in my chest as I looked at my brother. "Maybe we should stay here."

"No." His face hardened. "We're going. This could be our only opportunity to get me a knife."

"Cyrus is right. We're running out of time."

I rolled my neck, bothered by the sense of impending doom that weighed down on me. My eyes drifted between the two men. "This doesn't feel right."

"It'll be fine. You've been stuck in these damn woods for too long." Cyrus tapped his temple. "You're not thinking straight."

I locked my eyes onto Jax. He considered my concern for only a moment before motioning for us to follow him through the woods. I dropped my head and moved forward.

As we walked, Jax lectured us on how to act around a Collector. "If we run into any trouble, let me do the talking. They're masters of deception and trickery. It's easy to believe the lies that roll off their tongues." He stretched his legs over a piece of Clear Stone. "Don't hesitate if threatened. They see that behavior as a weakness and will use it to their advantage. Remember your training. And don't let your emotions cloud your better judgment."

We strolled through the forest in a single-file line, our eyes scanning every tree in sight. The manmade trail that led to the South Village appeared sooner than expected. Jax took a sharp right, heading away from the market. Our feet guided us into the unknown, Jax as our guide.

I flinched at a loud flapping sound—wings.

"Dragon," Cyrus stammered, dashing to my side, his head turning every which way. "I knew we'd find one."

Jax snickered, pointing to the darkening sky. A majestic bird with shiny black and yellow feathers soared through the forest. Its long, wispy tail fluttered in the warm breeze as it darted out of sight through a large gap in the canopy above.

"Winter's coming," Jax whispered.

"When?"

"Soon."

I sighed, eager for cooler weather. The warming sensation faded from my body and my eyes adjusted to the darkening woods around us. I eyed Cyrus. He nodded, confirming he could share my Lunin traits.

"We'll stay off the main path to avoid making contact with the others." Jax pointed to a cluster of boulders that appeared to go on forever. "The terrain gets a little rough, so mind your step."

Great. Of course, it does.

We struggled to keep up with Jax as he went up and over the jagged rocks. He moved like an expert climber, his hands finding the perfect gaps and ledges to assist with the challenging task.

I chuckled quietly to myself. *And I thought the walk to Starbucks was tough. Now, here I am, scaling boulders the size of small houses.*

I swore when my foot slipped against the smooth surface. Jax grabbed my wrist while Cyrus held my leg, leaving me dangling like a novice trapeze artist. Cyrus used one hand to raise the lower half of my body while Jax pulled me to my feet.

He smirked. "Do you see why I laughed during our walk to Starbucks?"

Ignoring his verbal jab, I asked, "How much farther?"

"It's just beyond those trees," he said, pointing to an area over a hundred yards away.

I cursed, shutting my eyes. My hands ached and half of my nails were broken or bleeding. Cyrus, equally exhausted, lifted himself over the edge of the white rock. He rubbed his forearms, loosening his tight muscles.

"I'm starving," I complained, touching my rumbling stomach.

"We'll eat soon. They serve food at the pub."

I groaned as we made our way over the last boulder. A small opening appeared between a cluster of trees.

Jax turned to face us. "It gets pretty busy during the evenings. Keep your heads down and stay close." He narrowed his eyes at my brother. "And don't talk to anyone."

Short minutes passed before we approached a large dwelling that rested only feet away from the manmade path we avoided on our journey. I glanced at the full moons that hung side by side in the purple sky. Unlike moonlit nights on Earth, thousands of twinkling stars surrounded the glowing orbs.

My head turned at the sound of rusted hinges. A tall Lunin with a full beard exited the pub. His blue eyes sparkled in the moonlight as he chatted with an even taller Solin.

The men shifted their features into neutral at the sight of Jax. They lowered their gaze and hurried down the stone steps toward the trail, never looking back. I shrugged when Cyrus shot me a curious glance. Jax pulled open the wooden door and waved a hand over his shoulder for us to follow.

My mouth watered as soon as we stepped over the threshold. The smell of fresh bread wafted into my nose, causing me to whimper like a hungry pup.

Cyrus's eyes widened at our new surroundings. Glowing lanterns illuminated the quaint space in a warm glow. Solins and Lunins dined across from one another, their lips touching the rim of their mugs between bites. I drooled, watching a man toss a piece of bread into his mouth. *That looks so good.* Over the past few weeks our diet had consisted of rooted vegetables and unseasoned dried meats.

My thoughts dissolved when I noticed Jax's elated expression. A huge smile swept across his unshaven face as he made eye contact with someone at the bar. He let out a long, relaxed breath and his eyes lit up with an emotion I had never seen—desire.

My heart sank when I followed his gaze.

A young Solin woman stood behind the bar, her eyes focused only on Jax. I did a double take. *She's the most beautiful woman I've ever seen.*

Agreeing with my inner dialogue, Cyrus murmured, "Holy shit," under his breath.

The Solin leaned over the counter to speak with a customer, her cleavage spilling out of her low-cut shirt. Cyrus cleared his throat. I stood motionless, enamored by her beauty.

The young woman's features mirrored a Victoria Secret model: tall, curvy—perfect. She tossed her layered, platinum-blonde hair behind her back, the tousled waves brushing against the bar top. The Solin's flawless complexion shimmered in the warm light and her deep-set, golden eyes sparkled when she met Jax's gaze. She whispered inaudible words near the ear of a Lunin man who stood beside her before leaving her place behind the bar.

Cyrus's jaw fell open and his eyes glazed over as the woman approached.

"Hey you," she purred to Jax.

I frowned. Even her voice sounded attractive.

I almost choked on my spit when she rested her delicate hands on the sides of Jax's face. He flashed her a seductive grin and before I could blink, she pressed her lips against his.

My posture deflated like a balloon with a slow leak.

The kiss, though brief, was filled with a strong sense of familiarity. *They've done this before—probably a hundred times.*

The young woman smiled as she pulled away. She touched her wet lips, then turned to face me and my brother. I stiffened; the ugly emotion of jealousy took over when Jax slid his arm around her tiny waist.

My brother's face beamed when Jax said, "This is the friend I was telling you about." He found my eyes. "I'd like you to meet Idalia."

NINE

I See the Sun

My brother's hand shot out. I rolled my eyes. He couldn't even introduce himself without stumbling over his words.

Idalia giggled as she wrapped her delicate fingers around his. "It's a pleasure to meet you, Cyrus."

I glared. Even her teeth were perfect: sparkly white and straight. My stomach tightened; I liked her less by the minute.

"And you must be Elara," she said, offering me her hand.

I gave it a quick squeeze but refused to make eye contact.

"So—" Cyrus lowered his voice. "You know about us, right? The reason we're back on Aroonyx."

Idalia nudged Jax with her hip. "Of course. He tells me everything." She leaned closer to my brother, her warm breath grazing his ear. "Don't worry, your secret's safe with me."

Cyrus shuddered at her proximity, his amber eyes igniting with lust. Jax narrowed his gaze when I huffed a breath louder than expected.

"I bet you're all hungry after your long journey," she said.

"I know Elara is."

I stared at Jax through the tiny slits of my eyes. "I'm capable of speaking for myself." His lips pressed into a tight line when I added, "You're distracted, I'll let it slide."

Idalia eyed the Lunin, curious about my sharp tone.

Playing the peace keeper, Cyrus said, "Well, I'm starved. Let's eat."

She pointed to a secluded booth at the back of the room. "Grab a seat and I'll bring over some plates."

The spark in Cyrus's eyes glowed brighter as he watched her stroll toward a door located near the bar.

"Men," I grumbled, storming over to the empty table.

A river of heat flowed through me, matching the way I felt around my brother during the day.

He slid onto the seat beside me and nudged me in the ribs. "You better cool it, sis."

"I'll cool it when the two of you stop drooling."

He added a flippant response while Jax took a seat across from us. His blue eyes searched for mine. Ignoring him, I focused my attention on the other side of the room.

Jax snickered at my behavior and clasped his scarred hands on the table. "Elara." I refused to meet his gaze. "Before you embarrass yourself, let me explain—"

I waved him away. "It's fine. None of it matters, anyway."

A heartbeat later Idalia returned, her arms filled with food.

"Let me help you," Cyrus said, banging his leg on the underside of the booth as he sprung to his feet.

Jax lifted his hands, allowing the table to steady itself before lowering them once more. I rested my chin in my hand, unamused with the ridiculous sight.

Idalia handed Cyrus two plates. My nostrils flared at the steam that rose from the warm bread and meats.

"I wasn't sure what you liked"—she paused to hand me a plate of food—"so I brought you one of everything."

I tossed it onto the table. Even her kindness irritated the hell out of me.

Jax cleared his throat and patted the seat beside him. "Thank you, Idalia." She smiled, sliding her perfect body next to his. "That was very considerate of you."

Their arms touched just enough to make me even more uncomfortable. Jax found my eyes. "Wasn't that a kind gesture, Elara?"

I plastered a fake grin on my face and through pursed lips said, "Thanks for the food, Idalia."

She nodded.

Taking my discomfort to a new level, Cyrus said, "Jax, why didn't you tell us about your beautiful girlfriend? All this time, we thought you were single."

My jaw clenched. I crossed my arms and leaned back in my seat. "He's right." I locked my eyes onto Idalia. "How strange? Jax never mentioned you at all."

The color drained from her face.

Jax inhaled a long breath through his nose, and in a quiet voice he said, "I only share information that's relevant to our mission. My personal life has nothing to do with either of you." Cyrus bowed his head like a submissive pup. "But if you must know"—he reached for her hand—"Idalia is just a close friend."

She batted her eyes, then motioned for us to eat. Cyrus reached for something that resembled a rack of ribs. I didn't budge. My appetite had vanished.

Eager for a distraction, I averted my eyes from the mouth-watering feast. Across the room, I noticed an attractive Lunin staring at our table. Tight black curls bordered her pale face and her light-blue eyes never left Jax as she leaned her back against the wall. I moved my gaze to the food that covered my plate. *She's probably another one of Jax's "close" friends.*

"Eat something," Cyrus pressed, his mouth full of food.

"I'm not hungry."

"You were starving right before Jax and Idalia—"

I slammed the toe of my shoe into his shin bone. My brother cursed, then coughed, nearly choking on his food. Recovering, he threw a piece of bread at me, hitting me square between the eyes. I grabbed my fork and tried stabbing him in the hand. Jax clicked his tongue on the roof of his mouth, an audible warning for us to cease our childlike behavior.

The others enjoyed their warm meals while I sat fuming, glaring at the beautiful Solin.

Idalia noticed Cyrus glance over his shoulder every so often. "You can relax," she said, dabbing a napkin to her mouth. "I'm not expecting any unwanted visitors tonight. The Collectors stopped by a few days ago."

"How do you know they were here?" he asked, taking a sip of water. "I thought they were masters at blending in with a crowd."

Idalia shrugged, picking at a piece of bread. "Over the years I've learned how to tell them apart from your average citizen."

More sarcasm left my mouth. "You act like you know one."

She eyed Jax. He nodded his approval.

"I did." She met my gaze. "My father."

Cyrus's forked clanged against the silver plate when it fell out of his hand. "Your father was a Collector?"

"Yes. He worked as one until they disbanded after Arun's death." A sadness filled her golden eyes as she spoke. "The life of a Collector was quite turbulent after the Clearing of the Seekers."

Jax cleared his throat as he looked at me and Cyrus. "This is the time period when Arun jailed and killed the Seekers."

We nodded our understanding while Idalia continued, "The citizens of Aroonyx disagreed with the Collectors' destructive ways. My father took shelter in the woods before meeting my mother. He wanted a fresh start, so they married and decided to live an honest life. The two of them built this place with their bare hands." She motioned to the aged wood. "My parents wanted to give the people an escape, somewhere to ease their troubled minds. I think it was my father's way of apologizing for the horrible things he did to those poor Seekers. I was seven when they murdered him."

Cyrus swore, dropping his head.

"Unfortunately, his past caught up with him. One morning I heard my mother screaming his name—Janus, Janus—over and over again. I ran down the stairs and when I opened the door"—she jerked her chin across the room—"I saw him restrained by two men he used to work with—ex-Collectors. They called him a traitor and slit his throat in front of me and my mother."

I sat motionless, unable to process the tragedy. Cyrus repeated a strong four-letter curse word as he looked at Jax. His expression remained vacant, already familiar with the violent story.

"They're not all bad," she said, lifting her head.

"Who?" my brother asked.

"Collectors."

I let out a sharp breath while tracing a set of initials carved in the wooden table. "I don't see us hanging out with one anytime soon."

"Elara, there's two sides to every story," she added.

My finger paused as it finished the curve of the letter S. "This is true." I looked up. "But still, I want nothing to do with those murdering bastards."

Idalia let out a deep sigh. "I understand how you feel. The Collectors have committed horrendous crimes, but the problem is—they don't know any better."

I shook my head. "Everyone knows right from wrong."

"That's the rub. These poor kids think they're doing the right thing. Zenith has them all brainwashed."

"I get it," I said, picking at my broken nails. "Regardless, I would never trust one—not even an ex-Collector."

"Never say never. People can, and do, change. My father was living proof."

The four of us sat in an awkward silence. Jax attempted to meet my gaze while Idalia stared at her half-empty plate of food. Cyrus kept his eyes glued to the Solin while I traced the numerous engravings on the table.

Long minutes passed before Idalia broke the silence. "I'm sure you're all tired. Why don't I show you your room?"

My brother slid out of the booth and stretched his muscular arms. "Thank you for dinner." He patted his full stomach. "It was delicious."

Idalia grinned and pointed to a staircase behind the bar. The two Solins chatted as they strolled through the fading crowd. I looked at Jax. His expression remained unreadable—blank. I wanted to chew his ass for not telling me about Idalia, instead I clenched my hands into fists, climbed out of the booth, and headed toward the stairs.

The steep steps led to a narrow hallway. There was a door to the right and a door to the left. Idalia pulled a small silver key from her back pocket and inserted it into the lock.

I scanned the cramped space as we stepped over the threshold. *Well, it's not the Marriott. But it's better than the woods.*

A full-sized bed rested near a window that overlooked the front entrance of the pub. Wooden floors, ebony in color, lined the quaint room. My fingers grazed a bowl that rested on a square table by the bed; the full moons' light reflected off the water inside the vessel. *Is that for us to wash our face and hands?*

"I'll be right back." Idalia turned and headed across the hall into the other room.

The old floorboards creaked under our weight as we inspected the temporary living space. Jax stood in the doorway, watching my every move.

"You can have the bed," Cyrus said, mid-yawn. "Jax and I will sleep on the floor."

"I won't be staying in this room tonight."

My head snapped toward the Lunin. Cyrus lifted a brow.

Before we could ask about his sleeping arrangements, Idalia squeezed past him.

"Here you go," she said, placing a small candelabra on the bedside table. "I thought you might want some more light."

I scowled. "In case you forgot, I'm a Lunin, I can see just fine in the dark, and thanks to me"—I inclined my head at Cyrus—"so can my brother." I plastered another fake grin on my face. "But I'm sure you already knew that, considering Jax tells you everything."

Cyrus flashed me a stern look and mouthed, "Be nice."

Idalia's face hardened as she removed the glowing candles. "Of course. How foolish of me to care."

Jax's eyes filled with disappointment when she stormed off into the other room. "I'm sleeping in Idalia's room tonight."

He met my gaze. "And I don't like interruptions, so make sure to knock if you need anything. After all, I would hate to see you embarrass yourself—again."

Bastard. Anger consumed me when Jax slammed the door shut behind him. I slipped off my shoe and threw it at where he once stood.

Cyrus grabbed my arm and spun me around to face him. "What the hell has gotten into you?"

"Idalia. That's what's gotten into me."

"She's done nothing wrong."

I poked him in the chest. "You're too blinded by her beauty to see why I'm angry."

"Oh, I know why you're pissed," he said, slapping my hand away, "and let me be honest with you, sis. Jealousy is not an attractive look for you."

I folded my arms across my chest and stomped across the room.

"Do you realize the way you acted tonight is the exact way Hillary acted? One of the reasons you wanted nothing to do with her."

I cringed, regret's claws digging into my back.

My brother sighed as he took a seat on the bed. "What's going on, sis? I thought you were better than that."

"I don't know." My eyes stung with unshed tears. I slid down the wall until I sat on the floor. "I've never acted like the crazy, jealous girl who throws shoes at closed doors."

Cyrus chuckled.

I pulled the hair tie from my bun and loosened the braid as I confided in my brother. "I guess I thought that Jax—I don't know what I thought, but obviously I was way off."

"Elara, you can care for more than one person."

"I don't believe that."

"It's true," he added, sliding off the bed onto the floor. "I started having feelings for you when I was dating Hillary."

I squished up my face, recalling our awkward conversation outside the Spanish portable.

"Sorry, that was a bad example—but it was the only one I had. Jax cares for you, Elara. I know he does."

A salty drop of emotion rolled off my cheek as I found his eyes.

"Hey, it's okay," he said, squeezing my hand. "I'm sure watching them kiss was a huge blow, but you heard Jax. They're just friends."

"Friends?"

"Let's look at it from his perspective. Jax is a twenty-two-year-old man, living a mysterious life alone in the woods. He's a handsome guy." I arched a brow at his honest remark. "I'm comfortable enough with myself to say that."

An unforced smile broke at the corner of my mouth.

"Did you think Jax had stayed celibate all these years? You saw Idalia, right?" I lowered my gaze. "Good Lord," he added. "She wouldn't have to twist my arm to hop in bed. I mean she could if she wanted to. Hell, I'd do anything she asked if that meant getting into—"

"Cyrus."

He laughed once more. "I'm just trying to ease your mind. I bet they're friends with benefits and nothing more."

I groaned, dragging my hands down my face.

"Jax has lived a rough life, most of which we know nothing about. It's obvious he trusts Idalia or he wouldn't have shared our secret. The guy's got like one friend, Elara, give him a break."

"Fair enough."

My brother smirked at my bare foot, and in a horrible British accent, he asked, "Shall I fetch your other shoe, my lady?"

I bowed my head. "That would please me, sir."

Cyrus hopped to his feet and jogged across the room. He froze when a gentle knock tapped on the door, his fingers dangling over the silver knob. A short breath later, he pulled it open, peered down the hallway, then bent down to retrieve something off the floor—a plate of food.

A smug grin crossed his face as he strolled over the aged floorboards. He handed me the note that rested on a slice of bread.

I unfolded the gray parchment and read the words aloud. "Elara, here's a little something in case you get hungry—Idalia."

My hand fell onto my lap. Cyrus smiled as he tossed me my shoe.

"I'll apologize tomorrow," I said, feeling less crazy and more like my old self.

We stayed up for hours chatting about everything from Jax and Idalia, to Cyrus's past relationship with Hillary. We laughed often, enjoying each other's company. My lips paused at the sound of footsteps coming down the hallway. They grew louder, then disappeared into the other room.

"At least Jax will be in a better mood tomorrow," Cyrus teased. "I know I'd be after spending a night with Idalia."

I curled my hand into a fist and punched him in his bicep. He sat there unfazed, smirking at my feeble attempt.

"That only works during the day," he said, dusting off his shoulder.

I rubbed my sore knuckles and shut my eyes, surrendering to the emotions that surfaced. Thanks to Cyrus's practical approach, I no longer felt jealous when I thought of the beautiful Solin. I accepted her role in Jax's life. *It is what it is.* At that moment, I decided to let go of the hidden sentiments I harbored for the Lunin. I valued his friendship too much to risk losing him altogether.

Cyrus let out a loud yawn. "We should get some sleep." He pointed at the window. "It's getting late."

I climbed off the floor and collapsed onto the bed, my eyes heavy with the weight of the day.

"I'm glad this floor is so comfortable," Cyrus said, letting his head bang against the wooden panels.

I patted the space beside me and scooted to the edge of the bed, allowing room for my brother. His massive frame took up almost every inch of the soft mattress.

I rolled onto my side and stared at the bedroom door, wondering how to apologize to Idalia. *Sorry for being a bitch?*

Sorry for acting like a crazy bitch? I hummed my agreement. *That seems like a good place to start.*

Long minutes passed. Cyrus snored and my body sank deeper with each relaxed breath that entered my lungs. Dreamland was just a heartbeat away. My rational thoughts mixed with fantasy when—BAM. The bedroom door slammed against the wall.

My eyes shot open. Cyrus sat up and spun around on the bed, confused about his whereabouts. Adrenaline surged through me as I sprang to my feet.

A shirtless Jax dashed into the room. He tossed his wet hair out of his anxious eyes and barked, "Get up!"

Cyrus hurried to stand, then stared at the Lunin with wide eyes. "Why? What's wrong?"

"They're outside." Jax motioned to the window while he pulled a shirt over his head. "And they'll be here any minute."

"Who?" I stammered.

A tangible fear grabbed hold of me when Jax found my eyes. "The Collectors."

TEN

A Painful Confession

My entire body went rigid.

Jax hurried across the room and with cautious eyes, he peeked out the window. "They're at the front door."

I turned at the sound of Idalia's quiet voice. "Use the back exit."

Dressed in different clothes, a loose-fitting shirt hung off her shoulder; her tiny shorts were barely visible under the long garment. She rubbed her red nose as she looked at Jax, her fingers clinging to his gray bag.

The Lunin focused his attention on me and my brother. "We'll go out the back door. When I say run, haul ass toward the spring. Your Lunin endurance will be tested tonight. Use the same route we came. Go over the boulders and stay off the main path. Don't stop running until I give the signal. Do you understand your orders?"

The severe, militant tone Jax used caused the hairs on the back of my neck to stand. My heart pounded in my ears. I breathed hard, unsure if I could obey his command.

I nearly jumped out of my skin when a loud knock thumped on the downstairs door. I looked at my brother, who kept his eyes glued to Jax. I flinched again. My anxiety increasing with each pound of a determined fist.

"Hurry, go now," Idalia encouraged.

She handed Jax his bag, then slipped a cloth-wrapped item into his hand.

A black folded knife appeared when he unrolled the package. The Lunin tossed it to my brother who caught it with one hand. He slid it into his back pocket, his eyes now fully alert.

Jax looked at Idalia and said, "Thank you—for everything," before kissing the top of her head.

She bit her lip, forcing back tears. A piece of her long hair blew into her face when Jax sprinted past her down the hallway. Cyrus hurried after him. As soon as I stepped over the threshold, she grabbed my wrist and said, "Promise me you'll look after him."

Unsure how to respond, my tongue tapped against the back of my teeth.

Her nails dug into my flesh. "He needs your help—in more ways than one."

Idalia spoke equally cryptic as the Lunin who waited impatiently at the top of the stairs.

"Go," she whispered, pushing me along.

As soon as our feet touched the last step, a deep voice bellowed, "Open up," from behind the closed door.

Jax inclined his head toward the exit at the back of the pub. The room, once bustling with noisy chatter, was silent, void of any sound other than our muffled footsteps tiptoeing through the quaint space.

Idalia hurried down the stairs. "I'm coming," she called.

Jax lifted a finger to his mouth, commanding our silence as he cracked open the door. We snaked our way through the narrow exit, one anxious body at a time, then hurried around the side of the establishment.

I slammed into Jax when his feet skidded to a stop. Unaffected by my ill-timed approach, he reached around his back and squeezed my wrist.

"What do you want, Leo?"

I blinked, baffled by the change in Idalia's voice. Her sweet and sultry tone transformed to raspy and direct, one filled with loathing.

The man said, "One of your customers gave us a tip. They said Jax was here with a young Solin and Lunin." His voice lowered. "The twins."

I lifted my free hand and bit my knuckles. Jax tightened his grip while Cyrus squeezed my shoulder, silent commands to stay quiet.

"It was a busy night. I stayed behind the counter."

The hidden figure let out a frustrated breath. "So you didn't see Jax or the twins?"

"Leo, I haven't seen Jax in months. And when I do, it's only in passing."

Damn. That sounded legit. She's a good liar.

"I hope you're not withholding information from us?" he pressed, his tone sharper than before.

"Come on, Leo," she purred in a seductive voice. "You're familiar with my father's past. I'm no different from you. We're on the same side—remember?"

The Collector paused and considered her comment for only a moment before saying, "Perhaps, but my hands are tied with this mission. I have direct orders from Pollux." The muscles in Jax's arm contracted. "He wants us to search the place," Leo added, letting out a high-pitched whistle.

Boots—and lots of them—shuffled out from the brush.

Jax held up a closed fist. We waited—listened.

"Very well," Idalia said. "If you must."

The rusted hinges squeaked as she opened the door wide enough for the Collectors to enter the pub.

"We won't be long," Leo said. "Pollux wants us searching every village tonight."

I tried to inhale a small breath, the reality of our situation suffocating me. *We don't stand a chance.*

Jax let go of my wrist and peered around the stone wall, then whispered, "Run," before sprinting toward the forest.

Without hesitation, our feet churned beneath us. Up and over the boulders we climbed, sliding down the steep descent to save time. My cracked nails bled more than our previous journey, but I never stopped—never dared to look back. The adrenaline that pumped through my veins, along with Leo's foreboding words, propelled me forward.

Long minutes passed before Jax motioned for us to stop. Cyrus skidded across a smooth piece of Clear Stone and nearly crashed into me. When he grabbed my shoulder to steady his balance, he ripped out a chunk of my hair.

"Sorry," he whispered, untangling the strands from his hand.

I touched the tender spot on my scalp. *It's cool. I needed a trim.*

Ignoring my misfortune, Jax scanned the vast space. "We can slow our pace now," he said, pointing to the flat grassy area near the manmade path that led to the South Village. "Stay close and keep your eyes peeled."

We nodded.

Cyrus helped me down the last boulder, and when he rested me on the ground, he nudged me with his arm.

"What's up?" I asked, curious about the concern that filled his amber eyes.

Jax turned. "I said we could slow our pace, not stop and chat."

My brother let out a frustrated breath, his feet glued to the ground.

"Come on. Let's go," I said, tugging at his arm. He hesitated, then moved forward when I added, "Boss man doesn't like to wait."

I eyed him as we walked. *Something's wrong—very wrong.* Cyrus's eyes burned a hole in Jax's back and his lips moved with inaudible words.

"What's wrong?" I asked, moving closer. Silence. "Cyrus. You're freaking me out. What's going on?"

He turned his head but kept his eyes fixed on the Lunin. "How does Leo know Jax?"

My mind raced, trying to find a plausible answer. "I don't know. Aroonyx has a small population. Maybe—"

"No. That's not it."

"Then what is it?"

"Think about it, sis. It takes hours to walk from the cliff-side to the South Village. Isn't it odd that as soon as we return to Aroonyx, four Collectors appear?"

I stammered, unsure of his implication.

Cyrus lowered his head and whispered near my ear. "And why did Jax let them chase him into the woods?"

"Because he didn't want them seeing us."

"Elara. No one knew we were back on Aroonyx—no one but Jax." My heart sank. "He said the Collectors aren't a concern unless a citizen has caused a disturbance or they're provoked. We weren't doing anything wrong on the cliffside. We look like every other Solin and Lunin."

"Shh." I inclined my head toward our guide. "He'll hear you."

Ignoring me, Cyrus went on, "We should have been able to walk right past those Collectors."

What is he trying to say? A thought crossed my mind. "Our Earth clothes."

"What?"

"Our old clothes," I said, fanning my shirt. "It would have been an instant giveaway if they saw us wearing what we had on that day."

Cyrus ran a hand over his chin as he considered my argument. "Yeah, you're probably right." A momentary relief washed over me until he added, "But something's fishy. I can smell it."

My head popped up when Jax whispered my name. "I need to speak with you."

I stole a glance at my brother. He waved me away.

My feet guided me toward Jax. His blue eyes scanned every tree in sight as we made or way back toward the campsite.

I shivered at the frigid gust that slapped me across the face. *Geez. Where did that come from?* Curious about the sudden change in temperature, I looked up and searched for the twin moons through the gaps in the swaying branches. They rested low in the night sky without a cloud to hide behind.

"Elara, I want to talk to you about Idalia."

I sighed, staring at the ground. "I screwed up, okay?" Jax turned his head toward me. "I'm sorry I acted like a"—I paused, omitting a five-letter word—"slightly unstable person back there tonight. I was going to apologize in the morning but—"

"That's not what I wanted to talk about."

"Oh," I stammered. "It's not?"

"No. I wanted to explain—" His words vanished as he pulled me behind his back.

My brother dashed to our side. In the blink of an eye, Jax pushed us behind a tree, our bodies pressed together as one. I held my breath and dug my bloodied nails into the soft bark when a man's voice sounded in the near distance.

"We've searched everywhere. They're not in the forest."

A different voice—a deeper one said, "We keep looking until we find them. Pollux's orders."

I could feel every ligament in Jax's body contract. He forced me closer to Cyrus, my back pressed into my brother's chest.

The first man scoffed. "Easy for Pollux to say, he's not out here chasing his tail. No, he's sitting on his ass with Zenith while we—"

Feet skidded to a stop. The deep voiced man said, "You better shut your *fucking* mouth. If Pollux heard that, he'd cut out your tongue and make you swallow it."

Another man snickered. "Or worse, take you to the basement."

I winced when Cyrus grabbed my arm.

"He won't have time." A different voice spoke. "As soon as we find Jax and the twins, Pollux and the rest of the IC will be dispatched to finish the mission."

The first man huffed a breath. "*If* we find them."

A wicked laugh rumbled in the deep voiced man's chest when he said, "Oh, we will. It's only a matter of time before Jax's past catches up with him. I'm sure he's getting homesick by now."

The men chuckled their agreement as they headed in the opposite direction.

Cyrus jerked my arm with so much force, I thought it would detach from my body.

I glared, turning my head. "That hurt," I mouthed.

His eyes filled with a nasty mixture of anger and anxiety.

Jax held up his fist, motioning for us to remain both still and silent. We waited for what felt like hours before emerging from our hiding place.

I did a doubletake when Cyrus bolted past us, knocking his shoulder against Jax.

The Lunin let out a long breath as he watched the Solin storm off toward the location of our first campsite. "What's up your brother's ass?"

I wrung my hands as the half-truth escaped my mouth. "I think he's just tired after the long day"

Jax shook his head at me and said, "Let me know when you think of a better lie," before hurrying to catch up with Cyrus.

I cursed, jogging after the two men.

My brother froze when Jax called his name.

"Spit it out, Cyrus. That Solin temper of yours is growing by the minute."

My brother whipped around, his eyes narrowing on the Lunin. "Fine. Then answer me these questions."

"Lay it on me," Jax said, crossing his arms and widening his stance. "I love a good interrogation."

The whites of Cyrus's knuckles showed as he squeezed his fists even harder. "Why do the Collectors know your name?" Jax's expression remained stone cold. "Who trained you in the art of combat? Why did the people in the market scatter when they saw you?" Jax tensed. "Yeah, that's right. You didn't think I noticed, did you? How could I? My head was too far up my ass—remember?"

My eyes darted back and forth between the two men, pausing on my brother.

"You're walking a fine line, Cyrus." The muscles in Jax's chiseled jaw twitched. "I'd advise you not to cross it."

"You see." My brother found my eyes. "Jax is getting a little defensive. People act that way when they're hiding something."

My chest rose and fell with quick breaths as I looked at Jax.

His voice lowered to a growl. "Watch yourself."

"Or what?" Cyrus asked, marching over to him. "You'll pull out your knife and put me in my place?"

"Cyrus," I called. "Stop it. What are you doing?"

Brushing me off, he circled Jax like a shark rising from the depths. His nostrils flared with each step, his eyes fierce, determined.

In a threatening voice, Jax said, "Don't do something you'll regret."

My brother stopped his circling. "Maybe you should take your own advice and tell Elara the reason you've lied to us for so long."

Rage consumed Jax. Through gritted teeth, he spat, "You don't have any proof."

A wicked smirk tugged at the corner of Cyrus's mouth as he got into Jax's face. "Yeah, I do. I'm looking right at it."

Jax held up his hand when I dashed forward. "Stay back," he warned. His pupils constricted as he glared at my brother. "I'm going to tell you one time and one time only—get the hell out of my face."

Shit. Cyrus stood his ground like a male lion securing his territory. The icy breeze blew Jax's hair into his eyes—he didn't bother to move it away. I watched my brother's hand slide into his back pocket. *What's he doing?*

Jax snickered when Cyrus flicked his wrist and exposed the blade of his black knife. "You can't be serious." The Solin sneered as he tightened his grip on the handle.

Jax stood tall and locked his eyes onto my brother. "Challenging me to a knife fight might be the last thing you ever do."

"Cyrus." I panted, winded from the sight of the inevitable brawl. "Please . . . stand down."

Ignoring my desperate plea, he rotated the handle in a taunting gesture.

Jax let out a long breath through his nose before speaking. "This isn't a fight you'll win."

"I wasn't planning on losing."

"You really want to do this? Right here—right now?"

"We won't have to"—he cocked his head to one side—"if you confess your deep, dark secret."

A heartbeat later Jax removed his knife, exposed the blade, and hurled it toward me. I flinched when it landed inches from my feet, the sharp blade wedged into the ground.

Cyrus glanced at the knife with curious eyes. Jax raised his scarred hands and tapped his chest, urging him to strike.

My hand shot to my mouth when Cyrus lunged with his armed hand outstretched. With little effort, the Lunin stepped to the side, sending my brother staggering forward. Quick to recover, he pivoted and aimed for the side of Jax's neck. I winced, watching him disarm my brother in one fluid motion. Once restrained, Jax twisted Cyrus's wrist. My brother cursed as the knife fell to the ground.

Jax kicked it across the grass before letting go of Cyrus. "It's over," he said. "You won't win this fight."

Cyrus cracked his neck and his voice erupted with anger when he yelled, "No, it's not over! Not until you come clean."

"That's enough!" Jax hollered.

I stumbled backward. We knew better than to push Jax. Cyrus of all people knew the consequences.

My brother jerked his thumb at the Lunin. "You see, Elara. He is hiding something." He glared at Jax. "Tell her . . . or I will."

The next few minutes passed by in a blur of fists and blood. Pushed to his limit, Jax swung his arm with enough force to kill a man. His knuckles slammed into Cyrus's jaw, the loud crack echoing in the vast space. I grimaced when my brother's head flew to one side. Buying time, he touched the joint near his ear, then threw an unexpected left jab—a cheap shot. Another crack. I covered my mouth at the sight of blood pouring out Jax's nostrils. Stunned by the surprise attack, he took a step backward and wiped away the red stream before lunging at my brother.

I stood motionless, but my mouth moved, screaming for them to stop. The two men wrestled on the ground for only a moment before Jax wedged his forearm under Cyrus's chin, blocking his airflow. Cyrus gasped and his eyes bulged.

I called the Lunin's name. "Stop it. He can't breathe."

Unlike that afternoon on the beach, Jax released my brother in an instant and hopped to his feet. Cyrus clutched his throat while reaching for the black knife that lay inches away from his outstretched hand.

Jax held his thumb over one nostril and blew hard, shooting mucus and blood onto the ground. I tried swallowing. *I'm going to be sick.* He repeated the sickening process with his other nostril, then moved his hands into a triangular position over his crooked nose. He sucked in a sharp breath before jerking his hands in a downward motion. The sound of bones resetting sent the bitter taste of bile up my throat. I looked away when he spit more blood onto the grass.

Jax pointed to the knife in Cyrus's hand. "You haven't had enough?"

Cyrus directed the tip of the blade at the Lunin's heart. "I'll do whatever it takes for you to tell her the truth."

Jax shut his eyes. His right hand trembled by his side.

No. This can't be happening.

Taking advantage of the situation, Cyrus made his move. My mouth gaped. All of his training had finally paid off. He stepped around Jax, held his arm behind his back, and pressed the blade to his neck.

"Tell her," Cyrus demanded, twisting Jax around to face me. "How do you know so much about the Collectors?"

His lips didn't move, but he met my gaze. A pain—a deep sadness grabbed hold of Jax. Time stood still. *Don't say it. Please don't say it.* My eyes filled with tears.

Cyrus pushed the knife deeper into Jax's flesh. Blood trickled from the wound. "Answer the question," he pressed.

My jaw fell open as the next event unfolded before my eyes. Jax slid his free hand into the small space between Cyrus's arm and his exposed neck. With the knife a safe distance away, he threw his weight into my brother, causing them to stumble backward. Cyrus's head slammed against the trunk of a tree. Disoriented, he loosened his grip long enough for Jax to flip around and disarm him. The Lunin wrapped one hand around Cyrus's neck while the other held the knife to his throat.

I shuddered. A darkness clouded Jax's eyes as his pale fingers dug into my brother's throat. *Any harder, and he'll crush his windpipe.*

"Please," I managed through half breaths.

Jax raised the tip of his knife to the side of Cyrus's throat—a kill shot.

My brother choked and sputtered. His eyes watered from the lack of oxygen. "Tell her," he mouthed.

Jax moved the knife away from my brother's neck. *Shit. He's not backing down, he's moving to strike.*

My voice bellowed through the forest. "Are you crazy? You'll kill him!" The Lunin froze. "Just answer the question,"

I begged, desperation oozing from my words. "How do you know so much about the Collectors?"

Jax shut his eyes as the knife fell from his hand, and in a quiet voice filled with remorse, he said, "Because I was one."

ELEVEN

Shattered Truths

Jax's confession sliced through my being like the sharp blade of his knife. A pained sound escaped my mouth as I collapsed onto my knees, the wind knocked out of me.

Cyrus's body slid down the trunk of the tree while Jax stood motionless with his eyes closed and pale hands trembling by his sides.

Everything outside of myself moved in slow motion, yet my mind raced, recalling every moment I spent with Jax. The troubled past he rarely spoke of, his hot and cold demeanor, his militant approach to combative training, the knowledge he shared about Zenith and the Collectors—all signs I had overlooked, signs I didn't want to see. My brother, wiser than he led on, had discovered the truth, pointed out the obvious. He had lifted the mysterious veil Jax hid behind.

Cyrus climbed to his feet and limped over to where I sat, frozen with shock.

"I knew something was fishy." He panted, winded from the altercation. "I've had my suspicions for a while—I didn't want to worry you until I knew for sure."

A single tear rolled off my cheek as I stared at Jax. "Why? How could you lie to us?"

"I had my reasons."

"That's a bullshit excuse," my brother snapped. "We trusted you. And for what? Just to be screwed over by you in the end."

Jax shook his head, regret smeared all over his face. "I had no choice. You would have never returned to Aroonyx if you knew the truth."

"You're damn right," Cyrus said.

"Everyone has a choice, Jax. And you chose wrong by lying. You betrayed us." More tears filled my eyes. "We . . . I trusted you."

He took a small step forward. "I'm aware of this. I never meant to blindside either of you. I keep that part of my life locked away. It's painful for me to revisit." He moved closer and stood above me and my brother, then squatted to my eye level. "I told you that day in the parking lot at school—and I meant what I said. I'll never be able to give you what you want." He shut his eyes and added, "I'm too . . . *fucked* up," before collapsing onto the ground beside me.

My chin hit my chest. Cyrus dragged a hand down the uninjured side of his face and let his body fall backward onto the grass. I glanced at the two men who lay on their backs. *How did I get here?*

Jax draped an arm over his eyes. "I'm not the same person I was back then." Cyrus huffed his disagreement while the Lunin went on, "I've spent years trying to detach myself from that part of my past. And you wonder why I'm so distant and closed off. Guilt occupies my mind 99 percent of the time. You can't imagine the disturbing shit I've seen—been forced to do by Zenith. It's impossible to erase from my mind. I'm imprisoned in a mental hell, one filled with regrets. And keeping this secret from the two of you sealed my fate. It threw away the key."

Did he choose wrong by lying, yes, but the amount of pain that radiated out of his being, out of his voice, tugged at my heart strings. I frowned, observing the Lunin. His once-confident posture had deflated and vanished. He looked as if he had run a physical and mental marathon.

Cyrus nudged me with his foot. "What if it's all a trap?" My brows raised. "What if he's working both sides and plans on taking us to Zenith?"

Damn it. That thought never crossed my mind. I eyed Jax, curious about his reaction.

His face fell at Cyrus's severe accusation, and in a quiet voice, he said, "If I wanted you dead, I would have done so the night I took you to Earth—the night Zenith ordered me to murder you both."

Silence surrounded us. My entire body went numb.

Cyrus pushed himself to a seated position and tossed up his hands. "Well, aren't you full of dark secrets."

My hair slapped at my face as the icy breeze swirled around us. I didn't move it away. Not because I didn't want to but because I didn't care. I didn't care about anything anymore. My chest felt empty as if my heart had been ripped out of it. The trust I placed in Jax unraveled like a loose thread, spilling into a pile of forgotten hopes and dreams. I rested a hand over my heart, curious if it still pumped blood through my veins. My fingers dug into my chest. Nothing happened—no pain, no sensation. I wanted to feel—something—anything other than the detached, altered state I found myself stuck in.

Jax's hair fell out of his eyes when he looked up at the swaying tree branches. Moonlight reflected off his pale skin, and for the first time, he appeared vulnerable—undone.

He inhaled the cool night air, then let a fogged breath of trapped emotions rush out of his lungs, along with words that changed my entire perspective. "I was six years old when Zenith took me from my home. Months before the Collectors arrived, I was playing outside and noticed a few older boys had captured a rare bird. They were torturing it by pulling out its feathers, so I ran over and grabbed it from their cruel hands. I shut my eyes, wishing I could help the injured creature, and before I knew it, I found myself standing on Earth."

"You . . . jumped?" I stammered.

"Yes, that was the first time, and it really took me by surprise. My head turned every which way as I wondered what had happened. The sights, the smells—it overwhelmed me. The bird flew out of my hands. I wish you could have seen my face when I saw the blue sky."

I smirked, thinking of my reaction when I noticed the green atmosphere on Aroonyx.

"A plane flew overhead," he said. "I had never heard or seen anything like that, so I fell backward and landed in a pile of fire ants. They bit and stung the hell out of me." I grimaced. "My parents' faces flashed in my mind, and in an instant, I was back on Aroonyx. The older boys were shocked, baffled by my disappearing act. They shook their heads in disgrace and ran back to their villages.

"I'll never forget the apprehension in my mother's eyes when I told her the news. She explained that Seekers were the only ones who had the power to jump to Earth, then shared the brutality they suffered during Arun's reign. My father, being the practical one in the family, insisted I told no one. They pulled me out of school, afraid I would jump in front of the other children. One night my father said to my mother, *We can't let anyone find out—especially Zenith.*"

Jax paused to shift his weight. The numbing sensation I experienced lessened with each truthful word that left his mouth. Cyrus, still uneasy, kept his eyes glued to Jax.

"Time passed without any disturbances, until my sixth birthday." Jax blew out a long breath. "There was a knock at the door and in walked the Collectors. My mother's desperate screams were the last thing I heard before a Solin struck me upside the head—knocking me out cold." His voice faded after he said, "I never saw my parents again. Zenith had them executed for treason. Harboring a Seeker was a crime punishable by death."

My mouth hung open as I looked at my brother. He was equally stunned by the tragic news.

"Jax," I whispered, unsure where to begin. "We had no idea. If you would have just told us—"

Ignoring me, he continued. "I woke up with a huge knot on my head, confused of my whereabouts. A different Solin dragged me out of this small room and into the Main Hall. I didn't speak, much less look at Zenith. I had never seen him with my own eyes. He was so much taller than I imagined. He circled me for a while, then lifted my chin, forcing me to meet his gaze. The bastard smiled. He actually smiled at me, like he had won a highly coveted prize. After a long pause he whispered, *I'm happy you're here Jax. You and I shall do wonderful things together.*

"I remember begging to go home. Without a drop of remorse, he pointed to the fresh pool of blood in the Main Hall and said, *Your parents are dead, this is your home now.*"

My heart broke for Jax. *This is insanity. No wonder he's so screwed up.*

"I started crying. Zenith doesn't allow Collectors to show their emotions, so he struck me over and over again until he got the point across. I lay there bloodied and bruised, my entire world turned upside down. Zenith stepped over me and motioned to the windowless room, then said, *Welcome home. From this point on, you will address me as father*."

Cyrus cursed, shaking his head in disbelief.

"He instructed the Solin who stood by with curious eyes to remove me from his presence. He said, *Take the boy to the basement, so he can think about his behavior.*

"The man tossed me into this blood-stained room. It had a window at the top, but I wasn't tall enough to see out of it. They starved me for over a week. A small cup of water was my only saving grace." Jax let his arm fall onto the ground beside him. "Something inside me snapped during that week of solitude. The kind, easy-going child transformed into an angry, aggressive soul who sought vengeance. I tried attacking the young Lunin who Zenith had sent to retrieve me." Jax shook his head. "That didn't go well. I could hardly stand, so weak with malnutrition. The teen Collector slammed me against the wall with zero effort while Zenith stood outside the doorway, snickering at my failed attempt. He then tossed a piece of food into his mouth before walking away. The Lunin stayed behind and kicked the shit out of me until I could hardly breathe.

"They left me in that hellhole for a few more days until I almost died of starvation. A Solin carried me into the Main Hall and tossed me a warm meal. I scarfed it down, then threw up everywhere." Jax swallowed. "The Collector made me clean it with my bare hands before Zenith appeared. He said, *You'll never have to see that room again if you show me your special powers.* Desperate for relief, I thought of Earth and shut my eyes. Nothing happened because my intention was selfish. I wanted to relieve my own suffering."

I hummed my understanding, recalling Jax's lesson about the "rules" of jumping.

"Infuriated, Zenith sent me back to the basement."

"Didn't he realize his mistake?" I asked. Jax turned his

head to find my eyes. "Forcing a Seeker to jump never worked for Arun. Why did he think it would work with you?"

"He was desperate. Zenith wanted everything Arun had achieved during his reign: the massive dwelling, domination over the people, and a group of men to do his evil bidding. But unlike Arun, he didn't have Saros." Jax tapped his chest. "He didn't have a Seeker."

Cyrus straightened as he massaged his sore jaw. I tucked my knees into my chest, the angst I felt toward the leader of Aroonyx growing at an exponential rate.

"This abusive cycle continued for months: starve me for days, bring me to Zenith, try to jump, back to the basement. This endless routine left me broken—hopeless. I spent those long hours pushing away the pain and anger until I felt nothing—no emotions at all." Jax sat up and adjusted his shirt. "Then one day everything changed."

"What happened?" my brother asked.

"A Collector took me to a private room near the Main Hall. It had a bed, wash room, closet filled with clothes." Jax's brows raised at the memories. "A table filled with food—and Zenith. He said, *These are your new living quarters. My son can't stay trapped in the basement all day.*"

I blinked hard. "I'm so confused. Why was he being nice to you?"

"He wasn't. Zenith doesn't have a kind bone in his body. I think in some disturbing way he thought I would express my gratitude and jump for him."

“Oh,” I murmured.

“Overnight, Zenith held me in high regard. He showered me with gifts, introduced me as his son to the Collectors. Zenith tutored me in every subject and trained me to speak in a way that commanded people’s attention.”

I thought of Jax’s direct approach to life, his rigid posture and firm tone. *Well, that explains a lot.*

“On my seventh birthday he forced me to train with the Collectors. They hated me: the Seeker boy—Zenith’s adoptive son who outranked them all. The older ones inflicted as much pain as possible. With nothing to lose, I learned to channel my anger and use it against them. Over the years I toughened up and advanced with each passing day. Zenith would count the number of new cuts on my body after each training session.” Jax showed us the scars on his wrists and forearms. “I never wanted him to find more than three.”

“Why?” I asked.

“Because each injury equaled the number of days I’d go without eating.”

“Damn dude. That’s intense.”

Jax shrugged, brushing off my brother’s comment. “Zenith’s method was ruthless, but it worked. At the age of ten, I could kill a man with my bare hands, cut out a tongue in three seconds, and hit a moving target over fifty feet away.”

Holy shit. At the age of ten, I was watching the Disney channel, daydreaming about being a princess.

“Zenith never expressed his sentiments, but he always watched me with prideful eyes. On my twelfth birthday, he named me the leader of the Inner Circle." Jax looked at Cyrus. "That's how I got my knife. It was gift from Zenith."

My heart skipped a beat. *The engraving on Jax's knife: For my son.* I shut my eyes. *He kept it. After all this time.*

Cyrus met Jax's gaze. "You told us there were nine members of the Inner Circle."

"There are now. I was the tenth."

I rubbed my eyes, trying to process the information he shared. Jax had mentioned he'd experienced a turbulent upbringing, but I never imagined anything to this degree.

"Jealousy ensued when I joined the ranks. I was five years younger than the youngest member of the exclusive group. The eldest ones expressed their concerns to Zenith, baffled with his decision to make a child the leader of the Inner Circle."

"They brought up a good point," I said. "Twelve is really young."

Another shrug from Jax. "I never wanted the damn job, but I didn't have a choice. Zenith silenced their complaints, and suddenly, I found myself going on missions with the others. I hadn't a clue what I was doing. I always made mistakes and slowed everyone down. One Lunin member in particular had it out for me."

A strong gust of wind caused goosebumps to spread across my body. I shivered, rubbing my hands over my chilled arms.

"Pollux was Zenith's most trusted Collector until I was awarded the high-ranked position."

Cyrus's head popped up. My mind raced. *Pollux. That's the name of the man Leo referred to outside of Idalia's, the same man who the unseen Collectors mentioned.*

CRACK. Jax sprung to his feet at the sound of the fallen branch. He scanned the dark forest. I followed his lead, our Lunin vision illuminated the area in a cool white glow.

Jax pulled his knife out of the ground, closed the blade, and slipped it into his back pocket before walking to retrieve the one he held at my brother's neck.

Cyrus helped me to my feet. His hand shot out, catching the folded blade that Jax tossed him.

"We should keep moving," Jax said, jerking his chin toward the cliffside.

I hesitated, looking at my brother. Apprehension filled his eyes, but acceptance filled mine.

"I still trust him," I whispered. "Regardless of the screwed-up situation."

"I don't know, sis. That was a shitty thing to do, keeping a secret like that from us."

Jax turned his head, the howling winds muffling our private conversation.

I pointed at my brother's pocket. "You have your knife. Don't be afraid to use it if he tries anything weird."

Cyrus nodded, patting the concealed blade.

I met his gaze and said, "I think we should hear him out. The more information he gives us about Zenith and the Collectors, the better."

"Okay, then let's go."

The two of us followed Jax through the forest, glancing over our shoulders every few steps. The air temperature dropped as we approached the cliffside. I squinted at the icy breeze and tucked my long hair into the collar of my shirt, irritated with the flying strands.

Jax slid his back down the smooth face of the same rock we hid behind on the day of our return. Cyrus lowered himself onto the grass beside me as I took a seat.

Eager to hear more about the mysterious Collector, I asked, "So you and Pollux didn't get along?"

"No. He never liked me. Pollux was the Lunin Collector who beat the shit out of me in the basement when I first arrived."

I bit my lip. "Right."

"He had done his time, worked his way up the ranks. Then I came along and took it all away from him. My close relationship with Zenith infuriated Pollux. It drove him mad. I was a threat to his position, so he took every opportunity to make my life miserable. He was like the brother I never wanted."

I stole a glance at Cyrus, relieved my relation had pure intentions.

Jax touched a scar on his neck. "He even tried to kill me a few times." He ran a finger across the jagged line under his cheekbone while saying, "Pollux is the acquaintance I ran into before we drove to Crystal Beach."

I nodded. He assembled another crucial piece of the puzzle. "What about your hand?"

Jax observed the scar that decorated his palm. "Courtesy of Zenith after I screwed up an important mission. I'll spare you the disturbing details of that horrible night. Inflicting harm on an innocent person was never something I enjoyed doing."

I shut my eyes. *There's a silver lining.*

"How long were you a Collector?" Cyrus asked, his voice hoarser than before.

"About six years."

I rolled onto my knees. "What made you leave?"

Jax inhaled a deep breath through his nose before finding my eyes. "You—Elara, were my reason for leaving."

TWELVE

Unraveled Trust

I stumbled over my words. "I'm sorry . . . what did you just say?"

Cyrus's eyes darted back and forth between me and Jax.

"You were the reason I left the Collectors."

"Can you elaborate?"

"It was the night Zenith ordered me to remove you from the situation."

Cyrus tossed up his hands. "Just say it. He ordered you to kill us. It's not like you didn't mention it earlier."

Jax let out a frustrated breath before continuing. "Very well. Yes, he sent me to murder you both."

I shivered and it wasn't from the frigid weather.

"Elara, do you remember that afternoon under the bridge when I told you your father caught me trying to steal food from your home?"

"Let me guess. Another lie?"

Jax nodded.

Cyrus muttered, "Bastard," before looking away, his posture uptight once more.

Ignoring my brother, the Lunin said, "One afternoon, I was giving Zenith the daily report when Elio, a Solin member of the Inner Circle, escorted a young woman into the Main Hall. She told Zenith she had valuable information he'd want to hear. I stood close by while she divulged the twisted news. The woman, Cressida, explained that the doctor she worked for had delivered twins: one Solin and one Lunin, only days before, during the bi-lunar eclipse."

The door to my memory bank flew open. *Jax mentioned Zenith was born during a Solar eclipse. He's the perfect combination of a Solin and a Lunin, both physically and mentally.*

"Cressida then sealed your fate by filling Zenith's head with a paranoid thought: *I wonder if these twins will grow to have powers equal—if not greater than your own?*"

I clenched my teeth. "So that's why he wanted us dead. Just the thought of us having more power sent him spiraling out of control?"

"The man's got some serious issues," Cyrus said.

"That's putting it mildly." Jax's voice trailed off as he glanced over my shoulder.

I froze, afraid to turn around.

"Let's keep moving," he said, climbing off the ground.

Out of habit, I reached for Jax's hand, but his earlier confession caused my fingers to recoil with hesitation. His blue eyes filled with regret as his arm fell to his side. Quick to act, Cyrus pulled me to my feet.

We walked side by side, following the curve of the steep cliff. My teeth chattered as I rubbed my arms. *Geez. It's getting colder by the minute.*

"So what happened after Cressida told Zenith about our"—Cyrus paused, using air quotes to finish his sentence—"magical powers."

"For some reason Zenith asked for the name of the doctor, which I found odd because he acted like he already knew."

"Who was it?" I asked.

"Iah was his name—or *is* his name." Jax ran a hand through his hair. "Who knows? He might not be around anymore. The way Zenith reacted when he found out makes me think he's dead."

Cyrus tucked his hands deeper into his pockets. "What did he do?"

"He lost his shit and started throwing things across the room."

My brother scoffed.

"Why?" I asked.

"I haven't a clue. I've racked my brain for years trying to answer that question. Something from his past set him off—something he wouldn't share. As soon as she said *Iah*, he demanded to know your whereabouts. Poor Cressida, realizing her error, stumbled over her words. He beat the living daylights out of her until she gave him the information he wanted, then slit her throat."

I shut my eyes.

"Zenith doesn't like leaving a, how do you say it on Earth?" Answering his own question, he added, "Ah yes, a paper trail. He didn't want rumors of your unique births spreading throughout the villages."

"How many people has the man killed?"

Jax flashed me a stern look. "Trust me, you don't want to know."

"Did Zenith send you to kill us after he murdered Cressida?" Cyrus asked.

"Yes, shortly after. He said it was a top-secret mission, and if I followed his exact orders, the other members of the Inner Circle would finally accept me as their own." Jax paused, watching my brother carefully. "It's important for you to understand how much I needed Pollux and the others' approvals. They made my life unbearable, and if killing two babies eased my suffering—then so be it."

"Wow," Cyrus chided. "Thanks for the honesty—for once."

Ignoring him, Jax added, "And plus, I was so brainwashed by Zenith, I'd do anything he asked."

We walked in silence for long minutes before he said, "It didn't take me long to find your house."

Cyrus scrubbed at his face, wincing at the tender spot. "Dude, I don't want to hear anymore."

"Well, I do. I need to know what happened. I need—"

"Closure?" Jax suggested.

I nodded.

My brother grumbled his agreement and waved a hand for Jax to continue.

"I snuck in through the bedroom window and found you both asleep in your cribs. Elara, you started crying, so I made my move."

My heart raced. *Okay, maybe I don't want to hear the rest of the story.* Cyrus clenched his fists, appearing more uncomfortable by the minute.

"I moved to strike but froze because you looked right at me." Jax paused. "No, you looked right through me."

My feet skidded to a stop. "How so? I was just a baby."

The Lunin faced me while Cyrus paused his casual pace.

"I'm not sure—but looking at you that night was like seeing my past, present, and future rolled into one giant slap in the face. This feeling, the one I mentioned under the bridge that afternoon, grabbed hold of me, and suddenly, I realized who I had become: a cruel and heartless person whose selfish desires controlled every decision. At that moment, I realized the people of Aroonyx were in grave danger with Zenith as their leader. I saw the trap . . . how easy it was—is, to follow his misguided ways and how easy it is to believe his deceitful tongue." Jax smoothed a crease in his shirt. "The idea of a better life vanished after Zenith murdered my parents, but seeing you that night shifted my entire perspective. Cressida's prediction echoed in my mind and a sliver of hope surfaced when I thought, *What if she was right? What if these twins do have the power to defeat Zenith?*"

Cyrus's lips pressed together. "So just like that, you decided to change your ways and not kill us that night? You made it sound like Zenith was crazy for believing Cressida, and now you're telling us you believed her as well?"

"Cyrus, it's not like the woman was an enchantress spouting a prophecy about the two of you defeating Zenith. She simply made an honest observation. Zenith was born during a Solar eclipse and shares both Solin and Lunin traits. The two of you were born during a similar celestial event—the bi-lunar eclipse. This had never happened before."

"It's crazy to think that hope changed your entire perspective."

A smile crossed Jax's face. "You took world history in school, did you not?" My brother nodded. "Good, then you remember learning that hope is what starts revolutions and hope is what ends wars."

I eyed my brother. He shot me an understanding glance. At eighteen, we left Earth to help free the people of Aroonyx. At thirteen, Jax left his old life behind to do the same.

"Your father was the one who found me standing over your crib with my knife in hand." I gulped, imagining his reaction. Jax jerked his chin at Cyrus. "Like your brother, he'd do anything to protect his family. He acted faster than I could blink and took me to the ground. Your mother dashed into the room and pulled him off. She demanded to know why I wanted to harm her children, so I confessed the details of my mission and explained my turbulent upbringing. Your father didn't give a damn about my life with Zenith. He wanted to kill me with his bare hands for trying to murder you that night, which is understandable."

Cyrus crossed his arms.

"But your mother"—the Lunin found my eyes—"she was the one who showed me compassion. She told your father that I was young, and that people make the best decisions they can at the time, regardless of the situation."

A comforting peace washed over me. I smiled, envisioning my biological mother.

"Your father didn't like the idea but agreed when his wife insisted I go with them. Vanish into the night and start a new life somewhere far away from Zenith and the Collectors. I didn't have to think twice. Not only did I fail a top-secret mission, but I divulged insider information about the life of a Collector, two crimes Zenith would not overlook." Jax let out a long breath. "He would have cut off my head and displayed it in the Main Hall as a warning to the others."

I cursed, rubbing the goosebumps on my arms.

"We were just about to leave when the rest of the Inner Circle knocked on the door."

My heart sank. "I thought the others didn't know about the mission. I thought Zenith wanted you to go alone."

"I never got a confirmation because I never spoke to Zenith again after that night, but I have a strong feeling that it was all some stupid test. The other members knew about the plan because Elio was the one who escorted Cressida into the Main Hall. He was there when Zenith gave me the orders. I think the others were instructed to trail me that night and wait—make sure I followed through with the mission." Jax's eyes clouded with regret. "And when I didn't, they made their move."

I shifted my weight. *He's getting to the part of the story I dread hearing the most.*

"No one survives an encounter with the Inner Circle unless Zenith wants to speak with the guilty party. Your parents knew this. That's why they wrote those notes."

I dropped my head, remembering my adoptive parents' confessions. My mother said the adoption agency found me with a note: This child was loved, and her name is Elara.

"Your mother hid me in the pantry with the two of you in my arms and said, *Keep my children safe, at all cost.*" Jax looked away. "Short minutes passed before Pollux found me hiding. I'll never forget the satisfaction that seeped from his pale blue eyes. He tried to grab me, but I jumped to Earth and seconds later found myself standing in front of the adoption agency. My intention had shifted from selfish to selfless. Keeping you safe was my top priority—my life's new mission."

Jax rolled his neck and touched the dried blood on his nose. He looked exhausted from the evening's confessions and even more so from revisiting his dark past.

Pain filled his eyes when he said, "I won't discuss the details of your parents' deaths. Some things in life are better left unsaid."

I swallowed a lump of grief down my throat, the knot expanding as it moved closer to my stomach.

My brother scratched the short hairs on his chin as he spoke to Jax. "This is a lot to process. This morning we thought you were"—he paused, searching for the right words—"you . . . but now you're—"

"An ex-Collector?"

"Yeah, and not just any Collector. You're the ex-leader of the Inner Circle and Zenith's adoptive son. That's a lot of information for us to take in."

"I understand, and I apologize for lying to you both, but I had my reasons." Cyrus watched the Lunin with cautious eyes. "If you want me to leave, just say the words and you'll never see me again."

"What? No. We started this journey together, and we're going to finish it together."

Cyrus shrugged, indifferent to my proposal.

I looked at Jax. "Yes, you made a poor decision by lying to us, but we'll see past it. Eventually." I motioned to my brother. "We wouldn't last a week out here without your guidance, Jax, much less devise a plan on how to defeat Zenith."

"Sis, I appreciate your practical approach to all of this, but I'm not like you."

"Yes, you are. You're better than me. You're the Solin, the optimist out of the group. You always see the glass half full."

"Not this time."

Once again, Jax pretended to blend into his surroundings while my brother and I argued.

"I just need some time to process everything—alone."

"Cyrus, are you crazy?" I waved a hand at the surrounding woods. "The Collectors are searching everywhere for us right now. We can't separate. You can't run off."

His amber eyes narrowed as his voice raised. "Damn it, Elara. I'm not running off. Unlike Jax, I don't hide from my problems."

The Lunin cleared his throat, an audible confirmation that he heard Cyrus's verbal jab. I gritted my teeth.

"I just want a few minutes alone to think everything over."

I shook my head back and forth with so much force I thought it would detach from my neck.

Jax rested a hand on my shoulder. "Let him go, Elara."

"No. You were the one who said we must stay together at all times."

"I know what I said, but things have changed."

"You're damn right they have."

I glared at Cyrus.

"Why don't you go to the spring? Elara and I will meet you there after you've had some time to yourself."

My brother straightened, pleased with Jax's suggestion.

I shook my head once more. "I don't like this. I have the same feeling—the one I had before we left for the South Village. It makes me—"

"It'll be fine," Cyrus said, tapping the knife in his pocket.

"No, it won't. You can't even see in the dark without me by your side. How are you going to make it to the spring?"

Cyrus pointed to the full moons. "I've got those two spot lights as my guide." He lowered his gaze. "Elara, if you want the three of us to continue on this journey together, then give me some space."

"Fine, if you insist."

"I do."

"Just be careful."

"I will." He looked at Jax. "If anything happens to my sister while I'm gone, I'll finish what my father started the night you broke into our home. Got it?"

The Lunin held up his hands and murmured, "Loud and clear."

"Okay, then I'll see you guys in a few."

We watched Cyrus stroll in the opposite direction toward the forest, his head held high, eyes scanning the vast area.

"He'll be all right," Jax said.

My lips pursed. *I hope so. I'll never forgive myself if anything bad happens to Cyrus.*

I shivered, blowing a cloud of warmth into my hands. "It's freezing. How did it get so cold?"

"There isn't a gradual shift between seasons on Aroonyx." He motioned for me to keep walking. "I planned on us staying at Idalia's until after the first snowfall. Unfortunately, that's no longer an option. We'll have to stick it out."

Perfect.

Jax smirked at my unenthusiastic reaction. "Don't worry, we can light a fire tomorrow because the Collectors won't be looking for us."

"Why?"

"Because no one is foolish enough to leave the warmth of their homes during the first snowfall. Not even the Collectors."

I groaned, feeling colder by the minute. "Is it like a blizzard or something? We had those in Maine."

Jax laughed. "Yeah, something like that."

I bounced up and down to stay warm while he observed the full moons in the night sky.

The smile across his face grew before meeting my gaze. "I want to show you something."

"What is it?"

"It's a surprise."

I looked over my shoulder, searching for my brother. "I don't want to leave Cyrus alone for too long."

"We won't, and where we're going isn't far from the spring."

I hesitated. *Is this a good idea?*

A wicked cackle sounded in my mind—the hidden figure. *Sure, it is. Cyrus wants his alone time, and your curiosity always bites you in the ass, so why not? I say go for it. Live a little.*

Jax cocked his head to one side, curious about my inner dialogue. I stilled, compelling the mysterious voice to go away.

"I hope you still trust me," he said, offering me his hand.

I hesitated until the voice slithered into my mind once more. *Do it, Elara. You know you want to.*

My eyes locked onto Jax as I slipped my hand into his. "I trust you." *For now.*

THIRTEEN

Needs vs. Wants

Jax led me into the forest, his hand never leaving mine. The temperature dropped, but my cheeks burned with heat. I eyed the Lunin.

What's happening right now? I sucked in a sharp breath when he laced his fingers around my own—an intimate gesture.

The only affection I ever received from Jax was a gentle pat on the back or a quick squeeze of the arm. This new approach left me questioning his intentions. *I don't understand. He has Idalia. Why is he holding my hand?*

I tried to play it cool by pretending I didn't notice his warm touch. I scanned my surroundings and glanced at the full moons, looking anywhere but our clasped hands.

Why is this freaking me out? I eyed him once more. *That's a stupid question. It's because you told yourself to let go of the romantic feelings you had for Jax, and now here you are—alone in the woods with the man who occupies your thoughts 90 percent of the time.*

I nearly choked on my spit when he asked, "Is there something you'd like to share?"

Busted. "No . . . not really."

Jax chuckled. The rough scar on his palm pressed against my own faded injury when he tightened his grip. "You really are a horrible liar, Elara."

"I wasn't lying. I do have something on my mind, but it's nothing I want to share."

"Fair enough. I won't pry."

We walked for long minutes in silence. I continued to glance at Jax, fascinated with his new demeanor. For the first time, he appeared relaxed. The muscles in his chiseled jaw didn't clench, and his eyes didn't drift to the faraway place he never spoke of.

Secrets are heavy burdens.

My head jolted forward when he halted our casual pace. When I turned, he let go of my hand and dropped his head.

I frowned. *Now what?*

"You can tell me," he said.

"Tell you what?"

"Whatever it is that's bothering you."

I rubbed my cold arms and moved closer. "Jax, nothing's bothering me."

"Then why do you keep staring at me?"

"I don't know." I motioned to his body. "You're different now."

"How so?"

"Normal?"

Jax's white teeth glowed under the moonlight when he let out a hearty laugh. "Wow, talk about brutal honesty. I never knew you found me to be so—abnormal."

"You know what I mean. It's like you've finally let down your guard."

"I have—for the first time in over sixteen years."

My eyes grew at this added bit of information. Desperate to stay warm, I twisted my hair around my neck like a scarf as he went on.

"Keeping my dark past a secret was one of the hardest things I've ever done." Jax reached for my hand once more. "Elara, I'm so sorry. Regardless of my reasons, I should have told you the truth."

"You're right, but I understand why you didn't tell us. Given the circumstance, you made the best decision you could." I glanced at our interlaced fingers. "Timing is everything, isn't it?"

Jax brushed his thumb over my chilled skin. "Yes, yes, it is." He smiled. "You remind me so much of your mother. She didn't judge me for my past or for the horrible crimes I committed. She saw me through loving eyes, and that alone changed my life. Your mother would be very proud of you, Elara."

My heart ached for the life I never knew. "What was her name?"

"Chandra," he said, tucking a stray hair behind my ear. I flinched at the unexpected gesture. "And like her daughter, she was a very beautiful woman."

I broke eye contact. Jax squeezed my hand and encouraged us to keep moving.

"How's your nose feeling?" I asked, eager to take the focus off me and my biological mother.

"It's fine." He touched the swollen area. "That wasn't the first time someone's broken my nose with their fist." He wiggled the cartilage back and forth. "I was impressed with Cyrus's quick jab. Honestly, I didn't see it coming."

"Men and their testosterone. Why do verbal arguments always lead to brawls?"

"We might use our fist instead of words, but at least we drop it afterward." Jax nudged me with his arm. "Women are vicious. They keep their emotions bottled up, then attack when you least expect it."

"Don't put us into one category."

"When it comes to women, there is only *one* category." A mischievous smirk crossed his cleanly shaved face. "It's called crazy."

My jaw fell open, but despite my amusement, I ripped my hand away from his. "You are such an asshole."

"I'm sorry." His shoulders bounced up and down with laughter. "That one was too easy."

I scoffed, rubbing my numb hands together. The wind howled around us, sending a shiver up my spine. Even the trees looked cold; their leaves trembled with every gust and their branches brushed against each other as if trying to stay warm. *I'd take the heat any day over this.*

"How much farther is the . . . surprise?" I asked.

"We're almost there."

I kept my arms wrapped around my chilled body as we walked, wishing I was brave enough to lean into Jax for warmth.

He lifted a hand and pointed to a cluster of trees on my left. The breeze grew stronger as we approached.

"Is this another part of the cliff?"

Jax nodded. "It's shaped like a peninsula. We jumped at the center of the formation. Beyond those trees is a clearing." Disoriented, I looked around. He used his hands to clarify. "If your back is facing the water, then this is the left side of the peninsula."

"Can you draw me a map sometime?"

He winked. "Sure thing, I'll get right on it." Jax moved his body in front of mine. "Your surprise is through those trees."

I craned my neck to get a better look.

He followed my every move, blocking my view. "But before we go any farther, I need to tell you something."

I gulped. *Oh no. I can't handle any more confessions.*

Jax inhaled a long breath and shut his eyes for only a moment before speaking. "Idalia and I have a complicated relationship. I met her shortly after I left Zenith—after I jumped with you and Cyrus to Earth. I was thirteen years old, all alone, living in the woods. She gave me food, her father's old clothes, and convinced her mother to let me hide at their place for a while. Besides your biological mother, Idalia was the first person to show me kindness. We grew closer as we got older, but I distanced myself after I turned eighteen." He ran his fingers through his hair. "For some reason, we always circle back to each other, but that time has come to a close." Jax paused, waiting for me to respond. When I said nothing, he asked, "Do you want to know why?"

"Um." I shifted my weight and stared at the ground. "It's none of my business."

"Oh, but it is," he whispered, closing the gap between us.

I breathed hard, my heart pounding in my chest. "Okay," was all I could say.

Jax hooked a finger under my chin. "Another woman has come into the picture, and words can't express the positive influence she's had on my life."

My eyelashes fluttered. *He's not talking about me—is he?* Jax took my hands into his. I held my breath. *Uh oh. Maybe he is.*

"Being around this woman makes me want to be a better man. Over the past year, she's given me the opportunity to see who I need—no, who I want in my life."

I let out a small gasp, overwhelmed by his honesty. Jax let go of my hands, then stepped behind me.

"What are you doing?" I asked, when his cold palm covered my eyes.

"Relax. I don't want you to see the surprise until we're there."

I shuddered a breath as he led me through the cluster of trees. One of his hands held my waist while the other obstructed my view. I sniffed the frigid air, taking in my new surroundings, and tried peeking through the cracks of his fingers. "Can I look now?"

"We've got to start working on your patience."

I groaned, my vision going dark once more.

Short minutes passed before Jax stopped his pursuit. His warm breath grazed my ear as he whispered, "Are you ready?"

"I guess." *The last time he said those words was right before we jumped to Aroonyx.*

My mouth gaped when Jax lifted his hand. Moon Drops—hundreds of them, glowed under the light of the twin moons. They covered every inch of the emerald grass that draped over the cliffside. I spun in circles, observing the stunning sight.

"Do you like your surprise?" he asked, bending over to pick one of the delicate flowers.

An inaudible stammer left my mouth, for I had no words. The Moon Drop Jax brought to Earth was beautiful, but it didn't compare to the ones found in their natural habitat. I lifted a hand to my mouth. *This can't be real. It's something out of a dream or a fantasy.*

I marveled at the flowers that surrounded my feet. The rose-shaped blooms opened to face the full moons, their stark-white petals fluttering in the breeze. At the center of each Moon Drop was a dust-like orb that illuminated the flowers in a shimmering light.

I glanced up. The violet-colored sky and twinkling stars created the perfect backdrop for the magical landscape. Jax offered me the delicate specimen.

"Can I touch it?" I whispered, afraid I would disturb the floating ball of light.

The irises of Jax's eyes grew brighter as he lifted the flower. He reached for my hand, then guided my finger through the glowing orb. I held my breath. The center remained untouched, as if a ghost had stepped in my place.

"Why can't I feel it or touch it?" I asked, mind blown that I failed the simple task.

Jax grinned as he watched my finger move back and forth like a child playing with a candle's flame. "One of Aroonyx's unsolved mysteries." He waved a hand at the surrounding space. "They'll turn to dust at sunrise." I frowned, remembering the heartfelt story of the Moon Drop. "But they always grow back and will bloom again during the full moons."

"Is this where you picked the Moon Drop when I asked if you could bring me something from Aroonyx?"

"Yes." Jax released the flower, letting it dance out of his hand on the breeze. "That's why it took me so long to get back to Earth that day. I jumped from the other side of the cliff. And considering your lack of patience, I sprinted the entire way here."

I smiled for only a moment before shifting my features into neutral. Jax had taken a step closer without me noticing. I let out a nervous breath, the white cloud mixing with his own. Every fiber in my body tingled with warmth; the cold weather no longer affected me. *Play it cool. Say something. Anything.*

I looked around the clearing. "Do you ever tire of being around so much beauty?"

"Never," he whispered, his eyes fixed only on me.

I swallowed. *Just tell him how you feel. It's now or never.* "Jax, I need—"

I never finished my sentence because his warm lips silenced my efforts. In a heartbeat, he had moved one hand to the side of my face while his other gripped my waist. I didn't stop him, and I sure as hell didn't hesitate when his tongue slid into my mouth. After months of pent-up tension, I surrendered to his gentle touch, allowing every romantic sentiment to surface.

My body felt weightless as he kissed me harder with each passing second. I hitched a breath when he pressed himself against me. My hands wandered, desperate to touch—feel every part of him. A spark of desire ignited inside me when Jax ran his fingers through my hair. I stifled a pleasurable moan. *I could do this for hours.*

A warm cloud left my mouth when he pulled away. Jax closed his eyes and rested his forehead on mine.

"That was unexpected," I whispered, still breathless from the intimate embrace.

"Not for me. I've wanted to do that for a while now."

This has been the craziest night of my life. After all this time, here we are.

As if reading my mind, Jax wrapped his strong arms around me. I rested my cheek against his chest, his heart thumping in my ear. The two of us stood in a comfortable silence, surrounded by the beauty of Aroonyx. Like the light of the full moons, a feeling of acceptance washed over me. *On Earth, I accepted Jax for who he was—a man with a troubled past, doing the best he could.* I sighed. *But now we're back on Aroonyx and everything has changed. Or has it?*

I lifted my head, surprised with a sudden awareness. *No, it hasn't changed. He's still Jax. A man with a troubled past, doing the best he can.*

"Elara, is everything okay?"

I smiled. "It's better than okay."

He kissed the top of my head. "I can't tell you how—"

My heart sank, watching the color drain from his face. In a flash, his serene posture shifted to the one I knew so well—rigid. Jax's fingers dug into my flesh when he pulled me behind him in a protective stance.

I tried looking over his shoulder. "What's going on?"

He stood tall, his senses on high alert. "Stay behind me. If I tell you to run, don't look back."

Breathless, I managed to ask, Why?"

"They're here."

My eyes grew to the size of bottle caps as I peered around Jax. Nine men emerged from behind the cluster of trees—four Lunins and five Solins. I cursed. My worst nightmare had manifested.

Their boots barely made a sound as they strolled toward us, the delicate Moon Drops crushed in their silent but deadly wake.

I observed the Lunin at the front of the group and repeated no, over and over again, until it sounded foreign on my tongue.

Jax's words hit me like a ton of bricks when he said, "Get back to Cyrus as fast as you can."

Unwilling to obey his command, I shook my head. "I won't leave you."

"You don't have a choice," he said, pushing me farther behind him.

I scanned the area for the quickest escape route. The sound of waves crashing against the white rocks below warned me that we were dangerously close to the cliff's edge. A ripple of fear passed through me as the men approached. *We're trapped. They're blocking our only exit.*

The Lunin who spearheaded the group walked with purpose and authority. Dressed appropriate for the bitter weather, he wore a long coat, the gray sleeves stretched over his well-defined biceps. My fingernails dug into Jax's arm. His spine straightened as he prepared to face his past.

The Lunin's short black hair barely blew in the breeze and his light-blue eyes flickered with spite as he moved closer to me and Jax. A vertical scar ran down his pale face, leaving a hairless gap between an eyebrow. Every time he blinked, the faded injury appeared on his eyelid, and formed a jagged line that stopped at his cheekbone.

This can't be happening. A tall Solin stepped beside him. The lines around his tangerine-colored eyes hardened as he crossed his arms. The man sneered at Jax, then looked to his left.

His counterpart stood tall. Not an ounce of fear flickered in the Lunin's eyes, only malice. And it spread across his scarred face when he flashed Jax a wicked grin. "It's been a long time, my friend."

Jax matched his stance and when he spoke, ice filled my veins. "Not long enough—Pollux."

FOURTEEN

A Fateful Decision

I didn't breathe. I didn't move. How could I? We stood face to face with the Inner Circle. Like a floodgate, the information that Jax shared about this elite group rushed into my mind: trained killers, Zenith's personal body guards, the men who murdered my biological parents—and Pollux, the person who made Jax's life a living hell. *We're doomed.*

The two Lunins stared at each other with enough angst to silence a crowded room. I stifled a mournful cry when the sun appeared over the horizon. As soon as the morning light touched the cliffside, the Moon Drops turned to dust. The strong winds scattered the black remnants, the ashes of our fallen comrades, around the clearing. My heart ached. The once-beautiful site had vanished into a tangible void, leaving a joyless, lifeless space behind.

"Well, well, well . . . what do we have here?" The wickedness that rolled off Pollux's tongue caused the hairs on the back of my neck to stand.

The Solin on his right snickered, his broad shoulders bouncing with amusement.

Pollux pointed a scarred hand at Jax. "Has the prodigal son returned?"

"I'm surprised he has the balls to show his face," the Solin muttered.

The Lunin's tongue tapped at the roof of his mouth. I ground my teeth at the annoying sound.

"Elio, where are your manners?" he asked, leaning to the side, his pale-blue eyes scanning me with ill intentions. "There's a lady in our presence."

Jax pushed me farther behind him, trying to block the Lunin's view.

"What an unexpected twist," Pollux said to Elio.

"It does add to the suspense, doesn't it?"

The Lunin tapped his chin as he met Jax's gaze. "Indeed, indeed it does."

The other members of the Inner Circle tightened their formation. I squinted, the sunlight exposing their features.

The seven men who stood behind Elio and Pollux were in their late twenties to early thirties. Their mature statures dwarfed the younger Collectors we saw that day on the cliffside. Flesh-colored scars covered their hands and faces, and their short hair didn't budge when a gust of wind whipped through the clearing. Only the chin-length locks of a stockier Solin's hair fought in the breeze.

I gulped when my eyes locked onto a massive Solin who moved closer to Pollux. He towered over the others, and his winter coat hugged his muscular frame. The age lines around his ginger-colored eyes made him appear older than the rest. I cursed. This member was different. The way he looked at Jax made me want to run for sanctuary or beg for mercy. He folded his arms across his muscular chest and widened his stance. The Solin's relaxed posture emanated a "I don't give a *fuck* if you live or die" vibe that chilled my warm blood.

"Where's your knife?" Elio asked, glancing at Jax's hands.

The irritating sound left Pollux's mouth once more before he said, "Unarmed? I'm shocked. Have you forgotten everything we taught you? Rule number four states"—I squeezed Jax's hand when the group spoke as one, an elite force of soldiers—"never leave for a mission without a sharpened blade."

A sarcastic smirk tugged at Elio's mouth as he pulled a black knife from his pocket. I flinched when he flicked his wrist. His smirk grew into a sneer as he ran a finger over the smooth side of the blade. "Unarmed? Tough break, Jax."

I glanced down at my protector's back pocket. *Why is he hesitating? He has his knife. I saw him pick it up after the brawl with Cyrus.* My heart pounded in my ears. *Cyrus? Where is he? Did he make it to the spring?*

Pollux's lips pressed into a tight line as he picked at his nails. "Has your boyfriend told you about his past?"

My knees wobbled. I had remained somewhat invisible until that moment.

A lethal calm filled Jax's voice when he said, "She already knows everything."

Pollux shrugged, dusting off his hands. "So she doesn't care that you've tortured innocent people or—"

"Don't listen to him," Jax whispered over his shoulder. "He's trying to get in your head."

I remained silent, desperate to blend into my surroundings.

Pollux flashed Elio an amused glance before addressing Jax. "I see." He snickered. "You told her about your past but left out the gory details."

Elio made an exaggerated pout face as he turned toward Pollux. "What a shame. That's the best part." His eyes sparked with malice. "I think you should fill her in on what Jax left out."

He nodded, then stretched his neck to get a better look at where I stood, immobile with fear.

"Did you know that Jax was worse than all of us combined?" He waited for me to respond, and when I didn't speak his voice sounded in a higher octave. "No? He didn't tell you?"

"He's lying," Jax said through gritted teeth.

Elio tapped the smooth side of the blade to his lips. "Shh."

The unspoken leader of the Inner Circle waved a hand at the men behind him. "Jax was always wanting our acceptance. He'd do anything Zenith asked. Lie, cheat, steal—hell, even murder." Jax tensed when Pollux's eyes narrowed. "But that's what a kiss ass does to get attention."

The tendons in Jax's arms quivered with rage.

Pollux wiggled his fingers at his archrival. "You're restricting my view. I need you to move."

Before we could react, two Solins dashed forward, pulled me from behind Jax, and restrained us in a locking hold.

A scream caught in my throat while I squirmed and twisted. With minimal effort the stout man pinned both of my arms behind my back. I winced at his firm grip.

Jax fought with all his might, but it was daylight and years of training along with Solin strength was no match for the unarmed Lunin.

The two men held us side by side, our arms brushing against each other.

Pollux's teeth glowed in the sunlight as his eyes roved over me. "There," he whispered, "that's much better."

Elio pointed to my body like it was an item on an auction block. "Looks like Jax has been holding out on you, Pollux. She's quite the pretty little thing, isn't she?"

His face twisted into a distasteful expression. "I don't like sloppy seconds, and I prefer blondes, but she'll do."

"Watch yourself Pollux," Jax warned. "Don't say something you'll regret."

Ignoring the threat, the Lunin looked at Elio. "I'm getting bored. Let's wrap this up."

The Solin nodded, then glanced over his shoulder at the others. They didn't budge, waiting for their orders.

Pollux used his fingers to count. "We've got Jax, the girl." He paused, looking around the clearing. "Now where is the other twin?"

My protective instincts took over, commanding my lips to move without thinking. "You'll never find him."

The Lunin's eyes grew with excitement. He clapped his hands like a villain from a horror movie while saying, "Ah, she speaks."

"She is a feisty little thing," Elio added.

"Good. Keeps it interesting," Pollux said, scratching the scruff on his chin. "I hate it when they don't put up a fight. Her screams will make it much more enjoyable for me."

Jax struggled in the Solin's arms as his voice erupted with anger. "Keep it up, Pollux. If you're not careful, I'll rip that foul tongue right out of your damned mouth."

"And how do you plan on doing that? You're unarmed and outnumbered."

"Tell Ishan to let me go, and I'll give you a demonstration."

Pollux's face twitched at Jax's sarcastic tone. Both Solins tightened their grip around us.

"As much as I would love to watch you try, I can't. Unlike you, I don't have time to dick around. I'm under strict orders from Zenith to bring him the twins. You know he doesn't like to wait." He looked at Elio, then inclined his head at me. "This one will have to do until we find her brother."

Pollux had issued me a death sentence. Jax told us that an encounter with the Inner Circle never ended well for the guilty party. He said Zenith enjoyed watching his victims suffer. I paled. *He's right. We're outnumbered and without Cyrus's help, we don't stand a chance.*

"You're not taking her to Zenith."

"Oh, but I am." Pollux's lips slid into a sadistic grin as he pointed at me. "After I've had some fun with your little play thing. After I've stuck her with something *other* than my knife."

Colorful words left Jax's mouth as he fought to free himself, and fury clouded his eyes when he spat, "You'll have to go through me first."

Pollux snarled and took a step forward. "I'd like that."

Elio's hand shot out, stopping the Lunin dead in his tracks. Pollux ripped his arm away, appalled by the gesture. The Solin recoiled but flashed Pollux a warning glance while mouthing, "Zenith wants him alive."

Pollux nodded but froze when his fingers moved to adjust the sleeve of his coat. His eyes grew while he laughed with vicious intent. "I get it now." He glanced over his shoulder at the others. "It appears I've hit a nerve with Jax."

Their expressions remained blank—unreadable, but the massive Solin's ginger eyes flickered with amusement.

"Yep, you sure did." Elio chuckled.

Pollux focused his attention on Jax but spoke to the Solin on his right. "I can see it in his pathetic eyes—in hers as well." He shook his head, disgust seeping from his pores. "Jax has fallen for the girl Zenith sent him to murder all those years ago." More wicked laughter left his mouth in white clouds. "Oh, the irony."

Sensing a build in tension, the other members of the Inner Circle shifted their weight.

As if a switch flipped, Pollux's entertained expression morphed into the face of a stone-cold killer when he said, "Too bad she'll be dead by the end of the day."

Jax hollered lethal threats mixed with curse words as he twisted in Ishan's firm grip.

"And that kiss you gave her earlier."

I shut my eyes. *They were watching us the entire time.*

Pollux snickered. "I expected something a little more exciting—considering your popularity with the ladies."

My eyes shot open at a gentle tap on my hand. Keeping my gaze ahead, I pretended to listen to Pollux's rant about Jax's romantic past while my fingers stretched to reach the unwanted item—Jax's knife. My heart shattered. Everything made sense. He kept his knife hidden because the odds of defeating nine members of the Inner Circle alone were slim to none. It wasn't out of frustration that he struggled in Ishan's arms. No, it was all an act so the Solin wouldn't notice him remove the folded blade from his pocket. I stifled a pained gasp when Jax slipped his knife into my hand. He made his intention known, without anyone knowing.

Tears filled my eyes. I knew what Jax wanted me to do. He wanted me to plunge the blade of his knife into my attacker's leg so I could get the hell out of there and find Cyrus. But, how do you abandon the person you love?

Short breaths entered my lungs, the gravity of the grim situation suffocating me. Sensing my gut-wrenching dilemma, Jax touched my fingers one last time. I shut my eyes, forcing back tears. *Stay strong. You must stay strong.*

My fingers trembled as I exposed the sharp blade, careful not to make a sound. I bit my lip. *No, I can't do this. I won't leave you.*

As if hearing my silent plea, Jax eyed me out of his peripheral vision. Courage mixed with acceptance radiated out of his being. His back straightened, and his eyes filled with a shared awareness that left me breathless. At that moment, Jax accepted his fate: imminent death.

I flinched at the evil laughter that flowed through the group. I had no idea what Pollux was talking about because I stopped listening when Jax handed me his knife. I sucked in a sharp breath, my fingers wrapped around the gray handle.

"But that's okay because you'll be dead," Pollux said to Jax. His pale-blue eyes narrowed at me as he licked his lips—a vulgar gesture. "And once I get my hands on her—"

"Do it now!" Jax yelled, his voice reverberating throughout the clearing.

As if guided by an unseen force, my hand moved on its own accord. I didn't have much room to work, so I made the attack count by jabbing the blade into the Solin's upper thigh, then twisted the handle before yanking it from his torn flesh. The stout man cried out in pain while falling to his knees.

Everyone froze, stunned by the surprise attack. My eyes darted between the bloodied knife in my hand and the injured Solin. Ishan tightened his grip around Jax.

Elio's eyes never left me as he asked the unspoken leader, "Orders?"

Pollux's nostrils flared and in a low growl, he said, "Bring me the girl. I'll take care of Jax."

FIFTEEN

A Living Nightmare

"Elara, run!" were the last two words Jax spoke before I sprinted out of the clearing.

I'll never know how I made it through the cluster of trees without a Collector grabbing me. Was it a miracle or a lucky break? Who knows? I didn't stop to ponder the question. Like a wide receiver at a championship game, I bobbed and weaved around the Solins and Lunins with an unwavering determination. I had to get to the spring. I had to find Cyrus.

The ground shook; boots and lots of them sprinted after me. *Don't look back, just keep running.* My body went into survival mode, propelling me forward. I leapt over a piece of Clear Stone and inhaled large breaths of the frigid air. *If only it were night.* The morning sun that shone through the canopy of trees was a cruel reminder that my Lunin endurance had faded. My lungs burned and side cramped, but I kept running. I had to.

"We'll catch you eventually."

I cringed at the familiar voice. It was Elio.

My pace quickened as I darted around the black trees, and short minutes passed before a familiarity washed over me. *This is the location of our first campsite. The spring isn't much farther.*

The sound of a man's heavy breathing sent adrenaline surging through my veins. *They're gaining on me.* My vision blurred. *You're almost there. Don't stop.*

A low-lying tree branch smacked me in the face as I slid down the gentle slope that led to the spring. I rejoiced at the warming sensation that moved through me. *Cyrus.*

My brother stood with his back facing me, staring at the secluded body of water. He whipped around at the sound of his name catching in my throat.

The color in his rosy cheeks lightened at the sight of three Collectors chasing after me. I wheezed and clenched my chest, nearly slamming into him. His amber eyes widened at the bloodied knife in my hand.

Without waiting for me to explain, Cyrus reached into his pocket and pulled out his own blade.

The Solin Collectors panted as they approached, winded from the long sprint.

Elio's eyes narrowed on me and my brother. "Drop the knives. You're coming with us."

Cyrus rotated the black handle. "Like hell we are."

My throat burned from the cold air when I cursed aloud. Until that moment, I hadn't noticed the identity of the other two Solins: the member with the long hair and the massive man with the flippant attitude.

The shortest Solin laughed at Cyrus's response while the one with the ginger-colored eyes sneered. "You don't want to challenge us, boy."

I scooted closer to my brother, Jax's knife dangling in my numb hand.

Cyrus directed the tip of his blade at the eldest Collector. "Try me."

The man snickered, and with a flick of his wrist he said, "Challenge accepted."

The next few minutes passed by in a blur of chaos. Two men rushed my brother while Elio snaked his way over to where I stood, frozen with panic.

The tallest Solin was leaner than the others but equally intimidating, and the hatred that clouded his tangerine eyes made me want to drop Jax's knife and run.

His bronze face hardened when he eyed the blood-soaked blade in my hand. "What are you going to do with that?" Every fiber in my body trembled. "Try to repeat the same cheap-ass shot you pulled on Levant?"

That was his name.

Elio checked the sharpness of his blade. "You've had . . . what? A month of training with Jax?"

Shit. Do they know how long we've been back on Aroonyx?

He tossed the knife back and forth between his hands while he spoke. "This is my job—this is my life." An evil grin crossed his cleanly shaven face. "Killing people is what I do for fun."

I didn't have time to process his words because he lunged like a snake going after its dinner. The air rushed out of my lungs when I hit the ground, my teeth knocking against each other. I squirmed underneath him, but I was no match for his Solin strength, even with my brother standing only feet away. He held me in a ground hold with his legs locked around my hips. *Go figure, the only combative exercise we didn't learn.*

With minimal effort, he twisted my wrist and tossed Jax's knife far out of my reach. I tried gouging his eyes with my fingers. This move only pissed him off, so he grabbed my arm and pinned it to the ground. I winced, the ligaments tight with tension. My free hand moved to strike. In a flash he held his knife to my throat. I grabbed his wrist and used all of my strength to keep the blade from digging into my cold flesh.

"You are a feisty little thing," he jeered. "I might have to join Pollux when he pays you a visit in the basement."

He pushed the knife closer when I mouthed, "Bastard," then turned his head at the sound of my brother's voice.

My eyes burned as I forced them to look in his direction; I couldn't turn my head. Cyrus held two knives in his hands. Miraculously, he had disarmed the long-haired Solin. Sensing my brother's emotions stir, the warming sensation inside my body intensified to an uncomfortable level. It hit me when my gaze shifted back to Elio. *The answer will reveal itself at the most opportune time.*

My mind raced, recalling Jax's prediction. Cyrus's foot was only inches from my outstretched hand. *If I can reach him, then maybe, just maybe our little trick will repeat itself.*

A pained gasp escaped my mouth as I reached for my brother. Forcing my compliance, Elio tightened his grip and pushed the blade into my throat. During our training, Jax mentioned that a knife could break the skin on the neck without causing a fatal injury because the main arteries were protected by a layer of muscle. I whimpered as the blade went deeper. I didn't want to test Jax's theory, but I had no choice. I had to reach Cyrus.

My vision blurred; the pain intensified as I stretched my arm. Tears filled my eyes when Elio slid the blade across my neck. Not enough to kill me but just enough to send a message. *It's now or never.* I used every ounce of adrenaline and screamed at the top of my lungs when my fingers touched Cyrus's ankle.

Just as before the warmth surged through me, concentrating in the hand that held Elio's wrist. I shut my eyes and released a wave of heat.

Elio hissed and dropped the knife he held to my throat. Taking advantage of the situation, I let go of his wrist and placed my palm over his face. His cool flesh turned warm and softened as I released more heat. He hollered in pain. My nostrils flared at the smoke that rose from his melting skin. Using Cyrus's shared Solin strength, I sat up and pushed the Solin off me. He fell backward and rolled into the fetal position, clutching his scorched face.

A stream of blood dripped down my neck. I covered the wound with my hand and scrambled to my feet. Silence surrounded me. I looked at Cyrus. He stood motionless, holding the two knives. The mouths of the other Collectors fell open as they observed their fallen comrade.

Without hesitation, I grabbed my brother's arm. He nodded, prepared to repeat our trick if necessary. We took a step closer to the other men. I let go of my bleeding neck and raised my hand in a threatening stance, aiming for their faces.

The long-haired Collector's eyes grew, making the connection. He turned his head. "Apollo, we aren't prepared for this."

"No, you're not," Cyrus said.

Apollo glared at my brother. "This isn't over."

"You're right. It's just getting started."

I gasped when the eldest Solin lunged at Cyrus. Without thinking, I grabbed Apollo's wrist and released another wave of heat onto his cool flesh. The knife fell from his hand. He called me every name in the book as he inspected the handprint shaped burn that wrapped around his wrist.

"Try that again," my brother warned. "And next time, she aims for your face." He pointed at Elio, who lay incapacitated with pain.

Apollo snatched up his knife, then barked orders at the Solin who stood in shock beside him. "Ravi, tell Elio to get his ass off the ground. We move—now."

The Solin nodded and dashed to his comrade's side. Apollo's eyes narrowed at my brother. "You've made a grave mistake by challenging us today." Cyrus didn't respond. "The next time we see each other, I'm going to make your sister watch while I cut off your fingers." He sneered in my direction. "And that's nothing compared to what Pollux has planned for you—you little bitch."

Cyrus took a step forward. "You should get the hell out of here while there's still time." He encouraged me to lift my hand higher, closer to Apollo's face. "Unless you want to look like your pal, Elio."

Apollo scowled, anger seeping out of his being. "Elio," he barked. "Let's go."

Ravi tried to help the fallen Solin to his feet but stumbled when Elio shoved him to the side.

"Get off me!" he yelled.

Without waiting for the others to catch up, Apollo turned and headed away from the spring. Elio squinted to see through the cracks in his fingers as he staggered after Ravi.

Tremors rippled through me like the aftershock of a massive earthquake. Unable to stand, I fell to my knees and clutched the wound on my neck.

Cyrus dropped the knives and kneeled beside me. He swore at the amount of blood that stained my pale shirt.

"Elara," he whispered, watching my eyes drift around the spring. "I need you to stay with me."

I tried to nod but grimaced at the pain. My brother removed his shirt and tied it around my neck like a makeshift bandage.

His eyes filled with concern as he applied pressure. "Sis, you've lost a lot of blood."

The loud pounding in my ears muffled his voice. My eyelids, like heavy weights moved sluggishly as I tried to blink.

"I need you to talk to me," he said, squeezing my hand.

The trees spun, my vision blurred. I wasn't sure if it was the blood loss, the fact we survived an attack from three members of the Inner Circle or that . . .

"Jax," I managed, my voice cracking.

Cyrus's eyes darted around the spring. "Where in the hell is he?"

A block of ice filled the space that once occupied my heart. "He's gone. They've taken him to Zenith."

SIXTEEN

Only Ally

Cyrus's face fell as he absorbed my painful words. Guilt's jagged claws dug into my back, leaving me incapacitated with grief. I abandoned Jax on the cliffside—sentenced him to a slow and painful death. Tears streamed down my face.

Cyrus murmured, "Oh, sis," while pulling me into a tight embrace. My emotions poured onto his shoulder, the salty drops warming his cool skin.

"What happened after I left?" he asked.

Through hushed sobs, I said, "He took me to this clearing and then the Inner Circle showed up." I wiped the snot from my nose. "They surrounded us. We were trapped."

Cyrus shut his eyes.

"Two Solins restrained us in a hold, and Pollux kept saying these horrible things, then Jax handed me his knife." I buried my face in my hands and cried, “They’re going to kill him, and it’s all my fault.”

“Hey,” Cyrus soothed, pulling my hands away. “Jax told us what to do if apprehended by a Collector. You did the right thing by getting the hell out of there.”

“No. I don’t care what he told us to do. I abandoned Jax, and in a few hours he’ll be dead.” I bit my knuckles. “And as punishment, I get to live with that guilt for the rest of my life.”

“Stop that,” he demanded, grabbing me by the shoulders. “Maybe they won’t kill him.”

Anger surged through me as I poked Cyrus in the chest. “You weren’t there. You didn’t see the way Pollux looked at Jax, you didn’t hear the twisted shit he said to him—to me.”

My brother pinched the bridge of his nose.

“Jax told us what happens if captured by the Inner Circle. Think of what Zenith will do when he gets his hands on Jax. It’s been nine years since they’ve seen each other. You heard the story. They didn’t part on good terms.” My anger shifted back to sorrow. More tears filled my eyes. “He’s not coming back.”

“You don’t know that.”

“You and your Solin optimistic attitude can go to hell.”

My brother collapsed onto the grass beside me, both stunned and hurt by comment.

“Cyrus, we don’t have time for hope-filled thoughts or pipe dreams. Jax is gone and he’s never coming back.” I tossed up my hands. “We can’t survive out here on our own. We haven’t a clue how to defeat Zenith, hell—we don’t even know where he lives. And to really top it all off, we don't have a way to get home."

My brother's chin hit his chest, the reality of our situation weighing down on him. After a few heartbeats of silence, he said, "You're upset. You're not thinking straight." I glared at his accurate comment. "I won't give up on Jax that easily. We have to stay positive and find a way to get him out of there."

My mouth fell open. "Were you not listening to anything I just said? Even if Zenith wanted to keep Jax alive as his prisoner, how do you propose we rescue him?" I paused, waiting for him to respond. Silence. "What are we supposed to do, Cyrus? Ask a random person for Zenith's address? Then stroll on over to his fortress-like home with a couple of knives in our pockets, and say, *Hey Pollux, it's nice to see you again. Is Zenith around? We're here to get our pal Jax. Can we stay for dinner?"*

"Okay, I get it, but regardless we can't toss in the towel and give up on the guy."

"I'm not giving up on him."

"It sure as hell sounds like you are."

I gritted my teeth.

"Elara, Jax would have never given up on us. He spent, what? Nine years watching over us." Cyrus waved a hand at the surrounding area. "Are you forgetting that you disarmed not one, but two members of the Inner Circle today?"

I looked at my blood-stained hand. "I can't guarantee our little trick will work on command."

"I bet it will if it means rescuing Jax."

I cringed, adjusting the fabric that clung to my wounded neck. "Maybe, but we still don't know where to find Zenith." I blew a white cloud of warmth into my hands. "And we don't have any money to buy winter clothes or food. Do they even use money on Aroonyx?"

The Solin shrugged.

"We don't know anyone. We have no allies."

"You're right."

I huffed a breath. "No shit."

"About most of it."

I raised a brow while applying more pressure over the makeshift bandage.

"No, we don't have directions to Zenith's or money for supplies, but we do know someone who has insider information about the Collectors."

I gasped. "Idalia."

"Mm-hmm. And I'm sure she'll help us. Especially after we tell her about Jax, and thanks to her father's dark past, I bet she knows where to find Zenith."

The glimmer of hope that sparked in my eyes vanished when I thought of Leo and the other Collectors who stood outside of Idalia's door the previous night.

Cyrus rubbed his chilled arms. "Don't tell me you're still jealous. I thought you let that go."

"No, I was just thinking about how Leo and the others were out looking for us." He nodded, his posture relaxing. "After our run-in with the Inner Circle, I'm sure the villages will be swarming with Collectors. How would we get to Idalia's without getting caught?"

Cyrus shivered; goosebumps covered every inch of his body. I reached for the shirt around my neck.

"No," he said, holding up his hand like a stop sign. "You need it more than I do. I may be freezing, but I'm not bleeding." He went on before I could protest. "The good thing is the other Collectors aren't aware of our identities."

I cocked my head to one side.

"Think about it, Elara. Everyone on Aroonyx looks the same. They're either Lunin or Solin." He inclined his head at me. "Black hair, blue eyes, fair skin." He tapped his chest. "Blond hair, orange eyes, tan skin."

"That's great, but Elio, Apollo, and Ravi saw both of our faces." I groaned. "And the entire Inner Circle saw mine."

"But how are they going to describe our exact features to the other Collectors?" Cyrus lowered his voice to mock Apollo's. "*Yes, Zenith, I believe the Lunin had a freckle above her left eyebrow and the Solin had a tiny scar on his wrist.*"

A smirk tugged at the corner of my mouth. His impression was spot on.

Cyrus added, "The average Collectors won't know it's us unless we're seen together."

"What are you saying?"

"We stay apart, fly under the radar."

I hopped to my feet. "Have you lost your damn mind? Look at what happened the last time we split up." His face fell. "That's the dumbest idea I've ever heard."

"I wasn't implying we go our separate ways. I'm simply suggesting we keep our distance when in the public eye. Stay close enough to see each other at all times but act like strangers so we blend in with the others." He watched a cloud leave his mouth as he let out a deep exhale. "It's not like they have wanted posters with our faces displayed everywhere."

"Not yet."

Cyrus's brows furrowed when he asked, "Do they even use paper on Aroonyx?"

I laughed before crying once more.

"It was an honest question. I wasn't trying to be funny."

"I know you weren't," I said, wiping a tear from my cheek. "My sanity is hanging on by a thin thread."

Cyrus rubbed his biceps. I frowned, watching his tan skin turn a light shade of purple.

"Your lips are turning blue."

He climbed to his feet. "Don't take the bandage off. I have another shirt in Jax's bag."

I shut my eyes. Just hearing the Lunin's name caused me pain. "Where did you find it?" I asked, remembering Jax had dropped it before the brawl.

Cyrus spoke with his back facing me as he walked around the spring. "I literally tripped over it on my way back from the cliffside." He blew out a breath while rummaging through the bag. "You were right. I couldn't see shit once I got into the forest. The trees blocked out all of the moonlight."

I bobbed up and down from the cold as he slipped a shirt over his head. "Well, you weren't the only one missing our shared traits. I could have used your Solin strength this morning."

Cyrus's head hung as he approached. "I'm sorry I wasn't there. I should have listened when you insisted that we stay together."

"It's not your fault. You saw the size of those Solins. I doubt the outcome would have differed."

"Hey," he said with wide eyes. "Look what's in the bag."

"Hell no. You're not shoving that powdered stuff in my wound."

"That's a serious cut, Elara. I think you need stitches."

"It's fine." I peeled the blood-soaked fabric off my neck. "See?"

"No, it's not fine. Look." He pointed to the stream that trickled down my shirt. I grimaced, touching the warm fluid. "This stuff helped clot the blood with your injured hand. Either you do it, or I will." He shook the jar. "Regardless, it's going in that wound."

"Fine. You do it."

I turned my neck so the injury faced my brother. He moved closer, powder in hand. A thought flew into my mind when my eyes caught the steam that rose off the water. *The spring did wonders for the knife wound on my hand. I wonder if it will help my neck?* I motioned for Cyrus to stop his approach.

"Elara, I have to do it."

"And you will but first—" I dashed to the edge of the spring and tested the water temperature with my hand. "It feels like a hot tub."

"Then I'm getting in because it's freezing."

"Don't," I said, grabbing his leg mid-motion.

"Why?"

"We don't have any towels. If you use your pants to dry off, they'll be wet and then you will freeze. As nice as it sounds, this water is a death trap."

"Then what are you doing over here?"

I lowered myself onto my stomach, tossed the makeshift bandage to the side, and stretched my aching neck over the water. "Let me know if it looks better after I soak it."

Cyrus folded his chilled arms across his chest.

I submerged my neck, moaning with relief. The water fizzed over the deep gash like it did with my hand. I shut my eyes, wishing the spring's magical properties could heal the aching in my chest.

Seconds later, I lifted my head. "How does it look?" I asked, using the blood-stained shirt to dab the water off my skin.

His nose crinkled. "It cleaned the wound, but I still think you still need stitches." He sat beside me. "Here, let me put the powder it now."

I gritted my teeth in preparation for the burning sensation I experienced when Jax administered the medicine. The healing properties of the spring worked because I didn't holler in pain when Cyrus pressed the powder into my wound.

"How does that feel?"

I shrugged. "Honestly, it's getting so cold everything feels numb."

"You can say that again." He re-tied the fabric around my neck and pulled it tight.

"Ow."

"You said you couldn't feel anything."

"I was exaggerating."

He rolled his eyes. "That should hold until we get to Idalia's."

"*If* we get there."

Cyrus snapped his fingers in front of my face. "Listen, I need you to be stronger than ever right now. You can't have an emotional breakdown and fall apart because I can't do this on my own." My shoulders sagged with defeat, but he pressed on. "I get it, okay? You're sick with a nasty mixture of grief and guilt. But the only way to move past it is to walk through those emotions and face them head on. If you don't, you'll be trapped on the other side."

"It's not that easy, Cyrus. Blame is something that's—"

"You can't blame yourself for what happened."

I stifled a groan. "Yes, I can."

"No, you can't."

"Why the hell not?"

"Because Jax never expected you to defend him against nine members of the Inner Circle. That would have been a suicide mission. Jax is a smart man. He did the right thing by giving you his knife." My brother raised his hand when my lips moved, silencing my efforts. "And you did the right thing by getting the hell out of there. Don't dwell on what happened today. If you do, you'll drive yourself mad. There's no point in feeling guilty because guilt exists in the past—and guess what? The past doesn't exist anymore, so let it go. Keep your attention focused on our new mission—rescuing Jax."

I stared at my twin brother. *Damn him and his practical advice.* A tiny smile broke at the corner of my mouth. *Leave it to Cyrus to see the glass half full when you're wandering around the desert without a watering hole in sight.*

Jax mentioned that Solins were known for their unwavering courage and determination, but Cyrus was different. He was more than a list of vague descriptions jotted down on a piece of paper—he was my better half and the true hero of the story.

My brother had the magical ability to calm my nerves when my emotions got the best of me, and he always steered me in the right direction when I got off track. Was it our strong bond? The special connection that only twins share? Who knows? Regardless the reason, I was grateful to call Cyrus Lofton my brother.

I flinched when he placed his icy hands on the sides of my face, and when he found my eyes, he whispered, "Everything is going to be okay. *We* are going to be okay."

"How can you be so sure?"

His hands fell into his lap. "Because the good in life always prevails." I forced a smile. "Zenith's reign can't last forever. The people of Aroonyx have forgotten what it's like to live without a ruthless dictator controlling their every move. Together, we can help them remember. I'll do whatever it takes to get that bastard to step down." He flashed me a warm smile. "I just hope you're by my side when it happens."

I stilled. The picture of our biological parents flashed in my mind. *He looks just like our father. I bet their voices even sounded the same.*

I nodded at my brother. He was right, right about everything. Even though the outcome seemed grim, I couldn't give up on Jax, and I sure as hell couldn't give up on the people of Aroonyx. I had to believe the man I loved was strong enough to face Zenith, and I had to believe the people were strong enough to face their darkest fears.

"Thank you."

He arched a brow. "For what?"

"For helping me see the situation in a different light."

"Anytime, sis."

Cyrus climbed off the ground, then helped me to my feet. Trying to stay warm, he bobbed and weaved like a boxer in a ring.

"So now what?" I asked, following his lead.

He faked a left jab. "We find a way to rescue Jax."

SEVENTEEN

Frozen in Time

"Okay. Let's get to Idalia's before we freeze to death."

Cyrus nodded while rummaging in the bag for articles of warmth.

I glanced up, watching the emerald atmosphere transform into an ominous sight. A sheet of nimbus clouds moved across the sky with such speed it looked as though someone tossed a gray down blanket over the forest. I shuddered a breath. *Yeah, this doesn't look like the weather in Maine or anywhere else on Earth.*

At that moment a gust of wind almost blew Jax's bag out of my brother's hand. I squinted, tucking my chin into my chest. The air temperature continued to drop with each passing second. *This doesn't look promising.*

My head snapped up when my brother called my name. His mouth gaped as he gestured to the sky. Snow—and lots of it—fell from the low-lying clouds.

"Cyrus we've got to hurry." I clenched my teeth. They wouldn't stop chattering. "Do we have any more clothes in the bag?"

He held up two pairs of shorts. "Just these."

"Well, that doesn't help."

"Here," he said, removing his shirt. "Take this."

"No. You already gave me the one off your back."

He tossed me the pale fabric. "I have more meat on my bones, and your shorts are like half the size of my own. I'll be fine."

Every muscle in my body trembled, begging me to slip it on, but my gut told me otherwise.

"You're wasting time, just do it."

Surrendering to his request, I pulled the shirt over my head, careful to avoid the injury on my neck, then kept my arms tucked inside the fabric like a caterpillar in a cocoon. Cyrus's large stature left the shirt hanging past my thighs.

My brother dusted the snowflakes off his bare skin before hurrying to collect the knives that lay around the spring.

He slid his blade and Ravi's into his back pocket before offering me Jax's knife. "He'd want you to have it."

With a heavy heart, I took it from his outstretched hand, wiped the blood off on my shorts, then secured the blade before slipping it into my pocket.

My brother loosened the straps of the backpack while inclining his head toward the forest. "Let's jog to keep warm."

"Sounds good to me."

The two of us turned our backs on the spring; our strides synced as one as we rushed up the gentle slope.

"We need a plan," I said, side-stepping a piece of Clear Stone.

"It's daylight, so we can use my Solin vision to watch for Collectors."

"About that."

Cyrus gave me a sidelong glance.

"Jax said no one leaves their homes during the first snowfall." I blew an ice crystal off my nose. "He didn't go into detail as to why, but I think we're about to see for ourselves."

I motioned to the evidence as we stepped through the cluster of trees.

"Holy—" Cyrus's voice faded.

A thin layer of snow covered the forest floor. My head turned. The cloud coverage cast a cool tone over the vast space, giving it a majestic quality. Even in the midst of our dangerous endeavor, I couldn't help but marvel at the stunning landscape. The black trees contrasted brilliantly against the glittering snow. We looked at the white tent that hovered above us, the green leaves draped in sheets of ice. I surveyed the dense brush. Silence. Only the howling wind dared to join us on our new mission.

Cyrus pointed to the trail of footprints behind us. "We don't have to worry about covering our tracks if what Jax says is true."

I nodded. "Let's keep moving."

As we hurried down the path toward Idalia's, I told my brother about the romantic moment I shared with Jax on the cliffside.

Cyrus stayed quiet and when my lips stopped moving, he said, "Well, that changes things."

It wasn't long before the gentle snow flurries turned into an aggressive blizzard—a whiteout. The strong gusts of ice-kissed wind burned my eyes, flakes sticking to my lashes. We kept our heads down as we trudged through the ankle-deep fluff.

I couldn't feel my extremities. I tried wiggling my toes, but nothing happened. It felt equally awkward as patting your head while rubbing your stomach. The motion was simple, yet my body refused to cooperate.

I stayed close to Cyrus, grateful that my skin still prickled with a mild heat. Like a dying flame it flickered through different parts of my body. A moment's relief and nothing else. The farther we went, the more it dimmed. I worried about my brother. Every time I looked in his direction, I found more ice and snow glued to his shirtless torso.

I shielded my face from another gust of wind. *This is insanity. Yesterday I was sweating, and now I'm turning into a block of ice.*

The winter on Aroonyx was like nothing I had ever experienced. There was cold, and then there was hell's version: a lethal cold that not only injected ice into your veins but also screwed with your head. My eyes felt heavy with sleep as if I had ingested a sedative, and my mind drifted to a bizarre world reminiscent of a fever dream. Stick figures without faces appeared before my eyes and repetitive voices filled my ears. I had never tried a hallucinogenic drug, but if the trip mimicked the twisted space my mind wandered, then count me out.

Time dragged by, one miserable step after another. Our casual jog lasted only minutes because we lacked my Lunin endurance. Both winded and exhausted, we stopped at the fork in the road.

My words came out in a tight whisper. "Do we go over the boulders or take the trail that leads to the South Village?"

I looked at my brother when he didn't answer. His entire body shook uncontrollably. *Shit.* His tan skin had turned a deep shade of purple, and his eyelids moved in slow motion when he blinked.

I cleared my throat. "Cyrus."

He swayed back and forth. I repeated his name, this time with more urgency. He turned, brushing the ice crystals off his face.

It took every bit of energy to speak. "I don't know if I can make it any farther. I'm so tired." I eyed the knee-deep snow that surrounded us. "Maybe we should rest for a while."

"No, we have to keep moving."

"Which way?"

With a trembling hand, he pointed to the boulders. "We can't take the trail." He paused to blink. "We don't know how to get to Idalia's from the South Village."

I shut my eyes as another gust slapped at my face. "How are we going to climb? We can barely walk."

"We don't have a choice."

Forcing my eyelids open, we started the second half of the painstaking journey. Our boots slid across the thin layer of ice that draped over each boulder like a tablecloth of death. My hands resembled those of a corpse lying in a hospital freezer: hard and morbidly pale. Once again, my fingernails chipped and bled, only this time I felt nothing. The only pain I endured was the thought of us not making it to Idalia's.

Even at his weakest, Cyrus had my back. He kept a close watch, catching me when I slipped and encouraging me to move forward, even though I begged him to stop.

Finally, we reached the last boulder. I groaned, staring at the rock like it was Mt. Everest. "We're almost there."

Silence. The flicker of warmth inside me dimmed to the point of non-existence. My head turned.

Cyrus's eyes were open, but they stared at nothing. His chest barely moved with the small breaths that entered his lungs.

I tapped his arm. "Are you okay?"

No answer. He just swayed back and forth.

I waved a hand in his face. "Cyrus."

"What's up?" His voice sounded further away than his gaze.

A strong four-letter curse word rolled off my tongue. "Listen, we have to hurry. The weather is taking its toll on us—and fast."

Like a scene out of a scary movie, my brother cocked his head to one side and blinked only once while saying, "Did you hear that voice?"

I cursed again. "Cyrus. That was me. I asked you a question. And I need you to answer me. Are you okay?"

Panic washed over me when he didn't respond. He just stood there like a drugged deer in the headlights.

I tugged at his arm. "We're almost there. I need you to follow me now, okay?"

He tried to nod. Not wanting to waste time, I compelled my feet to move forward. My boots sank with each step. Two strides later, we approached the last leg of our journey. *You can do this.* I winced, digging my fingers into the closest crevice, then froze when the last bit of warmth vanished from my body.

I yelled my brother's name as I ran—hobbled—to where he lay in the snow.

No, no, no. I fell to my knees beside him. His amber eyes glazed over as he slipped in and out of consciousness.

I pulled off the extra shirt, and grimaced at his blue torso before laying it over him.

"Damn it, Cyrus," I cried, patting his ice-cold cheeks. "We didn't come this far for you to freeze to death."

The wind howled, sending a sheet of snow scattering around us. "Stay with me," I begged, shaking him by the shoulders. "I've already lost Jax." Tears filled my eyes. "I can't lose you too."

The vice grip around my heart clamped shut. *No, please no.* My hand shot to my mouth, watching the last bit of light dim from his amber eyes.

Desperate, I tried sitting him up. *He's too heavy for me to carry without any Solin strength.* My head turned. *If I can make it over that boulder, I'll be at Idalia's in a few minutes.* I frowned at my brother. *I don't have a few minutes. Hypothermia has set in. If we don't raise his body temperature, he'll fall asleep and never wake up.*

That thought alone sent me on a mad dash to find help. My fingers dug into the rock, and my legs pushed me higher. I reached for another gap, then pulled myself over the ledge.

I remembered hearing stories about mothers who lifted cars off their children after an accident. Some refer to the anomaly as a display of *hysterical strength*, Western medicine either brushes it off or calls the occurrence an *adrenaline surge*, while the spiritual ones see it as an act of God. Call it what you want, but whatever helped me find Idalia's that day was something outside of my control.

The pub glowed like a building in a ghost town. Not a soul in sight. The absence of footprints around the dwelling confirmed Jax's warning about the first snowfall.

I flung open the door. The warmth of a crackling fire slammed into my face like a hammer. I squinted as ice crystals chased after me when I bolted into the near empty room.

Two men sat at the bar: an older Solin and a Lunin, close to my father's age. Their heads turned when they heard my dramatic entrance. The man's crystal blue eyes widened at my appearance. There I stood, winded after the exhausting journey with panic smeared all over my half-frozen face. Snow covered every inch of my body, leaving my black hair gray while the bloodied shirt around my neck didn't budge, glued by ice to my wound.

The age lines on the Solin's forehead creased with curiosity while the blue-eyed man hopped off the bar stool and shouted toward the stairs that led to Idalia's bedroom. "Honey! You better get down here."

The sound of feet thumping down the wooden steps caused my pulse to race.

A sweet voice filled the quiet space. "Callisto, you and Samson can get your own drinks. You don't need me—" Idalia paled when she noticed me standing near the doorway. My name flew out of her mouth as she dashed across the room, her golden eyes scanning me up and down. "What are you doing here?" She looked around the room. "Where's Jax and—"

I silenced her with my hand, and my voice cracked when I said, "Idalia, you have to help me. My brother's life depends on it."

She nodded.

In short sentences I told her of Cyrus's whereabouts and explained his grave situation.

"Got it," she said, sprinting toward the stairs. Over her shoulder she said, "Samson, Callisto. I need your help."

Without saying a word, the men grabbed their winter coats and rushed toward the door. Seconds later, the young

Solin appeared bundled up in a long jacket, another one draped over her arm.

"Take it," she said, tossing it to me as she walked by.

I slipped my arms into the fur-lined sleeves and fumbled with the buttons while following Idalia back into the cold. The two men jogged behind us.

Thankfully, the plush snow absorbed the impact when I slid off the boulder and fell over fifteen feet. Idalia and the Lunin hurried after me, eager to check for injuries while the Solin just shook his head, irritated by my misfortune.

Disregarding my throbbing head, I scrambled to my feet and sprinted toward my brother. His body was barely visible. The snow covered him like dirt on a fresh grave. I fell to my knees and yelled his name while dusting the white flakes off his face.

The Lunin dashed to my side and held two fingers to Cyrus's neck. He closed his eyes and counted. "There's a pulse, but it's faint." He looked at Idalia. "He doesn't have much time."

Idalia flashed the Solin a stern look. "Don't just stand there. Do something."

His burnt orange eyes shifted between me and my brother. I stilled when he met my gaze. Without saying a word, he bent down, picked up Cyrus, hurled me the backpack, and tossed my brother over his shoulder like he was leaving the market with a bag of grain.

My mouth gaped. I knew Solins were strong, but this man's strength resembled a Norse god. With minimal effort he climbed up and over the boulder with my brother dangling over his back, then jogged the rest of the way to Idalia's. *Am I the only one seeing this?*

We followed the Solin up the stairs and into the spare bedroom. As soon as he lay Cyrus on the bed, the Lunin checked his vitals.

Idalia pointed to her room across the hall. "Get some blankets."

The man with the orange eyes nodded, then hurried across the room.

Seeing my brother's half-frozen body sprawled on the bed left me incapacitated with grief. The familiar warmth that flowed through my veins while in his presence was gone—a distant memory of our time together.

I stood there in shock. I could hardly see straight because of the violent tremors. The tears that streamed down my face fell onto the black floorboards. I covered my mouth, muffling the sobs. *Hours ago, we sat in this room, laughing, enjoying each other's company, and now . . .*

My head jolted forward when the Solin knocked my shoulder as he darted past me, blankets in hand.

"We're losing him," the Lunin said, his fingers still pressed against my brother's main artery. "I can't find a pulse."

"We can't lose him, Callisto," Idalia said, grabbing the blankets from the Solin's outstretched hands. She stacked the patchwork quilts on top of Cyrus's body, the layers of her blonde hair fell into her face while she hurried around the bed.

Callisto climbed on my brother and began administering CPR. Using all of his weight, he forced his pale hands into Cyrus's chest.

"Move," the Solin barked, pushing him out of the way. "Let me do it."

My jaw fell open. There was a noticeable difference in strength. As if using a defibrillator, the forceful compressions caused Cyrus's body to rise and fall with sudden jolts.

Callisto sighed when he moved his fingers back to my brother's neck. "No pulse."

"Keep trying," Idalia pressed, eyeing me over her shoulder.

I couldn't breathe. The only sound came from Callisto repeating "No pulse" and the sickening crack of Cyrus's ribs breaking. Refusing to give up, the Solin pushed his hands harder and deeper into my brother's chest.

My vision blurred as the room spun like a horrific carnival ride I couldn't escape. What was left of my shattered heart turned to ash when Callisto shut his eyes and bowed his head.

"He's gone," he whispered, letting his arm fall to his side.

The room grew smaller by the second. *No, he can't be.* My eyes drifted to the bed, focusing on my brother's lifeless body.

I fell to my knees as a gut-wrenching darkness consumed me. *He's gone. Cyrus is dead.*

EIGHTEEN

Second Chances

The soft fabric of an even softer pillow pressed against my cheek. I lay on my side, stuck in a strange state of slumber mixed with awareness. No longer cold, I remained motionless, the tremors absent from my warm body. I inhaled a deep breath and rubbed Mr. Sandman's footprints from my eyes.

When I blinked, a Lunin man came into view. He sat with his eyes closed in a wooden chair only feet away from the bed. His smooth face had few wrinkles, and his black hair was neatly trimmed like a business executive on Wall Street. *Callisto.*

Life surged through me when I recalled my last encounter with the man. My brother's name flew out of my mouth in a raspy voice as I tossed off the covers and hopped to my feet.

Callisto's eyes shot open. I stumbled. The room spun. He was at my side in an instant, his hand gripped my arm.

"Easy," he soothed, motioning for me to sit down. "Your body needs time to adjust. You've been out for days."

"Days?"

He nodded.

I glanced around the unfamiliar space. Idalia's bedroom, larger than the one across the hall, had minimal furniture. The morning light illuminated a wooden desk in the corner of the room, a black chest rested at the foot of the queen-sized bed and a washroom was near the entryway.

My eyes darted back and forth with desperation. No sign of Jax's bag or evidence of my brother's existence. I clutched my chest, the remnants of my beating heart.

Callisto took a seat on the bed beside me, and in a quiet voice he said, "Elara, your—"

Don't you dare say it. I can't bear to hear the word.

A smile broke at the corner of his mouth as he met my gaze. "Your brother is alive."

My lip quivered and the tremors resurfaced, only this time with relief instead of grief. "What? How? I thought—"

The Lunin shrugged. "I haven't a clue how he pulled through that one. He didn't have a pulse, but Idalia wouldn't let Samson give up on him. She's with your brother now."

I dropped my face into my hands.

"He's a tough kid, I'll give him that much. You both are." Callisto stood and crossed his arms. "Can I ask you a question?"

I nodded.

"Why were you traveling during the first snowfall?"

My mind raced with unspoken questions. *Does he know who we are? Did Idalia tell him? Who is he? Can I trust him?*

Not waiting for a reply, he added, "Everyone on Aroonyx stays indoors during the first snowfall. The drastic drop in temperature is a shock to the body." He paused, watching my relaxed expression shift to concern. "But two people from Earth wouldn't know about this . . . would they?"

My knees wobbled as I stood from the bed. I reached for Jax's knife, then frowned at the empty pocket. I was dressed in different clothes. A thick, long-sleeved shirt and gray pants covered my pale body. The hours I spent training with Jax took over as my arms moved to the guard position without a conscious effort.

The Lunin's shoulders bounced up and down with laughter as he motioned for me to stand down. "Easy, Elara. I would never hurt you. Allow me to formally introduce myself. I'm Callisto, Idalia's uncle."

Feeling foolish, I lowered my guard and extended a hand. "Forgive me." He gave my fingers a gentle squeeze. "It's been a rough few days. I don't know who to trust."

"That's understandable. Cyrus filled us in." He shook his head. "I can't believe the two of you survived an encounter with the Inner Circle."

"Me neither."

He motioned for me to follow him toward the door. "But don't worry, you're safe now, and I won't tell anyone the reason for your return."

My skin prickled with heat the moment I stepped into the hallway. I sighed with relief. Cyrus was near. Callisto tapped his knuckles on the door to the spare room.

"Come in," Idalia called, sounding more chipper than the last time I heard her voice.

The Lunin had barely twisted the knob before I pushed past him and darted into the room. My eyes lit up when I found my brother sitting in the bed with Idalia perched at the foot. She looked more beautiful than ever. The Solin had gathered her tousled locks, more like handspun silk, over one shoulder, and her flawless complexion shimmered in the morning light that seeped through the bedroom window.

Grinning from ear to ear, I ran to my brother and threw my arms around his neck. Amused with my less than subtle salutation, he returned the gesture by giving me a tight squeeze. As if he had risen from the grave, I dug my fingers into his warm skin and sobbed on his shoulder. After a few seconds of an ugly cry, I pulled away and punched him in the bicep.

"Ow. What was that for?"

"Don't you ever do that to me again."

"Don't what?" His lips twitched with a smirk. "Freeze to death?"

My scoff turned into laughter.

Idalia stood and smiled at the two of us while straightening the comforter. "I'm going to head downstairs and see if the guys need anything." She looked at Cyrus. "I'll be back to check on you in a few minutes."

My brother gave her a warm grin before she headed toward the door. I called the Solin's name as her delicate fingers touched her uncle's arm. She turned, meeting my gaze.

"Thank you for saving my brother's life."

The irises of her golden eyes sparkled in the sunlight when she said, "You're most welcome."

After Callisto closed the door behind them, I twisted my body around on the bed and scanned Cyrus for any signs of permanent damage. Like me, he wore different clothes, but everything else appeared to be in working order.

I bit the inside of my cheek. "So . . . you really are okay?"

"Yeah, it took me a while to thaw out, but I'm good. My ribs hurt like hell." He touched the tender area. "I forgot about that little side effect of CPR."

I dropped my head, letting out an exaggerated breath. "That was the longest and hardest day ever."

"You're telling me," he said, scratching the patch of hair on his chin. "First, we run from the Collectors, then me and Jax kick each other's ass for a while, and then the two of you—"

I held up my hand. "It's cool. I don't need a recap of the worst day of my life."

We sat in silence for short minutes, our minds revisiting the details of that horrible morning.

Cyrus stared out the window while he spoke. "I'm sorry I insisted on splitting up that night."

"Stop apologizing," I said, rubbing my chest. A cold spot had appeared around the fragments of my heart when I abandoned Jax on the cliffside. "We've been through this. It's not your fault."

"Fine. Then I'm sorry I—"

"Died?"

"I was trying to find a better word." Cyrus pushed himself farther up the bed and leaned his back against the headboard before continuing. "I did have this strange thing happen in the midst of all the drama."

"What, like a near-death experience?"

"I don't know what to call it. I just remember looking down at my lifeless body like it was yesterday's laundry."

I squished up my face. "What in the hell is that supposed to mean?"

He paused, searching for the right words. "Not like actual clothes, but more like the attachment I had to my physical body vanished. I remember it all so well. Samson was administering CPR, Callisto was checking my pulse, Idalia was here, and you were over there, standing by the door." My eyes grew at his accurate account. "Here's the part where it gets weird."

"Is what you just told me considered normal?"

He laughed. "No, not at all."

I scooted closer and crossed my legs.

"I had this awareness wash over me. It's hard to explain," he said, his brows furrowing. "I think I could have left if I wanted to, and I almost did, but when I saw you collapse, something outside of myself pulled me back. It's like I had unfinished business. Before I knew it, I was awake with Idalia sitting beside me."

"Well, that story deserves its own chapter in our book of *Cyrus and Elara's Unexplained Events*." His pearly teeth glowed in the morning light when I added, "Just promise me you won't do it again anytime soon."

"I can't make any promises regarding things out of my control, but next time I'll wear a shirt when it's snowing."

I smiled, overjoyed to have my brother and his sense of humor back in my life.

He pointed to my neck. "How's your wound feeling?"

Having forgotten about the injury, my hand shot to the tender spot where Elio's blade drew blood. I grimaced, my fingers grazing the rough sutures. Feeling even more confused about my long nap, I asked, "When did I get stitches?"

"Right after you collapsed. Idalia said she gave you something to calm your nerves. It acted like a sedative, so she carried you to her room and stitched you up."

"Damn. That was some strong medicine because I remember nothing."

"I hear ya." Cyrus crossed his arms. "I know it appears like we've gone back in time, but the medicine they use on Aroonyx is way more advanced than anything found on Earth. I almost fell off the bed when I woke up and saw my feet."

"Why?"

He tossed off the covers. "Frost bite. They look a hundred times better now and only hurt when I walk."

"Ew. That's better."

"Thanks a lot, sis."

"I'm sorry." I tried muffling my laughter. "But your feet look like shit."

"Wow. You can be so mean."

"I'm just calling it like I see it." I bit my lip. "I might have to change your name to Gray Foot."

"Are you done making fun of me?" I covered my mouth. "Go ahead," he pressed, unable to hide his own amusement. "Laugh it up, sis. Hit a man when he's down."

I shifted my features into neutral. "I'm sorry, you were saying?"

My brother rolled his eyes before speaking. "Anyway—Idalia caked another strange powder on my feet, and within a few hours the black faded to gray."

He paused, watching me mouth, "Gray Foot," then added, "She said in a few days they'll be back to normal."

I wiggled my eyebrows at Cyrus. "I bet you've enjoyed having Idalia as your nurse."

"Hell yeah. The hot nurse. Every man's fantasy."

"You may have had an out-of-body experience, but that doesn't make you less of a ridiculous person."

My brother's mouth gaped. "You brought it up. How am I supposed to ignore the woman? She looks like a Greek goddess."

I shrugged. *This is true.*

Cyrus shut his eyes, his smile growing. "It's not my fault she's catering to my fantasy."

"Are *you* done?"

"Does this make us even?"

My lips paused at the sound of a loud knock on the bedroom door. Before we could answer, the knob twisted and in walked the Solin whose strong hands saved my brother's life.

The man turned sideways as he stepped over the threshold; his shoulders were too broad to fit otherwise. Now rested and not in a state of shock, I took a moment to observe his hard features.

Next to Apollo, the massive Solin who attacked us at the spring, this man was the largest person I ever laid eyes on. Not only did his height rival Jax, but his muscular physique dwarfed my brother's. The white hair he had fastened into a short ponytail matched his full beard, and the leather-like skin that covered his hands and face looked as though he spent a lifetime in the sun. I shifted my weight on the bed as he approached Cyrus. *He'd blend in perfectly at a biker rally if he had some tattoos and a motorcycle.*

In a raspy voice, the Solin said, "We're heading out." He extended his hand to my brother. "I'll keep you posted if we hear anything."

"Thanks again—for everything." Cyrus shook the man's hand with enough force to crack his knuckles.

The Solin didn't flinch. He only nodded, then turned and walked out of the room sideways once more.

I frowned, curious why he chose to ignore me. "Well, he seems friendly."

"Samson's a little rough around the edges," Cyrus said, staring at the closed door.

I snapped my fingers, remembering his name, then asked, "Why did he say, *I'll keep you posted*?"

My brother tensed. Refusing to meet my gaze, he turned his head and looked out the window. My heart hammered in my chest when Jax's face flashed in my mind. "Cyrus, what's going on?"

He hesitated before finding my eyes. "Samson and Callisto plan on scouting the villages for rumors about Jax."

"How would anyone know about his capture?"

"Think about it, Elara. The Inner Circle aren't the only Collectors. I'm sure everyone's talking about what happened." I shut my eyes as Cyrus continued. "I know Jax kept his head down and flew under the radar, but don't forget, he was the leader of the Inner Circle. You were there when he told us the story. Only the identities of those Collectors are known."

I nodded, my stomach tightening. "Idalia said Zenith took a lot of pride in claiming Jax as his Seeker, like Arun did with Saros."

"But Jax never jumped for Zenith—he had no proof."

"That didn't matter. Do you think anyone would have questioned Zenith's claim?"

I rolled my neck, the collar of the new shirt feeling tighter by the second.

"Idalia also said that after Jax jumped with us to Earth, Zenith sent every Collector on the largest manhunt since the Clearing of the Seekers." My eyes grew. "That's how they met. She said they stumbled across each other in the woods one day. He was in bad shape, so she—"

"Jax told me how she helped him out."

"When did he say that?" Cyrus asked. "I don't remember hearing that part of the story."

Regret's sharp claws dug into my back. "It was before Pollux and the others showed up."

"Right," he murmured.

A nasty mixture of frustration and anger surged through me, causing my words to hiss through tight lips. "He should have told us the truth, saved us the time."

"Exactly." Cyrus touched his bruised face. "And saved me a busted jaw."

"You're an idiot for pushing Jax into a corner. You know how he gets. He was this close"—I held my thumb and index finger a millimeter apart—"to killing you that night."

"I know, but he left me no choice. He needed to come clean and tell us the truth."

The mattress sagged when I collapsed onto my back. I draped an arm over my eyes. "I just don't understand."

"Understand what?"

"How did Jax manage to survive for nine years without being caught?"

"Idalia mentioned that after he left the Collectors, Jax grew out his hair and started living a low profile in the woods."

"I'm aware, but the guy still had to eat. You saw him at the South Village. Jax strolled through the market like he owned the place."

Cyrus pulled his foot onto his lap and examined the gray area while he spoke. "True, but you saw how everyone looked at him that day. Even the two guys who left the pub that night acted weird. Idalia said the people of Aroonyx are terrified of Jax. They recognize the close relationship he had with Zenith, and they also know the horrible things he's done to innocent people. She said an average Collector won't dare challenge him alone. The Inner Circle is his only threat."

I lifted my arm. "Is or was?"

Cyrus lowered his gaze. "I thought we were staying positive."

"I'm still working on it." Switching gears, I asked, "How did Idalia take the news?"

"Not well, but she refuses to give up and thinks we can figure out a way to rescue Jax."

"You Solins and your optimistic attitudes." *Must be nice.*

I sat up and gathered my hair over one shoulder, then stared at the comforter with wet eyes, my confidence from Cyrus's pep talk at the spring dissolving at a rapid rate.

He reached for my hand. "Stop beating yourself up about Jax. We don't know if he's—"

Our heads turned at another loud knock on the door. This time, Idalia entered the room. Her eyes darted between me and my brother before locking onto my own. I held my breath. *Something's wrong. It's written all over her face.*

The blonde locks of the Solin's hair trailed behind her as she dashed to the bed. She panted my name, winded from the sprint upstairs.

"What's wrong?" I managed, my voice shaking.

"It's Jax. He's alive."

NINETEEN

Brutal Honesty

"What?" I sprung to my feet. "Who told you? How do you know?"

Idalia's tongue moved so fast, I had to stare at her lips to grasp every word. "I heard someone mention his name while I was downstairs. A man sitting at the bar said to his friend, *I can't believe that after all these years, Pollux finally captured Jax. Poor bastard, I bet he didn't last a day.* The man beside him shook his head and said, *Zenith's keeping Jax alive until he tells him where the twins are hiding.*"

A strong curse word flew out my mouth as I looked at my brother.

He blew out a tight breath before saying, "I guess the cat's out of the bag." Unfamiliar with the phrase, Idalia cocked her head to one side. "Everyone knows we're back," he clarified.

She nodded, her eyes drifting between the two of us.

"But this is good news, right?" I asked her. "What the man said about Jax? He's alive."

She fidgeted with a loose thread on the comforter. "Yes and no."

"What does that mean?"

A gut-wrenching grief filled Idalia's eyes as she met my gaze. "Jax would never jeopardize the mission by putting your lives at risk. He'd let Zenith kill him before he did." My chest caved, and the whites of her eyes turned a bright shade of pink when she added, "Unfortunately, the leader of Aroonyx won't let him off that easy."

My stomach did a nauseating flip as I recalled Jax's early childhood with his adoptive father.

Idalia stared at her clasped hands. "Zenith will make an example out of Jax. He'll torture him to the brink of death before cutting off his head."

I tugged Cyrus's arm. "We have to go—now."

He eyed Idalia. She shook her head. "Elara, we can't—"

"Can't?" My voice raised. "What? All of a sudden you don't want to help Jax?" She winced as if I had punched her in the gut, but I pressed on. "You just told us that Zenith will torture him to death, and now you want me to sit on my hands and do nothing?"

Cyrus leaned forward in the bed and grabbed my arm. "Elara, that's not what she's saying. I can hardly walk right now. And you're not fully recovered. We sure as hell can't go wandering around Aroonyx in the freezing weather with our heads up our asses."

"Fine," I said, ripping my arm out of his tight grip. "You two stay here and take it easy. I have no problem going by myself." I glared at the Solins, my skin surging with heat. "Oh, how the tables have turned. You guys are all talk. Running your mouths about staying positive. But when push comes to shove, it's the Lunin who refuses to give up."

My head flew to the side when Idalia's warm palm slapped me across the face. Stunned, I touched my throbbing cheek. Cyrus rolled onto his knees, ready to play referee.

Idalia's golden eyes ignited with a fire lit by anger. She took a step closer, her heavy breathing mixing with my own. "How dare you," she spat. "I haven't slept a wink since you showed up on my doorstep because I can't stop worrying about Jax. I've accepted that the man I love has moved on—with you. But I won't sit here quietly while you put words in my mouth. Shame on you for thinking I'd give up on my best friend."

Idalia's honesty stung worse than the well-deserved smack across my face. Her no-nonsense approach verified that she and Jax had spent lots of time together because I felt scolded the same way I did after a tongue lashing from the Lunin.

I compelled my eyes to meet her gaze, and in a quiet voice I said, "I'm sorry. I shouldn't have said that." Her defensive posture softened. "I'm just so angry about everything. I feel like it's all my fault."

My brother relaxed and leaned his back against the headboard once more.

Idalia crossed her arms as she spoke. "All I wanted to say is that we can't rescue Jax until you're both fully recovered."

My chin hit my chest. *Good one. Way to overreact—as usual.*

Cyrus watched me carefully as Idalia went on. "Jax is mentally stronger than anyone I know. He won't break for Zenith." When my lip quivered, she added, "I know it's painful to imagine the horrible things they're doing to him, but it's a distraction. The three of us must stay focused. We get one shot at rescuing Jax. If we screw it up, Zenith will murder us all."

I looked at Cyrus. He nodded, the silent gesture making his intention known—he had sided with Idalia.

"Okay. So we let our injuries heal, then figure out a way to rescue Jax." My brows furrowed. "Slight problem. We don't know where Zenith lives. Do you?"

"Of course I do. Everyone does, but no one approaches his dwelling without an invite and an escort."

"You mean a Collector?"

She nodded. "Finding Zenith's isn't the problem. It's gaining access to his heavily guarded fortress that presents a challenge."

"Do you know anyone who can get inside?" my brother asked.

"Samson."

I raised a brow. "How would he know?"

"Because he was a Collector with my father during Arun's reign."

"Damn," Cyrus muttered. "These guys keep showing up out of nowhere."

"Figures," I mumbled, thinking of the Solin's tough appearance and detached demeanor.

"After my father's death, he and Callisto helped my mother raise me. Samson doesn't dwell in the past, nor does he reminisce about his time with Arun. He was the lead Collector during the Clearing of the Seekers. The man has a lot of blood on his hands."

I huffed a sarcastic breath. "Well, that's great. An ex-Collector knows why we returned to Aroonyx. Who else knows we're here?"

"No one, except for me and the two men who saved your brother's life."

"She brings up a good point, Elara. If Samson was working with Zenith, he would have let me die in the snow."

I sighed.

"He may come across as a cold and detached asshole," Idalia said, "but I trust Samson with my life. He would never tell anyone of your whereabouts. The man wants Zenith gone, just like the rest of us." The uncertainty in my eyes made Idalia say, "And Jax trusts him too."

Wondering if I knew the Lunin at all, I stammered, "They know each other?"

"Why do you think Jax is so skilled with his knife?"

I stumbled over my words once more. "Because he was the leader of the Inner Circle. Jax said Zenith started his training at a young age."

A tiny smile broke at the corner of Idalia's mouth. "Jax may have learned the art of combat and basic knife skills from Pollux and the other Collectors, but it was Samson who took him to an advanced level." Pride flickered in her eyes. "If you think Jax is skilled with a blade, wait until you see Samson in action."

I stood motionless, stunned by this added bit of information. *How many more secrets is Jax hiding?* I frowned. *Maybe I don't know him at all.*

Idalia's fingers twisted the locks of her platinum-blonde hair into a fishtail braid that draped over her shoulder while she added more details about Jax's past. *Geez. She makes it look so easy. Both the braid and being beautiful.*

"After I introduced the two of them, Samson took Jax under his wing. He respected Jax's courage to leave Zenith, so he started training him in ways even the Collectors shy away from using."

I gulped. "That's unsettling."

"His technique isn't for the faint of heart, but it lit a fire under Jax's ass. They trained from sun up to sun down for weeks. Samson wanted him to have a fighting chance in case he ran—"

"Into Pollux and the others?"

Unable to hold my gaze, she looked away.

Cyrus asked, "Do you think Samson will help us rescue Jax? After everything you told us, I doubt he'll volunteer to act as our guide and re-visit his past."

Idalia hesitated before saying, "It'll take some convincing on my part, but he'll come around."

I chewed on my nail as I looked at the beautiful Solin. "Can I ask you a personal question?"

"Sure."

"Jax lived with you and your mother after he left the Collectors, right?"

She nodded.

"Where did Samson train him?"

"Here."

"He stayed hidden the entire time? No one saw him, not even the customers downstairs?"

"He only lived with us for a short while. Jax stayed upstairs during business hours, then after we closed, he'd come downstairs and help me and my mother clean up. When he trained with Samson, they'd meet out back to stay away from prying eyes. Samson was the one who encouraged Jax to leave."

"Why?" my brother asked.

"It was too dangerous because the Collectors frequented the pub. We were committing treason by hiding Jax. He was a wanted man. If they found him, well, I wouldn't be standing here right now."

Still confused by their secrecy, I said, "But everyone saw you with Jax the night we visited the pub. Even Leo asked if you'd seen him."

"Things changed as we got older. This is a public house. Anyone can stop by for a drink. Pollux and the others aren't idiots. They knew I was seeing Jax. He dated a ton of women during that time.

"Zenith couldn't accuse me of harboring a criminal because the Collectors never found him when he stayed the night. They had no proof." Her eyes filled with memories of the past when she added, "I knew we were playing a dangerous game because I was dating a criminal."

"I see," I murmured.

"Also, the Collectors are familiar with my father's history. This gives me clemency in some of their eyes. And as far as Zenith goes, if he executed me for my relationship with Jax, the pub would close. If that happened, the people would add it to their list of grievances." She inclined her head toward the door. "It's the only place on Aroonyx that serves Maragin."

"What's Maragin?"

Idalia never answered my question because of the determined fist that pounded on the bedroom door.

She raised a finger to her mouth, urging us to remain silent. "Yes," she called.

"Idalia, you better get down here," answered an unfamiliar voice.

The urgency in the man's tone caused her to dash across the room toward the door. "Phoebus? What's going on?"

His voice lowered. "I'm not sure, but he's asking for you."

My pulse raced as I looked at my brother. He mouthed a four-letter curse word while climbing off the bed, then winced when his feet hit the floor.

The man behind the door went on. "Half the customers took off when they walked in." I mouthed, "They?" at Cyrus.

He shut his eyes and cursed once more. "Now I've got an empty house with only a few paid tabs."

"Who's asking for me?" Idalia pressed, her eyes never leaving the door.

"Pollux."

Profanity escaped Idalia's mouth as she motioned for us to hurry across the room. "Tell him I'm changing, and I'll be right down. Get them a round of drinks while they wait."

Phoebus sighed. "Okay, but you know how impatient they are."

"Just do it!" she barked, slamming her hand on the door.

"Oh shit" were the only two words that seemed appropriate for the situation, the only two words that slipped out of my gaped mouth. I couldn't breathe, much less move. Pollux and *they,* whoever else he brought with him, were downstairs—looking for us.

I eyed my brother. His expression mirrored my own thoughts. *We're trapped. He can barely walk, much less run through the snow.* I glanced at the window. *I don't even think it opens. There are only two exits out of this death trap, and both are downstairs.*

The casual four-letter curse word I repeated switched to a stronger one when Cyrus grabbed my arm and dragged me toward the entryway.

"Nope," I said, shaking my head. "I can't do this."

"Shh." Idalia cracked open the door. "Follow me and don't make a sound."

I shook my head again and mouthed, "I'm sorry, I can't," when my last encounter with Pollux flashed before my mind's eye. *His creepy voice and wicked laughter, the way he stared at me with that sadistic grin while licking his lips.* I shuddered. Everything about the man made my skin crawl.

My brother tightened his grip around my arm while his lips moved near my ear. "You're not alone this time." The warming sensation surged through me, a reminder of his truthful words. "I'm here now, and I won't let that bastard touch you."

I nodded, then followed Idalia over the threshold.

The three of us tiptoed across the hall into the Solin's bedroom. Cyrus closed the door without making a sound. My eyes followed Idalia as she hurried across the room. With little effort she removed three wooden panels from the wall, then motioned for us to step inside the confined space.

I glared at the squeaky floorboards. *Give us away and I'll make you firewood.*

The hiding place was large enough for only one person to fit comfortably—but comfort wasn't our priority. We needed to stay alive.

Cyrus stood rigid with his hands glued to his sides, while I pressed my body against his. My cheek rested on his brawny chest. It rose and fell with the quick breaths that entered his lungs. A wave of heat passed through me when Idalia repositioned the panels against the wall, locking us inside the upright coffin.

A tiny sliver of light shone through the small crack, allowing me to peer into the bedroom. Idalia straightened her clothes, patted her flushed face, and inhaled a deep breath before dashing out of the room.

Tiny shivers of terror caused my muscles to twitch involuntarily. Like a statue, my brother didn't budge, though his heart pounded in my ear. My fingers dug into his arm at the sound of muffled voices and feet thumping up the wooden steps. The entire upstairs shook when the door across the hall slammed into the wall.

I strained my ears while listening to Idalia speak in a calm and steady voice. "I already told you, there's no one here."

"Then who was sleeping in the bed?"

Hearing Pollux caused the hairs on the back of my neck to dance in a phantom breeze. I squeezed my free hand into a fist, the heat desperate to escape.

A half-truth rolled off Idalia's tongue. "Callisto stayed here a few nights. He didn't want to travel during the first snowfall. He left with Samson earlier this morning."

Pollux scoffed.

Another familiar voice said, "Let's keep looking."

I swallowed. *Please no. Not him.*

I held my breath as they approached the spare room and stifled a pained cry when Pollux stepped over the threshold, followed by Apollo and Ravi.

Cyrus tensed, for he too could see through the tiny gap in the wall.

The Lunin flicked his wrist at the others and said, "Search the place."

They nodded. Ravi's hair fell into his eyes as he looked under the bed. He then visited the wash room while Apollo strolled toward the window, his ginger-colored eyes scanning the snow-covered lawn. I gulped when he pushed up his sleeves, the handprint burn still wrapped around his right wrist.

"You should have a little chat with the person who keeps giving you false information," Idalia said, keeping the door open behind her, "because you never find Jax here."

Pollux's pale blue eyes narrowed as he whipped around to face her. "Don't play the dumb bitch. It's not a good look for you." He moved closer. "You know I'm not looking for Jax."

The Solin kept her expression stone cold, unreadable as she said, "I've only heard rumors. You know I rarely leave this place."

A wicked grin, the same one he gave Jax that morning on the cliffside resurfaced as he circled Idalia. I squeezed my brother's arm, begging him not to intervene.

"Would you like an accurate account of what happened that morning?"

Idalia said nothing, she only stared at the floor. Pollux crossed his arms as he walked around the brave Solin.

He snickered, pleased with her submission. "Well, after I dragged his ass home, I warmed myself by the fire while he got reacquainted with Zenith."

I shut my eyes, wishing I could shut my ears as well.

Pollux cackled like a villain from a horror film. "It's too bad you weren't there, Idalia. You really missed a great performance by your old boyfriend." He exaggerated a sigh while using his fingers to count. "There was screaming, blood, more screaming. Awe hell, there's no point in keeping track."

Idalia clenched her teeth.

Pollux grinned as he pushed a lock of the Solin's hair off her shoulder, then whispered near her ear, "Spoiler alert, Zenith won."

This can't be real. Maybe I'm dreaming. People aren't this cruel. Tears filled my eyes.

"But instead of helping Zenith force Jax to share the location of the twins, he ordered me to find them." Pollux waved his hands in a frantic motion that made him look even more disturbed. His voice raised. "So here I am, Idalia."

"They're not here," she whispered.

His tongue clicked the roof of his mouth as he looked at Apollo and Ravi. "I hate it when people lie to me."

I swore in the quiet space of my mind. Cyrus's heart thumped so fast, I thought it would fly out of his chest.

Idalia curled her hands into fists as she lifted her head. "I'm not lying. You've searched the entire pub, there's no one here."

Pollux tapped his smooth chin as he eyed his prey. "Apollo, Ravi."

"Sir," they answered.

"Why don't you wait outside." They nodded. "And close the door behind you."

Oh no. Obeying the Lunin's orders, the two men exited the room.

Idalia stood tall with her shoulders rolled back, ready to face Pollux head on. I held my breath. *I can't bear to watch.*

A crazed desire filled the Lunin's eyes as he traced the length of Idalia's arm with his finger. His tongue grazed her ear as he whispered, "When are you going to come visit me?"

She flinched and through tight lips said, "I don't have time. My work keeps me busy."

Pollux ran his finger across her collarbone and down her chest. My nails drew blood on Cyrus's arm when a wave of heat almost knocked me out. I shook my head as far as it would go in the confined space, silently beseeching my brother to stay put. He breathed hard, every muscle twitching with rage.

Pollux stepped in front of Idalia and stared at her breasts while he said, "You can always make time."

She shut her eyes. "I'll see what I can do."

He tossed the fishtail braid behind her back and pressed his lips to the side of her neck. Chills covered her body. The Lunin held Idalia's tan skin between his teeth and bit down before whispering, "You know I can please you better than Jax ever did."

My heart pounded in my ears. *It's like watching a disturbing scene from a movie I can't turn off. Make it stop. Make it stop.*

Idalia's eyes shot open with courage, not fear. Her voice lowered to a growl. "That's where you're wrong, Pollux." He sneered as he pulled away. "Regardless of the way you see yourself, remember this: Jax is ten times the man you'll ever be."

It took every ounce of shared Solin strength to keep my brother from bursting through the wall when Pollux back-handed Idalia across the face. His aggressive attack left blood trickling down her cheek.

All Solins displayed unwavering courage, but watching Idalia stand up to Pollux that day brought a tear to my eye. Her fingers touched the small gash, and with dry eyes she turned her head forward once more and met the Lunin's fierce gaze.

Anger consumed him. His lips twitched and nostrils flared. "The man Jax *was*—past tense," he spat. I shut my eyes, the fragments of my heart dissolving one flake at a time. "He'll be dead by the end of the day. *After* I rip him open and cut out his heart."

Pollux used the blood on Idalia's cheek to draw the shape of a heart on her face before licking his finger. The Lunin headed to the door, and when his hand rested on the knob he said, "I'll be sure to send it to you in a gift box when I'm done."

Bile crept up my throat. I tried to swallow. It only made it worse. *I'm going to be sick.*

Apollo and Ravi moved aside when Pollux opened the door. He looked over his shoulder as he stepped into the hallway. "We'll be back, Idalia. I wish I could tell you when"—malice filled his eyes as a smirk tugged at his mouth—"but where's the fun in that?"

The door slammed shut. Idalia stood motionless with her hands shaking by her sides. The emotions she hid from Pollux uncorked like a bottle of champagne, minus the celebration. Defeated, she collapsed onto her knees.

TWENTY

Without Conditions

My brother and I didn't budge until the downstairs door slammed shut. The wooden panel fell to the floor when Cyrus nudged it with his shoulder. Sharing his Solin strength, I followed his lead by removing the other two pieces with my foot.

Like poorly trained contortionist, the two of us unfolded out of the cramped space and hurried to help our friend who sat with her head buried in her hands.

"I'll kill that bastard the next time I see him," Cyrus murmured as he took a seat beside Idalia.

"That makes two of us," I said, heading to the wash room to find a towel for her injured face.

As I searched the cupboards, I listened to my brother share words of encouragement with the distressed Solin. Idalia stayed quiet while he showered her with praise. "That was the bravest thing I've ever seen," and "Jax would be proud," rolled off his tongue in a soothing whisper.

"Here," I said, offering her the damp rag. "Blood's dripping onto your shirt."

Cyrus took it from my hand and carefully dabbed the evidence that Pollux left behind before erasing the morbid heart he drew on her cheek.

I squeezed her hand. "Idalia, it took a lot of courage to stand up to Pollux. He barely spoke to me that morning on the cliffside with Jax, but when he did, I froze with panic." I stole a glance at the small gash on her cheek. "I don't know how you did it."

She shut her eyes and inhaled a deep breath. "Pollux and I have known each other for a long time . . . too long. I met him before Jax. For years he's asked me to pay him a visit." She rolled her eyes. "Like that would ever happen. The women who visit Zenith and his Collectors are known around Aroonyx as the PPs."

Our noses scrunched with confusion.

"Pleasure Payers," she clarified.

"Like prostitutes?" my brother asked.

"No, not at all. Zenith and the Collectors don't pay for their services. These poor girls pay *them* with their bodies in hopes of staying in their good graces."

"Does it work?"

Idalia found my eyes. "What do you think?"

I frowned.

"Exactly." She went on. "It works for Zenith and Pollux. They have their fun, tell the girls a few lies about how they can skip their next tax payment or other nonsense, then toss them out—literally. The PPs usually come back to the villages covered in bruises and with busted lips." She sighed. "Some never come back at all."

Cyrus shot me a look that screamed, *Is this real life?* I shrugged, equally baffled by Zenith's bizarre way of ruling.

Idalia sniffled as she turned her head. I eyed my brother for backup. He reached for her hand. "I'm so sorry this happened. Next time, I won't stay hiding in the wall."

She wiped away a tear. "I don't care about this injury. I care about what I said to Pollux."

I shut my eyes, thinking of Jax.

"Maybe he was all talk," Cyrus suggested. "Pollux can't kill Jax without Zenith's consent. Didn't that man downstairs say Zenith wanted to keep Jax alive until he disclosed our location?"

"Yeah, but I should have never said that to Pollux. By defending Jax, I sentenced him to the wrath of the most twisted man on Aroonyx." When she noticed the puzzled expression on my face, she added, "Yes, Zenith is a horrible man, but Pollux is worse. He's not right in the head."

"We're going to find a way to rescue Jax," my brother reassured her.

Idalia tossed the blood-stained rag to the side. "We have to convince Samson to help us. He's the only one who knows the layout of Zenith's dwelling."

I nodded. "Then we'll twist his arm."

A genuine smile tugged at Idalia's mouth when she said, "Good luck with that."

"Challenge accepted." Cyrus winked.

Idalia moved to stand. My brother beat her to the punch. I could tell he was hurting because his jaw clenched when he hopped to his feet, but he pushed through the pain so he could offer Idalia his hand. I smiled. Their striking features mirrored one another beautifully, as did their personalities: loving, kind, fearless; they were the perfect match.

She tucked a stray hair behind her ear as her eyes drifted between me and my brother. "Samson and Callisto won't be back for a few days. The two of you must go unrecognized until we decipher a plan."

"How do you suppose we do that?" I asked, climbing to my feet.

Idalia headed toward the wash room. "I think it's time for a little makeover."

I glanced at Cyrus. He shrugged, clueless about the Solin's comment.

A heartbeat later, Idalia appeared with a pair of dull scissors and an even duller straight razor—one you would find in an old barber shop. She motioned for me to step forward.

"Nope." I gathered my hair over one shoulder, protecting it from the menacing tools.

"Relax. It's just a trim." She giggled. "Only the Inner Circle knows your identity, but I'm sure Pollux has described your exact features to the others."

"We already talked about this." I waved a hand at my brother. "We look like every other Solin and Lunin on Aroonyx."

Idalia lowered her gaze. "Perhaps, but we can't take any chances. Your long hair is a dead giveaway."

I dropped my head and dragged my feet across the room while Cyrus laughed at my misfortune.

"Don't tease her too much," she said, flashing him the razor. "You're next."

He paled as he touched his overgrown locks.

Idalia ran her fingers through my hair, detangling the disobeying strands. I closed my eyes; the left-over tension I harbored after Pollux's visit dissolved at her gentle touch. I smiled, thinking of my adoptive mother. When I was a child, she would brush my hair every night before bed.

"I think we should bring it up to . . . here." She tapped my collar bone.

My eyes shot open. "You want to cut it that short?" I whipped around to face her. "That's like taking off fifteen inches."

"I know, but I need you to look less like . . . you."

I pouted, then faked a cry when the scissors made the first cut. The strands of my fallen comrades fell to the floor, blending in with the black wood.

"I have a thought," she said, my hair getting shorter by the second. "We can't rescue Jax without Samson's help, and I can't keep you locked upstairs until he gets back because the two of you will go stir crazy."

"So . . ."

She chuckled. "Jax was right." Another lock of hair fell to the floor. "You are impatient." I shrugged. "So, I think the two of you should work with me behind the bar."

"What?" I asked, turning to face her.

"Stay still," she snapped. "I almost chopped it off to your chin."

I grumbled, looking forward once more. Cyrus muffled his laughter. I kept my head motionless but used my hands while I spoke. "Idalia, that's a horrible idea. You're only cutting our hair, not giving us new faces."

She stayed quiet as she worked.

"What about Phoebus and your other employees? Won't they get suspicious if we're seen together? Especially after Pollux and the others were here looking for us."

"Elara brings up a good point, Idalia."

She nodded at my brother, keeping her eyes focused on my hair. "I only have three employees. None of them know you're here. Cosmo works in the kitchen. The man is so old, he can hardly see, much less hear. Phoebus works days and Hunter works nights. They're loyal employees, but I don't trust them with this secret." She tilted my head down. "For weeks, I've been talking about hiring more help, so it won't come as a surprise when the two of you show up for work. Cyrus, once fully recovered, will work with me and Phoebus during the day. And you will work with me and Hunter at night."

"When do you get a break?" Cyrus asked.

"When I'm dead."

My eyes widened. "Do you think it will work?"

"I hope so." She sighed. "The distraction will help keep your minds from wandering to dangerous places, and you can help me listen for rumors about—"

I shut my eyes. "Jax? And if he's still alive?"

"Yeah." Her throat bobbed.

My brother hobbled closer and asked, "What if Pollux and the Inner Circle show up?"

"Keep your eyes on the front door. They usually make a dramatic entrance, causing my poor customers to scatter like wildfire. You'd have time to make it upstairs and hide in the wall before they notice. That's what Jax used to do." Idalia dusted the hair off my shoulders. "I'm not concerned about the other Collectors because they don't have a personal account of your appearance. As long as you keep a low profile while downstairs, everything should go smoothly."

Idalia stepped back to admire her handy work.

I ran my fingers through my shoulder-length hair, then turned to face my brother. "How does it look?"

"I like it. Makes you look younger."

I frowned, unsure how to take the compliment. Idalia opened the trunk that rested near the foot of the bed and offered me a blue handheld mirror. I squinted at the faded *Made in the USA* imprint on the back. "This is from Earth," I stammered.

She nodded. "We don't have mirrors on Aroonyx. It was a gift from Jax."

I rubbed my thumb over the smooth plastic, admiring the item I always took for granted. "I didn't know he could bring things back from Earth."

More silence followed a long pause. I looked at Idalia. Her eyes filled with tears, and her voice cracked. "This was the only thing he ever brought to Aroonyx." She held up her finger. "Excuse me for a minute."

She hurried past me to the wash room, closing the door behind her. Cyrus dragged a hand down his weary face before meeting my gaze.

"She's trying to be strong," I whispered.

His eyes narrowed. "The Jax ordeal is bad enough but now she's risking her life to keep us safe."

"I know," I said, folding my arms across my chest. "So we need to pull our weight and act invisible when working downstairs. The last thing we want to do is cause her any unnecessary stress. I think if—" I held my tongue when the door opened.

Idalia cleared her throat and pointed to my hand. "What did you think?"

"Oh, I haven't even looked yet," I said, lifting the mirror to my face.

My jaw fell open at the person who stared back. I hardly recognized my own reflection. Cyrus was right, my short hair gave me a more youthful appearance. Unfortunately, the side-effects of nonstop worry mixed with anxiety aged my face ten years. I frowned, touching the permanent line between my eyebrows, then groaned at the dark circles that lined the underneath of my eyes.

Watching my expression change, Cyrus said, "It looks a hundred times better now than it did at the spring."

I adjusted the mirror, my fingers grazing the stitches that ran across one side of my neck. "I look like a creepy doll who lost her head and had it sewn back on."

Cyrus snorted. "You do. Like Sally, from *The Nightmare Before Christmas*."

I shot him a warning glare. "That's not funny."

"Then why are you laughing?"

"I hate you."

"Love you too, sis."

Idalia motioned for Cyrus to take my place. He limped the remaining steps and waved a hand at his head and face. "There's not a lot you can do with me."

"Hillary would say otherwise," I said, stifling my laughter.

My brother ripped the mirror out of my hand and raised it to his eye level. Spit sprayed onto the glass when he saw his reflection. "Damn, Cyrus." He couldn't stop laughing. "You've really let yourself go, bro."

Idalia covered her mouth while I let my amusement show. Cyrus's neatly trimmed, short blond hair had grown long—and not in the attractive way that Jax wore his. My brother's head looked like an overwatered Chia pet in need of a good trim. His face looked even worse. Tiny patches of hair covered his chin and cheeks. I laughed once more. *He looks like he tried to shave blindfolded.*

Cyrus kneeled so Idalia could reach the top of his head. She used scissors to cut off the majority of his hair, then shaved the rest with the straight razor, leaving only a small amount of fuzz behind. Her delicate hands moved the grooming tool to his face, taking extra caution around his jaw line. The coarse hairs fought against the dull blade, but Idalia's hand never shook. Her comfort level with the grueling task made it clear that Cyrus wasn't her first client.

I wonder if she shaved Jax's face before the Collectors showed up that night? I touched my lips, remembering the way his smooth skin felt against my own.

The memory faded at the sound of Idalia's voice. "That should do." Her eyes lit up as she observed my brother. "Much better, you look very handsome."

As if his celebrity crush had appeared out of thin air and asked him on a date, Cyrus's grin spread from ear to ear.

"You do clean up well." I rubbed a hand over the top of his fuzzy head. "And now you actually look like you joined the military."

My brother shot me an *isn't that ironic* glance before climbing to his feet. He quieted a pained groan.

Idalia touched his arm. "You should rest. We need you fully recovered sooner than later."

"She's right," I added. "I'll keep you company after I speak with Idalia."

The Solin blew a stray hair out of her face as she stooped down to collect the trimmings from our makeovers. My brother stood with his gray feet glued to the floor. I cleared my throat and eyed the door, encouraging him to give us some privacy. He nodded before exiting the room.

We worked in silence for long minutes. Not because we needed to stay focused on finding the fine strands of my hair that blended in with the floorboards or because Idalia appeared lost in thought. No, those weren't the reasons. The truth was that I lacked the courage to say the bitter words that gathered on my tongue.

I inhaled a long breath and let the air rush out of my lungs before taking a seat. "Hey, Idalia?"

She hummed her response while scooping the remaining bits of hair into a trash bag.

"I never apologized for my behavior the first night we met."

Her lips pressed together as she lowered herself beside me. "Elara, you don't—"

"Yes, I do," I said, finding her eyes. "So please, let me finish."

"Very well." She straightened, holding her clasped hands in her lap.

I rolled my neck, the walls of the small room closing in on me. *Just tell her the truth.*

I sucked in a sharp breath, then said, "It really took me by surprise when I saw you kiss Jax." She looked away. "I never knew you existed. Then all of a sudden, there you were, looking gorgeous as ever. I knew Jax had lots of secrets, but anytime he spoke about his life on Aroonyx, he always made it sound challenging—lonely." I sighed. "Idalia, you are the furthest thing from a challenge. You showed me kindness that night, and I treated you with disrespect." I squeezed her hand. "I'm truly sorry—for everything."

Her lips spread into a wide grin, the warmth matching the flecks of gold in the irises of her eyes. "Apology accepted, though I probably would have acted the same way had I been in your shoes. I had a strong feeling my relationship with Jax was about to change when he brought you here that night. He couldn't keep his eyes off you."

"That's because I was acting like a jealous"—I paused, omitting a four-letter word—"girl."

"That wasn't the reason. Do you remember when the two of you first spoke on Earth, and you told Jax to stay away?"

"He told you about that?"

She nodded. "Well, he took your dismissal pretty hard."

Confused, I cocked my head to one side.

"Jax had waited nine years to speak with you, Elara. He was so nervous, the poor man couldn't see straight. I encouraged him to relax and to jump from here when he was ready, but he refused and went to the cliffside." Idalia's fingers played with the gaps in her long braid. "Jax stayed away for a while after that first visit but knocked on my door when the two of you spent that afternoon under the bridge together. I didn't believe my eyes or my ears when I saw him. His entire perspective on life had changed. You know Jax, he usually keeps to himself, internalizes everything. But not after that day. Nope, he wouldn't shut up."

I chuckled, finding the humor in it all.

"He went on and on about you returning to Aroonyx and how you weren't like the other girls." Idalia tossed her loose waves behind her back. "The spark that Zenith dimmed had ignited once more—and you were the one responsible for this."

I shut my eyes, missing him more than ever. A peaceful moment of silence passed between us before she whispered, "He's crazy about you, Elara."

"Crazy is a strong word."

She shrugged.

The romantic moment I shared with Jax on the cliffside flashed in my mind. "But I do know he cares."

"That's putting it mildly." She winked.

"Idalia, I'm shocked at how well you've handled everything: the way you stood up to Pollux, the drama between you, me, and Jax. How do you manage to keep your emotions in check?"

"Solins are less dramatic than Lunins, so that helps. We don't keep our emotions bottled up inside." The blood rushed to her face. "Unfortunately, our tempers can get the best of us—as you witnessed earlier."

"I deserved it," I said, touching my cheek.

"Regardless, I shouldn't have lashed out. Having Samson in my life has toughened me up a bit."

"I can see that."

"He's also the reason I know how to handle Pollux and the other Collectors, and when it comes to Jax, it's simple."

"How so?" I asked.

"I love him enough to let him go." Idalia found my eyes. "Unconditional love means loving someone without conditions. It's wishing them the best in life without wanting to control the situation." She let out a small breath. "I can't change Jax or convince him to be the man he isn't. At the end of the day, I just want him to be happy. And he's happier with *you* in his life—so thank you, Elara. For giving my best friend what I couldn't."

The two of us stared at one another as if seeing each other for the first time. Call it fate, call it Jax—but something outside of ourselves had brought us together. A bond, forged by an unspoken awareness, locked its invisible chains around us that day, one, only women could understand.

"Friends?" I asked, extending my hand.

She slapped it away before pulling me into a tight hug. I winced at her Solin strength, then smiled when she said, "Always. Us girls have to stick together."

TWENTY-ONE

Rumors of Truth

The hands of life's elusive clock ticked by one agonizing second at a time. Some days, I wondered if everyone around me moved in slow motion, while my mind stayed in real time. Worrying about Jax was all-consuming, and helping Idalia behind the bar was nothing more than a temporary distraction from the mental hell I found myself living.

As an added precaution, she convinced us to use different names while working downstairs: Selene and Kyros. Not my first pick for a new alias, though my brother adored his, telling us that *Kyros sounded like the name of a badass superhero.*

Now fully recovered, Cyrus was back to his old self, annoying the hell out of me every chance he got—which wasn't often because we worked opposite schedules and only saw each other in passing. Still, my brother found ways to get under my skin. He'd hide behind the bedroom door and pull the scarf—the one that hid my stiches from prying eyes—off my neck as I walked out the room, then whisper, "Have a good shift, Sally. Don't worry, we're going to rescue Jack . . . I mean Jax."

I appreciated his fun-loving approach to life, but getting me to laugh during those dark times was a challenge all on its own. The days caused me physical pain. Forced to stay upstairs with guilt-driven thoughts as my only companion left my heart hollowed out like a rotten log; the fragile exterior remained, yet the innards were picked clean by parasites that fed on worry and anxiety.

Endless tension in my shoulders brought on pounding headaches that blurred my vision. I covered the window to block out the light—not to quiet the bass drum that thumped in my head, but to ignore the gentle rays of the sun. I didn't deserve a moment's peace, a second of comfort, or a flicker of forgiveness. Regardless of the others' skewed observations, I would always be the girl who abandoned Jax on the cliffside, the girl responsible for his torment.

At times, the guilt guided me to the closet, dressed me in warm clothes, then pushed me toward the stairs. *Go on, Elara* the hidden figure in my head would say, *Be the hero, rescue Jax, and then I'll go away.* I wanted to comply to the utter nonsense that swirled in my head, the black smoke I couldn't see through, but, how? I had Cyrus and Idalia to think about. If I had searched for Jax on my own, Pollux would have shipped pieces of my dead body along with the Lunin's heart to my brother and Idalia in that damn gift box he mentioned.

I rolled onto my side, the mattress groaning with my mental complaints. *It's been over a week. When will Idalia let us go outside?*

I stared at the fading light that bled through the blanket I hung over the window until my eyes burned—until the sun had vanished. Yawning with boredom, I stretched my leg and kicked the makeshift curtain to the side.

Minutes later the twin moons appeared in the evening sky. With little enthusiasm, I climbed to my feet and peered out the window. A fresh blanket of snow draped around Idalia's lawn, the tiny ice crystals shimmering in the moonlight. I blew out a breath, fogging up the old plate glass. Using my finger as a writing tool, I drew a frown face into the fading circle, tracing the previous day's image.

My head turned at the sound of the door opening. In walked my brother, his gray pants and crème-colored shirt stained with food and drink.

He wagged a finger at me before collapsing onto the bed. "I thought we talked about this. No more frown faces. Only smiles or complacent ones, remember?"

My lips formed a tight line, smothering the smirk that tried to escape.

Cyrus snapped his fingers. "I almost got a smile that time."

"Well, don't press your luck."

"How was your day?" he asked, draping an arm over his eyes.

"The same as it always is—miserable. How was yours?"

"Busy. I don't know how Idalia keeps working double shifts. I'm exhausted after one."

I cleared my throat, a horrible attempt at sounding casual. "So—"

"No," he interrupted. "I didn't hear anything about Jax."

I shut my eyes. The words that snapped out of Pollux's foul mouth were the last we had heard about Jax. Callisto and Samson had yet to return from the villages, and the bar patrons only yammered on about taxes and the weather—they actually talked about the damn weather.

A river of pent up emotions came flooding out of me, drowning my brother in its wake. "I can't keep sitting on my ass, doing nothing. It's affecting my sanity. I spend all day worrying about Jax, just to go downstairs and follow Idalia around the bar like a damn ghost, only to wake up and do it all over again."

Cyrus dragged a hand down his face before sitting up on the bed.

I spoke animatedly, adding to the dramatic performance. "I'm living in a mental hell with my life's remote stuck on repeat. I don't think—"

"Easy tiger," he said, motioning for me to lower my voice. "I get it. Cabin fever has taken its toll on you." When I didn't blink, he murmured, "In more ways than one." I rolled my eyes at his sarcasm. "But this is all temporary. Once Samson gets back, we'll figure out a plan. You know we can't try to rescue Jax on our own."

"What if he's already dead? You heard Pollux."

My brother lowered his gaze. "And what if he's not?"

Refusing to let our words chase each other in an endless argument, I headed to the closet and grabbed my shoes. "Do you need anything before I head out?"

The headboard knocked against the wall when Cyrus collapsed once more. "No. I'm good."

Without saying goodbye, I exited the room and hurried down the stairs. The pub was busier than usual, forks and dull knives scraped against the silver plates while mugs clinked together in celebration. I scoffed. *What is there to celebrate?*

I spotted Hunter running back and forth between tables, his arms filled with leftovers. From the kitchen, Cosmo yelled a slew of curse words mixed with, "Then tell them to eat at home if they don't like the food." A heartbeat later, Idalia rounded the corner, greeting me with an eyeroll followed by a warm smile.

Hands full, she jerked her chin at a Lunin sitting at the bar. "Can you get him a refill?"

I nodded and reached for a clean mug under the counter.

Idalia moved behind the bar with fluid grace while I stumbled to keep up. She chatted with customers as she filled their mugs, most of whom she already knew, and flirted with the men who stopped by just to say hello. My job was simple: keep the drinks coming and the bar top clean.

My nose crinkled at the sour smelling liquid that dripped onto my hand after a pitiful attempt at a free pour. I sniffed the green foam. "What *is* Maragin?" I asked Idalia, curious about the only beverage she offered besides tea and water.

"It's a powerful herb that grows a day's walk from the North Village." She took the mug from my hand and wiped off the rim before handing it to the Lunin with a smile.

I lowered my voice. "Is it like beer or wine found on Earth?"

"I don't know what those are."

"They're alcoholic beverages. They make people laugh or fight, depending on how much they drink."

She shot me a curious glance. "That sounds peculiar."

"Yeah, I guess it does."

Idalia grabbed another empty mug. "Maragin has a calming effect. It relaxes people—takes off the edge. Though sometimes people have an adverse reaction." She handed me the full cup and inclined her head at another man.

I pivoted and walked to the opposite end of the bar. The Solin tossed me a black object the size of a quarter found on Earth—a wooden coin. I smirked. *And to think I wondered if they used money on Aroonyx.* I tossed the payment into a jar behind the counter.

Remembering Idalia's warning, I looked to the door when it opened. A young couple entered the pub. The Solin woman scanned the crowded space, searching for someone—Idalia. When she eyed her mark, the woman's lip quivered. The Lunin who stood beside the despondent woman rubbed his pale hand across her lower back, a comforting gesture.

"Give me a minute," Idalia whispered.

I watched her hurry across the room. Idalia threw her arms around the woman's neck, and though her lips moved near the Solin's ear, her eyes scanned the young man who looked equally discouraged as his partner. The three of them spoke in hushed whispers for short minutes before Idalia told Hunter to grab them a round of drinks on the house.

"What was that about?" I asked as she walked past me to greet another customer.

She paused her quick pace. "Their union wasn't approved."

"I don't know what that means."

Idalia spun me around so our backs faced the bar patrons. Pretending to count jugs of unopened Maragin, she said, "Zenith is the only person on Aroonyx with the authority to approve a union between two people." I arched a brow. "There isn't a method behind his madness. No one knows the reason he approves some and not others." She looked over her shoulder at the disheartened couple. "They were denied today."

"Is this real life on Aroonyx?"

Idalia nodded.

"The people need Zenith's approval to marry?"

She pointed at the wet rings that decorated the bar top, then tossed me a rag. "Yep. He controls everything around here. Anyone who runs a business must pay a fee for his services."

"How much?"

The Solin smiled at an older man when he slid a wooden coin across the bar. She flicked it into the jar. "Sixty percent."

I almost choked on my spit as I stammered, "But that only leaves you forty?"

"I'm glad you learned basic math."

"You know what I mean. How do you manage to stay open after paying your employees."

"We get by. Their pay reflects the high tax. It all trickles down."

I stood lost in thought, the rag in my hand moving in endless circles across the bar top. Jax made it obvious that Zenith was a ruthless leader, but I assumed it had everything to do with the strict ordinances he passed and how the Collectors treated people. Taxes and union approval never crossed my mind.

"Selene . . . Selene." Idalia snapped her fingers, vying for my attention.

My lashes fluttered, still struggling with the new name.

"Can you handle the bar for a few minutes on your own?"

I scanned the men and women who chatted amongst themselves, drinks in hand. "Um. Yeah." A question, not a statement.

She sighed and ran a hand through her tangled locks. I frowned, noting her disheveled appearance. Signs of exhaustion shaded the thin skin beneath her eyes, and her worn posture reminded me of a cellphone running on 5-percent battery life.

Recovering, I said, "I mean, yes, I can handle it."

"Are you sure? I won't be gone for long."

I rested a hand on her shoulder. "Take all the time you need."

Relief filled her tired eyes. She turned and headed up the stairs.

A young Solin at the far end of the bar caught my eye when he blew out a sharp whistle while waving me over. I stifled a groan. *What am I? A damn dog?* Dragging my feet, I didn't rush to greet him.

"What can I get you?" I asked, plastering a fake grin on my face.

His orange eyes locked onto mine for only a second before he said, "A drink. What does it look like I want?"

"Noted," I mumbled, reaching for a mug.

The man blew out a frustrated breath as he cracked his knuckles. I watched him out of the corner of my eye while uncorking a fresh bottle of Maragin. *He has a lot of scars on his hands.* My heart skipped a beat. *And he's the only person in the pub sitting alone.*

I swore as the liquid overflowed onto my hand.

"Do you think I can get a drink before the sun comes up, or is that too much to ask?"

I swore again, only this time it wasn't for spilled Maragin. Across the bar sat a man who couldn't look me in the eyes, and his bronze face was a map of jagged lines created by knuckles and knives. I paled. The young Solin's hands were covered in scars, and his heartless demeanor knotted my stomach—made it impossible to swallow. A select group of men had this effect over me, and I was staring at one of its members.

His thumb tapped the bar like a metronome, prepared to time a death waltz. "Is there a problem?"

"No," I lied, handing him the mug. "You have a familiar face. I thought we might know each other."

The corner of his mouth twitched into a wicked smirk as he lifted the rim to his lips. *Maybe that's a requirement of all Collectors. One must smirk with enough malice to send your victims running for the hills.*

His Adam's apple bobbed as he drained every last drop. He slammed the empty mug on the counter. "Trust me, you don't know me." His orange eyes narrowed as he tossed a coin onto the counter. "When I pay people a visit, they always remember."

I gulped, longing for Idalia's company. *Just play it cool. Act like you're busy.*

I grabbed a rag, but when I pivoted, he said, "I'll take another."

I held my breath while reaching for a clean mug.

"When did Idalia hire you?" he asked, his fierce eyes burning a hole in me.

The half-truth skidded across my tongue. "Last . . . weekish." *Weekish? That's not even a word.*

"Interesting." The disguised metronome started once more. "What village do you live in?"

"Um." The full mug trembled in my hand, liquid splashing on my white knuckles. *Damn it. Just name a village—any village.*

"She lives up north, over by me," said a raspy voice.

I almost fell to my knees when Samson stepped up to the bar with Callisto in tow.

The young man went rigid as the ex-Collector took a seat beside him. Samson cleared the phlegm from his throat while reaching over the counter. He grabbed the mug out of my hand and took a long swig before addressing the Solin beside him. "You weren't planning on drinking this now, where you?"

Fear flickered in the young man's eyes. He stared at the scars on his hands. "No, sir. It's all yours."

Samson smirked as he ran a hand over his beard. *Yep, it's definitely a Collector thing.* "It's getting late, Inan. I think you better head home—while you still can." The young man cursed under his breath. Samson took another swig of the stolen beverage. "It's hard for a Solin to see at night, am I right?" His head turned to look at Inan, who stilled with panic. "Accidents happen. I would hate for Zenith to find one of his Collectors injured." He leaned closer and whispered, "Or worse—dead."

The bar stool toppled over when Inan scrambled to his feet. Without saying a word, he tossed another coin onto the bar and kept his head down while jogging toward the exit.

I stood motionless, stunned by Samson's intimidation factor. "Thank you," I mouthed, unsure what else to say.

Callisto gave me a subtle head nod as he took a seat, but the Solin stared right through me as if I didn't exist.

What the hell? Samson just saved me from a potential life-threatening situation, and now he won't even acknowledge me?

"So the rumors were true, they did catch Jax."

My head almost detached from my body when it snapped to the left. Grabbing a rag, I moved closer to the middle-aged woman whose lips paused when an older Lunin said, "Yep. Jax's past finally caught up with him."

I kept my eyes focused on a water ring that had stained the bar; the rag circling it matched the rhythm of my pounding heart. I strained my ears.

"Can you imagine the horrible things Zenith did to him?"

The Lunin wiped a thin layer of froth from his mustache before saying, "No, and I sure as hell don't want to. That's a bad way to go."

"Poor kid, he was so young."

My hand stopped mid-motion. *Was? Past tense?*

The man scowled at the woman's comment. "Young or not, the bastard had it coming to him. After the hell he put Sharik's family through." He raised his mug in celebration. "Good riddance to that one."

My finger nails cracked as they dug into the aged wood. The room spun. I didn't flinch when Idalia squeezed my arm.

"Elara," she whispered, her voice quivering. "When Hunter isn't looking, I want you to go upstairs and stay with Cyrus until we close."

How was I supposed to do that? My entire body felt numb. Idalia flashed Samson a pleading look. His expression remained blank as he took another sip.

She nudged me toward the staircase. "Hurry, go now."

Guilt no longer guided my footsteps—only grief. I didn't dry the tears that rolled carelessly off my cheeks or wipe the trickle of snot that dripped out my nose. I just twisted the door knob and stepped into the room like I did every other night.

My brother sat up, rubbing the sleep from his eyes. Through mid-yawn he asked, "Is your shift already over?"

I shook my head, unable to speak.

The blood drained from Cyrus's face when his eyes adjusted to my shared Lunin vision. He was at my side before I could blink. With wide eyes, he asked, "Elara, what's wrong?"

"He's gone."

Cyrus lowered his gaze to find my eyes. "What do you mean? Who's gone?"

The words I never wanted to say came out in a muffled sob. "It's Jax. He's dead."

TWENTY-TWO

Wake-Up Call

Cyrus guided my body toward the bed, encouraging me to a take a seat. I declined. If I sat down, I'd never get up again. His head turned when Idalia rushed into the room. Her arm knocked against his when she held me in a tight embrace. The flood gates to our emotional dams burst opened. Our sobs mixed as one, tears soaking each other's shoulders. Unsure how to console our grief, my brother wrapped his strong arms around the two of us.

Long minutes passed before he whispered, "Who told you the news?"

Idalia used the back of her trembling hand to blot her tear-stained face. "Elara heard a couple discussing what happened to Jax. Callisto and Samson confirmed it." My teeth sunk into my bottom lip as I squeezed my eyes shut. "They said everyone's talking about it."

"What if it's just a rumor?"

She looked at my brother. "Rumors tend to vary. My uncle and Samson said the stories about Jax are all the same." The Solin dropped her head into her hands and sobbed once more. "They killed him . . . the day Pollux paid me a visit."

My body swayed side to side in the phantom breeze that blew in from the land of shock and grief. I felt nothing—only emptiness. The rotted log that was once my heart had turned to dust.

"It's all my fault," Idalia cried. "If I had kept my mouth shut, Jax would still be alive."

"No." My voice sounded foreign—detached. "I hammered the nail in his coffin when I abandoned him on the cliffside."

"You're both wrong." We looked at my brother without a flicker of relief in our eyes. "I'm the one to blame. None of this would have happened had I not left Elara and Jax alone that night."

I curled my hands into fists. Anger is an interesting emotion. It can lift a person out of apathy and grief, light a fire under someone's ass, and send life surging through your veins. Like the magic in fairytales, wielding this sentiment doesn't come without a cost. Irrational decisions, tongue-flying regrets, and knee-jerk reactions are the tithes one must pay.

I tossed a coin to the hidden figure in my head who tapped its black claws together with excitement. *You may proceed, Elara.*

"That's it. It's settled. I leave for Zenith's tonight." My eyes narrowed at my brother. "With or without you."

"Like hell you will."

"Just try and stop me."

Two sets of hands grabbed my arms, holding me in place like a restricting seat belt.

A wild fierceness glowed in Idalia's eyes as she snapped, "Don't let your emotions cloud your better judgment. Lunins are known to overreact in traumatic situations." Her fingers dug into my skin. "You're not going anywhere, so cut the crap."

"Oh, but I am." I glared. "Let me go before I make you regret it."

My brother shot Idalia a warning glance. She let go of my arm in an instant, only for Cyrus to take her place. He grabbed my shoulders and shook me with enough force to make my eyes rattle in my head. "If you think for one second, I'd let you go to Zenith's without—"

"I don't care!" I shouted, my voice reverberating around us. "I don't care about anything anymore."

His amber eyes narrowed. "I'm calling bullshit. If you didn't care, you wouldn't be so upset right now—would you?" I clenched my teeth, twisting out of his strong grip. "Are you forgetting what Jax told us? With or without him, we must move forward with the plan. We must defeat Zenith."

"We never had a plan. You were the one who so gracefully pointed that out." I got in my brother's face. "I say screw Jax and his pipe dream. I'm taking matters into my own hands."

Idalia spun me around. "I'll be damned if Jax went and got himself killed so you could run and play the revenge card only to wind up dead." Her delicate finger tapped the creased line between my eyebrows. "You're not thinking straight,

Elara. The Collectors will have your head before you make it to Zenith's. You don't even know where he lives, so take off the vigilante mask and—"

The three of us flinched when the door slammed shut.

"What the hell is going on up here?" Callisto asked as he stormed toward us, Samson not far behind. "Are you trying to blow your cover? We can hear you all the way downstairs."

Idalia sucked in a sharp breath and held it. "I'm sorry, it's just—" More tears filled her eyes.

"It's okay, sweetie," her uncle soothed. He eyed the Solin who stood near the doorway. "We all cared about Jax."

Samson didn't say a word; his expression remained indifferent. Not a head nod of agreement or a hint of remorse sparked in those burnt-orange eyes—nothing. Looking more annoyed than concerned, he folded his muscular arms across his chest and narrowed his gaze. I shifted my weight, curious why this time he stared at me, rather than through me.

My brother flicked his wrist at Callisto and Samson before jerking his thumb at me. "Maybe one of you can convince Elara to rethink her idiotic plan of avenging Jax."

Staring at him through the narrow slits of my eyes, I mouthed a more vulgar version of, "Screw you," at my brother.

He waved me away.

Callisto raised a brow at Samson who returned the gesture with the world's longest sigh.

The Lunin found my eyes. "Honey, you seem like a smart girl, but that's the dumbest plan I've ever heard. Avenge Jax?" He looked around the room. "You and who else?"

I gritted my teeth and tossed the hidden figure another coin. It cackled, allowing the anger to boil over like a pot of forgotten water. "My brother and Idalia won't help, and I don't see you reaching for your coat." I pointed at Samson. "It's obvious 'smiles' over there doesn't give a shit about Jax, so I guess it's just me."

A muscle feathered in the Solin's jaw. Sensing a build in tension, Callisto said, "I get it. You've lost a friend, and you're upset right now."

I rolled my eyes. *Friend? Upset? What is this? A fucking therapy session?*

Callisto squeezed the bridge of his nose while he added, "Elara, you couldn't have left last week if you wanted to. You and Cyrus were still recovering."

My brother moved closer, then motioned to the other two men in the room. "You have no right to give them shit about any of this. They've done nothing wrong. You can't avenge Jax if you're not prepared." He squeezed my shoulder. "Think about it, sis. We're in no rush to go knocking on Zenith's door now that Jax is—"

"Dead?" I asked, getting into his face for the second time that night. "Say it, Cyrus. Jax is dead. And that changes everything. We can't defeat Zenith on our own. Hell, we never even finished our training." An unstable laugh left my mouth when I added, "Do you realize what this means?" Silence. "Fine, then let me break it down for you, bro. We are officially stuck on this *fucking* planet for the rest of our damned lives."

His face fell.

My eyes widened with a wicked smile that rivaled the Collectors. "Yeah, that's right—forever. And if we don't defeat Zenith, we'll either end up hiding in the woods like Jax, or worse, hopping into the grave with our parents."

When my brother's lips moved, I cut him off by saying, "So don't waste your breath with senseless words of encouragement because at the end of the day"—I motioned to the two of us—"our future looks pretty damn bleak."

Cyrus's nostrils flared. I knew my brother well enough to know that his Solin temper was about to throw off the gloves and hit me with a verbal hook. I stood tall, bracing myself.

"How dare you," he spat. "At least one of us is putting forth some effort into staying focused on the future rather than the past. You sit up here all day, locked inside that head of yours, consumed with irrational thoughts, but when I try to live in the now and share words of 'encouragement,' you crucify me for it. I am so sick of listening to you bitch about how life isn't going your way. Do you ever think of anyone other than yourself?"

I raised my closed fist without a conscious effort but froze when Samson shouted, "Damn it, that's enough!"

His arms fell to his sides as he stormed over to where my brother and I stood facing one another like boxers in a ring, ready to go twelve rounds. With little effort, Samson nudged Cyrus out of the way while locking his fierce eyes onto mine. "You better get your head out of your ass and start listening to your brother, because guess what? Everything he said is true."

I glared, the whites of my knuckles showing.

"Are you going to hit me?" He moved closer. "Do it, I dare you."

Idalia cleared her throat. I took a step back, unwilling to challenge the ex-Collector.

Samson inhaled a long breath as he ran a hand over his beard. "Jax was a smart man. Unlike you, he knew the difference between avenging and honoring someone. If you truly cared for your friend, then honor him by defeating Zenith. Avenging his death won't do a damn bit of good." His tongue tapped the roof of his mouth when a salty sentiment rolled down my cheek. "Pull yourself together, kid. You wouldn't last a minute in front of Zenith in your current state."

Idalia looked at her uncle for back up. He shrugged, refusing to take part in *Elara's intervention.* Cyrus crossed his arms and widened his stance, his amber eyes bouncing between me and Samson.

"Is your friend dead?" The Solin didn't wait for me to answer his rhetorical question. "Yeah, he is, but crying about it won't bring him back." I flinched when he tapped my forehead. "You better toughen up if you plan on going head-to-head with that man."

The bitter truth that shot out of Samson's mouth left me wounded like a prisoner with a blinded firing squad.

He lowered his voice to a normal speaking level. "The way you're behaving is exactly what Zenith wants. Go ahead. Unravel at the seams, fall apart, make yourself look even more vulnerable than you do now. What do I care? I don't give a shit, remember?" He glanced at the door. "If you want to go on a suicide mission, then go. I sure as hell won't stand in your way."

I shuddered a breath and shut my eyes, desperate to rebuild the emotional house of cards that had collapsed inside me. The Solin's tone rivaled the sharpness of Elio's blade as it slid across my skin that morning at the spring. My eyes shot open as I observed the ex-Collector in a new light. *He reminds me of Jax, only older and more of an asshole.*

"Or," he said, twisting the tip of his beard into a cone, "you can pull your head out of your ass, and let me teach you and your brother how to take down a murdering dictator."

Cyrus's jaw fell open. "You'd train us, like you did with Jax?"

"No. You'd end up dead if I used the same technique."

I eyed my brother, curious if we should back out of the offer. He mouthed a curse word with wide eyes.

"But you will train us—in some capacity?" I asked.

Samson nodded.

"And take us to Zenith, when we're ready?"

The ex-Collector pressed his lips together as he re-tied his short ponytail. "That wasn't the offer, Cyrus."

My shoulders slumped, the spark of hope extinguished.

"I'll train you in the art of combat and teach you everything I know about the mind of a ruthless leader, but that's as far as my offer goes. When I left Arun's, I vowed never to return to that hellhole." Samson crossed his arms. "And I plan on keeping that promise."

I looked at my brother. *We're out of options. Some help is better than none.*

Agreeing with my unspoken dialogue, Cyrus extended his hand to the Solin. "Fair enough. We accept your offer."

My brother winced as Samson tightened his grip. "Good, then I'll see the two of you tomorrow at sunrise. Meet me out back, behind the pub. We'll train before the doors open."

We nodded.

Samson turned to face Idalia. His entire posture shifted as he lifted her chin. The irritation in his eyes vanished, replaced by compassion. "Cheer up, Ida. You know it pains me to see you upset."

Forcing the grief off her face, she stood on the tips of her toes and kissed Samson on the cheek. "Thank you," she whispered, wrapping her arms around his neck. "They need you more than ever right now."

The corner of his chapped mouth twitched. I strained my eyes, wondering if they were playing tricks. *Was that a smile?*

Samson gave Idalia a gentle squeeze before heading toward the door.

Callisto's blue eyes drifted between the three of us. "Try to take it easy tonight, okay?"

Idalia sniffled, while my brother and I verbalized our agreements.

Samson let Callisto pass over the threshold before turning sideways to fit through the door. As he reached for the knob, he said, "Don't forget to bring your knives tomorrow."

I gulped. My brother only nodded.

Idalia blew out a quick breath after they left. She rubbed her swollen eyes before looking at me and Cyrus. "I'm shocked Samson offered to help. I thought I'd have to convince him on my own."

"I can see why," Cyrus murmured. "The dude's pretty intense."

"No wonder that Collector ran out of the pub tonight."

My brother and Idalia's head snapped in my direction. "Collector?" they asked.

My tongue moved with great speed, giving them a brief summary of my encounter with Inan.

Cyrus ran a hand over his shaved head as he glanced at Idalia.

"We may have to rethink this plan," she said. "I don't know if it's a good idea having you work downstairs." Her face fell as she hurried to the door. "Damn it."

"What's wrong?" I asked, grabbing her arm.

"I left Hunter all alone with a full house. I need to get down there."

I re-tied the scarf around my neck while saying, "I'll come with you."

"No, you've had a rough night. Just stay here and relax with Cyrus."

"Relax? I don't even know what that word means anymore. We're in this together. Let me help."

She squeezed my hand. "I appreciate your attitude adjustment, but I could use some time alone. Having you down there is just—"

"A distraction?"

She sighed. "No, a reminder."

"Right." I shifted my gaze to the floor.

"I'll see you guys in the morning," she said, rushing out of the room.

I stood motionless, staring at the closed door. I observed every crack and speck of imperfection in the aged wood. Dark knots swirled, leaking into the gaps like an oil painting. My head turned to one side. *Flawed but beautiful. That's what I'd name the door if it were on display in a museum.*

"Is it just me?"—I asked my brother as he collapsed onto the bed—"or does Earth feel like it's getting farther away with each passing day."

"I don't know, sis, but it sure as hell seems like it is."

I dragged my feet over to the bed when he patted the space beside him. The mattress sagged when my head hit the pillow. "For some reason, it doesn't feel like Jax is gone."

"I hear ya. Maybe it's because the shock hasn't worn off. When my grandfather died, my mom kept her cool until after the funeral. That's when it hit her."

I shut my eyes. More words of truth fired from his mouth, only this time they struck me in the chest.

"I hope he didn't suffer for too long." Cyrus grimaced when I went rigid. "Sorry, I shouldn't have said that."

"Well, he's not suffering anymore so—"

My brother reached for my hand as I wept. He didn't say a word while I grieved the loss of Jax. Long minutes passed before the tears ran dry. I had nothing left to give. Exhausted,

I rolled onto my side and drifted off to sleep. Cyrus never let go of my hand.

My fingers grazed the gritty but oily surface as I walked. A dimly lit hallway lined with doors appeared to go on forever, like a maze of mirrors minus the reflections. The soles of my shoes slapped against a sticky residue as I ventured farther down the narrow path. *Where am I?*

Using my Lunin vision, I scanned the unfamiliar space, then lifted my foot, bothered by the foreign matter that covered the bottom of my shoes. *Blood. And lots of it.* My pulse quickened. *It's everywhere.* The floors, the walls, even the ceiling dripped with the red liquid. *I have to get out of here.*

My hand reached for the first door on the right, blood-soaked fingers sliding against the cool knob. I used my shirt like a rubber grip opening a jar and stumbled into the room. More blood, only this time it covered a man who sat in the corner, his expression cold—lifeless. The light of the twin moons illuminated his bruised and battered body. Lacerations decorated every inch of his pale skin. My breath hitched when his head turned toward me, the light exposing his jet-black hair and piercing blue eyes. *It can't be.*

"Jax?" I called, rushing forward.

I winced, slamming into an invisible wall. Like a mime in a house of horrors, my hands patted the phantom barrier. I called his name again, only this time with more desperation—panic.

He stood, blood dripping from his parted lips, his ears . . . My hand shot to my mouth. *Dear God.* Even his eyes leaked with evidence of suffering. I stilled as he approached.

The Lunin cocked his head to one side, observing my shocked expression. He didn't blink. The whites of his eyes matched the blood that continued to drip onto the floor. My heart sank. The light that fueled Jax had dimmed—vanished, replaced by a heartless, tormented soul.

I whimpered when his hand slammed on the invisible wall between us. Jax's nostrils flared and blood sprayed onto my face when he spat, "Wake up Elara, you should have never come for me."

TWENTY-THREE

A Twisted Plan

Disoriented, I flew out of the bed, stubbing my toe on the nightstand.

Cyrus was at my side in a heartbeat. "Easy, sis. You're dreaming." He rested a hand on my back and grimaced at the sweat-soaked shirt.

I clutched my chest, gasping for air. The smell of iron-rich blood still stung my nose. Desperate to shake the vivid nightmare, I dug my fingers into my scalp and squeezed my eyes shut.

"Bad one, huh?"

"Only the worst dream ever." I checked my palms for traces of the oily residue. "It felt so real. Jax was right there but—" My voice cracked.

"It was just a dream, Elara, and dreams aren't real."

I shivered, Jax's heartless expression etched into the wall of my memory bank. "But you didn't see his face or hear his voice. Jax blamed me for what happened, Cyrus. And now his ghost will haunt me forever."

"Hey," he soothed. "That's not true. Jax never blamed you for anything."

"You don't know that."

"Yes, I do."

"How?"

"Because that's not the kind of man he is—was." I looked away. "Elara, this nightmare has everything to do with the unnecessary guilt you keep carrying around. You didn't abandon Jax that morning on the cliffside, so let it go."

I wanted to agree with my brother, but the dream was unlike anything I had ever experienced.

My Lunin vision faded as the morning light seeped through the bedroom window. Our heads turned when Idalia cracked open the door.

Cyrus's eyes lit up. Dressed for the day, the Solin wore a pair of tight-fitting, khaki-colored pants and a light gray long-sleeved shirt that accentuated her perfect figure. Her platinum-blonde locks were twisted into a loose braid that hung over her shoulder. The exhaustion and grief that clouded her golden eyes couldn't disguise her inner beauty.

"Samson will be here soon," she said, walking toward the bed.

"Why didn't you come get me last night?"

"I tried, but you were sound asleep." She motioned to Cyrus. "I figured your brother wouldn't mind you staying in his room for the night."

He squeezed my shoulder. "Of course not."

"The two of you should get dressed. Samson isn't a very patient man."

We followed the Solin across the hall and into her room. Cyrus headed into the washroom while Idalia kneeled beside the bed. She banged her fist on a weathered floorboard, and like a seesaw, one side popped up.

Curious, I scooted closer. My eyes grew when she opened the black wooden box that rested in the hiding place.

"How did you get these knives?" I asked, admiring the small arsenal of weapons.

"Samson has his connections with the men on the black market. Here." She handed me a familiar blade with a gray handle. "Jax would have wanted you to have it." My chest tightened as I took it from her hand. "I wasn't trying to keep it from you," she said, meeting my gaze. "I found it the day you showed up with Cyrus, so I hid it in this box. I didn't want the Collectors getting their hands on it."

I slid the knife into my back pocket and smiled. "Thanks for keeping it safe."

"Hold onto Jax's knife for sentimental value," she said, searching through the pile. Her eyes glowed as she offered me a folded blade with a stark white handle. "But use this one as your own."

As if holding a delicate artifact from a museum, I marveled at the expert craftmanship. "Wow, it's beautiful."

No larger than my palm, the folded blade was the perfect

fit. My finger traced the minute engravings that decorated the handle: two crescent moons and three star bursts.

"It was my mother's. My father had it made for her." She pointed to the stars. "They represent the past, present, and future."

"No." I handed her the knife. "I can't take this. It's a family heirloom. It should stay with you."

Idalia curled my fingers around the folded blade. "Consider it a gift. I want you to have it—use it."

I shut my eyes, her generosity leaving me more emotional.

"The bathroom is all yours, sis," Cyrus said, lowering himself beside us. He did a double take. "Damn, that's a lot of knives."

❧

"No wonder I almost froze to death."

I nodded, rocking back and forth in the snow that covered the forest floor behind the pub.

Cyrus blew a cloud from his mouth. "And *this*"—he sliced through the white haze with his hand—"is warmer than the first snowfall?"

I shrugged. "How would we know? This is the first time Idalia's let us step outside."

"True."

I glanced at the morning sun that rested in the cloudless sky, mocking us with warmth we would never feel. *So close and yet so far.*

Our heads turned at the sound of boots crunching through the snow—Samson. The tails of his winter coat trailed behind him as he stomped toward us, his orange eyes drifting back and forth between me and my brother.

His calloused hands re-fastened the tie around his ponytail while he asked, “Did you bring your knives?”

We nodded with our entire bodies, the bone-chilling cold sending shivers down our spines in nonstop waves. I squinted when my short locks slapped me in the face, and my brother cursed, stuffing his hands deeper into his pockets.

Samson’s brow furrowed at our reactions. Unfazed by the weather, he stood tall with his hands resting by his sides; the coarse hairs of his beard danced in the breeze.

“Are the two of you done acting like little girls?” We stilled. My brother’s lips moved, but Samson cut him off by adding, “First lesson: don’t let the weather affect your aim.”

I mouthed, “What is happening right now?” to Cyrus when Samson took off his coat and tossed it onto the snow-covered ground. Brushing me off, my brother’s hands flew out of his pockets. I snorted. *Way to look tough, bro.*

Samson took it one step farther by pushing the sleeves of his shirt over his muscular forearms. My eyes widened. *Geez. And I thought Jax had a lot of scars.* Almost every inch of his bronze skin had evidence of his time with Arun. Flesh-tone and light pink in color, the jagged lines created a twisted path that led to nowhere. I halted my observations when the ex-Collector spit a ball of phlegm near the toe of my boot. *Ew. Was that necessary?*

Ignoring the disgust that smeared across my face, he said, “In the summer, a sweaty palm can make you lose your grip around the handle, and in the winter, the numbness in your fingers can affect the precision of your throw." He looked at me and my brother. "The two of you need to learn how to cope with the physical discomforts. Everything I'm about to teach you will hurt like hell." I gulped. "But remember." Samson moved closer, finger aimed for a good flick at my forehead. "It's all mental."

I flinched when he made contact with my cold skin.

Samson pivoted, the snow compacting under his weight. He waved a hand over his shoulder as he walked deeper into the forest. "You're up first, Cyrus."

My brother hurried to catch up with our new teacher, but before I lifted my foot, Samson spun around and restrained him in a headlock.

Cyrus's amber eyes found mine, a mixture of shock and concern. His Solin strength was no match for the ex-Collector. Samson wrapped his right arm around Cyrus's neck, locking it into the crease of his left arm that forced my brother's head to look down. Cyrus's eyes bulged, his air flow restricted.

The gentle heat that flowed through me transformed into a fiery river as I took a step forward.

"Don't come any closer," Samson warned. "I need to see if Jax taught you kids anything useful."

I froze, my eyes never leaving my brother.

"Come on," Samson barked, tightening his grip. "Escape the hold."

Cyrus twisted and turned like a new puppy on a leash, but Samson didn't budge. The harder my brother fought, the more he struggled to breathe.

I looked over my shoulder when Idalia cleared her throat. "Samson, I thought you were going to start with something simple.

"This *is* simple."

Idalia mumbled, "Here we go," as she took her place beside me.

"Pull your head out of your ass, Cyrus. Think about your training with Jax. How do you escape this hold?" Samson squeezed his arms tighter while my brother continued to struggle. "All you're doing is flopping around like a damn toddler throwing a tantrum. I can do this all day, but in about fifteen seconds you'll lose consciousness."

My brother hesitated for only a moment before using all of his strength to squat, taking Samson with him. Cyrus swung his left hand to the ex-Collector's groin, then stood upright, slamming his fingertips into Samson's forehead, purposely avoiding the eyes. After a quick twist, my brother had freed himself from the hold, hands held in the guard position.

Idalia and I stood with wide eyes as if we had just witnessed a man escape from a strait jacket. The eldest Solin nodded at my brother, impressed with his quick reaction time.

"Is Samson smiling?" I whispered.

Idalia chuckled. "Don't get used to it."

"Well I'll be damned," he said, clapping Cyrus on the back. "It looks like Jax did teach you a few tricks of the trade."

My brother stared at his hands. "Honestly, that's the first time I've escaped that hold."

"It takes practice—and lots of it. In a few weeks these maneuvers will feel like second nature." Samson ran a hand over his beard as he eyed me and my brother. "Arun was a smart man, but Zenith's smarter—more vindictive. Unlike his predecessor, Zenith never intended on helping anyone other than himself."

"Yeah, Jax—" I paused, clearing my throat. "He mentioned that." Samson watched me with curious eyes. Bothered by his intense stare, I added, "Idalia said we shouldn't ask about your past. But if there's any information you're willing to share about the Collectors or how things worked during Arun's reign—we're all ears."

The Solin took a step closer. "What do you want to know?" He didn't wait for my response. "That I've killed more innocent people than all of Arun's Collectors combined? That I have enough blood on my hands to last a lifetime? Or, how I haven't enjoyed a peaceful night's sleep in over twenty-five years because the faces of my victims haunt my dreams?"

I tried to swallow but my tongue stuck to the roof of my mouth. Like a sponge, his brutal honesty had absorbed the saliva.

Samson scowled at my reaction. "Or would you like a firsthand account of what I learned during my time with Arun?"

My shoulders sagged. *Bastard. He could have left out the other parts.*

Samson motioned for us to follow him through the woods. My brother hesitated, leaving ample space between himself and the ex-Collector.

"Are you scared?" I teased.

Cyrus glared, pushing me in front of him. "After you, sis."

"Have fun," Idalia said, waving at us over her shoulder. "I'll be inside if you need anything."

The two of us trailed behind Samson, our boots sloshing through the snow. A few breaths later, he stopped in front of a massive tree. My hand slid across the fuzzy bark, fingers grazing the deep grooves—knife marks from previous target practices. I touched my back pocket. *I wonder if this is where Samson trained Jax.*

"You can't win a knife fight unless you learn your opponent's weakness. Right now, the two of you know nothing about Zenith." Samson lifted his hand when my lips moved. "No. What Jax told you doesn't count. Have you met Zenith? Seen him with your own eyes?" I shook my head. He went on, "I didn't think so. The way he treated Jax was one thing. What he plans on doing to you—is another."

I sighed while Cyrus crossed his arms. The wind howled around us, loosening a sheet of snow that clung to the canopy of leaves overhead. Me and my brother dusted the white fluff off our hair and coats while Samson just blinked the snowflakes out of his eyes.

"Zenith cares about one thing and one thing only: his own well-being. He doesn't give a damn about anyone else.

Selfish people will stop at nothing to get what they want. Add a bit of delusional paranoia to the mix, and they'll kill whoever gets in their way."

Jax's face appeared before my eyes. I turned my back on the tree, focusing my attention on Samson while he spoke.

"Zenith has zero attachment to the Collectors or his precious Inner Circle. They're merely his pawns, and he uses them to get what he wants without risking his own life. The man is nothing more than a coward who hides behind the tough façade he created. Now don't get me wrong, the guy's not an idiot. Every decision he makes is precisely calculated. Zenith has brainwashed each Collector into believing that without him, they'd have nothing—*be* nothing."

A shiver rippled through me. *It's too cold. I can hardly think straight.* Desperate to stay warm, I rocked back and forth but froze when Samson shook his head at me. *Busted.* Cyrus shot me a smug grin, amused with my failed attempt.

"Zenith won't step down without a fight. The two of you are a threat to his position. He'll stop at nothing until you're both dead. Killing Jax was his way of playing dirty."

My throat tightened, and my eyes closed for a split second before Samson's fingers dug into my shoulders. I winced when my head jolted forward.

"Pull yourself together, kid. You can't let your emotions show around Zenith. If you do, he'll use it to his advantage and get inside your head. Manipulation is a wicked talent—a trap he loves to set for the weak minded and fainthearted."

I bit my lip, forcing the tears away. Sensing my inner struggle, Cyrus moved closer. The heat intensified when his arm brushed against mine.

Samson let me go and took a step backward. "That's why he murdered your friend. Zenith knew Jax would never disclose your whereabouts, so he used him as bait. He wanted the two of you to come to him. Why would Zenith leave the safety of his dwelling? He has everything he needs: The Collectors, a plethora of knives, and if he stays put, he doesn't risk losing face in front of the people."

My head spun. *This is insanity. Why did Jax think we could defeat Zenith? How can Samson?* I looked at my brother. *There is no way in hell we can do this alone.*

Cyrus blew out a sharp breath as he rubbed the blond fuzz on his head. "Samson, I mean no offense when I say this, but the idea of me and my sister knocking on Zenith's door with two knives in our hands sounds like a suicide mission."

"It is. You wouldn't even make it through the door in the wall."

I tossed up my hands. "Then what's the point of trying to defeat Zenith on his own turf?"

"There isn't one. Good thing that was never the plan."

I eyed Cyrus. He shrugged, equally baffled by Samson's harsh truth.

"You don't want us defeating Zenith at his dwelling?" I asked.

"No. The two of you will do it in broad daylight, so everyone can see." A smirk twitched at the corner of Samson's chapped mouth when he said, “We’re going to force that bastard to come to us.”

TWENTY-FOUR

The First Collector

Our jaws fell open. More concerns formed on my tongue. "How in the hell are we supposed to do that? You made it sound like Zenith doesn't like leaving his dwelling."

"He doesn't, but if we piss him off, he'll show his face in the villages."

Cyrus's eyes clouded with confusion. "Can you elaborate?"

"I'm going to train you and your sister harder than ever. Once I'm convinced you can hold your own against the Collectors, I'll send you into the villages."

My brother let out a sarcastic laugh, the cloud dissipating around Samson's face. "Your average Collector is one thing, but what about the Inner Circle?" Cyrus waved a hand at me. "I think you're forgetting our team has two members—they have nine."

"Thank you for the update, Cyrus. There's only two of you? I had no idea." Samson slapped a hand over his face, exaggerating his performance. "And nine members of the Inner Circle?" His tongue clicked on the roof of his mouth. "We should quit now while there's still time. I'm sure you and your sister can find a cute little home in one of the villages and live a peaceful life."

I snickered, covering my mouth. *Why am I laughing? It's not funny. Maybe it's because I'm hanging onto my sanity by a thin thread.*

Cyrus glared at my behavior while Samson added, "Zenith wants to murder the two of you with his bare hands, so it's the Collectors job to attack when you least expect it. By the time I've finished your training, the average Collector won't be a concern." Samson found my worried eyes. "Yes, the Inner Circle poses a threat, but Zenith won't dispatch this elite group unless he's certain of your whereabouts."

"He already sent Pollux, Apollo, and Ravi searching for us. What makes you think he won't send them again?"

"He will. Make no mistake about that." I dropped my head. "Elara, I'm trying to ease your mind by saying Zenith won't dispatch all nine members of the Inner Circle at once." Samson lowered his gaze. "He did that morning on the cliffside, because Jax's combative skills rivaled Pollux and the others."

My brother asked, "What do you want us doing in the villages?"

"I want the people of Aroonyx to witness your shared Solin and Lunin traits. Use this unique ability along with your training to stand against the Collectors. This will prove that you and your sister are not afraid of Zenith."

I laughed again, though I felt like crying. "Samson, this plan makes no sense—whatsoever. What good will that do?"

"They'll join your side."

"Our side?" I blinked. "Are we going to battle? There's no way in hell the people of Aroonyx will offer to help us defeat Zenith just because we're different."

Samson smirked as he stroked his beard. "Yes they will, along with the average Collector."

A loud barking laugh escaped my mouth. "Like that would ever happen."

Even my brother expressed his amusement with a quiet snort.

Samson shifted his weight and asked me, "Why do the Collectors follow Zenith?"

"Because he's Zenith."

"No, they follow the illusion of an all-powerful man. I was here when Zenith gained control of Aroonyx. Everyone, including myself, was enamored by his ability to use both Solin and Lunin traits, and not only that, but he looked different."

I nodded, remembering Jax's description of Zenith: bronze skin, black hair, one blue eye, and one orange—the perfect combination of a Solin and a Lunin.

Samson went on. "He used this to his advantage, and it wasn't long before everyone believed Zenith was special—destined for leadership."

"Won't the people recognize their mistake when they see us using our shared traits?" I asked.

He let out a long breath. I cocked my head to one side, curious about the heavy weight that rested on his shoulders.

"No. Unfortunately not. They're all too brainwashed, especially the Collectors. The people have no attachment to Zenith, only to the façade he's created. If his followers see two people sharing traits like their current leader"—Samson huffed a breath—"you're damn right they'll join your side."

"How can you be so sure?" Cyrus asked.

"Because I fell into that trap with Arun. Instead of listening to my gut, I followed someone out of curiosity. I put all of my trust into a man who was nothing more than a bag of lies."

A thick cloud left Samson's mouth as he shut his eyes. I could tell he was debating whether or not to share a part of his past because the tendons in his arms contracted and his hands clenched into fists.

Hoping to ease his discomfort, I tried switching the subject, but his raspy voice cut me off.

"In my late teens, I remember looking at Saros and the other Seekers like untouchable beings: the special men and women who could jump to Earth, the ones Arun awarded with fancy titles, land, and privileges. They lived a glamorous life, and over the years I became jealous."

Ignoring Samson's stern glance, my brother and I bounced in the snow to stay warm while he continued his story.

"My family was poor. I helped my father farm the fields around our small home because my mother died when I was just a boy. I was a huge pain in the ass. From an early age, I loved starting fights and getting into trouble. Rumors about Arun starting an exclusive group spread throughout the villages. Eager to feel a part of something bigger than myself, I joined and was named the first Collector."

I eyed my brother, amazed by this bit of information.

Samson cleared his throat. "I craved acceptance, and Arun took advantage of this, making each one us feel special—entitled. That's how I met Ida's father. We were in our early twenties and thicker than thieves, the world was at our fingertips."

Samson paused. The line between his eyebrows deepened, and his Adams's apple bobbed in his throat when he swallowed a lifetime of regrets.

Ignoring the strong gust that whipped around us, Cyrus stood tall. My toes danced in secret, hidden under the snow that dusted my boots. A sadness grabbed hold of me as I observed the haze of grief that surrounded the eldest Solin, thick enough to cut with a knife.

I shivered when he spoke, and it wasn't from the bone-chilling cold.

"I was the first Collector to murder a Seeker." Samson stared at the swaying tree limbs, his voice barely above a whisper. "I hated doing it, and to make matters worse, it wasn't a clean kill. Arun never trained us in the art of combat, so we had to teach ourselves how to end a man's life. I used my Solin strength to restrain the Lunin Seeker I captured and slid my blade across his throat, thinking that would get the job done. Novice mistake." He glanced at the two of us. "I hope Jax taught you how to perform a clean kill."

We nodded. Cyrus gave me an all-too-familiar look, reminding me of his brawl with Jax.

"I made a huge mess, trying to push that damn blade deeper into his neck." Samson grabbed the thick mass of muscle that shielded the main artery in his throat. "This shit is hard to get through with a sawing motion."

I gulped, my stomach churning with nausea.

"It took me well over three minutes to cut the main artery. I know that doesn't sound like a long time, but when you're covered in someone else's blood, and your victim's screams have silenced because neurogenic shock has taken over—three minutes can feel like a lifetime."

I had to look away. It was too much to process. Cyrus blew a tight breath through pursed lips.

Unfazed by our reactions, Samson added, "So there I was, holding the Lunin's half-severed head in one hand and my knife in the other. I just stood there, looking back and forth between the blood-soaked blade and the man's frozen expression." He spit a wad of phlegm into the snow. "I'll never forget the way his lifeless eyes stared through me, mouth open mid-scream."

"Shit," Cyrus muttered, unable to hide his true feelings.

The eldest Solin shrugged. "After the shock wore off, I blew chunks everywhere—all over the Lunin's dead body. Arun reassured me that I did the right thing by killing the Seeker. He said, *We must find each and every one. End the lives of those who disobeyed my orders. End the lives of those who pose a threat.*"

I recalled my chat with Jax under the bridge on Earth. Arun wanted the Seekers to return to Earth so they could learn more about the tools he wanted to use as weapons—protection to defend himself if an uprising occurred. When they failed, he took it personally, unaware of the Seeker's unspoken rule: only those with a pure intention are permitted to jump.

My mind drifted back to the present at the sound of Samson's voice. "Sometimes I wonder why I stayed working for Arun. Torturing an innocent person to the brink of death, only to end their lives didn't feel right. It never sat well with me. But Arun gave me a purpose, and this helped justify my behavior.

"Over time, the killings got easier—quicker, but with each brutal murder, I drifted farther away from the truth." He tapped his chest. "The small bit of good left inside, begged me to stop. But how could I? Death and destruction had become a way of life.

"Every night when my head hits the pillow, I hear the screams of my victims and see those beautiful blue and orange eyes."

My mouth gaped. *Idalia mentioned Samson had blood on his hands—but not that much.*

Cyrus stole a glance at the ex-Collector. "I'm at a loss for words, Samson."

"Good thing I didn't ask for your opinion." He smirked. "I wanted you to hear the reason these young Collectors follow Zenith. He does the same thing as Arun did with us. Praises them for committing crimes, celebrates torture and murder as a success."

"How long did you work for Arun?" I asked, surprised how small my voice sounded.

"The last five years of his reign. It's funny, I was the first one to show up and the first one to leave."

"Why is that?"

Samson spit more phlegm onto the snow before looking at my brother. "I left that hellhole after I stumbled across Arun's body."

"Jax said he took his own life. Is that how he died?" Cyrus asked.

"Yep. I found him sprawled out on the floor in his bedroom." Samson cracked his neck. "Stabbing yourself in the heart takes dedication, that's for sure. I'll never know how he managed to do it without going into shock before the blade penetrated his chest cavity. He was lying on his back, so he didn't fall on the knife. I guess the bastard wanted to take his sweet time."

"That's disturbing."

I nodded at my brother's accurate description.

"Nah, not really. Not after the shit he did to those poor Seekers. A knife to the heart lacked the flair he used on the others."

"What did you do with his body?" I asked.

"Not a damn thing. I just stood there, staring at him. I felt nothing. No remorse, no grief . . . no relief. I walked out the bedroom, closed the door behind me, said goodbye to Janus, and never looked back."

Cyrus's shoulders sagged while I swayed side to side in the strong breeze, lost in thought. I always wondered how Jax knew so much about Arun and the first Collectors on Aroonyx. I observed Samson with a new set of eyes. *And now I know why.*

"I told you this story to help you understand why young, impressionable people"—he cleared his throat—"specifically the Collectors, are so eager to follow the next big thing. When you use your shared Solin and Lunin traits to stand against them, they'll second guess their loyalty to Zenith. He's old news now that the twins have returned." Samson used his fingers to count. "You're younger, mysterious, and have the knowledge of Earth under your belts." A huge grin crossed his face. "It's the perfect trifecta . . . one Zenith can't touch."

TWENTY-FIVE

It's All in the Wrist

And just like that we had a plan—a blue print that showed how to disrupt the foundation Zenith stood upon.

My brother's eyes locked onto mine, and using our unique bond to communicate without words, we agreed to take the next step in our journey.

Pleased with the acceptance that flickered in our eyes, Samson pulled a black knife from his pocket and exposed the blade with a quick flick of his wrist. "I hope you're ready," he said, motioning for us to take off our coats. "Because your training starts now."

The reality of our new endeavor hit me in the face like a brick of ice when I removed the only article of warmth from my body. I cursed, tossing it onto the ground beside my brother's coat.

My hand paused as it reached for Jax's knife. I remembered how comfortable the white one felt in my hand. Trembling, I unfolded the blade from the handle.

Samson grumbled his complaints while taking it from me. "What are you doing? That's not how you open a knife." He folded the blade before tossing it to me. More sounds of irritation left his mouth when it fell into the snow.

I groaned, bending over to pick it up.

"Great. You can't open a knife much less catch one. Elara, were you napping when Jax was training you or did you just not give a—"

"Don't be an asshole," I snapped, dusting off the snow. "I've tried. I can't figure out how to open the damn thing without cutting myself."

Samson looked at Cyrus. "Is she always like this?"

"What? Sassy?"

He nodded.

"No—usually she's worse."

I flashed my brother a vulgar gesture that only made him laugh.

"Well, it's time you learn how to open a blade with one hand." Samson demonstrated with his own knife. "See, it's all in the wrist. Quick flick, away from the body." He moved beside me and wrapped his strong hand around my own, guiding me through the motions. "Stop flinching. The blade won't cut your skin if you trust the process. Don't hesitate. That's the fastest way to meet an early grave."

Fourteen tries and twelve colorful words later, I learned how to open a knife with one hand.

Satisfied with my progress, Samson turned to face my brother. "Go on, show me how much time I need to spend coddling you."

With a smug grin plastered on his face, Cyrus exposed the blade of his knife with zero effort. I scoffed and mouthed, "Kiss ass."

"Are you sure the two of you are twins?"

I shifted my features into neutral after faking a laugh. "Wow. Mr. Smiles has a sense of humor."

Thick white clouds blew out of Samson's mouth as his broad shoulders bounced up and down. Rubbing it in, Cyrus opened and closed his knife in a repetitive motion, his smug expression growing with every swish of the blade.

"Are you done?" I pressed, shifting my gaze between the two men. "Or should I tell Idalia about your lack of maturity?"

The color drained from my brother's face, the swishing of the blade stopping quicker than it started. Samson's brow furrowed as he cleared his throat while I stood tall, the only one left smiling.

"What's next on the agenda?" I asked, moving my wind-swept hair out of my face.

Samson adjusted his pants by the belt loops before looking at my brother. "There's something I want to try."

"Oh, hell no." Cyrus touched the scar on his neck. "Jax said those exact words to me on Earth. I'm not falling for that trick again."

I chuckled, watching my brother squirm in his boots.

"All right, why don't you sit this one out. Being the loving sister that she is, I'm sure Elara won't mind standing in your place."

My face fell but Cyrus's beamed with delight. "I think that's a marvelous idea, Samson."

My feet slid through the snow as the ex-Collector placed my body in front of the tree.

I glared at my brother. "A part of me hates you right now."

"Hate is a strong word, sis. Where are your manners?"

"In two seconds, why don't you look up your ass because that's where I'm about to shove them."

"Save that angst for your visits to the villages, Elara. You'll need it. Right now, it's time to have a little fun."

"Let's not," I muttered, staring at the man who towered over me. *I wonder who's bigger? Samson or Apollo? Scratch that thought. I don't want to see a side-by-side comparison.*

He pointed to Cyrus. "When it comes to courage, Solins don't think, they just act. Lunins, on the other hand, overthink everything and tend to hesitate—or worse, do nothing at all. This little exercise will help you overcome that problem."

This doesn't sound good.

"First, I need you to hand me your knives."

I gulped, touching my back pocket. "Why?"

"Don't waste time asking stupid questions."

Adding to his golden-boy performance, Cyrus offered Samson his folded blade. With little enthusiasm, I tossed him my white knife, which he caught with one hand.

"I'll take Jax's knife too."

"How did you know I had it?"

The ex-Collector raised a wiry brow. "More questions?" I lowered my head. "Elara, I may be older than your father, but I'm not an idiot. I can see it in your back pocket."

"Fair enough," I murmured, handing it to him.

Samson's massive hand held all three knives with room to spare. He rested his left hand on the tree and leaned closer, forcing my back against the fuzzy bark. "Here's how the game works. You stand right here with your arms held by your sides"—he looked over his shoulder and pointed with the knives—"while I stand over there. There are two rules: Keep your eyes open." He pushed himself to the upright position and rotated his arm, warming the muscles in his shoulder. "And whatever you do . . . don't move."

I swallowed hard when Samson turned and walked at least sixty feet away from where I stood, panic-stricken. My heart pounded in my ears as the gentle heat surged through me.

"And that's my cue," Cyrus said, taking four steps backward, his boots sloshing through the snow.

"Thanks for having my back, bro."

"I'm right here. Just a few feet away." He muffled his laughter. "Holler if you need anything."

Choice words mixed with a white cloud when Samson flicked his wrist, exposing the blade of my white knife. Eyeing my brother out of my peripheral vision, I said, "If I get out of this alive," I paused, watching the ex-Collector raise his armed hand over his shoulder, "I'm going to kick your—"

My words merged with a shriek when he hurled the knife at the tree—at me. Sharing Cyrus's Solin vision didn't help because the blade launched out of Samson's hand like an arrow from a bow. Every muscle in my body contracted when the lethal part of the knife pierced the bark, its handle swaying only inches above my head.

Nope. I don't want to play this game. Twisted sideshow carnivals were never my thing.

Quick breaths entered my lungs, and my hands buzzed with heat. Snapped out of his light-hearted mood, my brother took a step forward.

To my dismay, the unforgiving wind blew a strand of hair into my eyes. I lifted a hand, only for another knife to thwart my efforts: Cyrus's blade. A strong four-letter word shot out my mouth; the precise throw had pinned the sleeve of my shirt to the tree.

"I told you not to move!" Samson shouted.

"Easy, Elara." My brother took another step closer, his tone severe. "He's not messing around; don't you dare move."

Not risking a head nod, I shut my eyes. The sharp whistle of another blade soaring through the air signaled my body to tense. I held my breath when it connected with the tree, the black handle thumping against my cheekbone. *Maybe I should run? No, that's a horrible idea. Knowing Samson, he'll use me as target practice.*

"You broke another rule!" he yelled. "You're not allowed to close your eyes."

"Focus, Elara," my brother encouraged. "You can do this. He's testing you, don't let him win."

Leave it to Cyrus to kick my ass into gear. My pulse raced, but I stood tall, chin lifted and eyes open. Samson watched me with a curious expression as his fingers rotated the gray handle—Jax's knife.

I stilled, ignoring the shivers of terror that zipped through me. Fear and the cold would have to wait. Cyrus said I needed to be stronger than ever if I wanted to rescue Jax, but that time had passed. Samson said to honor Jax by defeating Zenith—and so I would because that's all I had left to give. If I couldn't handle a trust exercise with Samson, how could I face a man who wanted to kill me with his bare hands. *It's time. It's time to take a stand.*

As if hearing my internal dialogue, Samson nodded as he raised his armed hand. The overwhelming fear I experienced transformed into courage when he hurled the knife harder and faster than the others. The sharp blade grazed the side of my neck before it wedged itself into the tree. I didn't flinch. I didn't blink. A trickle of blood warmed my cool skin, but I refused to lift a hand, allowing it to drip onto the collar of my shirt.

Cyrus stood wide-eyed as if he had witnessed the underdog in a boxing match throw an unexpected jab for the knockout win. Samson reminded me of Jax, the afternoon he walked out of the surf on Crystal beach. Grinning from ear to ear, he jogged toward me, applauding my performance.

I touched the cut on my neck. A cat scratch compared to the damage Elio did at the spring. Lifting my shoulder to my ear, I wiped off the blood, then turned and pulled the knife that pinned my shirt to the tree, along with the others.

"Well, who would have thought," Samson praised. "A Lunin acting like a Solin. Maybe you and Cyrus are related."

I rolled my eyes, offering him the weapons.

He took his, then shooed away the others. "Let that be the last time anyone takes your knife."

"Copy that." I handed Cyrus his before slipping the other two into my back pocket.

My brother hid a shiver when the wind whipped through the forest. I glanced at my body, wondering if someone had thrown a blanket around me. A warmth moved through me and it wasn't because of my brother's proximity. Something inside had changed—something I wouldn't understand until the very end.

Samson circled his arms, then popped his knuckles. "I want to start with some basic attack moves. Knowing Jax, I bet he focused on defense maneuvers."

My brother and I nodded. The ex-Collector took a moment to observe the two of us. His burnt-orange eyes scanned our faces as he twisted the end of his beard into a cone.

"Question." We met his gaze. "The two of you fought off three members of the Inner Circle: Elio, Ravi, and Apollo, is that right?

I eyed my brother, unsure where Samson planned on steering the conversation.

Cyrus crossed his arms. "Yeah, that's right."

"Next question. How in the hell did you survive? Earlier, you squirmed like a little girl in that headlock, and at the time, your sister couldn't open a knife."

Another nervous glance at my brother. We never told Idalia or anyone else about the little trick we used on Elio and Apollo at the spring. We called our escape from the dangerous encounter *a lucky break—a near miss.*

We trusted our new friends, but our unique ability was unpredictable, and we didn't want to share it with the others until I could will it on command.

Samson's posture tensed. "You're hiding something from me, I can tell."

We looked away, unable to meet his gaze.

He moved closer, gesturing to the three of us. "This relationship won't work unless we trust each other."

I sighed. Jax's voice echoed in his words.

"I'm only going to ask one more time. How did you escape from three Solins during the day?"

I tucked a hair behind my ear and reached for my brother's hand.

"You want to show him?" Cyrus asked.

"If we can get it to work. Do you think it will?"

Heat surged through me faster than I could blink. Cyrus flashed me a warm smile. "Hell yeah, sis. Let's do it."

Samson's brows raised. "Do what?"

"A trick," I said, shifting my weight. "One Zenith doesn't have."

His brows raised even higher. "All right. You've got my attention."

"I have no idea how this little trick works, but here goes nothing."

Focus. On what? You always focus on negative emotions. What happens if you tap into something greater? I shut my eyes and visualized Jax, allowing every sentiment to surface. Grief and regret dug their sharp claws into my back when I thought of abandoning him on the cliffside. Fear and anger knocked on the door of my mind when I thought of Pollux and Zenith. I cringed, the heat growing to an all-time high.

Cyrus tried letting go of my hand. I squeezed it tighter, forcing his compliance. *Stop running from your fears. Face these emotions head on. There's beauty behind the madness.*

And there it was—the small payoff I received from harboring negativity. This was the bitter truth, and it stared me right in the face. Anytime I experienced an undesirable emotion, I always justified it by placing the blame on others. *The guilty party caused my suffering. I'm the victim.* I smiled. *No. That's not how it works. There's no one to blame but myself. I'm responsible for the way I react to a situation. I have a choice. I can see the situation for what it is and move forward or live my life stuck in reverse.*

With this realization, the raging river of heat calmed to a babbling brook. Like a phoenix rising from the ashes, the fragments of my shattered heart took shape once more. The damage was visible, but it thumped with life—with love when I thought of Jax.

I gasped, inhaling a full breath for the first time in weeks. Cyrus turned his head when my eyes shot open.

“Show him,” he said, pointing to Samson’s hand.

My lips spread into a large grin as I grabbed the Solin’s wrist. “This might sting a bit.”

TWENTY-SIX

A Hidden Truth

The blood that colored Samson's cheeks drained faster than a popped water balloon. His orange eyes glowed with a combination of curiosity and bewilderment as he stared at my hand. "Can you turn up the heat?"

The line between my brows creased with apprehension. "I don't want to hurt you."

"Elara, you couldn't hurt me if you tried."

Cyrus inhaled a deep breath as he shifted his weight in the snow. "You may regret saying that."

Another wave of warmth rippled through me. Compelling my body to relax, I used the same technique as before to release the heat that concentrated in my hand.

Samson winced, the muscles in his forearm contracting.

"Have you had enough?" I asked, tightening my grip.

Bearing through the pain, he clenched his teeth while motioning with his free hand. "No. Give it all you've got."

"Don't kick our asses afterward," Cyrus said, rolling his neck. "You asked for it."

Another burst of heat shot from his body into mine. My vibrating hand became a pale blur around Samson's bronze skin. I opened the floodgate, letting it pour out.

He hollered and fell to his knees. I let go, clutching my hands near my heart. The Solin cradled his injured wrist, then buried it in the snow. A loud hiss followed by steam rose from the white fluff.

"Damn," Cyrus mumbled, his eyes lighting up with pride. "Way to go, sis." He offered me a fist bump. "Nailed it."

Concerned about the damage I did to our friend's wrist, I forced a smile when our knuckles connected, then asked the ex-Collector, "Are you okay?"

He pulled his hand from the snow and looked up. "Kid, I'm better than okay. This little trick of yours is a real game changer."

Samson climbed to his feet. I cringed, watching him touch the melted skin on his wrist, his index finger sinking into the scorched flesh.

"That's going to leave one hell of a scar."

The Solin eyed my brother. "I stopped counting after I left Arun." He tapped his fingers to his palm, checking for any hidden injuries. "So that's how you survived that morning at the spring. You unleashed hell out of your hand."

I shrugged. "Yeah, but today was the first time it worked without me experiencing pain."

Samson rubbed his hairy chin as he scanned my brother. "Does it work both ways? Can you release heat from your hand?"

"No, it just passes from me to her. I feel this surge of heat build in my body, then it rushes out of my arm and down my hand into Elara's. It's like she drains my powers."

Samson snickered. "Family has a tendency to do that."

Amused, I nudged my brother in the ribs. He returned the gesture by flicking me in the arm.

The eldest Solin let out a long breath as he adjusted the short hairs of his ponytail. "This is quite the twist. Not only do you share each other's traits, but one of you can absorb the other's power."

"That's what Jax said," Cyrus added.

"For the time being, let's keep this our little secret. I don't care if Idalia or Callisto find out, but don't show the people in the villages—not yet. Not until Zenith makes his move. The element of surprise is crucial in the art of combat."

We expressed our agreement with a unanimous, "Got it."

"Speaking of combat. Let's start working on those attack moves."

Cyrus hopped from one foot to the next, warming up like he did with our previous teacher.

"These training exercises need to feel real so you know what to expect when a Collector attacks."

I snorted, visualizing our encounter with the Inner Circle. *If that didn't feel real, then I don't know what does.*

"Elara." Samson lowered his gaze. "That was one time, and your little trick saved your ass, not your combative skills. The villages will have Collectors lurking around every corner. I won't let you use your special power during these visits, so hand-to-hand combat is your only option if you want to survive."

I dropped my head. "Noted."

He moved behind me and rotated my body to face my brother. "I want the two of you to spar, but instead of using—"

I choked, my spit went down the wrong pipe. "We've never trained together like that. Cyrus was the one who sparred with Jax." I cleared my throat. "I usually just watched."

"Figures," Samson said, pushing the sleeves of his shirt farther up his arms. "Good thing I'm your new teacher. Jax's easy-ass training method would have left you six feet under." He pointed to our pockets. "Take out your knives."

"I thought we were sparring?" Cyrus asked.

"I swear, if you or your sister ask one more idiotic question, I'm going to lose my shit."

Not pressing our luck, we pulled out our knives.

"Before you interrupted me, Elara"—Samson shot me a stern glance—"I was trying to say that instead of using your fists, I want you to use your knives."

My eyes almost fell out of my head. "Samson—"

He held up a closed fist. "Sweetie, I think you should stop talking now." The Solin encouraged us to begin. "Guards up."

With zero desire to go blade to blade with my brother, I raised my hands in slow motion. He took one look at my reluctant eyes before folding the blade back into the handle.

"Sorry, Samson. I can't do this." Cyrus waved a hand at me. "I won't hurt my sister."

A low growl rumbled in the Solin's throat as he got in my brother's face. "Listen to me very carefully. I don't volunteer my time to those who plan on wasting it. You have a decision to make, Cyrus. Give your sister a few scrapes and bruises today or toss dirt over her mutilated body after the Collectors are done with her." His voice lowered. "And trust me, you would rather kill Elara with your bare hands than let Pollux have his way with her."

My brother's nostrils flared. Just hearing the Lunin's name put him on edge.

"He's right," I said. "We don't have time to mess around."

Samson nodded and took five steps backward, leaving us ample space to move. "That a girl. Now let's get to work."

⁂

There's pain, and then there's agony. You know, the kind that makes your teeth feel fuzzy. The kind that drives away tears because any small movement excites your nerves like a live wire, ready to zap you in an instant.

The physical exertion was unlike anything we had ever experienced. I vomited twice, Cyrus only once. Bloodied and bruised, Samson pushed us harder with each gust of wind.

Panting, I held my head between my legs while he sparred with my brother. A red stream dripped out of my mouth onto the snow when I lifted my gaze.

I grimaced at the morbid site. Blood mixed with mucus poured out of my brother's nose. He cursed when the ex-Collector's blade sliced through the sleeve of his shirt, leaving a large gash on his lower bicep.

"Careful," Samson taunted. "One inch lower and I would have cut the tendon in your arm."

Cyrus spit a wad of bloody phlegm onto the ground before charging the Solin.

The sound of boots sloshing in the snow caught my attention. I whimpered, trying to turn my head.

Idalia's white-blonde hair trailed behind her like a flag of surrender, and her golden eyes narrowed as she called the ex-Collector's name.

Samson dodged my brother with a spin maneuver, then held up his hands in a surrender stance.

She stormed toward him, snow spraying in her wake. "What in the hell have you done to them?"

"Ida, listen."

I did a double take at his gentle tone.

"No, you listen," she demanded, poking him in the chest. "I told you to train them, not break them." She inclined her head at the two of us. "I can't let them work behind the bar now. They're a mess. Customers will think I beat my employees."

I chuckled in my mind because any sudden movement kicked my pain receptors into high gear. *Idalia's right.* I looked at my brother before glancing at my own battered body.

Evidence of Samson's advanced combative skills decorated my brother's face. Deep cuts that would eventually scar covered his hands, and his long-sleeved shirt was torn, splattered with patches of blood. I glanced at the lower half of his body. A large rip in Cyrus's pants exposed his muscular thigh, and he balanced on one foot, his eyes scanning the discolored snow. *When did he lose a boot?*

I wiped the oily residue from my lips while observing the swollen mass on my wrist. *At least I didn't lose my hand.*

My shoulder-length locks were matted together with enough tangles to rival the time I let my little cousin use my black hair as a track for his Matchbox cars. The sleeve of my shirt had vanished, gone forever. I looked around. *Maybe it's with Cyrus's lost shoe.*

My fingers grazed the injuries on my face and body. A busted lip, split eyebrow, and numerous lacerations were gifts bestowed by Samson. A swollen eye, throbbing wrist, and bruised ribs were compliments of my brother.

Samson ran a hand over his beard while he spoke. "Honey, I know they look a little rough right now." Idalia arched a brow. "Okay, they look like shit," he corrected, "but I have to train them this way, so they have a fighting chance against the Collectors."

"I get it, but that's enough for one day. We're about to open. I can't let anyone see them like this."

"Fair enough." He pointed at the scarred tree. "I'll be back tomorrow so we can work on your aim."

I didn't say a word; my sour expression voiced a lack of enthusiasm.

Cyrus grunted like an old man as he reached down to collect our coats. He tossed the largest one to Samson. "Thanks again."

A mischievous smirk twitched at the corner of the Solin's chapped mouth. "You won't be thanking me when the two of you wake up in the morning."

My brother mumbled inaudible words as they shook hands goodbye.

"Elara." My head snapped up and arm shout out when Samson tossed me Jax's knife. I caught it with one hand.

"Good girl." He winked.

My brow furrowed. "When—and how did you take this out of my pocket?"

His smirk expanded into a playful grin. "You're not the only one with a few tricks up your sleeve."

I scoffed, waving him away. Samson squeezed Idalia's shoulder before stomping through the snow, his coat hanging over one shoulder.

"Come on," Idalia said, motioning for us to follow. "Let's get the two of you cleaned up."

ණ

My brother and I lay sprawled on our backs, our wounds covered in strange powders and ointments whose healing properties we didn't bother asking about.

Idalia barely made a sound as she closed the bedroom door and headed down the stairs.

Cyrus swore when his shirt snagged on the bandage around his abdomen. "And we thought Jax was a hard ass. Samson's technique is brutal. I don't think trained soldiers could keep up with him."

"Not likely. Though the Special Forces would give him a run for his money."

My brother slapped a hand over his injured face. "That's who he reminds me of."

I grunted, turning my head to face him. "Who?"

"A badass Green Beret or SEAL."

"Well, you are supposed to be at boot camp—"

"So are you."

I huffed a breath, staring at the ceiling. "It all makes sense now, doesn't it?"

"What?"

"The way Jax acted—all serious and shit. I guess it's an ex-Collector thing."

Cyrus's eyes widened. "I know, right? Samson's like an older version of Jax, only grumpier and more screwed up in the head."

"Speaking of heads. That story about the Lunin Seeker—"

My brother's face squished up as if he had smelled the inside of Samson's boot. "Don't get me started."

"Okay, then how about his mad knife-throwing skills?"

Cyrus held a hand over his sore stomach as he laughed. "I wish you could have seen your face."

I glared. "He threw those damn knives at me like I was the opening act at some twisted circus."

"Your face"—he laughed harder—"just sheer terror."

I curled my injured hand as best I could into a fist and punched him in his bicep.

He frowned, squeezing his eyes shut. "I probably deserved that."

"Yeah, you do, considering you punched me in the eye today."

His mouth gaped. "Don't make me feel guilty for following Samson's orders. The dude held a knife to my back until I took the first swing."

"Easy. I was just teasing you."

Cyrus draped an arm over his eyes. His words mixed as one when he mumbled, "You gave me a bloody nose."

"I'm going to tell Samson you're acting like a little girl again."

"Fine, then I'll tell him you paid more attention to Jax's physique than the lessons he taught."

My humorous mood dissolved. *It's one thing to bring him up in casual conversation, it's another to crack jokes. I'm not ready. It's too soon.*

Cyrus quickly switched gears by offering me praise. "I'm proud of you, sis. You did good today."

I ignored his compliment, counting the cracks in the ceiling.

My brother turned his head. "I never got the chance to ask. What's the secret behind our little trick?"

I hesitated, debating if I should share the details about my transformational shift. *You never keep secrets from your brother. Don't start now.*

I spent long minutes trying to articulate my new posture on life. Cyrus listened quietly, absorbing every word.

Through mid-yawn, I finished my story with, "So there you have it."

"I'm glad you found the key that unlocks our trick because it might save our asses one day," he said, finding my eyes. "But I'm even more thrilled to hear you've let go of those negative emotions." He squeezed my hand. "Your eyes look brighter—like you've made peace with everything."

"I don't know if peace is the right word, but I've accepted what happened to Jax." I swallowed a lump of grief. "Letting go of an attachment is hard." Cyrus verbalized his agreement with a loud sigh. I closed my eyes, resting a hand over my heart. "The good news is, I'm willing to try."

TWENTY-SEVEN

Don't Make Him Angry

I gasped, tossing off the covers. Like a sleep-deprived mother, Idalia's eyes remained closed as she grabbed my arm, anchoring me in place. "Elara, you're dreaming. Go back to sleep."

A hushed apology rolled off my tongue as I scooted under the covers.

Why do I keep having the same nightmare? I flopped onto my side and rubbed my tired eyes. *I thought the madness would stop after that transformational shift. A lot of good that did.*

Every night I dreamed of the blood-soaked hallway and tasted the iron tinge that lingered in my mouth when Jax uttered those cruel words through the invisible wall: *Wake up Elara. You should have never come for me.*

I shivered, gathering the thin comforter around the cold spot in my chest. Eager for a distraction from the morbid images that haunted my mind, I reflected on our time with Samson. We had spent the last two weeks training in the bitter weather.

Thanks to his unorthodox lessons, our combative skills had advanced leaps and bounds. We learned how to escape all the basic holds and dodge jabs and left hooks. The ex-Collector even taught us the art of wielding a blade. After a few private lessons, I could hit a target farther than Cyrus.

I always used the white knife when I trained but kept the gray one in my back pocket as a reminder of my new mission: honor Jax by defeating Zenith.

Idalia mourned the past: her first love and best friend. Meanwhile, I mourned the future: thoughts of what could have been. Cyrus reminded us, *Time has the power to heal.* We always voiced our agreements, but behind his back we'd asked each other, "Does it really?"

The mattress sagged as my rational thoughts mixed with dreamland. Idalia's curvy figure morphed into Samson, who then turned into a tiger with my father's head. I giggled in my sleep, watching him chase his tail, paws batting at the orange and black blur. With a mouthful of fur, he called my name. The vivid dream blurred but he continued to say, "Elara," over and over again.

I almost went into cardiac arrest when my eyes opened. Like a creepy statue, my brother stood over me. "Elara," he repeated. *Ah, that was the voice in the dream.* "You need to get up."

Not wanting to disturb Idalia, I whispered, "Geez, Cyrus, you almost gave me a heart attack. What are you doing in here?"

He blew out a tight breath, hands trembling by his sides. "I've got some bad news." Pollux's face flashed in my mind. "Sis—"

I sat up, eyeing the secret hiding place in the wall. "What's wrong?" Suddenly parched, the words got caught in my throat. "Are the Collectors here?"

"No." His eyes never left the headboard as he lifted a hand. "I've been tracking him for hours. There's a little brown monkey sitting right behind you."

Baffled, I spun around on the bed. Only an empty wall stared back. My posture relaxed. *Glad I'm not the only one having silly dreams about animals.* I turned back around. "Cyrus, you're sleepwalking. Go back to bed."

"No, I'm not. I'm wide awake, and you need to get up"—he tugged at my arm—"because I don't trust that little bastard."

I covered my mouth, muffling my laughter. "Stop it. You're going to wake up Idalia. Just go back—"

"Get down." Cyrus gasped, pulling me to the ground. "He's about to pounce."

My tailbone slammed onto the hardwood floors, teeth clattering in my head. "What the hell is wrong with you?" I asked, patting his cheek. "Wake up."

"I'm not asleep." Defying the laws of personal space, my brother placed his face only inches away from mine. "Look at me. I'm wide awake."

"Okay," I whispered, wiping the spittle that sprayed onto my chin. "Just scoot back."

He stretched his neck to see the headboard.

What is wrong with him? I scanned Cyrus's troubled face. The whites of his eyes were bloodshot, his brow furrowed, and his chest moved up and down with heavy breaths. *He's right. He is awake.*

My brother cursed, hitting the deck. Following his lead, I pressed my cheek against the floor. "Cyrus, you're starting to freak me out."

He tried to meet my gaze but couldn't keep his eyes off the damn headboard. I called his name once more. This time with a little more urgency.

Finally, he acknowledged me and said, "You're freaked out? That monkey has been giving me the stink eye all night."

"When did you first see him?" I bit my lip, feeling like an idiot for asking such a stupid question.

"Earlier tonight. I went downstairs to get a drink of water but grabbed the wrong jug. I chugged the entire thing before I realized it was Maragin. It tasted like—" His words faded when he hopped to his feet. Dashing across the room, Cyrus yelled, "He jumped out the window."

Idalia sat up, squinting to see in the dark. "Elara? What's going on?"

I climbed off the floor and took a seat beside her. "Hell if I know." I pointed to the window where my brother stood with his nose pressed against the glass. "Cyrus is acting crazy."

She reached for the lantern on the night stand. "How so?"

The cool light that filled my vision shifted to a warm glow when she lit the wooden wick.

I stumbled over my words, flicking my wrist at him. "He's not making any sense, and—"

"Elara." Cyrus's eyes lit up with joy as he tapped the window pane. "He's okay. The snow broke his fall." A huge grin crossed my brother's face when he added, "What a clever little guy. He's building a snowman."

Idalia grabbed my wrist, her voice filled with concern. "Who's building a snowman?"

I sighed. "The monkey is."

"What's a monkey?"

I burst into laughter, amused by the absurdity of the situation. *How did I get here?*

Idalia shot me a stern look.

"I'm sorry," I recovered, wiping a tear off my cheek. "A monkey is a furry animal that lives on Earth. They're smart and can climb trees." I cocked my head to one side as I observed my brother applauding the invisible primate. "Though, I've never seen one build a snowman."

"How did it get here on Aroonyx?" she asked, crawling across the bed to get a better look.

I wrapped my fingers around her arm. "It's not here. Cyrus is seeing things. He said he got thirsty, so he went downstairs and made the mistake of drinking Maragin instead of water."

"He's so cute." My brother's voice raised an octave as he waved out the window. "He's smiling at me."

Idalia groaned, dropping her head.

"What's wrong?"

"It appears your brother is having an adverse reaction to Maragin."

"You mentioned that could happen. What are the side effects?"

Idalia's face squished up as she ran her fingers through the layers of her hair. "It varies. Some lose their inhibitions, others become detached from reality." She inclined her head toward my brother. "The majority hallucinate."

Cyrus bounced up and down like a young child watching the circus roll into town. My lips pursed. "How long does it last?"

"Depends on how much the person drank, their body weight, and how much they ate prior to ingesting the herb."

"Idalia—how long?"

She grimaced. "Six to nine hours."

My jaw fell open.

"Come on," she said, motioning for me to follow. "Let's get Cyrus downstairs and see if we can get him to eat anything. That should help."

Idalia reached for her robe while I walked toward my brother. As if speaking to a distraught patient at a mental hospital, I softened my words with a gentle sweetness. "Hey, bro. How's it going?"

He yanked my arm, pulling me beside him. "Look at my little buddy down there. Not only did he build that snowman, but he made that igloo too, which we're going to hang out in later, after we race around Aroonyx in those two pedal cars he crafted with his little furry hands. He wants to ride to Zenith's later." Cyrus found my eyes and in a stern voice added, "But I told him that wasn't a good idea."

I shut my eyes.

"Isn't Rico the coolest little monkey? I bet you want one now."

"You named him?"

"Obviously. Why wouldn't I?"

I don't have the patience for this shit. "Come on, Cyrus. I need you to follow me downstairs."

"No," he snapped, glancing at the door. "I can't go out there."

"Why?"

"Hillary's standing in the hallway, and she's still pissed that I broke up with her, which is all your fault by the way."

I snorted and mouthed, "Ex-girlfriend," at Idalia. She bit her lip, heading into the hallway.

I stood on my toes and held Cyrus's face with my hands, commanding his attention. "Listen, Hillary is not in the hallway or on Aroonyx, and neither is your little furry friend. You're having an adverse reaction to Maragin, and it's making you hallucinate." My brother looked at me like I was the crazy one. "You need to come downstairs and eat something."

My arms fell to my sides when he took a step backward. "No, I can't leave Rico. He gets mad if he's left alone for too long and trust me"—his voice lowered—"you do *not* want to see Rico get angry."

"Then tell him to come with us." I chuckled, unable to keep a straight face.

Cyrus ran a hand over his short hair. "I don't know about that, sis. Rico is pretty happy playing in the snow."

Adding to his delusional thoughts, I cupped my hand near my ear and said, "Listen, I think he came inside." My mouth gaped. "Yes, he's downstairs now."

My brother paled when he looked out the window. "Rico!" he yelled, knocking my shoulder as he sprinted across the room.

Quick to react, Idalia sidestepped the Solin as he bolted past her.

"This is going to be a long night," I murmured, following Idalia down the stairs.

"I'm afraid it will. Should we pass the time with a cup of tea?"

"Sounds good to me."

Idalia headed into the kitchen while I stood with my brows touching my hairline, watching my brother chase after his invisible friend.

His behavior defines the word bizarre. Cyrus jumped on top of tables and crawled on his hands and knees, begging Rico to calm down. Apparently, the monkey was angry with my brother for not riding the pedal cars to Zenith's. I held my tongue, listening to Cyrus express his apologies to thin air.

Idalia rested a plate of food on the bar: dried meats and a couple of rolls, before offering me a cup of tea. She jerked her chin at a small table in the center of the room. "Let's sit over there so we can keep an eye on him."

The legs scraped against the floor as I pulled out a chair. I crossed my legs, leaned my back against the wooden slats, and blew into the silver cup, inhaling the sweet menthol fragrance.

"It's called Minlav," Idalia said. I blinked at the foreign word. "It's great for settling an overactive mind." I raised my cup in a celebratory gesture, then took a small sip. "And it's toxic unless steeped in boiling water." I spit it back into my cup. She laughed, taking a large swig of her own tea. "I wouldn't poison you, Elara."

I lifted the rim to my lips once more. "Good to know."

She turned her head. "Hey, Cyrus." He froze, looking at her upside down through his legs. Trying to hide her amusement, she said, "You and your friend should grab a bite to eat. I put a plate on the bar."

My brother stood upright and spun around. As if noticing the beautiful Solin for the first time, he dashed across the room and knelt beside her,

Getting comfortable, I slouched in my chair. *This will be fun to watch.*

Cyrus's eyes lit up with desire as he reached for her hand. I shook my head when he spoke in a voice deeper than usual. "Idalia, I think we should get married."

I bit my knuckle while she patted his shoulder. "Okay honey, we'll start planning tomorrow."

Adding to his embarrassment, Cyrus ran the back of his hand down her arm in an inviting way that would make any girl blush. Idalia kept her cool.

"You're the most beautiful woman in the world—in any world."

She tossed her hair behind her back, eyeing me with a look that said, *He's really trying, isn't he?*

I nodded.

"I think about you in ways that I shouldn't," he added. *Oh no, don't say it, bro.* "Like when I'm alone in the—"

"That's very . . . special," she interrupted, her cheeks flushing with heat.

Cyrus tucked a stray hair behind her ear. "I can't help it. Your eyes are stunning." His thumb brushed her warm skin. "Your face is beautiful." His gaze wandered to the Solin's cleavage that peeked out of her robe. "And your perfect figure makes me want to—"

"Okay, Casanova," I said, pulling him to his feet. "Best to stop while you're ahead."

Idalia twisted in her seat and laughed into her shoulder. Cyrus's elated expression dissolved as I dragged him away from the new love of his life. Hoping to distract my brother from his lust-filled thoughts, I suggested, "Why don't you hang out with Rico? I bet he's hungry."

Cyrus stopped dead in his tracks, ripping his arm out of my firm grip.

"What is it now?" I asked.

Terror washed over him, the lust vanishing from his eyes. "He's pissed." Cyrus pointed at the bar. "Look at him."

"Who?"

The same amount of frustration that seeped out my brother's pores the day I told him we were twins resurfaced in a flash. Voice raised, he grabbed me by the shoulders. "Rico, that's who, and he's angry because I left him alone at the bar." My eyes rattled in my head when he shook me twice. "This is your fault, Elara. You need to make things right between the two of us."

"How is this my fault?" I blinked after asking the question. *Are we really talking about an imaginary monkey?*

"You were the one who told me to come downstairs. Rico was perfectly happy playing outside in the snow. He wanted us to ride the pedal cars."

My patience slammed into a brick wall, causing my voice to rise. "I don't want to hear another word about the damn pedal cars."

"Elara, I can't take him yelling at me again." His fingers dug into my skin. "Please, you have to talk to Rico for me."

I sucked in a large breath and held it. I could hear Idalia's muffled laughter from across the room. *Just play along, it will all be over in the morning.*

"Where is he?"

"The seat on the left, near the plate of food."

"Stay here, I'll be back."

Cyrus nodded, a thin layer of sweat beading his brow.

I headed toward the bar. *How am I going to swing this? Improv? Yes, that's it. I can finally put that theater class I took in Maine to good use.*

I cleared my throat, speaking loud enough for my brother to hear. "Hey Rico, how's it going buddy?" I waited, then gave the air a fist bump. “Yeah, he told me. I know, racing those pedal cars to Zenith’s sounded like good clean fun, but there’s a slight problem.” I paused, leaning closer to the plate of food. “We don’t know where he lives. That’s why we should wait for Samson.” I hummed and moved my head up and down with great enthusiasm. “Exactly. We don’t want Samson getting angry, do we?” I shook my head. “No, we most certainly do not.”

My teeth dug into my lips when I glanced at Cyrus. He stood rigid with his blood-shot eyes glued to where I sat, chatting to an invisible monkey.

“You do?” I gasped, touching my chest. My brother took a step forward, ready to play mediator. “Okay, I’ll tell him.”

I hid an eye roll while hopping off the barstool.

“Well, what did he say?” Cyrus asked as I approached.

“That’s between me and Rico.” He shifted his weight. “But he does want you to join him at the bar.” I lowered my voice to a whisper. “And—he’ll forgive you about the pedal car race if you eat all of your food and drink some water.”

I could have sworn a ray of sunshine shot out of my brother’s eyes, or maybe his ass, when he looked at me. “Have I ever told you that you’re the world’s best sister?”

I groaned while he pulled me into a hug, lifted me off the ground, and spun me around in circles. “Stop it,” I begged. “You’re going to make me throw up.”

My head spun when my feet hit the wooden floors. “You better go,” I said, pointing at the empty barstool. “Rico’s waiting. You don’t want him to get angry again.”

Cyrus tripped over his own feet as he hurried across the room.

I collapsed onto the chair across from Idalia. "Allow me to apologize on my brother's behalf."

"It's fine. He's sweet and perfectly harmless." She sipped her tea. "That's the second proposal I've gotten this year."

"Really?" *Why do I sound surprised? I'm sure Idalia has men falling at her feet.*

"Yep, but your brother's was by far the most entertaining. Too bad he won't remember it in the morning."

I froze, the rim of my mug grazing my bottom lip. "What? Why not?"

"One of the side effects."

"Oh man." I grinned, watching Cyrus offer the air a piece of bread. "I can't wait to have a little chat when he wakes up in the morning."

"Be nice, Elara."

I flashed her a tiny smirk before sipping the lukewarm beverage. "I will, after I remind him how he laughed at me during Samson's courage exercise."

"Fair enough." Idalia rested her cup on the table. "Speaking of Samson, how's everything going?"

"Good." I grimaced. "Perhaps painful is a better word. He wants to send us to the North Village in a few weeks."

"I trust Samson's plan, but it still makes me nervous to think about you and Cyrus wandering around the villages."

I nodded. "Especially since he won't let us show anyone our trick."

Idalia's golden eyes glowed with the fierceness of a feral cat as she reached across the table. I winced when her nails dug into my wrist. "Elara, promise me that you'll use it if necessary."

"We can't, Samson—"

Her nails went deeper. "I don't care what Samson said. He has a bad habit of seeing things from one perspective. If you find yourself in a life-threatening situation, please promise me you'll use it."

The fear that flickered in Idalia's eyes was the kind that makes someone look over their shoulder in a dark alley, the kind that makes children check for monsters underneath their beds.

"Okay, I promise."

Our heads turned at the sound of Cyrus's bare feet thumping on the wooden floor. His chest heaved. Not from exertion but from excitement.

"It's Jax." His eyes shifted between the two of us. "He's alive. Rico just told me."

Idalia's lip quivered. Coming to her aid, I said, "That's not funny, Cyrus."

"I'm not laughing," he countered, appalled by my accusation. "We don't have a lot of time. Rico said we need to leave for Zenith's—right now, if we want to rescue Jax."

My nostrils flared as I rose to my feet, kicking the chair out from underneath me. Our tea spilled everywhere when I slammed my hand on the table. "Damn it, Cyrus, that's enough!"

He bowed his head like a scolded child and whispered, "Geez, don't shoot the messenger. I was just telling you what Rico told me."

My voice lowered to a growl as I pointed a finger at him. "And I'm telling you to get your ass back to the bar."

Without saying another word, my brother dragged his feet away from the table.

"I'm so sorry," I said, picking up my chair. "Cyrus is out of his mind tonight."

Idalia forced a smile, though her eyes watered with tears.

We sat in a partial silence for long minutes while Cyrus whispered to Rico about snowmen and Hillary.

"It doesn't feel like he's gone," she said, using the spilled tea as ink to draw on the table.

"I agree. I bet it's because we didn't get any closure."

She shrugged.

"Can I ask you a question?"

Another shrug.

"The couple at the bar that was talking about Jax mentioned a man's name—"

"Sharik?"

"Yeah. What happened between the two of them? The man said something about Sharik's family."

Idalia shut her eyes. "That's a skeleton in Jax's closet he never wanted to let out."

"I see." *I'll add it to the list.*

"I swore I'd never say anything to you or Cyrus." She sighed. "But I guess that doesn't matter now."

"You don't have to tell me."

"No, it's okay. I don't mind sharing, as long as you promise not to think less of him afterward."

"I won't. I'm aware of his troubled past."

The Solin tapped her chin, her eyes burning a hole in my face. A moment later, she leaned across the table and whispered, "Okay, so here's what happened."

TWENTY-EIGHT

Guilt & Mild Regrets

"Rumors about Sharik leading secret meetings spread throughout the villages. Treason is not tolerated on Aroonyx, so Zenith sent Jax to rectify the situation."

I scooted closer, my curiosity piqued. "When did this happen?"

"About nine years ago. Right before Jax took you and Cyrus to Earth. He was still the leader of the Inner Circle."

"It blows my mind to think Zenith let a thirteen-year-old boy lead the Collectors."

"It does sound crazy, if not foolish, but Jax was Zenith's Seeker, his prized possession. When we first met, I thought Jax was seventeen."

"How old was he?"

"Almost fourteen."

The Solin gathered her hair over one shoulder and used her fingers as a comb to brush through the white-blonde locks.

"Even though we were close in age, Jax towered over me. I don't know if it was his rough upbringing or what, but he matured a lot faster than the other boys his age."

I nodded.

"He fit the part of a Collector: tall, strong, fierce." She looked at her nails. "I think that's another reason he and Pollux didn't get along. Jax embodied the traits of a lethal killer, but for some reason, the ladies fell at his feet. Pollux, on the other hand, has never had that problem."

"I can't see why," I muttered.

Idalia huffed a sarcastic breath. "So Jax showed up at Sharik's home with Pollux and Elio as backup. Zenith told him to 'rough' up the accused just enough to get the point across, so the other men attending these secret meetings would see what happens when someone defies their leader."

I held my breath, afraid to hear the rest of the story.

"Jax knocked him around a bit, and Sharik tried to fight back. He was a Solin but that didn't matter because it was late in the evening. Jax slammed Sharik against the wall and held him by his throat."

My pulse raced as I remembered how he used that same maneuver on Cyrus during the night of their brawl. A knot formed in my stomach. "What happened next?"

"Jax said this darkness came over him, something he couldn't control. There he stood, squeezing the life out of Sharik while Pollux and Elio just watched. Those bastards didn't bother interfering."

"Why?"

"I'll get to that later."

My heel tapped against the wooden floor. Idalia shut her eyes for only a moment before saying, "This next part is what the couple at the bar was referring to."

I bit my nail, eyes glued to Idalia's lips.

"Curious about all the commotion, Sharik's family—his wife and son, who was only four at the time—rushed into the living room. When Jax saw the fear in the young boy's eyes, he snapped out of his trance and let go of Sharik." She clasped her hands.

"And?"

"It was too late. Sharik's son stood there in shock, watching his father's dead body fall to the floor."

I cursed, dragging both hands down my face. "That's a horrible story."

She nodded. "Jax said everything hit him at once. Realizing his error, he tried to resuscitate Sharik, but the Solin's wife flipped out and tried to attack. Elio beat her to the brink of death. She lost consciousness, so he tossed her body next to Sharik's, all while that poor little boy watched."

I rested my forehead on the table, the spilt tea soaking my warm skin.

"Elara." Idalia drummed her fingers near my ear. "You promised me."

My head popped up. "I don't think less of him. After hearing Samson's story, I figured Jax had a lot of blood on his hands too. It's just a messed-up story. That poor kid."

She leaned back in her chair and glanced at Cyrus, who continued to whisper to his imaginary friend.

"How did Zenith take the news about Sharik's death?"

Idalia blew out a long breath that sounded like a low whistle. "Not good."

"Why?"

"The mission was based on rumors. Zenith had no proof of Sharik holding secret meetings. He dispatched Jax to threaten the Solin, not kill him. Zenith's smart. He didn't want the people questioning his leadership, wondering why their ruler killed an innocent man in front of his family. The incident just added to his fear of an uprising."

"He hits the mark of every other paranoid dictator in Earth's history."

"Glad we only have one to worry about."

I picked a piece of lint off my nightshirt. "True."

"Are you familiar with the scar on Jax's hand?" she asked.

"The one on his palm?" She nodded. "The one he refused to talk about."

Another head nod. "As a punishment for failing the mission, Zenith sliced open Jax's hand with his own knife while Elio and Pollux held him down." She met my gaze. "That's why they didn't interfere that night. They wanted Jax to kill Sharik so Zenith would react the way he did."

"Jax kept so many secrets from me. Sometimes I wonder if I knew him at all."

She patted my hand. "You did, Elara. You knew the good part of Jax—the part he always kept hidden."

Remembering his confession, I looked my brother. "I think Cyrus helped speed up the process."

"Look at him over there, laughing with himself. Do you think he's still talking to that monkey?"

"His name is Rico," I said, biting my lip. "Don't forget or he might get angry."

Idalia's chuckle morphed into a yawn as she stretched her toned arms.

"Why don't you go back to bed?" I suggested.

"No, I don't want to leave you alone with Cyrus all night."

"It's fine. I'll tell him it's Rico's bedtime."

"Sounds like a plan." Idalia grinned as she reached for our tea cups. She stood and while walking toward the bar, she said, "Goodnight Cyrus, goodnight Rico."

My brother knocked a bar stool to the floor as he hurried to stop her. "Don't go," he begged, taking her hand.

She gave it a gentle squeeze. "I'm tired, Cyrus. It's been a long day."

"Then why don't I go to bed with you?"

Idalia eyed me as I approached. *Oh boy. Here comes Casanova's second attempt.*

"I can keep you company," he added, lacing his fingers around hers. "And instead of talking we could—"

"Not tonight, bro," I said, grabbing him by the arm.

Cyrus frowned, then pouted when I dragged him away from Idalia.

"Sleep well," she said, heading up the stairs.

My head jolted backward when Cyrus slammed on the breaks.

He whistled while patting his thigh. "Here, boy."

My mouth gaped at the bizarre spectacle that unfolded before my eyes. Cyrus's smile grew as his imaginary friend climbed up his leg. He then giggled like a school girl when the invisible monkey moved to his shoulder, apparently Rico's tiny paws had gotten the best of him.

I shook my head when he nuzzled the empty space near his ear. *I'm going to end up tossing Rico out the window before the night's over.*

It took longer than necessary to get up the short staircase because we had to let Rico relieve himself in the men's room, which was located across the pub; he refused to use the women's, telling Cyrus it offended him.

My brother motioned to the bed. "Are you cool sleeping on the floor? There isn't enough room for the three of us."

"Please tell me you're joking," I said, the mattress sagging underneath me.

He gasped, yanking me off the bed. "Elara, how could you?"

"How could I what?"

"You just sat on Rico." He ground his teeth while shaking his head at me. "Great. Now he's angry again."

A low growl rumbled in my throat. Enough was enough. Rico had to go.

"Cyrus, you need to tell Rico that your sister is about to get angry. If he doesn't cool it, I'll get Hillary from the hallway and let her deal with him."

My brother stood there slack jawed; the color fading from his pink cheeks. "You wouldn't dare."

"Try me."

Defeated, Cyrus crouched down beside the bed and explained the severity of the situation to Rico.

Pleased with my improv skills, I settled under the covers, a victorious grin lingering on my face. Only minutes passed before Cyrus collapsed beside me. The bus to Dreamland picked him up within seconds. I fell asleep giggling; Cyrus's arm wrapped around Rico was the last thing I saw before dozing off.

❧

I squinted. *How is it already morning?*

Yawning, I stretched my arms, the lack of sleep from the previous night taking its toll. My eyes, which felt like sandpaper, blinked as I looked at Cyrus. *I'm going to have so much fun when he wakes up.*

The floorboards moaned their complaints in creaks and squeaks as I walked around the bed. I looked out the window. The morning sun kissed the horizon. A pleasurable explosion of warm hues illuminated the space around the pub. My eyes darted from the emerald grass to the black trees. *No way.*

The snow had vanished. Not a trace of winter left behind. I pressed my palm against the glass—warm. *What the hell?* Like a mime, my hands glided across the pane with gentle strokes—still warm. *Geez. I guess Jax was right about the short seasons.* Only three weeks had passed since the first snowfall.

My head turned as I heard my brother stir. He tried to sit up, only to collapse back onto the pillow, his fingers massaging the area above his eyebrows.

"Hey there, bro." I smiled, taking a seat beside him. "How ya feeling this morning?"

Eyes closed he murmured, "Like shit. My head's killing me."

"Tough break." I watched his expression carefully as the next sentence rolled off my tongue. "How did Rico sleep?"

He squinted, the whites of his eyes even more bloodshot than the previous night. "Who's Rico?"

The world's largest grin grew across my face. "That's a silly question to ask, considering how much time the two of you spent together last night."

"Sis, I don't know what the hell you're talking about, but could you lower your voice? It's extra loud and slightly irritating this morning."

My shoulders bounced up and down. "You really don't remember anything about last night?"

"What is there to remember? I went to bed and woke up with a pounding headache."

"You did—after giving us an Oscar-worthy performance." He arched a brow. "Would you like the short or long summary of the evening's events?"

Cyrus groaned, pushing himself to the seated position. "Elara, I don't even know what you're talking about."

"Idalia and I wondered the same thing about *you* all night."

His blank stare confirmed the side effect of Maragin—memory loss.

My lips moved with quick words as I described every detail: Rico's short temper, the pedal cars, his proposal to Idalia—the list went on and on.

Cyrus didn't move, he hardly breathed. "Please tell me you're joking?" I shook my head. "Is this some cruel trick to get back at me for laughing at you during the courage exercise?"

I held up three fingers. "Scout's honor. It really happened." The deepening concern in my brother's eyes caused me to ask, "You really don't remember anything about last night?"

"No. I went downstairs to get a drink of water and that's it."

"Well, lesson learned. Stay away from Maragin."

Cyrus faked a cry, massaging his temples.

"We should get dressed," I said, standing from the bed. "Samson will be here soon."

"There's no way I can train today." He covered his face with a pillow. "My head hurts so bad, I can hardly see straight."

"That won't fly with Samson. The word *excuse* isn't in his vocabulary. You better man up and—" I paused at the sound of knuckles tapping on the door.

"Can I come in?"

"Absolutely," I called, my voice sounding in a higher octave. *Oh, this will be fun to watch.*

Trying to blend in with the bed, Cyrus pressed the pillow harder over his face when Idalia stepped over the threshold.

"I just wanted to make sure the two of you were up. Samson will be here soon." She pointed at Cyrus and mouthed, "Is he awake?"

I nodded, snatching the pillow from his red face. My brother cursed, draping an arm over his eyes.

"I brought you something that will help your headache," she said, moving beside the bed.

Cyrus didn't budge, his body immobilized with embarrassment.

"Here." She slipped a vial of liquid into his hand. "Drink this. You'll feel better in no time."

Cyrus forced himself to meet her gaze and whispered, "About last night."

Realizing my presence only made the situation more uncomfortable, I said, "I'll see you outside in a bit."

After freshening up in the washroom, I slipped on a pair of shorts and sleeveless shirt. I circled my arms and lifted my knees to my chest. *Ah. This is so much better. I can actually move now. I'll take the heat any day over the cold.*

I changed my tune when I opened the back door. The heat hit my face like an oven pre-heated to four hundred degrees. It was only daybreak, yet the temperature felt warmer than late August in Texas.

I did a doubletake when Samson rounded the corner. His short-sleeved shirt hugged his biceps, making them look twice the size they did under his winter clothes. Thick scars decorated his ashy forearms, and the patches on his gray pants mirrored poorly placed tiles in an abstract mosaic. Tight cords of muscle showed through the thin fabric that clung to his chest and abdomen, and his well-defined trapezius gave the illusion of a missing neck. The closer he got, the smaller I felt. *Damn, the man's as thick as a tree.*

Not one for warm greetings, he asked, "Where's your brother?"

I couldn't hide the amusement that tugged at my lips. "He'll be down in a minute. He had a . . . rough night."

"Explain," he demanded, retying his short ponytail.

Samson got a good chuckle when I disclosed every detail of my brother's performance.

He crossed his arms. "A buddy of mine had a reaction like that once. I spent the entire night chasing after his dumb ass. He wouldn't shut up about this damn tree. He kept saying it wanted him to tickle its branches." He rolled his eyes. "The idiot even gave it a name—Twigs."

I tossed my head back to the cloudless sky. "Rico Twigs. That sounds like the name of an indie band."

Samson's brow furrowed. "What's a band?"

"Sorry. Earth reference." It was only then that I realized music had been void of my life for over six weeks.

Our heads turned when Cyrus exited the back door of the pub. Dressed in summer clothes, he hurried to catch up.

Ready to give him hell, Samson asked, "How ya feeling lover boy?"

My brother shot me a fierce look. "You told him?"

Eager to remind him of the reason for my swollen eye, I touched my chest and said, "I had no choice. He held a knife to my back."

"Keep laughing, sis. The line's been drawn. I see whose side you're on now."

I slid my feet closer to Samson.

Cyrus tried to glare, but his light-hearted sense of humor got the best of him. He flashed me a warm grin.

"I hope your head's feeling better because we have a lot of ground to cover today."

"It is. Idalia gave me—"

"Will Rico be joining us today?" I glanced around the wooded area. "It's not snowing but he can dig in the dirt."

"I hate you right now."

"That's enough," Samson snapped, giving me a stern look. "I've got some news we need to discuss."

Our playful banter ended there. We straightened, our eyes focused on the Solin who twisted the end of his beard into a cone.

"It doesn't sound good."

Samson turned to face my brother. "Depends on how you look at it. On my way here this morning, I heard a few whispers." *That's never a good sign.* "It sounds like working downstairs with Idalia has bit you in the ass."

I stole a glance at Cyrus. He stayed focused on Samson.

"Someone tipped off the Inner Circle. I'm sure Pollux and the others will be here any day now."

A colorful four-letter word shot out my mouth. My hands buzzed with heat as I sensed my brother's emotions stir. "So what's the plan?"

"I'm sending you to the villages tomorrow."

Cyrus shook his head. "Samson, we're not ready."

"Yeah, I thought you wanted to train us for a few more weeks?"

His nostrils flared. "Yes, Elara, I did, but things have changed. Do you want to stick to the old plan and have a standoff with the entire Inner Circle, here at Idalia's? Or do you want me to advance your training today, so you have a fighting chance in the villages tomorrow?"

My stomach knotted with anxiety. Cyrus moved closer, a silent gesture of comfort.

Not waiting for us to verbalize our agreement, Samson reached into his back pocket and exposed the blade of his knife with a quick flick of his wrist.

"Things are going to work a little different today." He checked the sharpness of his blade with his thumb. "The time for casual training is over." I frowned as he circled his arm. "Knives to the ready."

TWENTY-NINE

A Glitch in Time

Cyrus winced as he swept crumbs from underneath the table while I groaned, stacking clean mugs behind the bar. Every muscle in our sore bodies screamed in pain.

Our day with Samson left us bloodied and battered as if he'd thrown us into a ring with a mixed-martial artist. Every few seconds, my eyes darted to the front door. I felt like a diver in a shark cage with chum floating around me. It was only a matter of time before Pollux and the rest of the Inner Circle rose from the depths.

"I think that's good," Idalia said, tossing a dirty rag into a silver bin.

Cyrus pushed a stool under the bar. "Are you sure? I didn't finish sweeping."

"It's fine. I can take care of it in the morning before we open." She blew out a lantern attached to the wall. "It's late. Let's head upstairs."

Eager to rest my aching muscles, I limped up the wooden staircase with Cyrus and Idalia in tow. My feet skidded to a stop when I reached the landing. The door to Cyrus's room was closed. *That's not how we left it.*

The hairs on the back of my neck danced in a phantom breeze as I turned around. My finger moved to my lips, silencing the two Solins. Quick to act, Cyrus stepped beside me, his amber eyes narrowing at the door.

The saliva in my mouth evaporated as I dug my nails into my brother's arm. *Something's wrong.*

Cyrus stood tall, his Solin courage emanating from his being. "Stay close," he whispered.

Remembering my training, I reached for the white knife in my back pocket, but my fingers found the gray handle. I tossed Jax's folded blade to Idalia before following my brother down the hallway.

I cursed in the quiet space of my mind. *I don't want to know who's waiting on the other side of that door.*

Cyrus inhaled a deep breath and in one smooth motion, slammed his boot against the wooden panel. The two of us dashed into the room, my armed hand outstretched.

My breath hitched. A young Lunin, no older than thirteen or fourteen, stood near the bed. His black hair was shaved close to his head, and his bright blue eyes darted back and forth while his scarred hands trembled at his sides. The window, which I never knew opened, swung back and forth in the summer breeze.

Before I could blink, Cyrus dashed forward and restrained the teen in a grueling headlock. "Who sent you?" he barked, locking his arms in place.

Idalia's hand shot to her mouth when she ran over the threshold. The Lunin fought against Cyrus's strong grip. He gasped, his eyes bulging from the lack of oxygen. Out of desperation, he met my gaze, his mouth moving with words I couldn't hear.

"Cyrus. Let him breathe so he can tell us."

My brother loosened his hold around the Lunin, just enough for the adolescent to choke and sputter.

Cyrus's lips moved near the young man's ear. "Was it Pollux—Elio?"

"No," he panted. "The other Collectors don't know I'm here."

Unwilling to play games, Cyrus leaned back and jerked his arms in an upward motion. The Lunin squirmed but held my gaze.

Curious, I took a step forward. "Then why are you here?"

"To give you a message."

Anger surged through my brother. He tightened his grip once more. "Kid, my patience is wearing thin. Who told you to give us a message?"

The Collector's eyes clouded with a mixture of anxiety and grief as he whispered, "Jax."

The pained cry that left Idalia's mouth was a morbid reminder of the dark days that had haunted us for weeks on end. My taunt muscles turned to mush, my armed hand falling to my side.

"You've got about two seconds to come clean," Cyrus warned. "Enough with the lies. We know Jax is dead."

The Lunin twisted in my brother's arms. Unable to catch his breath, choppy words formed into a sentence that sent a shiver up my spine. "No, he's not. Zenith spread those rumors in hopes that you would come to him to avenge Jax's death."

Shit. My mind flashed to my knee-jerk reaction the night I heard the rumor downstairs.

"Let him go," I demanded. "He's telling the truth."

"You don't know that, Elara."

"Yes, I do. He can look me in the eyes."

My brother gritted his teeth, and with great reluctance agreed to my request.

The Collector fell to his knees, his hand clutching his red neck. Cyrus counted to three before he grabbed the teen by the collar of his shirt and dragged him to his feet. "I'll make you pay with your life if I find out you're lying to us."

In a hoarse voice, the Collector said, "I'm not." He adjusted the shirt over his lean torso when Cyrus let him go. "Jax said you wouldn't believe me, so he wanted me to tell you this: Cyrus, remember Crystal Beach and Elara, remember the walk to Starbucks." The young man blinked, unsure of the words that left his own mouth.

I shut my eyes. The room spun so fast, I thought I would vomit. A cold sweat formed on my brow. *This can't be true.* I held a hand over my pounding heart. *Jax is alive?*

As if hearing my private thoughts, Idalia collapsed onto her knees. Muffled sobs filled the quiet space as she buried her face in her hands.

The past few weeks flickered through my mind like the season finale of a popular TV drama ending with Jax's death. As gut wrenching as it played out, I had accepted what happened, allowed myself to grieve the loss of the man I cared for—the man I loved. The negative emotions I let go of—anger, guilt, grief, and resentment—all resurfaced in an instant.

Without thinking, I rushed toward the Lunin, dug my fingers into his shoulders, and shook him with enough force to scare the living daylights out of him. My voice trembled, eyes stinging with unshed tears. "Where is he?"

"Zenith has him locked in one of the rooms in the basement."

I stilled as my heart sank into the bottomless pit of my stomach. *The nightmare. It wasn't a dream.* I shook my head back and forth, not wanting to accept the truth. *It was a warning—a vision.*

Through short breaths I panted, "Cyrus, Idalia, we have to go—now."

The Solin climbed to her feet, ready to rescue her friend but my brother said, "No, not yet. We'll leave in the morning after Samson hears the news. I'm sure he'll—"

The tight breath that passed through the Collector's pursed lips interrupted my brother.

"What is it?" I pressed.

"I don't think Jax will make it through the night."

Idalia rushed over. “What do you mean?”

“He’s in bad shape. Zenith and Pollux did a real number on him.”

The tinge of blood sparked on my taste buds, the nightmare manifesting before my eyes. “What did they do to him?”

The Lunin ran a hand over his short hair and stared at the ground while he spoke. “Ever since his capture, they switch off, taking turns in the basement.” Bile crept up my throat. “He refused to talk, so things got messy. Zenith brought out the tools we use during torture training.”

Idalia covered her mouth with both hands while I stood there in shock. Over three weeks had passed since that horrible morning on the cliffside, meaning Jax had endured a living hell for over twenty-one sunrises. *I’m going to be sick.*

Forcing the nausea away, I stammered, “He’s just sending you to find us now?”

“No. He asked me to come the first day they brought him in.”

Cyrus caught my swinging arm, stopping my palm before it slapped the Collector across the face.

My voice erupted with anger. “You let them torture him for three weeks before coming to find us?” Every fiber in my body trembled with rage. “Do you mean to tell me that Jax has been waiting for us to rescue him this entire time?”

The Lunin’s face fell. “No, that wasn’t the plan.” With cautious eyes he glanced at my brother. “I tried to leave, honestly, I did. You don’t know what it’s like living at Zenith’s. It’s nearly impossible to escape without getting caught. I’ve spent every second of every day trying to figure out a way to get here."

"Why are you helping Jax?" Cyrus asked.

"Because I admire his courage. He was at the top, the leader of the Inner Circle, and left it all behind for a greater cause." His pale hands curled into fists. "I hate being a Collector. My older brother forced me to join. Zenith treats us like the dirt he walks on. He's a horrible man." His voice faded into a breathless whisper. "I'm terrified of him—and after tonight, he'll have my head."

The hands of compassion cradled my aching heart as I touched his arm. "What's your name, kid?"

"Archer."

"Can you take us to Zenith's? Will you help us rescue Jax?"

"I can't let you go inside. It's too dangerous." He chewed on his lip. "No one is guarding the door, so I should be able to sneak downstairs to the basement."

Idalia cleared her throat. "Why aren't the older Collectors on watch?"

"It's not necessary. Zenith or Pollux are usually down there with Jax."

"Then how are you going to go unnoticed?" Cyrus asked.

"If we hurry, there's a small window of opportunity. I've been noting their schedule and they take a short break a few hours before sunrise."

I slipped my folded blade into my back pocket. "How long will it take us to get to Zenith's?"

"Not long. It's just past the West Village."

"I'm coming too."

Cyrus's head snapped toward Idalia. "Like hell you are." Her lips moved in protest, but my brother cut her off by saying, "It's too risky. The Collectors have no proof that we were here. The last thing you need is Pollux seeing you with us."

"He's right," I added.

She stood tall, unwilling to back down.

Cyrus's face hardened. "No. You're not getting in the middle of this. Thanks to Samson's training, we're more prepared than ever." He rested a strong hand on her shoulder. "Idalia, you've done more than your fair share. It's best you sit this one out. We'll send word as soon as we rescue Jax."

She swallowed a lump of grief. "You promise?"

"Cross my heart."

I smiled at their silent exchange, then frowned when my brother asked Archer, "So you're willing to risk your life to help us?"

"Yes, sir." I flinched when he popped to attention. "After speaking to Jax, I believe the two of you have the power to defeat Zenith. I'm convinced you need Jax's help to do this, so I'll do whatever it takes to complete the mission."

The sincerity in which he spoke caused me to act without thinking. "Archer—when this is over, I want you to come with us and start fresh."

A spark ignited in his blue eyes for only a second before dimming. "Elara." My brother gasped. "Absolutely not. He's a Collector. You do remember what Jax told us, right?"

"I do remember. He was in a similar situation the night he met our parents." Cyrus shut his eyes, an awareness washing over him. "And it was *our* mother who said, *people make the best decisions they can at the time, regardless of the situation.*"

My brother dragged a hand down his face before extending it to Archer. "Okay kid, it looks like you're one of us now."

The Collector smiled—he actually smiled—as he shook my brother's hand, accepting his offer.

Adrenaline surged through my veins when Archer's blue eyes locked onto mine. "Then let's go rescue Jax."

THIRTY

A Heartfelt Goodbye

"I'll be right back." Idalia spoke over her shoulder as she rushed toward the door. "I'm going to grab the extra knives and pack a bag."

The three of us nodded. I flinched when the window banged against the wall, its rusted hinges creaking like nails on a chalk board.

Cyrus slammed it shut before addressing Archer. "Okay, we need a plan. I refuse to walk blindly into Zenith's waiting hands." He crossed his arms. "You said the other Collectors don't know you're here?"

"Not that I'm aware of. Zenith keeps us on a strict curfew. Everyone was asleep when I left."

"What about your brother? Won't he know you're missing?"

Archer shook his head at Cyrus. "He's in a different group. They sleep on the floor above me."

"Okay. We can mark that one off the list." My brother stole a glance at me before asking, "How do you plan on accessing the room in the basement? Isn't it locked?"

"Only from the inside. Anyone can open the door from the hallway."

I stifled a gasp. *In the dream—vision, the door wasn't locked.*

My brother shifted his weight. "How are you going to get Jax out of the basement? You said he was pretty beat up."

"I'll have to carry him."

"No offense Archer, but you don't look like the strongest person."

I could have sworn the Lunin stood taller and puffed out his chest.

"I might not have your Solin strength, but I can do it—I must. The only problem I face is getting Jax up the stairs and to the exit. There's only one way in and one way out."

Noting my anxious eyes, Cyrus said, "Archer, if they catch you trying to sneak Jax out of the basement—"

"I understand the risk."

"What if we go in with you?" I asked.

"No. The two of you must stay hidden until I bring him out."

Idalia interrupted our conversation as she rushed toward us with Jax's gray bag in her hand. She offered it to Cyrus. "I packed everything you need: clean clothes, food, water, and the extra knives I kept hidden in that box."

My brother adjusted the straps before slipping his arms through the loops.

"There's also a jar of powder that helps clot blood and a vial of liquid for pain relief." She squeezed her shaking hands. "I don't know if it will do any good but—"

"Hey," I soothed, wrapping my arms around her neck. "It's going to be okay. We're going to get him out of there in one piece."

Idalia sniffled, pulling away. "Please be careful." She pressed Jax's folded blade into my hand.

"No. Why don't you hang onto it?"

"Because it's time Jax got his knife back."

I smiled, sliding it beside the white one in my pocket.

Archer glanced out the window. "It's getting late. We should go."

Idalia watched us hurry toward the door. Cyrus turned when she called his name. Like a scene from a romantic drama, the beautiful Solin jogged toward my brother, her layered locks trailing behind her in a golden wake.

Without saying a word, she stood on the tips of her toes and placed her delicate hands on the sides of Cyrus's face. My jaw almost hit the floor when she pressed her lips against his.

Stunned by the intimate gesture, Cyrus stood wide eyed with his arms glued to his sides. *Oh, come on, bro. Here's your chance. She's giving you the green light.*

A heartbeat later, his natural charm kicked his ass into gear. My face beamed when he pulled her into a tight embrace.

I lifted my eyebrows at Archer, who stood in the doorway, intrigued yet perplexed.

Idalia's voice quivered as she held Cyrus's hands close to her chest. "Please come back to me."

His pearly teeth glowed when he said, "I wouldn't have it any other way."

She batted her eyes, flashing him a coy smile. That was all it took for my brother to make his move, only this time he kissed her with a little more passion and desire than before.

Archer and I turned to face in the opposite direction. I stared at the wall while he observed the door that had detached from its hinges, thanks to Cyrus's less than subtle entry.

I looked back at the newly minted couple when Idalia said, "Now go, hurry."

As if struck by Cupid's arrow, my brother glided over the floorboards, his eyes glowing.

"Oh, and Cyrus." He spun around, eager for another heartfelt goodbye. "Tell Rico I'm sorry for not believing him about Jax."

Cyrus's bronze face turned a bright shade of pink.

I shook my head in disbelief. "Damn monkey was right all along."

Archer's brow furrowed. The poor kid looked more confused by the minute.

I waved a hand over my shoulder, motioning for him to follow. "Don't concern yourself with our strange ways. We're not your average Solin and Lunin."

The line between the Collector's eyebrows deepened, doubt clouding his eyes.

Spirits lifted, Cyrus threw an arm around the Lunin, who tensed at the unexpected gesture. “Lighten up, Archer. Our journey together has only just begun.”

THIRTY-ONE

Insider Information

The crescent moons hung side by side in the late evening sky. Their casual grins mocked our deadly mission with a shimmering glow as the three of us followed the worn path that led to Zenith's.

My lungs expanded as I inhaled a breath of the summer air. Irritated with the tiny beads of sweat that formed on the back of my neck, I slipped the hair tie off my wrist and gathered my sticky locks into a low ponytail. I frowned when it scratched my damp skin like a bristly brush. *I miss my long hair.*

Cyrus's fingers rotated the knife handle as we walked. "Archer, keep your eyes peeled for your pals hiding in the woods."

Ignoring the verbal jab, he whispered, "If only I could. It's too dark. I can't see anything."

"What about your night vision?" I asked, hopping over a piece of Clear Stone.

"I don't come of age for four more years."

"Right."

"Then keep your ears open," Cyrus said, surveying the area.

We walked in silence for long minutes before my curiosity moved my tongue. "Hey Archer?"

"Mm-hmm."

"Why does Zenith recruit underage Collectors?"

"I'm not sure. If I had to guess, I'd say it's because he wants us trained before we turn eighteen. Zenith doesn't allow the Inactive Members or IMs, as they call us, to go out on missions."

"Why not?"

He shrugged. "We're not a lot of help without our Solin and Lunin traits. Our job is to collect taxes and scout the villages for talks of treason. We report noncompliance and *lethal whispers*—that's code for treason—to the Upper Level, the AMs. That's my brother's group." Archer looked at Cyrus while he spoke. "He's an Active Member. They're at least eighteen years or older. The ones Zenith sends on missions. That group reports to the Top Level, the IC, or as you know them, the Inner Circle."

When I gave my brother a sidelong glance, he mouthed, "What the," followed by a strong four-letter word.

"We had no idea it was so structured," I said.

Archer tucked his scarred hands into his pockets. "It wasn't always like this. In passing I heard Apollo say that Zenith formed these subgroups after Jax left."

"Why?"

"No one is brave enough to ask."

Curious about the tangled web of the Collectors, I continued my casual interrogation. "So your brother's group reports to Pollux?"

"Only after getting an approval from Apollo or Oberon. No one is allowed to bother Elio or Pollux unless there's evidence of treason or . . ." The Lunin's voice faded as he shifted his gaze to the ground.

"News about us?"

He nodded, refusing to meet my gaze.

"Do Elio and Pollux share responsibilities? Are they joint leaders of the Inner Circle?"

Archer snickered, amused by my naïve questions. "No. Pollux is the unspoken leader of the IC. If you were a Collector, he'd toss you into the basement for asking that question."

"Noted."

"Pollux and Elio have worked together for years, but I wouldn't call them friends. If push came to shove, Pollux would use Elio as a shield to save his own ass."

That sounds about right.

"They are the ones who report to Zenith," he added.

Jumping in on the conversation, Cyrus asked, "Do you see him a lot, or does he hide out in his room?"

"Who? Zenith?"

"No, your brother." The Solin rolled his eyes. "Yes, I'm talking about Zenith."

"He usually keeps to himself, but sometimes he'll come downstairs and watch a training exercise. He doesn't stay for long. His presence puts everyone on edge, even the Inner Circle. At an early age, we're taught to avoid making eye contact with Zenith. If he acknowledges one of us, we're instructed to say, yes sir and do exactly as he asks."

"Is he trained in the art of combat?"

Archer let out an unstable laugh. I folded my arms across my chest, a chill climbing up my spine.

"Is that a joke?" he asked Cyrus.

"No. It's a serious question."

Archer ran a hand over his shaved head before speaking. "Zenith's combative skills are more advanced than all of the Collectors combined." I gulped. *Does that include Samson?* "And sharing both Solin and Lunin traits only adds to his skill set," the Lunin added.

"How is he with a knife?"

Archer laughed even harder at Cyrus's question. "Like nothing you've ever seen. Zenith can hit a direct target farther than Oberon, which is crazy, because that man knows how to wield a blade."

Perfect. In a few minutes, we'll be knocking on his door.

"There was this one time he came downstairs to watch Pollux and Elio teach us this advanced attack move." Archer pointed ahead when the path forked. "Stay to the left. It will take us to the West Village."

We nodded.

"You were saying?"

He cleared his throat. "Right. So Zenith was standing in the corner, minding his own business when he suddenly lost his cool." Archer kept his gaze forward. "He rushed toward them while yelling, *You're doing it wrong*, then disarmed Elio and threw him across the room. His head slammed into the wall, knocking him unconscious."

"What did you do?"

"What could we do? We just stood there in shock. And if that wasn't enough, Zenith decided to hurl his own knife along with the other one at the incapacitated Solin. The blades pierced Elio's thigh, leaving only the handle exposed."

"Well, that answers my question," Cyrus muttered.

"Did Pollux do anything to help?"

Archer flashed me an incredulous look. "Not a damn thing. He just stood there like the rest of us and watched Zenith pull his knife out from Elio's leg—only after giving it a good twist, then wiped off the blood on the Solin's shirt, turned, and exited the room."

I eyed Cyrus, my courage dissolving at a rapid rate. He tightened his grip around the black knife in his hand.

"The two of you need to understand that *no one,* under any circumstance, challenges Zenith. A few years ago, four Collectors were foolish enough to try. They thought an ambush would work."

"I'm guessing that didn't go over well?" I asked.

"No. Not at all. Zenith displayed their severed heads around the perimeter wall for weeks, until they were just skulls with brittle skin. He made us disassemble the bodies and string the pieces around the property as a warning to the other Collectors."

Cyrus clapped Archer on the back. "Thanks for the mental picture."

The Lunin shrugged. "Elio will do whatever Zenith asks, even after the incident in the training room. I don't know if it's because he's—"

"Brainwashed? Disturbed?" my brother suggested.

Archer didn't answer. He just lowered his head, feet guiding him down the beaten path.

I used my shirt to wipe the moisture off my brow. "I had the pleasure of meeting Elio the day he tried to kill me."

Archer turned his head, and when he met my gaze, an unspoken gratitude flickered in his eyes. "He was so pissed when he got back that morning. Someone made the mistake of asking him what happened." His tongue tapped the roof of his mouth. "Elio took out all of his angst on an eleven-year-old in my group. He dragged him down to the basement, and we never saw the kid again." Archer gestured to me and Cyrus. "He didn't want Zenith knowing what you did to him that day. My brother was on watch near the Main Hall and overheard Elio telling Zenith that you threw a torch in his face."

I snorted. "Yeah, it was something like that."

"Everyone knew he was lying, including Zenith. A torch doesn't leave a handprint burn on your face."

"What did Zenith do?" Cyrus asked.

"Elio, Apollo, and Ravi were punished for letting you escape. He's not as hard on the Inner Circle as the other

Collectors because they hold more value to him, but they all got a good lashing." Archer stretched his leg over a fallen branch. "Zenith calls his whip the *undresser*."

I raised a brow. "Do we even want to know what that means?"

"No, but I'll tell you anyway. The accused must keep their shirt on during the lashings. Zenith won't stop until the whip has shredded the fabric, leaving your shirt in pieces."

I shut my eyes. "So he undresses you with the whip."

"Yep." Archer stopped his quick pace, turned his back, and lifted his shirt.

My hand covered my mouth while Cyrus choked on his spit. As if someone had played tic-tac-toe and disregarded the O's, massive scars in the shapes of X's covered Archer's toned back.

I gritted my teeth as I looked at Cyrus. He shook his head, nostrils flaring.

Overstepping my boundary, I touched one of the raised lines. The muscles in Archer's back contracted. I apologized, recoiling faster than a snake after a failed strike.

Looking more uncomfortable than ever before, Cyrus encouraged us to keep walking.

"Why did you get that lashing?" I asked.

Archer let his shirt fall over his torso before syncing strides with my brother. "I made the mistake of asking for seconds during meal time."

I massaged my temples, wishing I could forget everything I just saw and heard.

Switching gears, the Lunin said, "Zenith praised Pollux for capturing Jax." I swallowed. *I'm not ready to hear this part of the story.* "That was the first time I ever saw Zenith in a *good* mood. A few of us heard Pollux and the others come through the door, so we hid and watched. Until that day, every Collector saw Jax as this untouchable being, the prodigal son who slipped through Zenith's fingers. There were rumors about Jax's combative skills outmatching the IC, so it took us by surprise when Pollux dragged him into the Main Hall."

I steadied my heavy breathing and my footsteps quickened, matching the pace of my pounding heart. *I can't ask what happened next.*

Too late. My brother jumped the gun. "What did Zenith do when he saw Jax?"

"I didn't see his initial reaction because Pollux closed the door. It may have kept us from seeing the bloodshed, but it didn't drown out the screams."

My fingernails dug into my palms. The anger I felt toward Zenith and Pollux burned a hole in my stomach. My boots thumped against the dirt, the casual pursuit turning into a militant march.

Unaware of my emotional turmoil, Archer added, "The screaming lasted for hours. When the door opened, I saw Zenith with his knife in hand, standing over Jax. Blood covered Pollux from head to toe. I'll never forget the wicked grin on his face when he dragged Jax downstairs to the basement." Archer blew out a long breath. "Zenith made my group clean up the gory mess in the main hall."

My voice cracked. "Archer, I can't hear anymore."

He nodded, shoving his hands back into his pockets.

The time for tears had passed, but I couldn't remove the black veil of grief that draped over me. My heart ached for Jax. He spent most of his childhood tormented by Zenith, and he escaped, only to circle back and do it all over again. *How screwed up is that? We're coming Jax. Please hold on a bit longer.*

A gust of the evening air swirled around us. The tree branches were like a swaying cathedral, housing a choir of leaves. Their bone-chilling voices sang in different octaves: a gentle swoosh, a firm swish. On any other occasion, I may have found their song soothing—but no, not during that night—the night everything changed. A failed soloist tumbled to the ground. As if paying his respects, Archer stepped over the leaf, refusing to disturb it.

We walked . . . and walked . . . and walked. When Archer mentioned Zenith's wasn't far, I assumed he meant a quick stroll through the forest—not a marathon.

Using my Lunin night vision, Cyrus scanned the wooded area. Archer's posture remained relaxed as he continued to share insider information about his life as a Collector until we approached our first stop. He raised a closed fist.

"That's a big village," I whispered, admiring the homes built from blocks of Clear Stone.

Wooden roofs capped the tiny dwellings, and glowing lanterns hung from silver hooks on each porch. Were they an invitation to come inside or a warning to stay away? The sight was peaceful—still. *Where is everyone?*

Answering my unspoken question, Archer said, "Inside their homes. People who live in the West Village don't wander around Aroonyx at night. Zenith's dwelling is only a stone's throw from the edge of town."

He sidestepped his way down the gentle slope; our boots slipped on the moist grass.

"There are four villages, right?" I asked.

"Yep. North, South, East, and West."

My head turned as I tried to get my bearings.

Cyrus kicked a cluster of dirt with the toe of his shoe, sending it flying into the dark. "Is the South Village the one with the large market?"

Archer nodded. "Idalia's is northeast of the South Village and southwest of the East Village."

My head spun with coordinates I couldn't follow. "So that means the cliffside is south of the South Village?"

"Yep, that's right."

Cyrus nudged Archer in the ribs. "I wish you would have found us earlier. You're full of useful information."

The Collector forced a smile.

"When did Zenith hear of our return?"

He let a gust of wind pass before answering my question. "I'm unaware of the exact date."

"An estimate works."

"A while back an elderly man came to Zenith and told him he saw a Lunin Seeker jump from the cliffside, only to return with a young man and woman. He dispatched four Solin AMs that afternoon to scout the area."

Slack jawed, I looked at my brother. "That's why those Collectors were there the day we jumped. Zenith knew we had returned." I shook my head. "He's known the entire time."

"So much for us flying under the radar."

Archer slowed his pace as we approached the village. "So you've been on Aroonyx for—"

"Um. What do you think, Cyrus? About two months?"

"Elara, I stopped counting after week one. If what you say is true, then four months have passed on Earth."

My adoptive parents' faces appeared before my mind's eye. That night on the beach, Jax told us we had six months to defeat Zenith. We now had four. A heavy weight rested on my shoulders. *How in the hell will we defeat a man whose name alone makes my heart skip a beat?*

Archer's hushed voice redirected my attention back to the present. "The quickest way to Zenith's is through the West Village. If we take the road less traveled, we risk missing our opportunity to rescue Jax."

My brother's lips moved along with his boots. "Then what are we waiting for? Let's go."

The footpath widened as we neared the center of town; a desolate, road-like route, straight as an arrow, cut through the middle of the village. Large establishments—businesses constructed of black wood and Clear Stone—flanked our sides as we walked.

There was something familiar about the foreign space, something I couldn't put my finger on. I eyed Cyrus, his expression mirrored my own: confusion mixed with possibility.

"Elara. Do you think?"

"Maybe?"

Our eyes went on a visual scavenger hunt, searching for the home of our birth. I reflected on my vision at NASA: old furniture, black wooden walls, the warm light of a lantern. A moment later I noticed an abandoned house on top of a hill. Lost and forgotten, it sat near an old windmill, the blades spinning in the summer breeze. Unlike the other homes, no lantern hung from its silver hook, and the windows were boarded up.

I squinted, wishing it were morning so I could use my brother's powerful eyesight to see the hidden details of my past.

Reaching around Archer, I tapped Cyrus's arm while pointing with my free hand. "Jax said he buried our parents by the windmill near our home. I wonder if that's it?"

"I bet it is. Look"—he motioned to the vast space—"that's the only windmill in the West Village."

"It's weird to see it, right? It's always felt like a dream."

He nodded. "After we defeat Zenith, we'll go and pay our respects." A smile tugged at his mouth. "Hell, we could even live there."

I blinked, taken aback by his change of heart. "You'd stay on Aroonyx?"

"I would if Idalia asked me to."

"That sounds like a good plan, bro."

I marveled at the businesses we passed, each one resembling the set of an old western with a medieval twist. An apothecary selling vials of liquid and jars of powder filled the space on my right, and a general store, offering anything from dull tools to the mugs found at Idalia's stood on my left. A tall establishment without windows sat at the edge of town.

"Archer," I said, pointing to the faded lettering. "What's that place?"

"Union Services."

"Thank you, I concluded that much when I read the sign. What's it for?"

"It's where a couple applies for a union."

I thought of the distraught woman Idalia comforted at the pub. "How does it work?"

"You fill out a form, stating your intention to marry. Then the clerk gives you a date to appear before Zenith."

"Like a court date?"

"I don't know what that means."

I pulled the hair tie from my ponytail. "Does Zenith go to Union Services to meet the couple or do they go to him?"

"Zenith rarely leaves his dwelling. All meetings are held in the Main Hall."

"What happens next?" Cyrus asked.

"He reviews the couple's letter of intent, asks a few questions, and makes his decision."

I nodded. "Do you know why he approves some couples and not others? Idalia said no one understands the process."

"I haven't a clue. It probably depends on his mood that day."

Cyrus's voice lowered as we headed deeper into the forest, the West Village a speck of light behind us. "Do you know why Zenith never filled Jax's spot?"

Archer shrugged. "A few of the older Collectors, the ones who worked with Jax, think it's because Zenith wants to fill his position with another Seeker."

I tossed up my hands. "Why is he so obsessed with Seekers?"

"Zenith idolizes Arun's reign. He's not an idiot. Over the last ten years, he's lost the favor of the people. Everyone hates him, and he knows it. If he can get a Seeker to jump to Earth and bring inventions back to Aroonyx, then he'll have something to dangle over their heads. He could create a desire that only he can fill."

Cyrus blew out an irritated breath. "The guy is so delusional."

"Perhaps, but he's always ten steps ahead of everyone else." The Lunin glanced over his shoulder before adding, "That's why the two of you are driving him mad."

"How so?" I asked.

"The IC always hits their mark when dispatched by Zenith. The guilty party is silenced and that's it." A smirk crossed Archer's pale face. "But capturing the two of you is like trying to catch a cloud of smoke. You can close your hand around it—but poof—it's gone."

I hummed my agreement while Cyrus said, "You're a clever kid, Archer."

The Collector didn't nod or smile at the compliment, he only pointed at the enormous structure ahead.

A clearing of trees stood like soldiers on watch, guarding the fortress-like dwelling. My eyes followed a wall made of Clear Stone that surrounded the perimeter. I shivered, wondering where Zenith had placed the decapitated heads of the Collectors.

"There's no windows," Cyrus whispered.

"And I don't see any doors."

In a hushed voice, Archer said, "Like I mentioned earlier, there's only one way in and one way out."

Perfect. The entire place gave me the creeps. It reminded me of an old asylum from a show about paranormal hunters.

Archer took a step forward, then turned to face us. "I wish I could say this with more enthusiasm." He waved his hand in a dramatic gesture at the structure and said, "Welcome to Zenith's."

THIRTY-TWO

Not What We Expected

Archer's blue eyes drifted between me and Cyrus as he spoke. "Okay. Let's keep this simple. I'll sneak in, get Jax out of the basement, and meet you over there." He pointed to a cluster of trees that faced a wooden door, the only way in and out of the fortress. "Stay hidden. Don't come to me, I'll come to you."

I rolled my neck. The heavy burden had given me a crick. "Archer are you sure you want to do this?"

"I made a promise to Jax, and I don't plan on breaking it."

"I understand," I said, resting a hand on his shoulder, "but we're here now, so if you want us to come with you just say the words."

"No. The risk is too great. You could get trapped."

"He's right, Elara. Don't forget what Samson told us. We can't defeat Zenith on his own turf. Let Archer go inside alone so we can rescue Jax the smart way."

I found the Lunin's eyes. "Thank you—for everything."

He shrugged. "My brother is the bravest person I know, but you're a close second."

Archer's entire body went rigid when I threw my arms around his neck.

He cleared his throat when I pulled away, unsure what to make of the kind gesture. An apology rolled off his tongue, followed by, "I haven't had a hug in over"—he paused, counting on his fingers—"eight years."

A piece of my fractured heart shattered when it hit the pit of my stomach. He was so young, and even without a loving upbringing he wanted to do good—he wanted a fresh start.

Channeling his Solin optimism, Cyrus stepped in front of the Lunin. "Keep your chin up, Archer. Zenith and the other Collectors have no power over you. True courage is found within." He patted the Lunin's chest. "And you have more in here than all of those idiots combined."

Our faithful guide extended a hand to Cyrus, who shook it firmly, initiating Archer into our group. Without looking back, the young Lunin jogged toward the wooden door.

We skirted the perimeter wall until we arrived at the designated location. My heart pounded in my ears as I peered around a tree, trying to get a better look.

"How long do we wait?" I whispered. "What if Archer doesn't come back?"

"I'm not sure. I'm starting to rethink this entire plan. What if it's a trap?"

I gasped. My head turned every which way until the practical side of me took over. "No. It can't be. Archer knew those things about Jax. He could look me in the eye." My brother lowered his gaze. "He did," I pressed. "That says something about his character."

"Let's hope you're right because if not, we're *fucked.*"

We waited for what felt like hours. Cyrus kneed me in the back of my leg every few minutes, encouraging me to stay still. Every fiber in my being screamed, *what are you doing? This is a horrible idea.* I flinched each time a branch snapped, fearing a surprise attack. *Okay, think of something else to occupy your thoughts. What about Jax? No, that doesn't help. Screw it. That's the only thing on your mind right now. I wonder how bad his injuries are. Oh no.*

I whipped around to face my brother.

His eyes grew at my grave expression. "What is it?"

"Where are we taking Jax?"

"What do you mean?"

"Where are we taking him after Archer brings him out?"

"Back to Idalia's?" I raised my brows at his idiotic suggestion. "Right. That's a horrible idea. The pub is the first place the Inner Circle will look for us. I don't want to put Idalia in danger."

"No shit," I snapped. "Nor do I. That's why I'm asking." I dragged both hands down my face. "Cyrus, we didn't think this through—like not at all."

He glanced over his shoulder. "Should we take him back to the spring?"

"Do you know how to get there? Because I don't." I lowered my voice. "Also, Archer said Jax is in bad shape. What if he needs a doctor?" Blood surged through my veins, flight or fight mode kicking in. "Can you carry Jax? You don't have your Solin strength."

"Elara, you need to calm down. I get it, okay? We screwed up by not thinking this through. Let's stick with the facts, not the hypothetical."

I sucked in quick breaths, my fingers clinging to the tree's fuzzy bark.

Cyrus tapped one of the straps around his shoulder. "Idalia packed us some medicine, which we can give to Jax. Hopefully it holds him over for a while. Archer is with us now, so he can act as our guide. I'm sure he knows where to find a doctor. And if I get tired of carrying Jax, he can help."

A moment of relief washed over me until I thought of Jax's familiar face. "Do you think we can stroll into a village with Jax over your shoulder and go unnoticed? The Collectors will be there before sunrise."

Cyrus's chest rumbled with irritation. "No, I don't. Do you have a better plan?" Tears filled my eyes. Recovering, he grabbed me by the shoulders, and said, "Everything is going to be okay. *We* are going to be okay, remember?"

I let his soothing words play on repeat in my mind while counting to ten.

"Better?"

"A little bit." I motioned to the bag. "Why don't you let me carry it? One less thing for you to worry about."

Agreeing, he swung it off his shoulders. I crouched to the ground and opened the flap. My fingers fumbled around a pair of shorts and a loaf of bread, stopping once they reached the tiny arsenal of weapons. "Let's split up the knives."

"Good thinking," he said, taking a knee beside me.

I handed Cyrus five of the ten folded blades. His large pockets accommodated them with ease while mine struggled to conceal the hidden items. I tightened the straps, then stood before slipping my arms through the loops.

Tired of waiting, my brother cracked his neck and circled his arms as if preparing for a training exercise. I glanced up at the amethyst-colored sky that peeked through the canopy of trees. Only one of the twin moons smiled back. I gulped.

An impending sense of doom washed over me, the same feeling I experienced when Pollux and the others appeared on the cliffside.

My head snapped toward the door, the sound of rusted hinges breaking the silence.

I held my breath. Out walked Archer—scratch that—he ran, as fast as he could, while supporting the majority of Jax's body weight on his back. The ex-Collector's legs dragged behind the determined Lunin as he hurried toward us.

Cyrus's arm shot out when I dashed forward. A reminder of Archer's stern warning. I waited.

Time stood still when the Collector approached, winded from the exhausting task. My brother reached out his hands.

I cursed over and over again, my entire body trembling. I didn't even recognize Jax. Both of his eyes were swollen shut, and the features of his striking face were distorted by deep lacerations and countless bruises. His pale shirt was torn by the *undresser* and soaked with blood. I couldn't swallow. I couldn't breathe as my eyes assessed the damage. His right hand had swollen to twice its normal size, and chunks of flesh hung from the underside of his biceps.

I bit my knuckle. *I'm staring at a corpse. We're too late.*

"He's still breathing," Archer panted.

I watched Jax's chest. It contracted with each shallow breath.

Cyrus squatted, then lifted the injured Lunin. He didn't flinch or make a sound when one of his ribs snapped in two.

My brother cringed. "Sorry, Jax." He adjusted the ex-Collector's tall frame over his shoulder and patted his back. "We're going to get you out of here now."

Desperation clouded Archer's eyes as he waved us away. "Hurry. You need to get the hell out of here." I followed his gaze toward the wooden door that swung in the breeze. "They know you're here. The IC is coming."

THIRTY-THREE

An Arrow of Courage

"Cyrus, run," was my only response.

Without hesitation, my brother pivoted and sprinted through the woods with Jax over his shoulder.

A familiar voice, one filled with rage, reverberated around us. "ARCHER."

Grabbing the Lunin by his arm, I whispered, "Come on, let's go."

"No."

One word—one syllable was all it took to shatter my piecemealed heart.

My fingers dug into the scars on his forearm. "We talked about this. You're coming with us."

Archer twisted his arm away from my tight grip and stood tall. "I'm sorry, Elara. That was never the plan." He swallowed. "Go. I'll hold them off and give you a head start."

A haze of grief surrounded me; I squinted through the burning mist of salted sentiments to see the young man who wanted nothing more than a fresh start. “Archer, please.” Determined footsteps pounded against the dirt on the other side of the wall. I breathed hard, the words expanding in my throat. “You’ve done enough for us. This part of the story doesn’t need a hero.”

A cold sweat mixed with nausea overwhelmed me when a Lunin and Solin exited the door. Pollux’s pale blue eyes stared at Archer with enough malice to knock a man dead while Elio sneered at me with vicious intent, the tip of his blade directed at my heart.

The three Collectors, including the Lunin beside me, froze when a loud bell sounded around the fortress. I covered my ears, nearly hitting the deck.

The small amount of color in Archer’s face drained. “The alarms.” He grabbed my arm, spun me around, and shoved me in the direction of Cyrus. “Hurry. Get out of here while you still can. Zenith’s coming.”

I searched for my brother, a silhouette in the near distance, then pivoted to face the Lunin and the two Collectors who approached. My feet danced underneath me like a thoroughbred’s hooves in a starting gate. “Archer, I won’t let you do this.”

“I know”—he pulled a folded blade from his pocket—“Jax told me you’d say that.”

I stumbled backward when Archer swiped the air with his knife, missing my abdomen by a hair. I dodged another attack as he forced me away from Zenith’s—away from him.

My eyes watered with a bitter truth. *Jax knew this would happen. He knew they'd catch Archer sneaking into the basement. The Collector told us he made Jax a promise, and the determination in his eyes proves it. He's not coming with us.*

"Just go!" he hollered, the knife trembling in his hand. When I shook my head, he lowered the blade and said, "It's okay, Elara. *This* is the type of mission I always wanted—a selfless one."

A single tear glided down my cheek when the brave Lunin turned to face his demise. I closed my eyes for only a moment and accepted the decision he made for me: sacrifice one to save the lives of hundreds.

Thanks to Jax, Archer understood the big picture—the purpose behind our endeavor: Only my brother and I had the power to defeat Zenith—the power to free the people of Aroonyx. Archer's selfless act was based on hope, and that alone gave me the courage to move forward.

Without saying goodbye, I spun around and sprinted after my brother. Three strides later my feet skidded to a stop when a pained cry sounded behind me. I turned. When Pollux caught my eye, his lips slid into an evil smirk. He pulled Archer closer, twisting his knife deeper into the young Collector's chest. Like a morbid dance, he then circled the brave Lunin around to face me. Blood dripped from Archer's mouth, his shirt stained with the oily residue. He gasped for air as he met my gaze. I held my breath, watching the light dim from his blue eyes.

Archer stayed strong, even during those final moments. He whispered, "Go," one last time, before meeting death with open arms.

My body quivered with rage when Pollux yanked the embedded blade in a downward motion, slicing Archer wide open from his chest cavity to naval. The smell of death—iron-rich blood—engulfed my senses. I looked away when Pollux pushed Archer to the ground, the young Collector's intestines hanging out of him like shredded ribbons.

Elio snickered at my terrified expression, unfazed by the brutal murder his counterpart committed. Pollux didn't bother wiping the blood from his blade. He stepped over Archer and used the toe of his boot to push the innards of the deceased Lunin closer to me, a cruel reminder of who I was up against.

Bile crept up my throat when Pollux lifted the rope of intestine with his foot. "What a mess." He kicked it to the side.

Wicked laughter left Elio's mouth as he inspected the mutilated torso. "Nah. It's no big deal. We'll make his brother clean it up, along with what's left of her."

The unspoken leader of the Inner Circle cocked his head to one side as his pale blue eyes roved over my trembling body. He dragged the smooth side of the bloodied blade down his chest and hissed, "You're next, sweetheart."

My feet moved without a conscious effort, guiding me with great speed in the direction of my brother. I didn't look back when two pairs of boots followed.

Elio wasn't a concern because like every other Solin, he would eventually tire, but Pollux could run forever. *I have to find a way to slow him down.*

The hours I spent training with Samson caused my body to react without thinking. I reached for a spare knife and exposed the blade while dodging a low-lying tree branch. I grunted, hurling the knife behind me.

Pollux didn't skip a beat or slow his pace as he dodged my failed attempt. The attack only propelled him forward, Elio not far behind.

My fingers gripped another black handle. Pollux ducked, cackling at my poor execution.

"You're going to run out of knives, Elara," he taunted. "And when you do, I'll be right here—waiting to play."

I pushed myself harder and farther with each stride. I zigzagged around the trees like a wild deer evading a pair of tigers who decided to team up for their next meal.

Elio's heavy breathing faded behind me. I expressed my gratitude to the universe, along with a silent plea while reaching for another knife. *Third time's a charm. Please help me.*

Hoping to catch Pollux off guard, I stopped dead in my tracks, spun around and hurled the knife through the air. The Lunin's eyes grew to the size of silver dollars but he didn't holler in pain when the blade of my spare knife embedded in his upper left abdomen. Elio hurried to catch up when his comrade fell to his knees.

I stood motionless, equally stunned as the Solin who kneeled beside Pollux with wide eyes.

The Lunin's nostrils flared, and he gritted his teeth while reaching for the knife. He shut his eyes and with great care he pulled the blade out of his stomach.

"Bring her to me," he snarled, applying pressure over the wound. "Alive."

I ran faster than ever that night. I had to get to Cyrus, the tiny spec in the distance. Elio voiced his complaints—a slew of hateful words—as he chased after me. Short minutes passed before his burning lungs halted his pursuit.

I glanced over my shoulder and found him holding his head between his legs, his chest rising and falling with sharp breaths. He lifted his gaze. The handprint scar on his face tightened as he ran the smooth side of his blade across his neck. "You're going to pay," he panted.

Ignoring the threat, I continued my journey. The remaining four knives shifted in my back pockets. I touched the gray handle and let out a deep sigh. *I'm safe—for now.*

I slowed my pace to a speed walk once I caught up with Cyrus. "They're gone," I whispered, breathless from anxiety.

My brother was covered in sweat, his face beet red with exhaustion. "I'm glad you're here, sis. I can't go any farther without sharing your Lunin endurance."

"I tried to hurry," I said, eyeing Jax's battered and broken body. "Pollux and Elio slowed me down."

"What?" The Lunin's torso swung to the side when Cyrus whipped around, his amber eyes scanning the forest. "Where are they?"

"They're gone." I urged him to pick up the pace.

Cyrus froze. "Where's Archer?" I shut my eyes. "Elara? Where is he?"

"Dead," I managed, fighting back tears. "That was their plan all along: give us a head start." I covered my mouth and spoke through muffled sobs. "Only I didn't take it. I just stood there and watched Pollux gut him like a fish."

"Damn it." Cyrus kicked a tree branch. It splintered when it slammed into a nearby trunk. "I'm going to kill that bastard with my own hands."

"Get in line," I sniffled, wiping the snot from my nose.

I stilled when Jax's body jumped with a quick jolt. Cyrus adjusted the Lunin over his shoulder. "Let's keep moving. We're still too close to Zenith's."

We jogged for hours through the forest, our eyes scanning every tree in sight, desperate to find the exit to the never-ending maze.

I waved a hand at the surrounding space. "Cyrus, where are we?"

"I have no idea. I thought if we headed in this direction, we'd end up by the cliffside."

I nodded, wiping the sweat off my brow. "It all looks the same—just trees. Why haven't we come across a village?" He shrugged. "It's almost sunrise. What are we—" My words faded when I looked at Jax. *Oh no.*

Cyrus's eyes grew, unsure what to do with the Lunin who went into convulsions.

"Put him down!" I yelled.

Cyrus squatted and eased Jax off his shoulder. I glanced at my brother, then pointed at the bloody foam that poured out of Jax's mouth like a volcano science project.

"What's happening?" I cried, kneeling beside him.

"He's having a seizure. Help me roll him onto his side."

"Should we put something in his mouth?" I asked, grimacing at the fluid that formed a puddle on the grass.

"No. That's a myth. It's impossible to swallow your tongue. It will be over soon."

I gnawed on my knuckle, waiting for it to stop. After a couple of minutes, the seizure subsided.

Cyrus rolled the Lunin onto his back after checking his airway. Jax wheezed with every shallow breath that entered his lungs.

My brother paled when he rested his ear on Jax's chest. "Elara, I think he's suffering from cardiac tamponade."

"What the hell is that and when did you become a doctor?"

"I signed up for this program at school that let me volunteer with the local fire department on weekends. On my first day, we got a call, involving a head-on collision. The air bag had malfunctioned, so the steering wheel crushed the guy's chest. When the firefighters got him out of the vehicle, they started to triage the patient. The man's heart sounded like Jax's does now: muffled—like it's trapped in a bag of water." I wrung my hands. "Cardiac tamponade is a serious medical condition—pressure on the heart from an accumulation of fluid."

"How do you fix it?"

"I don't know. They put the guy in the ambulance and took him to the hospital."

I cursed, my voice rising. "Cyrus. What are we supposed to do? Pick up the phone and dial 911? Find the nearest emergency room?" I gestured at the trees. "Look around, we're on another planet, in the middle of nowhere."

I started to hyperventilate when Jax's muscles contracted—another seizure.

Cyrus rolled him onto his side once more. A deepening concerned filled my brother's eyes as he stared at the Lunin. "Seizures aren't related to the heart condition. Something else is going on with him." Cyrus moved in front of Jax and peeled open one of his swollen eyelids, then checked his pulse. "Quick, hand me the vial of liquid Idalia packed us."

I swung the bag off my shoulder and hurried to find the desired item. After uncorking the stopper, I handed it to my brother.

Cyrus forced open Jax's mouth and poured the liquid down his throat.

"Should you have given him the entire dose?"

"Probably not, but it can't hurt, right? Idalia said to use it for pain." He rested a hand on Jax. "The guy looks like he could use some relief."

I groaned, scooting closer to the two men. "Let's hope he doesn't overdose."

Cyrus tossed the empty vial to the side. "At this point, it's worth taking the chance." He reached for his knife. "Let's see the extent of his injuries."

My brother sliced through the pieces of torn fabric, then peeled the remnants from Jax's bloody torso. I grimaced at the Velcro-like sound—dried blood sticking to flesh.

Cyrus blew out a low whistle while I threw up on the grass. Jax's mutilated body resembled a silicone mannequin that special effects artists use in horror films.

Deep gashes lined his chest and abdomen. Ribs poked through his pale skin, and his collar bone was snapped in two. Bruises in every shade painted his body like a morbid watercolor. Cyrus's fingers slid in the warm liquid as he inspected each wound.

"There's so much blood," he whispered. "I don't know which injury it's coming from."

I wiped the vomit off my chin and wrapped my arms around my midsection, rocking back and forth. *I can't handle this. It's too much.*

Cyrus looked at the stream that trickled out Jax's mouth. "I wonder—" He pulled the shreds of fabric off the Lunin's back as he rolled him onto his side. "Shit." Grief clouded my brother's eyes.

"What is it?" I asked, crawling around Jax to get a better look.

I would have thrown up again had I not just emptied the contents of my stomach. Evidence of the *undresser* was written all over his back, along with puncture wounds. I shut my eyes. The disturbing pattern looked as though Pollux and Zenith had used Jax as target practice.

"That, right there"—Cyrus pointed to a massive gash below the ex-Collector's rib cage—"is the problem."

"What do you mean?"

"The fluid around his heart is one thing—along with the other injuries, but this is our biggest concern." My brother wiped the oily residue with his hand. "Look how much blood is pouring out of the wound." He found my eyes. "Elara, if we don't find a way to stop it—he'll bleed out."

I touched the scar on my neck. "What about the powder Idalia packed?"

The muscles on Jax's back contracted when Cyrus applied pressure over the gash, blood leaking through the cracks of his fingers. "I don't think that will help. This wound is too deep." He glanced around the forest, searching for the answer. "I wish we had a match or something to cauterize the skin."

My head snapped up. Like a beacon of hope, the sun peeked over the horizon, illuminating the forest in a gentle glow. The familiar warming sensation flowed through me as I looked at my brother. "Give me your hand."

His eyes lit up as he gripped my fingers. "Brilliant."

"We're going to try something." I spoke near Jax's ear. "It's probably going to hurt like hell."

I pushed Cyrus's hand out of the way, replacing it with my own. Blood stained my pale skin. I shut my eyes and allowed every emotion to surface: fear, anger, resentment, apathy, but when I thought of Archer those sentiments dissolved. Hope and love filled the void.

The heat passed from Cyrus's body into mine, concentrating in the hand that covered Jax's wound. The Lunin's body writhed in pain while my warm palm melted his bloody flesh.

"Hold him," I snapped, refusing to let up.

Using his Solin strength, Cyrus restrained Jax with his free hand until I gave the signal.

With his mouth gaped, Cyrus fell backward when I lifted my fingers. "You actually did it," he whispered.

I inspected our handiwork. "No, *we* did it." The gash had closed, the skin glued together by a blistering burn.

A moment of relief washed over me until Jax's body convulsed for the third time.

Cyrus sighed. "We may have solved one problem, but I have a strong feeling these seizures are related to something internal. We need to find the spring. Maybe the water can do something to help—"

My brother's name came out in a tight whisper. He turned, following my extended arm. Nestled behind a cluster of trees was a small home.

"Who do you think lives there?" he asked.

A familiarity, the same one that knocked me upside the head in the West Village, resurfaced.

"I don't have a clue, but I think we should ask for help."

Cyrus ran a hand over his head. "It'll go one way or the other."

We looked at Jax when he coughed, choking on his own blood. It sprayed my face, the iron-rich drops stinging my taste buds. I didn't wipe it away, I only stared at my brother with pleading eyes. "We have to try."

Cyrus nodded, climbing to his feet.

"Please hang on," I whispered, resting a hand over Jax's heart. "I won't lose you again."

THIRTY-FOUR

The Eyes Hold the Key

Cyrus's Solin strength allowed him to carry Jax without breaking a sweat. We slowed our pace to a crawl as we approached the residence.

"Do we just go up and knock?"

I remained silent, observing the details of the quaint home. The frame was constructed from blocks of Clear Stone, stacked together in a checkerboard pattern. Wooden shingles decorated the chimney. My eyes darted around the front porch, noting two chairs near the windows. *I wonder how many people live here.*

"I'll go and knock. Why don't you take Jax and hide on the other side of the house? That way if something goes wrong, you can get a head start."

"Elara, that's a horrible idea."

"It'll be fine. I have a couple of spare knives along with the other two in my pocket. And plus, Archer—" I swallowed a lump of grief down my throat. Saying the young Collector's name caused me physical pain. I inhaled a shaky breath. "He said the Collectors live at Zenith's. It's not like Apollo will answer the door."

My brother's lips vibrated with uncertainty. "Okay, fine. Just make sure to yell if you need me."

I waved him away before jogging toward the porch steps. Taking extra caution, I peered into the closest window. A fireplace, couch, coffee table, and oversized armchair decorated the front room. I squinted to see through the sun's glare. A dining area housed a black wooden table with four chairs, and a tiny kitchen was tucked away in the back. I pressed my forehead against the glass and eyed a dark hallway to the right. *Great. It doesn't look like anyone's home.*

Unwilling to give up on Jax, I tapped my bloodied knuckles on the door, held my breath, and counted to five before repeating the process. Only this time, I slammed my palm on the wooden panel when the words, *I won't lose you again*, echoed in my mind.

My heart thumped in my ears when the knob turned.

An older Lunin poked his head around the door, his blue eyes heavy with sleep. He blinked once, twice, then asked, "Can I help you?"

I stilled. I knew the man's voice—but how? I scanned his unfamiliar face. Deep wrinkles lined his pale skin, gathering around his eyes, and white and gray streaked his jet-black hair, a gentle pattern of aging.

The man shielded his eyes, squinting to see me in the sunlight. "Miss, could you please state the reason for your visit?"

"My brother and I need your help. Our friend has suffered a grave injury." My voice quivered. "Please, he doesn't have much time left."

He flung open the door and scanned the front yard, the residual sleep fading from his eyes. "Where is he?"

The man gasped when I called my brother's name. Unsure of his reaction, I focused my attention on Cyrus as he rounded the corner of the house. Realizing I wasn't in danger, he climbed up the steps, his shirt covered in Jax's blood.

"Elara. He's barely breathing."

The elderly Lunin glanced at me and my brother before observing Jax's battered body. "Hurry," he said, motioning for us to follow. "Bring him inside."

We dashed over the threshold and into the home. I chased after Cyrus with my arm outstretched, trying to catch the blood that dripped from Jax's mouth with my hand. I missed. A thick stream, clotted with red lumps, splattered onto the black floorboards.

The man pointed toward the hallway. "Take him into the room on the left. I'll be there in a minute after I grab some supplies."

Cyrus rushed out of the living room and down the hall.

A flicker of hope sparked inside me when the man cupped his hands around his mouth and yelled, "Orion. Get up. We have a patient."

Patient? Doctors have patients. With wide eyes I asked, "Are you a—"

"Yes, now help me gather what I need to save your friend's life."

Tired of the extra weight, I tossed the backpack onto the couch, then jogged to catch up with the Lunin. In the kitchen he stood on his toes to reach the top shelf of a cabinet and tossed me various items that looked as old as dirt: rolls of gray gauze, clouded vials of liquid, a long tube attached to a glass syringe, and jars of powdered substances.

"Put these on the bedside table. I need to get my medical bag from the closet."

I nodded and darted toward the hallway, never taking my eyes off the life-saving supplies.

SMACK.

Everything flew out of my hands when I collided with a young man who happened to exit his bedroom right as I walked by. Not bothering to apologize, I crouched to the ground and used my shirt as a makeshift bucket to gather the items. The man followed.

"Forgive me," he whispered in a calm and soothing voice.

I looked up when he handed me the gauze—and blinked, only once. The Lunin, not much older than myself, met my gaze and pressed a vial of liquid into my hand. My mouth moved, but no words came out. I blinked again, transfixed on the young man's sharp features. His pale skin was flawless. Not a worry line or scar anywhere in sight, and his chiseled jaw rivaled the high-fashion models found in Europe.

His jet-black hair hung into his sapphire-blue eyes when he reached for a jar of powder. *Wow. His eyes sparkle. They actually sparkle.*

The Lunin's full lips spread into a warm grin when he offered me his hand. I couldn't look away even as he pulled me to my feet. *He looks like Jax, only younger.*

The sound of my brother yelling my name, followed by, "I think we're losing him," sent me darting past the stranger.

I grabbed the doorframe and swung my body into the room. Three strides later I was at Jax's side. I dumped the supplies on the bedside table, then turned and assessed the damage. His bare chest constricted with each shallow breath, and his skin felt warmer than the heat that buzzed through my veins.

I squeezed his hand that dangled off the bed and whispered, "Stay with me, Jax. You have to stay with me."

A heartbeat later, the doctor rushed into the room with his medical bag in hand, the young Lunin not far behind. Cyrus dragged me away from Jax to allow the men ample room to work. We stood with our backs glued to the wall like two medical students about to witness their first procedure.

The eldest Lunin moved with grace and ease while checking Jax's vitals.

"Should you tell him about the heart thing?" I whispered.

My brother cleared his throat. "I think the trauma to his chest has caused cardiac tamponade."

The doctor eyed his assistant and jerked his chin at the medical bag. "Hand me the needle."

"Pericardial synthesis?"

The eldest Lunin nodded.

I looked at Cyrus. He shrugged, unfamiliar with the medical terminology.

The doctor pointed to his patient. Without exchanging words, the young assistant grabbed Jax by the shoulders and moved him to the seated position. I frowned, watching the ex-Collector's head fall forward like a rag doll.

"That's a correct diagnosis," the doctor said to Cyrus while tapping his fingers around Jax's sternum.

My eyes went on a frantic search for medical devices found on Earth: oxygen machines, ventilators, defibrillators—life-saving devices. I scowled at the dated room. *This isn't a hospital on Earth. Aroonyx doesn't have advanced technology.*

"The fluid around your friend's heart is causing pressure." I stifled a gasp when the doctor inserted a long needle into the soft tissue of Jax's chest—he didn't budge. "So I'm going to drain it with this needle."

I grimaced as fluid filled the large tube. The medical assistant lifted the ex-Collector's head and held it with his hand. Blood pooled from Jax's mouth onto the bed. *Good Lord. It looks like he's holding a corpse.*

I shifted my weight and inhaled a deep breath. Perhaps a subtle preparation for the next few minutes of hell.

Before I could blink, Jax's limp body went rigid. As if possessed by an evil spirit or strapped to an electric chair, he twisted and turned while foaming at the mouth. More convulsions, only this time with greater intensity. The two men tried to restrain the ex-Collector, but their combined strength was no match for the violent seizure.

A colorful word left Cyrus's mouth when Jax's body fell onto the bed. My hand shot to my mouth. The needle inserted in Jax's chest had snapped in two. The doctor's eyes grew as he looked at the sharp piece left in his hand. Quick to act, his assistant pulled the jagged end out of Jax's sternum.

Working through the bloody foam that sprayed onto his face, the eldest Lunin touched Jax's forehead while scanning the other injuries. "When did he eat last?"

Answering for the two of us, Cyrus said, "I don't know. Why?"

The doctor pressed on Jax's abdomen, ignoring the chunks of flesh and gaping wounds. He looked at his assistant and pushed down harder. Jax's broken hand curled into a fist, the first sign of life.

I looked at the young Lunin when he said, "You don't think—"

The doctor nodded. "Seizures, fever, tenderness in the abdomen." He peeled open both of Jax's eyelids. "And look, subconjunctival hemorrhages."

I gasped. "What the hell is that?"

The doctor turned, his expression grave. "Bleeding in the eye." He used his forearm to wipe a bit of sticky foam off his face. "But in your friend's case, it's severe. The blood has penetrated the sclera—the white part of the eye. Watch." He turned Jax's head. Red fluid dripped from his tear ducts. I stilled.

It's just like the nightmare.

The doctor rubbed a bloody hand over his chin. "There's only one thing on Aroonyx that can cause this symptom, and of all the ailments I've treated over the years, it's the toughest one to cure."

Cyrus took a step forward. "Why?"

"Because the survival rate of Minlav poisoning is less than one percent."

My brother dropped his head while I stood there in shock. *Minlav. I know that name. The tea. The tea I drank at Idalia's. She said it was toxic if not boiled in water.*

A tear rolled off my cheek. It wasn't the lashings, the cardiac tamponade, or the endless broken bones and knife wounds that had put Jax's life in danger. No. It was something we never saw coming.

"Poison," I breathed. "The bastards poisoned him."

THRITY-FIVE

I Can't Watch

An eerie silence swept over the room.

Without asking me why or how, the doctor turned to his assistant and said, "Bring me the tube."

The young man nodded and jogged out of the room while the doctor shifted his gaze between me and my brother.

"The procedure I'm about to perform is not for the faint of heart. Your friend's body must absorb the antidote on an empty stomach, so I need to remove the contents with a pump." I gulped. *That sounds unpleasant.*

He went on. "Minlav is a highly toxic herb if ingested raw. A large dose will kill a man in a matter of minutes." He observed his patient. "It appears they gave Jax a small amount over a period of time."

We never mentioned his name. I guess he recognizes Jax's familiar face.

The doctor looked at my brother. "How long was he held captive?"

Cyrus stumbled over his words.

"Over three weeks," I clarified.

The doctor hummed while rubbing the stubble on his chin. "I've never treated a patient with this much toxicity in their blood."

"What are the complications?" Cyrus asked. "Will the antidote work?"

The Lunin checked Jax's vitals for the fourth time while answering my brother's questions. "It's hard to say. This is a first for me." He paused, listening to Jax's heartbeat. "Patients who ingest a small dose of the herb typically recover in a few days *if* their body accepts the antidote."

"If?"

The doctor found my worried eyes. "Yes. In most cases, a patient's body rejects the medication."

My pulse raced. "How do you know? What happens?"

"The adverse reaction occurs a few seconds after administering the dose. The poison attacks the antidote in an aggressive way. Internal bleeding in the stomach causes projectile vomiting."

I grabbed my brother's hand.

"And the pain is excruciating," the doctor said, tapping his head. "A complication with Minlav antidote rejection is hemorrhagic stroke."

My breath hitched. "What is that?"

"Bleeding inside the brain."

"Can you fix it?"

"It's a messy procedure. If Jax's body does not accept the antidote, I'll have to drill a hole in his skull to drain the fluid."

I eyed Cyrus, my knees wobbling. At a loss for words, he squeezed my hand.

Our heads turned when the young Lunin entered the room. He carried a long tube with a hand pump attached to the end. My eyes grew when he tossed a silver corkscrew onto the bed.

The doctor faced my brother. "I need your assistance."

"How can I help?"

"This is a very unpleasant procedure for the patient. I need you to use your Solin strength to restrain Jax while I insert the tube down his throat." He looked at his assistant. "My son will work the pump."

Son? I did a doubletake. How did I not catch the resemblance?

My brother hurried to the bed and with great care climbed on top of Jax. Using the ground-hold technique Samson taught us, Cyrus pinned Jax's bloodied arms to his sides while wrapping his legs around his hips.

"Are you ready?" the doctor asked Cyrus.

My brother tightened his grip. "Yeah. Let's do this."

I sucked in a sharp breath and held it when the doctor inserted the tube down the ex-Collector's throat. Had it not been for Cyrus's strength, Jax's writhing body would have thrown him off the bed.

I covered my mouth, unable to look away from the madness that unfolded when the doctor's son started the handpump. Bloody mucus with chunks of debris filled the container. *I'm going to be sick.*

"Keep him still," the doctor instructed, holding the tube steady.

My brother's fingers dug into bits of bone and torn flesh as he pushed Jax deeper into the mattress.

"Orion. Hurry, the antidote."

A foul-smelling odor filled the room when the doctor's son unscrewed the vessel that housed the contents of Jax's stomach. I gagged. The fluid spilled all over the floor when Orion rested it on the nightstand. He then retrieved a large vial from the medical bag and poured the clear liquid into a fresh container before screwing it back onto the pump.

I shuddered a breath when the doctor said, "Okay. Here goes nothing."

Orion flipped a switch, reversing the process. My eyes followed the antidote as it traveled from the pump to the tube and down Jax's throat. I bobbed up and down, counting down from ten. I only got to three before hell unleashed its demons.

The assistant cursed, and the doctor froze.

"Get back," Orion demanded, motioning for Cyrus to move.

My brother sat up, his legs still wrapped around the ex-Collector's hips. The doctor worked faster than he had all day, and in one smooth motion, he pulled the tube from Jax's throat.

Words can't describe the horror I witnessed that morning. Black vomit the color of death shot out of Jax's mouth in a violent stream, covering my brother from head to naval. He fell backward onto the bed, the chunks dripping from his gaped mouth. The smell was atrocious. I turned my head and emptied the rest of my last meal onto the floor.

The doctor barked commands at my brother. "Cyrus, roll him onto his side so he's facing the wall."

My brother nodded, then paled. Another round of onyx-colored vomit splattered his face. Powering through, he wiped his eyes and followed the doctor's orders.

"Orion, hand me the tool."

What about anesthesia? I trembled. *Please don't tell me they're going to drill a hole in his head while he's awake.*

The doctor rolled his wrists, then checked the steadiness of his hands. A surgeon's dream; they didn't shake, they didn't move. I gulped. *He's going to do it.*

"Point of entry?" Orion asked, handing his father the corkscrew.

He paused, then said, "Left side," after Jax's right arm twitched involuntarily.

The young Lunin nodded and placed a bed pan on the floor in front of his father when he kneeled beside Jax. The doctor moved into position, pressing the sharp end of the tool against the back of Jax's head. I bit my knuckles, the sour taste of retch lingering in my mouth.

He looked up at Cyrus. "Your friend's life is in grave danger. This procedure can cause neurogenic shock. It's crucial that you keep him still. There will be blood—and lots of it. Are you up for the task?"

My fearless twin eyed me over his shoulder, and when I met his gaze, he said, "Absolutely. I'll do whatever it takes."

THIRTY-SIX

Full Circle

I saw stars, flecks of silver and gold, when the doctor twisted the handle. Over three weeks had passed since I heard Jax's voice, and the sound of his bloodcurdling screams sent me falling to my knees.

Without stopping the procedure, the doctor said, "Orion, get her out of here."

The young man climbed to his feet, grabbed my arm, and dragged me out of the bedroom. One of his hands held my waist, steadying my trembling body. I winced at the shouting that echoed down the hallway.

"Hold him tight. I'm almost through the skull."

Orion guided me toward the front door. "Come on, let's get you outside."

The dry heat knocked me in the face like a two by four when we stepped onto the porch. I held my head between my legs. *I can't breathe.*

"Easy," Orion soothed. "Deep breaths. In and out."

I focused on his voice, my shoulders rising and falling.

"I know it looked pretty bleak back there, but my father is—was, the best doctor on Aroonyx."

"Was?"

"Yes, he's retired now. If anyone can save your friend's life, it's Iah."

I stilled. "Your father's name is Iah?"

He nodded, helping me move to the upright position. *Iah. That was the name of the doctor Cressida worked for, the name that sent Zenith spiraling out of control. He's the doctor who delivered twins during the bi-lunar eclipse—the doctor who delivered . . . us.*

Orion touched my shoulder. "Are you okay?"

That's why I recognized his voice. The reason I felt safe knocking on the door.

The Lunin repeated his question.

"I'm not sure."

He gestured to a chair by the window. "Why don't you take a seat? I think you're experience a bit of post-traumatic stress."

Like a lost soul, I floated across the porch, my feet dragging behind me like heavy chains. The wooden slats creaked underneath my weight as I collapsed onto the chair. With a numb mind, I stared into the forest.

Orion rested his hand on top of mine. I didn't flinch at his gentle touch. "Waiting is the hardest part," he said, patting my clammy skin. "You're not alone, okay? I'm here now."

The kindness in his voice draped over me like a warm towel after a shower on a winter's night. We had never met, but his calming presence lifted the fog of hopelessness that engulfed me.

We sat in silence; mindless chatter wasn't appropriate under the given circumstance. Beads of moisture formed on the back of my neck and brow. I gathered my matted hair, crusted with blood, into a low ponytail, then used a layer of sweat to keep the stray pieces from falling into my eyes.

I glanced at the Lunin, amazed at his comfort level with the warm weather. His hands rested casually on his lap, and his crème-colored shirt and toned forearms were free of moisture—save for the blood and vomit that stained his pale skin. Pleading with the universe, I leaned my head against the back of the chair and shut my eyes. *Please let him live. We've come so far. I can't bear—*

The front door swung open. Out dashed Cyrus, his hands and face covered in blood. "Your father needs help with the—" He snapped his fingers at Orion.

"Sutures?"

My brother nodded.

Like a doctor paged at a hospital, Orion hopped to his feet and rushed into the house.

Cyrus watched him go, then dropped his head. He pressed the blood-stained heels of his palms into his eyes after lowering himself onto the seat beside me.

"That was the hardest thing I've ever done."

"Did he drain the fluid?" I asked.

My brother fanned his stained shirt. "Yeah, and he tried something new that—" He shut his eyes.

"What did he do?"

"A new procedure. One he's never performed on a patient." I straightened. My brother scrubbed his weary face. "Elara, it was horrible. After he drained the blood from Jax's brain, he grabbed a syringe and filled it with more antidote."

"Why? I thought his body had already rejected the medication."

The Solin shrugged. "He said Jax's heart was failing, along with his other internal organs, so he had to try." Unshed tears stung my eyes. My brother leaned forward and dropped his head in his hands. "The doctor inserted the antidote directly into Jax's brain."

I swore, squeezing my eyes shut. "Is that even possible?"

"It is now."

"Did it work?"

Cyrus shifted his gaze to the woods. The ball of grief lodged in my throat expanded. I tried to swallow. No luck.

"Only time will tell," Cyrus whispered. "That's what the doctor said."

I sat there in a state of shock, my mind flipping through a photo album of memories, both pleasant and painful: the day I saw Jax standing outside my bedroom window, the first time Cyrus tapped me on the shoulder at school, our life-changing night at Crystal beach, and the shit storm that hit us after jumping to Aroonyx. I had lost Jax only to fear losing him again. An expression of the memories rolled off my cheek.

"Cyrus, how did we get here?"

Staring at the motionless tree limbs, he murmured, "I was just wondering the same thing."

"After today's drama, I don't think I can handle any more."

My brother's strong and optimistic attitude faded as he reached for my hand. "I know, sis. It's wearing on me too."

"The doctor's name is Iah."

Cyrus twisted in his seat. "What did you say?"

"You heard me."

"Wait." He blinked. "Does that mean—"

I nodded.

Cyrus blew out a low whistle. "Damn, it's like we've come full circle."

I looked up when a sudden gust of wind whipped through the forest, the tree branches hollering their complaints. The air temperature dropped, cooling my tepid skin. Ominous rain clouds gathered in a dense formation, their gray puffs blocking out the morning sunlight. I flinched at a flash of lightning, preparing for the crack of thunder.

BOOM.

It shook the entire house. I eyed Cyrus, an uneasiness settling in my bones.

"You're right about us coming full circle," I whispered. Another streak of silver danced across the sky, the light glowing in my brother's eyes. "Let's hope history doesn't repeat itself this time."

THIRTY-SEVEN

A Tangled Past

The heavy downpour slapped at our faces with each gust of wind. I didn't shield myself from the cleansing rain. I just sat there, soaking wet.

Cyrus's hand gripped the wooden armrest. The blood that dripped off his tan skin onto the Clear Stone floor, reminded me of a ruined canvas, one a painter destroyed by dousing it with water.

I shifted my weight. The rain thumped against the roof of the small home, and every so often the rolling thunder interrupted its efforts.

Long minutes passed before the front door opened. We groaned, climbing to our feet, our muscles stiff from sitting for so long. I wiped the water from my face while Cyrus stretched and popped his neck. The two of us kept our heads down as we approached Iah and Orion.

The doctor slid his gaze between me and my brother as he dried his bloodied hands on a gray rag. "Jax is stable." Our heads popped up. "His body accepted the antidote after it was administered through the brain."

I threw my arms around Iah's neck. He stumbled backward, surprised by my Solin strength.

Making the connection, he said to Cyrus, "Had I known, I would have asked your sister to help you restrain Jax."

My head shook back and forth with great speed. "You saw me in there. I wasn't much help at all."

"How do you know we're related?" Cyrus asked, crossing his arms.

"I knew when Elara called your name. I've assisted with many births on Aroonyx, but I'll never forget the twins I delivered during the bi-lunar eclipse. Your parents named you the moment they held you in their arms."

"Told you it was him," I said, nudging Cyrus in the ribs.

"How did you discover my identity?"

I jerked my chin at the house. "Jax. He told us the story about what happened with Cressida. When Orion told me your name, I put two and two together."

"I'm so sorry," he whispered, grief clouding his eyes. "Had I known, I would have stopped her from going to Zenith."

I touched his arm. "It's okay. It was out of your control."

"I'll keep telling myself that." Switching gears, he turned his attention to my brother. "You kept a clear head during a stressful procedure. Have you ever thought of practicing medicine?"

Cyrus arched a brow, followed by a sarcastic laugh. "No. And after today—hell no."

"Understood." Iah smiled, patting him on the back. "The medical field isn't for everyone."

I rocked back and forth. The question formed on my tongue faster than I anticipated. "So doc, what's the final diagnosis?"

"Get ready to take notes." Iah handed Orion the blood-soaked rag. "Besides the Minlav poisoning and the cardiac tamponade, your friend has suffered the following injuries: nine broken ribs, a broken clavicle, a fractured nose, shattered hand, blunt trauma to both eyes, internal bleeding, and numerous lacerations and knife wounds that took over 127 stitches to close."

"And he's still alive?" Cyrus stammered.

"Yes. I'm aware this list sounds—"

"Horrible?" I added.

"It does, but over time Jax will recover."

"Can I see him now?"

"No."

I sighed, wrapping my arms around my mid-section.

"Your friend needs time to rest. I gave him something to induce a mild coma. He'll be out for a few days. The antidote is strong, and the side effects of a direct injection into the brain are unknown. This was a new procedure for me, so I must watch him carefully."

Orion stole a cautious glance at his father.

"What is it?" I asked, my eyes darting between the two men.

Iah cleared his throat. "There's something you must understand about the healing process."

"We're listening." Cyrus widened his stance.

"Over the past few weeks, Jax has experienced more physical and mental stress than most people could handle." He tapped his chest. "I'm only a medical doctor, but I've spent enough time studying the human body to know the mind takes the longest to heal."

Damn. I never thought about his mental state.

The doctor found my eyes. "Elara, Jax's path to recovery will be long and hard. Probably tougher than anything he's ever faced."

"Right," was all I could say.

"I'm assuming the two of you need a place to stay while he recovers?"

Cyrus grimaced when I caught his eye.

"We appreciate the offer, Iah, but the last thing we want to do is put you and Orion in danger." I motioned to me and my brother. "We're sort of on Zenith's shit list right now."

The young Lunin chuckled, a flash of lightning shimmering in his sapphire eyes. "We live in the middle of nowhere." He waved a hand at the surrounding trees. "The Collectors won't find you here."

"That's why it took me so long to come to the door," Iah added. "We never have visitors."

"Can you give me a general idea of where we are?" Cyrus asked, craning his neck around the porch railing. "I've lost all sense of direction."

"We're southeast of the East Village."

Slack jawed, I turned to my brother. "We ran clear across Aroonyx."

"Figures."

"We'll stay, as long as you're comfortable housing wanted criminals."

More quiet amusement sounded in Orion's throat.

"I'm serious," I added. "If Zenith finds out, he'll have your heads for committing treason."

"Let's not worry about the hypothetical, my dear. We'll cross that bridge *if* we get there."

"Listen to the doctor," Cyrus whispered, a smirk tugging at his mouth. "He's a smart man—like your brother."

I scoffed, punching him in the arm.

He smiled for only a moment before frowning. "What about Idalia? We need to send word and tell her we're safe."

"Do either of you know her?" I asked the two men.

Orion's face lit up like the Fourth of July when he said, "Yeah, everyone does."

The muscles in my brother's arms tensed, his eyes narrowing on the Lunin. *I guess I'm not the only twin who gets a little jealous.* I bit my lip, trying to contain my laughter.

"Idalia was kind enough to let us stay with her after the Inner Circle captured Jax. We promised to call—send word once we were safe."

"I can leave tomorrow," Orion suggested. "It's always nice to pay her a visit."

A wave of heat rippled through me. I eyed my brother. His nostrils flared like a bull searching for a matador.

"Thank you, Orion," I said, amusement plastered all over my face. "That means a lot to us." I turned my head. "Doesn't it, Cyrus?"

"Mm-hmm."

I snorted at his ice-cold response.

Orion cocked his head to one side. "What's so funny?"

"Oh . . . you know . . . life?" Both Lunins flashed me questionable looks. Recovering, I added, "It's been a long day. I'm pretty tired after—"

"Then let's get you inside so you can freshen up." Iah clapped a hand on his son's back. "Orion will show you to the washroom, and when you're finished, feel free to join us at the table for lunch."

"Thank you," I said. "This is the first time I've felt safe in weeks."

The age lines around the doctor's eyes creased. "It's my pleasure, Elara." His smile grew as he glanced at me and my brother. "And if it's not too bold for me to say—the two of you look exactly like your parents."

His simple words warmed my heart. Even Cyrus, still fuming about the Idalia comment, returned Iah's kind gesture with a grin.

"Why don't you guys come with me?" Orion said, waving a hand over his shoulder.

Cyrus waited for the Lunins to step over the threshold before pointing both of his middle fingers at the door. "After you, sis."

I laughed hard. This rare opportunity left me no choice. I had to remind him of the words he shared with me the first night we met Idalia, the night my jealousy showed its ugly face.

Lowering my voice to mock my brother's, I said, "Orion has shown us nothing but kindness."

He glared and stepped in front of me right before I moved through the doorway. Over his shoulder he asked, "Are you done with your performance, or should I expect an encore?"

"Depends on the audience."

Scowling, he tried to close the door in my face. I caught it right before it slammed into my nose. Wanting to end on a high note, I shoved Cyrus into the wall while hurrying to grab Jax's bag from the couch. My head snapped backward when he yanked my ponytail. I whirled and slapped him in the chest. He stuck out his tongue, then snatched the bag from my hand.

The two of us poked and elbowed each other like a pair of six-year-olds until we reached the hallway—the private wing in Iah's temporary hospital.

Our humor, along with the bloodstained rainwater on our clothes, dripped onto the wooden floorboards. Not wanting to disturb Jax, we tiptoed down the hallway after Orion.

The Lunin twisted the second doorknob on the right, then waved a hand at the world's smallest bathtub. "Pump the handle a few times to get the water running." He pointed to the cabinet above the toilet. "There are clean towels in there and—" His voice faded as he observed my appearance.

"I have clothes," I said, patting the bag in Cyrus's arms.

He let out a relieved breath as he ran his fingers through his black hair. "Good, because that's one thing I can't help you with."

My cheeks flushed when he caught my eye, a tiny smirk tugging at his lips. Cyrus cleared his throat.

"Right." Orion shoved his hands into his pockets and spun around. "I'll be in the kitchen with my dad." He spoke over his shoulder while he walked. "Join us when you're done."

My brother stilled until Orion rounded the corner. Before I could blink, he grabbed my arm and pulled me into the washroom, closing the door behind him.

"What was that, sis?"

"What was what?"

He flicked my pink cheeks.

"Stop it," I said, slapping his hand away.

"Is it because he looks like Jax?"

My mouth gaped. *Bastard.* I slammed my fist into his gut.

"Damn it, Elara. That hurt."

"Keep it up, bro. Next time my knee finds your balls."

He used his hand as a talking puppet while mocking me in a high-pitched voice. "Keep it up, bro."

"Shut up," I muttered, pushing him toward the bathtub. "Go get cleaned up."

"Okay, mom," he said, the talking puppet speaking for him once more.

"And you might want to rinse twice. You smell like shit."

"So do you," he said, pulling off his shirt.

I gagged when he threw it at me with a direct hit to the nose.

Cyrus burst into laughter while I wiggled out of the washroom like a spider had climbed down my back.

"Love you, sis."

I shut the door without responding, the taste of bile lingering in my mouth. *I can't wait to brush my teeth.*

My head turned to the left. I strained my ears to hear the whispers coming from the kitchen.

"They seem like nice kids."

Kids? I feel like an old lady after everything we've been through.

"Yeah. Elara's very nice."

The warmth returned to my cheeks.

"And her brother?" Iah asked.

"He's cool, but I can tell he's very protective of his sister."

Someone let out a long sigh followed by a pat on the back. I slid my feet closer, cupping my hand around my ear.

"Orion, you know Solins have short tempers."

"Did you see how upset Cyrus got when I mentioned Idalia?"

My jaw cracked open. *Clever, boy. He picked up on it.*

"No, I didn't notice, son."

I got comfortable and leaned against the wall, eager to hear more, but the sounds of food preparation drowned out their quiet voices. A pot clanged against the grate of a stove, drawers opened and closed, and liquid filled mugs. *I hope that's water and not Maragin. The last thing we need is another appearance from Rico.*

Tired of standing in the hallway, waiting for Cyrus to finish freshening up, I weighed my options: hang out with Iah and Orion or check on Jax. *The doctor said to let him rest.* I leaned against the wall with my neck turned ninety degrees to the right. *But it's not like I'm going to wake him. I just need to see him with my own eyes—make sure he's okay.*

Like a stealth snake, I slithered down the hallway and peeked around the door. My pulse quickened. Jax lay on his back with a clean gray comforter pulled just above his hips. His torso was wrapped in enough gauze to rival a mummy at a museum. A splint concealed his broken hand, and the lacerations on his face were compacted with different colored powders. More gauze circled his head, and his eyes were still swollen but free of blood.

My chest quivered with a small breath as I pushed open the door. *Damn it.* I froze, the rusted hinges creaking loud enough to blow my cover. Moving in slow motion, my feet guided me toward the bed. I stood beside the Lunin with a heavy heart.

"Jax," I whispered. "I don't know if you can hear me." His eyes moved behind closed lids. I glanced at the door. Steadying my breathing, I rested a hand on his bandaged bicep and said, "You're safe now. Everything is going to be okay."

Taking my chances, I leaned over the bed and pressed my lips against the gauze on his forehead. The muscles in his face twitched. *Uh oh.* I pulled away right as Orion stepped into the room.

"Elara," he whispered, hurrying to the bed. "You heard my father. Jax needs to rest. It's crucial that his brain activity stays limited right now. His body needs to focus on healing, not chatting."

"Sorry. I just needed to see him in a better state than he was in when you dragged me out of here."

Orion looked at Jax before finding my eyes. "I understand," he said, touching my arm. "Come on, lunch is ready. You'll feel better after you eat."

The Lunin's prediction proved true. The weight of the past twenty-four hours lightened when my teeth sunk into a warm roll. I moaned. The soft dough tasted like a sweet pretzel.

With a full mouth I said, "Thank you so much, Iah. I don't know the last time I ate."

He smiled, pouring a ladle of stewed meat and vegetables onto my plate. My eyes blurred with desire when I held my face over the steam and inhaled. The fragrant aroma was like nothing I had ever smelled. I dove in. Roll in one hand, fork in the other.

My brother stepped around the corner with wide eyes. "Oh man, that smells amazing."

"You better hurry before I eat it all."

Cyrus's blond hair glistened with beads of water as he pulled out a chair. I chuckled. He started reaching for food before taking a seat.

"Did you get enough?" I asked, taking a sip from the silver mug.

He shook his head, food falling off his plate. "I'll probably go for seconds, thirds, and fourths."

"My father is an excellent cook," Orion said, lowering himself onto the chair across from me. We knocked knuckles while reaching for a roll. "Ladies first." He grinned.

I ignored my brother when he cleared his throat for the second time in less than an hour.

Iah rested his elbows on the table and blew into his tea cup before asking, "Care to share the details of your plan?"

I stopped mid-chew. "What plan?"

"Defeating Zenith."

Orion smacked my brother on the back when he choked on his food. I blinked, taking another sip of water. "Not one for small talk, huh?"

Iah lifted the thin rim to his lips. "Just a curiosity."

My brother hit his chest, trying to dislodge the piece stuck in his throat. I grimaced when he let out a loud burp. "How do you know we plan on defeating Zenith?" he asked Iah.

"Rumors have spread throughout the villages about these twins from Earth stirring up trouble. I'm curious about the details of your plan because I know what Zenith is capable of doing."

"I think everyone does."

Iah met my gaze. "Perhaps, but I knew the man for the first half of his life. I saw the horrors with my own eyes."

Speaking as one, my brother and I stammered, "You knew Zenith?"

"Yes. For the first eighteen years of his life."

No way. I rested my fork on the table. "Were you the doctor who delivered him?"

"No, at the time I was an apprentice, though I was present for his birth."

I eyed Orion. He picked at the meat on his plate, already familiar with the story.

"I worked for his father," Iah said, "his adoptive father, Taurus."

Cyrus sniffed the liquid in his cup.

"It's water," I reassured him.

He took a small sip, then asked, "What was his dad like?"

"Taurus was the most highly sought out doctor on Aroonyx, and the medical advancements he discovered saved many lives. He was the one who crossbred two herbs and created Yarfrey, the powder we administer in wounds that helps the blood clot and prevent infection."

It's about time someone told us the name.

"Everyone respected Taurus, including Arun." My brow furrowed. Iah clarified by adding, "This was at the beginning of Arun's reign, when he still had a positive impact on the people."

The lines on my face softened as I reached for my fork.

"Taurus and Arun were very close." Iah's eyes drifted to the past. "Their romantic relationship blurred into their professional one—giving Taurus an advantageous position."

My brows lifted to my hairline. "Wow. I had no idea Arun was—"

"Homosexual?"

"Uh—"

"Does it matter?" Iah asked.

"No," I stammered. "It just took me by surprise."

Cyrus nodded with wide eyes.

"Arun kept it a secret until he met Taurus."

I scooted my chair closer to Iah, fully engaged in the story while Cyrus added more food to his plate.

"My life changed when Taurus selected me as his apprentice. It was the opportunity of a lifetime. More mature than most eighteen-year-olds my age, I couldn't wait to get started." Iah rested his cup on the table. "Back then doctors treated patients out of their homes or made house calls. The first clinic opened after Zenith became leader."

"How was it working for Taurus?" I asked.

"Eye opening. The man was a genius in his field. I would have never tried that new procedure on Jax had I not worked under Taurus's guidance. He always pushed the boundaries with medicine." His lips pursed. "Along with every other aspect of his life."

I pushed away my plate, and it wasn't because of my full stomach. Noting the change in Iah's tone, Orion straightened, his sapphire eyes glued to his father.

"Being a Lunin, Taurus had a sharp mind, but a bad habit of internalizing his emotions. He was quite moody unless Arun was around. Time passed, and everything took a turn for the worse when Saros showed up."

I shifted my weight on the hard seat. "What happened? What did Saros do?"

"Nothing, but at the same time—everything."

"Care to elaborate?" my brother asked.

"When Arun learned of Saros's ability to jump to Earth, he presented him with the title of Seeker."

"Yeah, Jax told us about the history of the Seekers."

"But did he tell you Saros is the reason Zenith turned out the way he did?"

My hands fell into my lap. "No. No he didn't."

"It's not a story Zenith cares to share," Iah said. "Arun put all of his energy and time into Saros and the other Seekers. This created a rift between him and Taurus, and their relationship ended when Arun named Saros his closest advisor."

"Were him and Arun—"

"No. They were just friends. Saros was dating a woman at the time."

Indifferent, Cyrus reached for another roll.

"Let's see"—the doctor counted on his fingers—"ah yes, I was around twenty-two when Taurus started acting strange."

"How so?"

"His casual mood swings shifted to aggressive. The two of us would be working on an experiment, and the smallest thing would set him off. For example, I dropped a beaker. It didn't break, but that was all it took for him to erupt with anger. He threw everything across the room, then made me clean it up." The doctor blew out a tight breath. "I started dreading going to work."

I thought of the story Archer shared about Zenith's reaction to the training exercise with Elio. *Taurus is sounding very similar to Zenith.*

"One morning a woman knocked on Taurus's door. I stumbled backward when it opened because she was holding her stomach and bleeding everywhere. I brought the woman inside and laid her on the bed, then yelled for Taurus, telling him we had a patient in labor.

"The woman screamed at the top of her lungs while he prepared for the delivery. The room got dark—really dark, like night had fallen. Confused, I ran to the window and saw the twin moons blocking the light of the sun."

I mouthed, "The solar eclipse," to my brother.

He mouthed back, "Damn."

"The celestial event lasted for long minutes, and during this time, Taurus delivered the child. I'll never forget the look on his mother's face when she saw her son. Bewildered by his strange appearance, she touched his jet-black hair, then brushed a thumb over his bronze skin. Taurus was the one who pointed out his eyes: one orange and one blue."

"Zenith." I sighed, sinking in my chair.

Orion rested his hands behind his head as he leaned back, and when he found my eyes, he gave me a subtle head nod, confirming my theory.

Intrigued, my brother leaned forward and asked Iah, "Did his mother die after childbirth?"

"No, Taurus allowed her to stay the night. She left with the infant the next morning. Four years later, my mentor brought home a young boy with black hair and tan skin. I knew it was the same child when I saw his unique eyes. Taurus explained that the woman could no longer care for her son, so he adopted the boy and decided to raise him as his own."

The doctor paused to take a bite of food. His mouth moved slower than a cow chewing its cud. I watched his lips, anxious to hear the rest of the story.

He swallowed, took another sip of tea, then dabbed his chin with a napkin before speaking once more. "The two of you have had a long day. Why don't we finish this conversation at a later time?"

I knocked my knee on the table as I rose to my feet. "No, we want to hear the rest now."

Orion smirked at my overzealous behavior.

"I mean, if you're willing to tell us, that is."

"Very well," Iah said, motioning for me to take a seat. "Taurus treated Zenith with great kindness for the first few years. He gave the child everything: private tutors, expensive clothes, handmade toys from popular vendors, and then suddenly it stopped."

"Why?"

Iah turned his attention to my brother. "Jealousy."

My face squished up with a mixture of disgust and confusion. "Of his own kid?"

"No—he was jealous of Arun's relationship with Saros, so Taurus took all of his anger out on Zenith." I gulped. "He beat that poor child throughout the day. Taurus would take 'breaks' only to come back with bloodied fists. I made the foolish mistake of voicing my opinion one day." Iah stared at the tea in his cup. "Unfortunately, I made it worse for Zenith.

Taurus locked the child in the attic and starved him for days, weeks at a time."

A cold spot formed in my stomach when I thought of the way Zenith treated Jax as a child. I shook my head in disbelief. *It all makes sense now.*

"The man even performed experimental procedures on the child. Things we would only try on cadavers, things too dangerous to try on the living. The screaming was unbearable. I couldn't focus on my work, and patients stopped visiting Taurus because of the distraction."

Cyrus leaned back in his chair. "Well, no wonder Zenith's so *fucked* up." He grimaced at Iah. "Sorry about the language."

The doctor shrugged. "I'm sure it has a lot to do with the way Zenith is now."

"Besides speaking with him, did you ever try and stop Taurus from torturing Zenith?"

"That's one of my biggest regrets in life, Elara." A deep sadness filled his blue eyes. "I was a coward. One day, Taurus brought me to the attic. It looked like something out of a nightmare. Chains crusted with blood hung from the ceiling, beakers filled with tissue samples lined the perimeter of the room, the smell of waste and vomit was as thick as fog, and that poor boy was strapped to a blood-stained table."

I pushed my plate farther away as my stomach churned with nausea.

"Taurus wanted me to assist him with a procedure. He was determined to change the color of Zenith's orange eye to blue."

"What is wrong with people?" Cyrus found my eyes. "Taurus sounds like Dr. Mengele."

I nodded, remembering the evil man who performed twisted experiments on children in concentration camps during World War II.

Unfamiliar with Cyrus's reference, Orion clasped his hands and rested them on the table while Iah continued.

"I couldn't do it. Not because my hands trembled while holding the syringe, but because I couldn't torture a child."

"Then how does that make you a coward?"

"Because I didn't do anything to stop him. I stood there and watched Taurus perform the gut-wrenching procedure."

I shut my eyes, the courage exercise with Samson replaying in my mind. *Lunins tend to hesitate, or worse, do nothing at all.*

"That was the day Zenith lost all respect for me."

"How old was he then?" Cyrus asked.

"Ten. Taurus started torturing him at the age of six and didn't stop until he came of age."

I stumbled over my words. "He treated him that way for twelve years?" Iah nodded. "Because he was jealous? That seems a little intense."

"Yeah, I'm confused," Cyrus added. "Why did Taurus adopt Zenith? Did he want a child?"

"I have my theory, if you care to hear it." Our heads nodded with great enthusiasm. "The jealousy he harbored about Arun's relationship with Saros only festered over the years. Before the Seeker came along, Taurus escorted Arun to public events. They were attached at the hip, inseparable. Arun had something special—a Seeker. Taurus thought if he had something equally special—a child born during a solar eclipse who looked different than the others—then maybe, he could repair his broken relationship with Arun."

My head spun, baffled by the chain of events. "But Taurus didn't know that Zenith could share both Solin and Lunin traits."

"That didn't matter. The man was desperate. He brought the child to Arun—an unexpected visit that didn't go well. Saros told Arun to stay away from the boy. He sensed a darkness around him."

My eyes lit up with an awareness. *The Seeker's powerful intuition. Jax said he gets these strong feelings—gut feelings that usually prove true.* I stifled a gasp. *Saros knew Zenith would turn.*

Catching on, Cyrus said, "I bet Taurus didn't take the news well."

"No. That was the first time he beat Zenith. He realized he was stuck with a reminder of his failed relationship with Arun."

"This is mind blowing," I said, using my hands to demonstrate. "Everything makes so much sense now. I feel bad for thinking it, much less saying it, but damn—poor Zenith."

Cyrus scowled. "Poor Zenith, my ass. You do realize that because of that man, your boyfriend is hanging onto life by a thin thread."

Orion's head popped up. I winced, my brother's words punching me in the gut.

"Yes, Cyrus. I was there when we rescued him, and I was there when Pollux sliced Archer wide open." He looked away. "All I'm saying is that it's messed up to think about Taurus torturing Zenith for his entire childhood. Jax spent half that time with Zenith and look how screwed up it left him."

You could have cut the tension in the room with the knife in my back pocket. Everyone looked in opposite directions, pretending to blend in with the walls or the rug under the table.

Iah inhaled a slow breath, then cleared his throat. "Elara, if it makes you feel any better, Zenith got his revenge when he came of age."

"I don't like revenge. It leaves a bad taste in my mouth."

"Unlike my sister, I'm okay with it."

I pinned Cyrus with a long stare.

Ignoring me, he asked the doctor, "What did Zenith do?"

"He poisoned Taurus—with Minlav." Our mouths gaped. "Shocking, I know. That's why, when triaging Jax, I mentioned that ingesting a large dose of Minlav at once can kill a man in a matter of minutes. I know this, because I witnessed it with my own eyes."

"You saw Zenith poison Taurus?"

Iah found my curious eyes. "Yes. Zenith was in charge of preparing his father's meals, and one evening as I was leaving, I watched him grind an herb, which I later discovered was Minlav. He sprinkled it into his father's cold stew. At the time, I didn't think anything of it, but when I returned to work the next morning, Taurus didn't answer the door. Zenith did, and he was wearing his father's clothes, the same shirt and pants Taurus wore the previous night—the night he was murdered."

My throat bobbed. *This story is getting a little creepy.*

"I asked for Taurus, and in a calm and silky voice, Zenith said, *Your services are no longer required.*"

On the edge of my seat, I asked, "What did you do?"

"I left, only to turn around when I got halfway home."

"Why?"

"My medical bag. I didn't bother to take it with me the night prior because I thought I still had a job. Working for Taurus didn't pay a lot, and medical supplies were costly back then. If I wanted to start my own practice, I had to get that bag."

I rubbed my clammy hands on my shorts. "So what did he say when you came back to get it?"

"Zenith had left for the day—or at least I thought he had." Goosebumps covered Iah's arms as he let out a deep sigh. "I opened the front door and called his name—no answer, but a flicker of light caught my eye from the attic. It was a direct shot from the foyer, straight up the stairs." He shifted his gaze between me and Cyrus. "The door was cracked open."

I stilled.

"Please tell me you didn't go up there," Cyrus murmured.

"I did." The doctor shut his eyes while he spoke. "I should have turned and ran for the hills that day, but my curiosity got the best of me. You see, the attic door was never left open."

I wiggled in my seat, my eyes glued to Iah.

"Working with Taurus in the medical field taught me to ignore what most find grotesque or gory." His eyes shot open. "But I forgot everything I learned the day I walked into the attic."

I held my breath. *This can't be good.*

"The smell of Minlav overwhelmed me, confirming my theory about Taurus's death. Zenith had mutilated his adoptive father's body—in ways that are unimaginable. Parts were pieced together in abstract ways: fingers replaced with toes; an arm attached to the chest cavity; Taurus's pale hand holding the heart; and his mouth had been sliced from ear to ear, then sewn shut in a disturbing pattern as if Zenith had tried to spell a word—lies—yes, I think it said lies. The strangest part was that Zenith had successfully changed the color of Taurus's blue eyes to black, but they were no longer in the sockets."

"Then how did you know he changed the eye color?"

Apprehension clouded Orion's blue irises as he looked at his father.

Ignoring his son's silent request to skip over the next part of the story, Iah said, "Because Zenith was holding them in his hand when I turned around."

A four-letter curse word shot out Cyrus's mouth. I repeated it with minimal effort. *I'm listening to a morbid audiobook I can't turn off.*

Breathless, Cyrus asked, "What did Zenith do?"

"In the same calm and silky voice, he said, *Iah, perhaps you should get your ears checked. Did I not say, your services are no longer required?* I stood there trembling. He moved closer, rotating Taurus's black eyes in his hand like marbles. When I told him I forgot my bag, he said, *I'm aware of this. I put it outside on the doorstep after you left.*"

My mouth gaped. "You walked right past it?"

"Yes. Sometimes we're oblivious to the obvious." I cursed again and the doctor added, "Zenith's posture shifted, and a fierceness filled his eyes when he spoke. He said, *You are to leave this house and forget everything you saw here today. If not, I will hunt you down and make you pay for the crimes you committed against me.*" Iah massaged his temples. "Crimes. That's when it hit me. Zenith saw me as a coward, the man who could have saved him but didn't.

"So I ran downstairs, grabbed my bag, and moved to the opposite side of town—the West Village. News of Taurus's death traveled throughout the villages. This was years after the Clearing of the Seekers and Arun's death. Zenith planted rumors about his father's demise." Iah used air quotes to say, "Natural causes," then added, "and seven years later Aroonyx had a new leader."

I tossed up my hands. "I don't even know what to say."

"There's nothing left to discuss," Orion said, speaking for the first time since our collision at the bread basket.

The sound of an agonizing scream caused Iah to scramble to his feet and rush toward Jax's room.

Orion looked at my brother. "Why don't you take Elara outside?"

"Come on, sis. Let's go."

I covered my ears, not wanting to add a soundtrack to the horror movie I found myself starring.

The two of us collapsed onto the porch chairs. I leaned forward and rested my head in my hands. Staring at the Clear Stone floor, I said, "That was the craziest shit I've ever heard."

"Agreed." My brother mirrored my defeated posture.

I waited for a gust of wind to pass before asking, "What's the plan, Cyrus? How *are* we going to defeat Zenith? Rescuing Jax has changed everything. We can't go into the villages now. You heard Archer, Zenith knows we burned Elio's face with my hand. He knows about our little trick."

For the first time ever, uncertainty fogged Cyrus's amber eyes, and in a voice saturated with doubt, he whispered, "I don't know, sis. I don't know about anything anymore."

THIRTY-EIGHT

Never Play with Matches

We scratched Samson's plan after our eye-opening conversation with Iah. Jax was the missing piece we needed to defeat Zenith. Both men had troubled pasts, though the latter surpassed the first with flying colors. *Fight fire with fire* were Cyrus's words of wisdom. I agreed, for I was in no rush to see Pollux or Zenith anytime soon.

Over nineteen sunrises had passed since our daring rescue. My brother's observation about the advanced medicine on Aroonyx proved true because Jax's injuries recovered faster with each day. He was never coherent for more than a few minutes at a time, and everyone kept me away, which drove me mad. I wanted a reason, but they always brushed me off by saying *Jax needs his rest.*

I groaned, unable to get situated in the confined space. With Jax staying in the spare room, my brother slept on the couch while I lay sideways in the armchair.

I giggled. His large stature left him hanging off the sofa, the blood draining to his head. *Figures. Leave it to Cyrus to look peaceful while sleeping in an awkward position.*

I played with the ends of my hair while reviewing the past few weeks. Cyrus bided his time with Iah, learning everything he could about medicine. *Saving someone's life is all it takes.* That's what Iah told me anytime I teased my brother about his new role as medical assistant.

Every morning we trained in the woods around Iah's home. We tried to mimic Samson's teachings, though we didn't spar with knives or knuckles. Hell, most of the time we just stood in the woods and chatted about random events while perfecting our aim.

I spent my free time with Orion while Cyrus attended to Jax's injuries with Iah. We would relax in the shade of the tall trees or swim in the nearby spring to stay cool. The young Lunin was a kind and gentle soul who always listened to my never-ending rants: how much I missed Earth, how I longed to see my adoptive parents, how challenging it was for me to leave Archer behind. The list of complaints went on and on, but Orion never showed a flicker of irritation, and he only interrupted to share words of encouragement. Not the type Cyrus offered. Orion's words had a softer quality—a less harsh approach.

The only problem with Orion was his striking resemblance to Jax. I constantly made an effort not to call him by the wrong name. Unlike the ex-Collector, Orion was raised in a loving home, and it reflected in his caring and warm personality. This Lunin didn't keep any secrets from me.

I blew a hair out of my eye. *I can't sleep. I shouldn't check on Jax, but everyone else is in dreamland. What's the worst that could happen?*

I started down the hallway, then paused, remembering his blade. *Idalia was right. It's time Jax gets his knife back.*

Careful not to make a sound, I reached into the gray bag that hung near the front door. I chuckled. *Oh Cyrus.* His entire upper body had fallen off the couch, arm wrapped around the leg of the coffee table. Unfazed, his eyelids twitched with REM sleep.

Hoping to go unnoticed by Iah and Orion, I tiptoed down the hallway. When I got to Jax's door, I glared at the hinges. *Make one sound and I'll pull you apart with my bare hands.*

My threats worked. They didn't squeak when I opened the door. Thanks to my Lunin vision, I could make out every detail of the dark room: the window, nightstand, closet, even the colors of the bedding.

My heart warmed as I approached Jax. He looked like a new man compared to the day we rescued him from Zenith's. Fresh scars covered his pale face, but the jagged lines couldn't hide his striking features. His black hair fell into his closed eyes and his muscular chest rose and fell with slow breaths.

Stop it. That's inappropriate. The man's sleeping. Too late. My eyes wandered to his toned abdomen, the eight-pack flexed even while he slept, accentuating the sharp V lines that traveled under the covers.

I scolded myself once more before placing the knife on the bedside table. As if playing spin the bottle, I flicked the handle and watched it rotate counterclockwise. My breath hitched when it pointed to Jax.

I rested a hand on his bicep, careful to avoid the tender scars. His skin tightened. *I'm in deep trouble if Iah finds me in here.*

Throwing caution to the wind, I reached for the piece of hair that hung in Jax's face. His eyes shot open.

Everything moved in slow motion when he grabbed my wrist. I whimpered at the pain that radiated down my forearm.

"Jax," I begged. Silence. No response. I winced as he tightened his grip. *He's going to break my wrist.*

Before I could scream for help, he dropped my hand, flew out of the bed, and reached for my neck. A second later, he slammed my body against the wall. I saw stars when the back of my head collided with the wooden panels. My lips moved, but no words came out. I choked and sputtered, my feet dangling off the ground.

"You." Jax's nostrils flared. "You . . . did this to me."

My eyes bulged. I tried tugging at the hand wrapped around my neck—no luck, he squeezed harder. I gasped, hitting his arm.

"Jax," I mouthed. "You're not . . . at Zenith's."

Hearing his adoptive father's name sent a river a fury surging through his veins. As if shocked by an electric current, his body twitched, causing my head to twist in an awkward angle. My vision blurred.

Jax blinked, equally surprised by the sudden jolt. He shook his head, and when he moved his face closer to mine, I noticed his pupils constrict to the size of tiny pin holes. In a threatening tone, he growled, "And now you're going to pay . . . for your crimes against me."

The Lunin's face darkened along with the rest of the room. *Crimes. That's what Zenith told Iah the day he found Taurus's body.*

My brother hollered Jax's name as he rushed into the room, then plowed his shoulder into the Lunin, sending him tumbling to the ground. My limp body slid down the wall.

Jax held his ribs and spit blood onto the floor before crawling to reach my neck once more.

My brother yelled, "Snap out of it, Jax!" and dove to the ground, restraining the ex-Collector as best he could in a reverse ground hold. Two heartbeats later, Orion and Iah rushed in, their eyes wide with shock.

"Get Elara out of here!" Cyrus hollered at Orion.

"Hold him," Iah instructed, filling a syringe with a clear liquid.

My brother wrapped his arms tighter around Jax, who struggled with every breath to break free.

Orion scooped me up in his arms and ran out of the room. The last thing I saw were Jax's heartless eyes watching me go.

Orion lowered me onto the porch chair, then kneeled in front of me. "May I take a look?"

I didn't nod, and I couldn't speak. The pain was too much.

I winced as his cool hands pressed on my neck.

"Sorry," he whispered. "I'll be gentle."

I shut my eyes. Orion turned my head to the left and then to the right before making me look up and down. After the short examination he asked, "Can you open your mouth?" while massaging my sore jaw. When I did, he said, "Now say ah." Orion looked into my mouth, his eyes squinting at the back of my throat. "Your airway is clear, but your neck is swelling. I think your larynx has some mild bruising." He brushed my hair off my shoulders. "I can give you something to help ease the pain."

I waved him away. *Pain? He thinks my neck is causing me pain?* My eyes welled with tears.

"Or not," he murmured. "It will take a few days to heal. My father has some sublingual drops you can take for the swelling. Your voice will sound a little hoarse for a few days, and don't freak out if you cough up some blood."

I huffed a raspy breath. *Like a little blood bothers me anymore.*

Orion took a seat beside me, and after a few minutes of silence he said, "Elara, this is why we didn't want you going in there."

I glared at the trees, and in a hushed voice that sounded like I suffered from laryngitis, I said, "Because you knew Jax would try to kill me?"

"No, but my father and I are aware of his fragile mental state, and we haven't a clue about the side effects of an antidote injection to the brain."

I clenched my fists.

"Jax is not in a good place, Elara. He was tortured for over three weeks, and that was the first time he's been out of that bed since he arrived. He probably thought he was still at Zenith's."

"No. He knows he's not there anymore. He knew who he was holding against the wall."

The Lunin twisted to face me. "Please don't listen to anything that comes out of Jax's mouth right now. He's unstable. That's why my father and I must keep a close eye on him at all times."

I winced, trying to swallow. "Why?"

"Several years ago, Zenith released a man after torturing him to the brink of death. My father treated his injuries. Physically, the Solin recovered, but mentally"—Orion paused, tossing the hair out of his eyes—"the damage was irreversible. A farmer found his body on the rocks at the bottom of the cliff."

"He took his own life?"

"Yes. He jumped."

Through gritted teeth, I said, "I hate Zenith. This is all his fault."

"No, it's not."

Outraged, I hopped to my feet and whirled on the Lunin. "Are you mad? He's the one to blame." I coughed blood into my hand. Ignoring it, I cradled my neck and said, "Zenith tortured Jax for most of his childhood, only to do it all over again. He abuses the Collectors, murders innocent people, and has brainwashed most of Aroonyx. He's a monster."

"I never said he wasn't." Orion's voice raised. "All I'm saying is this: placing the blame on others leaves you playing the victim card for the rest of your life."

My shoulders sagged as I recalled the transformational shift I experienced outside of Idalia's. *That feels like another lifetime.*

Mistaking my silence for passive aggressive behavior, Orion added, "If you blame Zenith for how Jax turned out, then you might as well blame Taurus for the way Zenith ended up." He rose to his feet and tossed up his hands. "Hell, you could even blame Saros or Arun for Taurus's behavior." He circled his finger in the air. "You see, blame is an endless circle that goes on forever."

I crossed my arms and met his gaze.

"We all face challenges in life, Elara. It's how we react to those challenges that define us."

I blinked but didn't look away. Orion's simple yet impactful words knocked the breath right out of me.

"Taurus and Zenith chose the path of jealousy and revenge. Look where it led them. Jax could have justified his turbulent upbringing and chose the same path but he didn't—and that makes all the difference."

He's right. If you blame others for your current situation, you accept the role of victim: a person stuck living in the past, a person living the life they wanted to escape.

In a hoarse voice, I said, "Thanks for the reminder. I had forgotten the obvious."

"Anytime," he said, squeezing my hand.

My matted hair brushed against my shoulders when I looked at the door. Cyrus had stepped onto the porch without us knowing. His eyes darted between me and Orion before glancing at our clasped hands. The Lunin's fingers fell from mine as he crossed his arms.

"How's Jax?" I asked, meeting Cyrus halfway.

"Iah gave him something for sleep." He scratched the stubble on his chin before finding my eyes. "Elara, I don't want you stepping foot in that room. It's off limits right now. And when Jax wakes up, under no circumstance are you allowed to be around him without me, okay?"

I nodded, my fingers cradling my swollen neck.

Orion waved a hand at the morning light that illuminated the forest. "Elara, would you like to take a walk with me? Get out of the house for a while?"

"Yeah, that sounds nice."

Cyrus shifted his gaze between the two of us. "Sis, we need to have a little chat first." He looked at Orion. "Alone."

I rolled my eyes at his father-like tone.

"Okay. Elara, why don't you meet me at the spring when you're done?"

After flashing Orion a thumbs up, he turned and headed down the steps of the front porch.

I counted to five before asking my brother, "Is there a problem?"

He didn't answer. He just stood there, his eyes burning a hole in the Lunin's back.

My hands buzzed with heat when he moved closer and whispered, "What are you doing with Orion?"

I hesitated, confused by his interrogation. "Going to the spring like we do every day."

"Cut the crap, Elara. I'm not an idiot and neither is Jax."

"What the hell is that supposed to mean?"

"Don't play dumb. You know exactly what it means. Do you even care for Jax anymore?"

A wave of heat rushed through me as I took a step forward, closing the gap between us. "How dare you. You have no right."

"Oh, but I do. You're my sister and Jax is my friend. I have every right to ask that question. What if he would have stepped outside and saw you holding Orion's hand, huh? Talk about a slap in the face after everything he's been through."

My mouth gaped at his accusation. "Holding hands? What the hell is wrong with you? We weren't holding hands. Orion shared something that really knocked some sense into me, and when I thanked him, he squeezed my hand. We're friends—that's it."

"Does Orion feel the same way?"

"Yeah . . . why wouldn't he?"

"Because he doesn't know the details about your romantic history with Jax."

I scoffed. "When we were sitting at the kitchen table, listening to Iah tell the story about Taurus, you called Jax my boyfriend."

"Did you confirm it with Orion?"

My eyes stung with tears as I stared at the front door. "No."

"Why?"

"Because things change when your 'boyfriend' tries to kill you, Cyrus."

"Elara, Jax pulled the same crazy-ass move on me in the woods when we had our brawl."

"And that's supposed to make me feel better?"

"Yes, it is," he argued. I huffed a breath at his response. "Unlike tonight, with you in the bedroom, Jax knew what he was doing during his confession. He purposely attacked me that night, and that's not what happened with you." My brother sighed. "He needs time to heal. You can't give up on the guy."

I glared. "You think I'm giving up on Jax?"

"I think you're considering it after tonight's incident." Cyrus glanced at Orion's distant silhouette. "I see the way the two of you look at each other. Orion's smart, easygoing, and hell, he even looks like Jax." I gritted my teeth. "I get it, okay? He's the lesser of the two evils. The obvious choice for a rebound."

I gasped. My brother's words punched a hole through my fragile heart. "You think I want to move on with Orion?"

"I don't agree, but I can understand why you would."

"You, of all people, know how I feel about Jax. You saw how it crushed me when they captured him that morning on the cliffside, and you watched me sink into a pit of despair when I found out he was dead. I lost Jax, only to fear losing him again, and now he's alive, but instead of feeling at peace,

I'm living in fear because the man I love just tried to kill me with his bare hands."

"That wasn't his intention."

"Bullshit. You didn't hear the cruel words he said to me back there. Jax blames me for what happened, just like I knew he would. Crimes, Cyrus." My voice cracked. "That's what he said. He told me the same twisted shit that Zenith told Iah when he found Taurus's body."

My brother cursed, then rested his hands on my shoulders. "Listen. I don't want to get involved with your personal life."

"Then don't."

Cyrus let his arms fall to his sides. I could feel the disappointment in his eyes. He couldn't read my private thoughts, but our strong connection allowed him to see why I searched the forest for Orion, why I didn't look in the direction of Jax.

My brother lifted my chin. "Elara, as your brother, it's my obligation to warn you about the dangers in life." I found his eyes. "And I'm telling you right now . . . you're playing with fire."

THIRTY-NINE

Blurred Lines

Bothered by Cyrus's earlier lecture, I opened my eyes for the fourth time that night. I sat up in the armchair and tucked my knees into my chest, watching the moonlight dance on the coffee table.

Thanks to my brother, the visit to the spring with Orion turned awkward in two seconds flat. I overanalyzed everything: the words that left his mouth, the small gestures of kindness, every . . . damn . . . thing.

Lashing out, I gave Cyrus the silent treatment for the rest of the day. This lasted until he asked if we saw Rico at the spring. I couldn't stay mad at him for long, but it hurt like hell knowing he thought I was willing to give up on Jax so easily.

I grimaced, stretching my stiff muscles, then flashed the armchair a one-fingered gesture while walking toward the door. *The first snowfall will be here soon.* I yawned. *I better enjoy the warm weather while I still can.*

Not wanting to wake Cyrus, I opened the door just a hair and slipped through the small crack. I faced the wooden panel and held my breath as I twisted the knob, sealing it shut.

Success. Sucking in the evening air, I spun around. *Fuck.*

There sat Jax on the porch steps with his back facing me.

Adrenaline surged through my veins, my senses on high alert like a rabbit who took a wrong turn into a fox's den. *What do I do? Yell for help?* I stilled. *Play it cool. Maybe he doesn't know you're here.*

At that thought, Jax leaned forward and rested his forearms on his thighs, his scarred hands clasped together tighter than Samson's grueling headlocks.

The Lunin stared at nothing. A gust of wind blew a piece of hair into his eyes. He didn't bother to move it away.

I cleared my throat. *Shit. Why did I do that?*

He tensed.

Without thinking, I slid one foot in front of the other until I stood next to Jax. *Please don't kill me.* Remembering our little game we used to play in the woods, I lowered myself in slow motion onto the porch step beside him.

I froze when he let out the smallest of breaths. *Is that relief or preparation for an attack?*

The two of us stared into the forest, one soul tormented with thoughts of the past, one with thoughts of the future.

The trees mirrored Jax's posture. Their strong trunks stood motionless while their leaves danced in the breeze.

I watched him out of the corner of my eye, unsure if I should stay quiet, chat about the weather, or bring up the topic of attempted murder.

My hands trembled along with my voice when I asked, "How are you feeling?"

Silence. He kept his gaze forward. I shifted my weight, the Clear Stone digging into the back of my thighs. *I guess ignoring me is better than him trying to kill me.*

Mustering every ounce of courage, I turned my head and said, "I put your knife on the bedside table."

No verbal response, though his knuckles turned white.

Deep breaths. Keep it simple. "Jax," I whispered. "I'm so sorry for everything that happened." With a quivering hand, I touched his arm. "I can't imagine—"

The strange twitch—the jolt that looked like a glitch in a videogame flickered through Jax. He jerked his arm away from me, whipped around, and said the words I never wanted to hear. "Wake up, Elara. You should have never come for me."

A pained cry escaped my mouth as I stared at Jax's cold and heartless eyes. The same eyes that haunted me in the vision.

The front door swung open. My brother dashed onto the porch and was at my side in an instant. Never taking his eyes off the ex-Collector, Cyrus pulled me to my feet and pushed me behind him.

"Jax." His voice was calm—cautious. "What are you doing out here?"

Silence.

Cyrus repeated the question. Ignoring him, Jax stood and headed into the forest.

"Stay here," Cyrus whispered before hurrying after him.

My eyes grew when my brother made the mistake of grabbing Jax by the arm. He spun and charged him.

Cyrus dodged a closed fist, then held up his arms in a surrender stance. "Jax. It's me, Cyrus."

Another jolt of the unseen energy rattled the Lunin. He looked down at his shaking hands before storming past my brother. Cyrus mouthed, "Stay," in my direction before jogging after him.

"What's going on?" Orion asked, pulling a shirt over his toned abdomen. "I heard voices. Is everything okay?"

I pointed to the forest. "You heard Jax."

"What?" Orion scanned the front yard.

"Cyrus is with him."

The Lunin relaxed, taking his place beside me. "Good. We can't leave him alone right now." Orion paled when he saw my vacant expression. "Are you okay? You look like you've seen a ghost."

"It sure feels like I did."

"Did Jax say something to you?"

I nodded, refusing to meet his gaze.

"Remember what I said, you can't listen to—"

My own voice sounded foreign on my tongue when I whispered, "It doesn't matter. None of it matters anymore."

The two of us stood on the porch in silence for long minutes before Orion suggested, "Should we take a walk?"

I shrugged, indifferent to his proposal—indifferent to everything.

My feet dragged across the grass, guiding me toward nowhere like an underpaid tour guide on an excursion. Every part of my body felt numb, except for the chains that bound my heart, the chains that Jax forged without my consent.

"What's the one thing you miss most about Earth?"

I blinked, surprised by the light-hearted question. *He knows I'm hurting. Sure. I'll play the small talk game.*

"Um." I looked around the forest. "I miss a lot, but mostly the evening sounds."

"What does that mean?"

"There are animals on Earth that make sounds at night: crickets, frogs, cicadas. They get noisy once the sun goes down."

"Doesn't that get annoying?" He waved a hand at the surrounding space. "Isn't it better when it's quiet?"

I huffed an amused breath. "I used to think that until we jumped to Aroonyx, but now I miss it. It was a subtle reminder that life exists."

Orion shoved his hands into his pockets. "Do you plan on returning to Earth after you and Cyrus defeat Zenith?"

His question tugged at the chains on my heart. The intimate moment I shared with Jax on the cliffside before Pollux and the others showed up made me question what I wanted after the story ended, but now . . .

I stopped my leisurely pace to face Orion and tossed up my hands. "I don't know." He recoiled at my harsh tone. "It's really none of your damn business."

"I'm sorry. I didn't mean to pry."

"Well, you did. So next time, don't."

My hand shot to my mouth, for Jax had said those exact words to me the day in the parking lot at school.

Recovering, I touched Orion's arm. "Forgive me. I'm a complete mess right now."

He forced a smile. "You don't have to apologize."

We looked to the sky when wings fluttered overhead. A bird with black and yellow feathers soared through the forest like a colorful bullet, its wispy tail trailing behind. Before I could blink, it dashed through a hole in the canopy above.

"Winter's coming."

I stared at Orion with a gaped mouth. *Wow. Now we're both repeating Jax's words.*

"Do you think you could swing by Idalia's and pick up some warm clothes for me and Cyrus?"

"Sure thing. I'll leave after the first snowfall."

I expressed my gratitude with a tiny smile.

Orion inclined his head toward the house. "We should head back and get some sleep."

"Right." *Like I'll catch any z's tonight.*

Orion kept the mood light by asking questions about the weather on Earth, then shared the details of his childhood on Aroonyx. His calming presence lifted my spirits, and by the time we stepped onto the front lawn, I found myself laughing at his amused expression when I mentioned Cyrus's adverse reaction to Maragin.

"I think my father has a jug locked away in the pantry." He winked. "We can save it for a rainy day."

"I don't know if you can keep up with Rico. He's a clever little monkey."

Orion raised a brow. "How is he with combative training?"

"He lacks my skills, but I still don't want to piss him off."

The Lunin tossed back his head, his sapphire eyes glowing in the moonlight. "No offense, Elara." He tapped his chin, scanning me up and down. "You don't look like a very tough girl."

In a flash, I moved behind Orion, wrapped my arms around his neck, and jerked them in an upward motion. He lost his balance when I knocked my knee into the crease of his leg. Unable to breathe, he tapped my arm.

The Lunin spun around with wide eyes when I let him go. "Damn."

I chuckled. "Do you still agree with your previous observation?'

Orion shook his head back and forth with great enthusiasm. "No, ma'am," he said, placing a hand over his heart. "Allow me to retract that statement."

"Good man."

"But how are you with a surprise attack?"

Caught off guard, I stumbled backward and fell to the ground. Orion held me in a lazy ground hold with a smug grin plastered on his handsome face.

His tongue tapped the roof of his mouth. "Looks like someone needs a little more training."

His eyes grew when I rolled him onto his back, reversing our positions. He winced as my thighs squeezed his hips.

"Any final request?"

His full lips curled into a smirk as his eyes locked onto mine, and my pulse raced when his warm breath grazed my lips. "Yes, but you're not ready to hear it yet."

I shuddered a breath. My head turned at the sound of a deep sigh. There, only feet away, stood Cyrus and Jax with their arms crossed.

Shit. I scrambled to my feet as if Jax had walked into the bedroom and found me and Orion in the ground-hold position without wearing clothes.

My brother shook his head in slow motion. Jax glanced at me for only a moment before narrowing his eyes on Orion. His right hand clenched into a fist, and without saying a word, he turned and headed into the house.

Orion took one look at my brother's tense posture, then said, "I'll see you in the morning, Elara."

I nodded, watching him go.

Cyrus's chest moved with quick breaths as he stormed toward me. "Sis." He paused, calming the anger that fought to surface. "I tried to warn—"

"We're not having this conversation again."

"Yes, we are. You have no idea what Jax has been through. If you only knew the messed-up shit that's running through his mind right now—"

I shoved my brother in the chest. He didn't budge. "And how would I know that, Cyrus?" My voice raised as I motioned to the house. "Jax only speaks to me with hate-filled words. He doesn't want to talk to me about what happened. Why would he? I'm the reason for his suffering. He blames me for—"

"No, he doesn't."

"Yes, he does."

"You're wrong, Elara."

"How would you know?"

Cyrus's voice reverberated around the forest when he yelled, "Because he told me—he told me everything!" My chin hit my chest like a heavy weight. "Sis, Jax isn't right in the head. He needs time to heal. The man cares for you, I know he does." My brother glanced at the front door and sighed. "He's just too screwed up to see it right now."

A strong gust whipped around us. I shivered at the drop in temperature.

In a small voice, I said, "The first snowfall will be here soon. We should get inside."

My brother grabbed my wrist when I walked away, and I didn't turn around when he said, "Don't be like this." I twisted out of his grip, but he pressed on. "Don't close yourself off to the world."

I stood motionless, more confused and hurt by the minute. I thought of Jax before our encounter with the Inner Circle and after his capture, then thought of Orion, and the ease, the simplicity, he had to offer.

"Just give it some more time, Elara."

I found Cyrus's eyes as I spoke over my shoulder. "Funny, huh? How timing is everything."

FOURTY

A Shade Darker

Have you ever had a dream where you're trying to run and your legs won't move? You know—the frustrating one that leaves you looking like an idiot because your arms are pumping, but your feet aren't going anywhere. That's a great depiction of how I felt during the days that followed my argument with Cyrus.

The first snowfall hit Iah's home with a relentless fury, leaving the five of us trapped inside the confined space.

Iah busied himself in the kitchen with food preparation or spent his time cleaning medical supplies while Jax stayed locked in his room, surfacing only for bathroom breaks. My brother and I milled around the living room and dining area like hungry sharks, leaving poor Orion looking uncomfortable in his own home.

Iah tried to keep us occupied with small talk about his career as a doctor. I didn't listen to a word because I was too busy yelling at my brother. The term "up my ass" described Cyrus's irritating behavior to a T. Like a damn dog, he followed me everywhere. Trailed me to the kitchen, the window, the couch, the table—hell, he even waited outside while I used the restroom. The only time I got a break was when he visited Jax. Their long walk, the one they took after Jax uttered those bone-chilling words from my nightmare, brought them closer than ever. *Figures. Bastards.* They'd spend hours locked in the spare room, chatting about Lord knows what. It was like I didn't exist, like I never had a relationship with the Lunin. *Bastards. Did I already say that?*

My leg bobbed up and down. I had to pee, but I held it, refusing to let my shadow follow me for the third time that day. I waited another minute before hopping to my feet.

My brother stood from the couch.

"Damn it, Cyrus." He flinched at my sharp tone. "I'm not a child that needs potty training. I am fully capable of going 'pee pee' all by myself."

Orion snickered from the kitchen, then frowned when Cyrus flashed him a warning glare.

My brother waved me away before collapsing back onto the lumpy cushion. Colorful words tumbled off my tongue as I stormed out the living room and down the hallway. *I'm so sick of Cyrus and his—*

SMACK.

I ran head first into Jax. He gritted his teeth, holding his ribcage. Our eyes locked for a spit second when I mumbled, "Sorry."

He didn't accept my apology. The two of us knocked arms trying to walk into the bathroom at the same time.

Jax steadied his breathing and flicked his wrist at the door. "After you . . . *Elara.*"

I growled at the sarcastic way he said my name, then pushed past him, slamming the door in his face.

I took a seat on the toilet and rested my elbows on my thighs, dropping my head in my hands. *This is ridiculous. I can't keep living like this. Cyrus and Jax are driving me mad.* My head popped up. *Maybe I can live with Idalia?* I scoffed at my irrational thoughts and flushed the toilet.

I glared at the toes of Jax's boots that peeked under the crack of the door while washing my hands. *Asshole. I see how it is now.* The chains around my heart tightened as I rested my hand on the doorknob. *Why won't you talk to me?*

I found Jax in the same position I left him: rigid, arms glued to his sides, brows furrowed, stone-cold expression. I rolled my eyes, and said, "Let me know when you're done acting like a child."

No answer. I flashed him a vulgar gesture, letting my middle finger hang in front of his face for about two seconds before spinning around.

Lacking my flair, Jax responded by slamming the washroom door shut. He got his point across when the entire house shook.

❦

We stood with our foreheads pressed against the living room windows.

"Do you see him?" I asked.

"Not yet."

Using Cyrus's Solin vision, my eyes locked onto our target. "There he is."

"It looks like he got it all," Cyrus said, tapping the glass.

"Hopefully she packed us a few sets so we don't have to wash clothes every day."

"It's Idalia. I'm sure she did."

The frigid wind slapped at our faces when Orion opened the front door. He shook the snowflakes from his hair.

"Sorry it took me so long," he said, tossing the bag onto the floor. "The snow was knee deep up north."

I watched him hang his coat. He dusted more ice crystals off his face.

"Thank you so much. I can't wait to step outside."

"You might regret saying that. It's a little chilly out there."

I shrugged, helping Cyrus dig through the bag.

Orion crossed his arms. "Idalia wanted me to tell you that the villages are swarming with Collectors, and Pollux stops by every few days."

A wave of heat caused me to lose my balance. I grabbed my brother's arm when my knee hit the ground. "Easy. They have no proof we were there. Samson will keep her safe."

Cyrus nodded, then tossed me a pair of pants, a long-sleeved shirt, boots, and a fur-lined coat before carrying the bag down the hallway.

Orion frowned, watching him go. "Should we ask Cyrus if Rico wants to build a snowman?"

"Don't push him, he's a little cranky these days."

"You all are."

I rested a hand on his shoulder. "And that my friend is a true statement."

"Do you want to go for a walk after you change?"

"Yes." My lips spread into a wide grin. "Cabin fever set in—like two days ago."

"Okay. Then I'll see you in a bit."

I slipped into the washroom and hurried to get dress. The winter clothes hugged my body like a warm glove. I slid the white knife into my back pocket before putting on the heavy coat, then brushed my cheek against the soft lining as I opened the door. *Ah. Much better.*

That casual thought dissolved when I heard raised voices coming from Jax's room. Curious, I tiptoed down the narrow hallway and pressed my ear against the wooden panel. Not wanting the toes of my boots to disclose my location, I pushed the lower half of my body away from the door and strained my ears.

"I keep telling Elara the same thing." My brows furrowed at Cyrus's voice. "You have to give it more time."

"No. I've done enough damage."

"She still thinks you blame her for everything."

"I don't give a *fuck* what your sister thinks."

I held my breath.

"Watch it," Cyrus warned.

The Lunin muttered his complaints, then said, "None of this shit matters anymore anyway."

"How can you say that?"

Footsteps moved closer. *Get out of the way.* I froze when Jax answered my brother's question. "Because the person she once knew is dead."

I fell into the room when the ex-Collector opened the door. Not catching my fall, he stepped backward and let me hit the ground. Jax verbalized his irritation with inaudible words as he stepped over my sprawled-out body. His boots thumped down the hallway. I flinched when the front door slammed shut.

"Geez, Elara." Cyrus scowled, offering me his hand.

I slapped it away and climbed to my feet.

"What in the hell is wrong with you?" He pointed at the door. "You're eavesdropping on us now?"

"With good reason. What are the two of you hiding?"

"It's none of your business."

My jaw fell open. "When did we start keeping secrets from each other?"

"Elara, Jax needs someone to confide in right now."

"Then he should talk to me!" I yelled, tossing up my hands. "I'm the one he had the relationship with, Cyrus—not you."

"He doesn't feel comfortable—"

"I don't give a *fuck* if the topic of conversation makes him uncomfortable." My voice continued to raise. "Or if *I* make him uncomfortable. He owes me that much."

"You don't understand—"

"Why are you taking his side? Why are you defending him?"

"AND WHY ARE YOU NOT?"

The walls shook with the rage that shot out my brother's mouth. Breathless, I stumbled backward, then rushed out of the room.

Orion stood at the end of the hallway with his jaw cracked open. He didn't try to stop me when I stormed past him toward the front door.

Thick clouds of warmth left my mouth as I scanned the yard on a mad hunt for Jax. The sound of a knife whistling through the air signaled his location. I turned.

He stood tall while holding four spare knives in his scarred hand. With a quick flick of his wrist, he exposed a sharp blade, then hurled it at the tree. It pierced the bark, landing right beside the other knife.

I wrapped my arms around my waist and stomped through the snow. Cyrus and Orion hurried onto the porch. I could feel my brother's eyes watching my every move. I held up a hand, a silent gesture that screamed, *don't you dare intervene.*

I inhaled a deep breath of the cool air and widened my stance as I faced the Lunin.

"Jax, we need to talk." Silence. He checked the sharpness of another blade. "I know you can hear me."

"Yeah, Pollux didn't cut off my ears," he muttered.

I gritted my teeth at his sarcastic remark.

Jax raised his armed hand and said, "I have nothing to say to you," before releasing the knife.

"Well, I have plenty." I lost my cool when he lifted his arm, preparing for another throw. "Damn it, Jax. Can you stop that for like five minutes and look at me when I'm talking to you?"

The vein on his neck pulsated as he spun around, fingers gripping the handles of the knives. "What do you want, Elara?"

"I want to talk."

Jax stared at the blade in his hand while he spoke. "Do you not understand that I have nothing to say to you?"

My arms fell to my sides. "What the hell did they do to you?" More silence. *Geez. He can't even look me in the eyes.* I stood on my toes, desperate to meet his gaze.

I should have kept my mouth shut but my anger boiled over. In a flippant tone, I asked, "What? Did being with Zenith revert you to your old ways?"

He moved closer. "Yeah, maybe it did."

Not backing down, I reached for his hand. "Can you please"—I shut my eyes when he pulled away—"just tell me what happened?"

The wind blew my hair into my face; I didn't bother moving it away.

Jax glared at me with enough loathing to knock a man dead when he said, "Because of you, I was tortured for weeks, in ways that are unimaginable." His eyes filled with resentment as he turned toward the tree. "Allow me to spare you the gory details."

"And that's my fault?"

"No." He whipped back around. "I made that mistake all on my own."

"So this is it," I said, pointing at his armed hand. "*This* is who you are now?"

Jax would have killed me with the knife had I been standing in front of the tree. He threw it with enough angst to chill my warm blood. The blade wedged itself between the other two at the exact moment he spun around and yelled, "Yes! This is who I am, this is who I've always been—and being back with Zenith and Pollux reminded me of that bitter truth."

I shook my head. "Why are you lying to yourself?"

Jax exposed the blade of his gray knife and used it as a pointer while he spoke, the sharp end directed at my face. I hissed, taking a step backward.

His entire body twitched—the glitch. He waited for it to pass, then tightened his grip around the handle and said, "You, of all people, should be happy that for once, I'm telling the truth."

I knew better than to push Jax into a corner, but I refused to cower before him. My mouth moved with quick words as I followed him through the snow. "No. This isn't who you are. I won't accept it."

"Acceptance?" His face squished up in a sour expression. "What makes you think I'm looking for your acceptance? When this mission is over, I'll take you back to Earth, and you'll never have to see me again."

A low growl rumbled in my throat. He hit a nerve. "That's great you can predict the future, Jax. But did you ever think, what if you can't take me back?" He stopped his quick pace and found my eyes. "What if I'm stuck here on this damn planet for the rest of my life?" My brows raised. "Then what?"

Without a drop of emotion, he answered, "Then you'll have to move on."

"You can't be serious. After everything we've been through over the last year." I followed his gaze when he turned his head. "You're willing to throw it all away? Just like that."

"And just like that you're willing to move on with Orion?"

"That was low."

"Yeah, I heard about that," Jax said, pointing the tip of his knife at Orion, who stood with his arms crossed on the porch. "I get it. He's smart, doesn't have any baggage, and hell, as a bonus, he even looks like me."

"You're such an asshole." He shrugged. Anger surged through me as I moved my body in front of his. "Why do you and Cyrus think I want to be with Orion?"

He snickered, slipping the folded blade back into his pocket. "Oh, so even your brother agrees with me?"

My mouth gaped at the low blow. "I am so sick of everyone telling me to move on."

"Then maybe you should take the hint."

My eyes grew in disbelief. I waved a hand at the house. "I don't want to be with Orion."

"Doesn't matter to me."

"I don't want to move on."

"Ask me if I care?"

Tired of the endless banter, I dropped my head.

The wind howled around us, a referee yelling calls I couldn't hear. My frustrations and anger drowned out the noise. Hell, it made everything outside of myself disappear. I didn't shiver when the icy breeze snaked down the collar of my coat or bother to notice how the bottom half of my pants were soaked through from the shin-deep snow. *Enough with the mind games. Just tell him how you feel.*

"Do you want to hear the truth?"

"Do I have a choice?" he asked, his back facing me.

My hands shook as I took a cautious step forward, and my voice got caught in my throat when I whispered, "I want—" I paused, wrapping one hand around his bicep while the other touched his back. He froze when four little words rolled off my tongue. "I want . . . you Jax."

FOURTY-ONE

Broken Promise

Jax shut his eyes as he absorbed my desperate plea, and when he turned to face me, the chains around my aching heart tightened with enough tension to leave me breathless. I stole a glance at Cyrus, who nodded his approval before encouraging Orion to follow him back into the house.

Closing the gap between us, Jax took a hesitant step forward. His hands trembled by his sides, and for the first time in weeks, he met my gaze and held it.

I breathed hard. The white clouds that left our mouths formed one pained breath when he whispered, "I have nothing left to give you."

"I don't need anything," I said, placing my palm on his chest.

Jax's expression hardened as he pushed my hand away, and his voice raised when he said, "I don't even know who I am anymore, so how do you?"

I motioned to his body. "Because this guarded, jaded person isn't who you are."

Recoiling, he took a step backward, his nostrils flaring.

I dragged a hand down my chilled face before saying, "I don't need the details of what happened at Zenith's."

"Good, because I didn't plan on sharing."

I sighed, reaching for his hand. "But we can get through this—together."

He stared at my pale fingers like they were toxic waste. Disgusted, he twisted out of my tight grip. "Together?" I held my breath when another jolt rushed through him. He let it pass, then cracked his neck and said, "There was never a *we*, Elara." He poked me in the forehead. "You might want to get that through your thick-ass head. I made a foolish mistake one [illegible]ht, and now I must suffer the consequences—end of story."

Jax turned on his heels and stormed through the snow. *Oh, hell no.* [illegible] *tion isn't over.*

I chased after him, the [illegible] me down. I tripped over my own feet while trying to catch up [illegible] and through gritted teeth, I said, "So this is your decision. I don't get a say?"

"No, you sure as hell don't."

"Yeah, that makes sense, considering I never had a choice with any of this—did I?"

Jax scrubbed his face with both hands while muttering, "Here we go."

Side by side we walked through the snow, a pointless journey to nowhere. My mouth moved equally fast as my hands while I spoke. "Jax, did I ask you to take me to Earth eighteen years ago?"

"Nope."

"Did I ask you to appear out of thin air and turn my world upside down?"

He rolled his eyes. "So now we're playing twenty questions?"

"Yeah, maybe we are." Jax stopped his quick pace as I stepped in front of him and scowled at my finger when it poked him in the chest. "And did I ask you to kiss me that night on the cliffside?"

No answer. He only looked away. My lip quivered. *How? How can he be so cold?*

The Lunin widened his stance and crossed his arms, a posture I knew all too well. His heartless eyes stared right through me, a silent gesture that asked, *Are you done*?

I inhaled a long breath to collect my emotions, and before I could blink, the truth spilled out of me. "Jax, it crushed me when they took you that morning."

"Imagine how I felt."

I winced at the emotional bullet he shot at my heart. "I spent weeks"—my voice cracked—"overwhelmed with guilt, thinking it was all my fault."

"Are you going to cry about it?" he asked, making a pout face.

My chest caved. This careless remark filled my eyes with moisture. I looked up, willing the tears away. *Just keep going; ignore his jabs.*

I pointed at the house. "When we heard you were dead, I grieved and realized the only way I could move forward was to accept what had happened. And then I hear you're alive, only to fear losing you again." I paused as a salty drop rolled off my cheek. "And now, it's like you've risen from the grave. And what sucks, what really, really sucks is that instead of feeling at peace"—I took a step forward and slammed the backs of my hands into Jax's chest—"it feels like you've ripped out my heart with your bare hands."

The ex-Collector stilled. A darkness grabbed hold of him as he moved forward. *Shit.* My eyes darted toward the house. The porch was empty, help was nowhere in sight.

Jax spoke in a silky-smooth voice, one that oozed a lethal calm. "Touch me again, and I will."

A threat? He's threatening me? Livid, my arm swung with enough force to snap a tree branch. Not skipping a beat, he grabbed my wrist, stopping my open palm right before it smacked him in the face. I winced at his firm grip. Standing his ground, Jax tossed my arm to the side. My boots slid in the snow, following the motion of my failed attempt.

Defeated, I turned my back on Jax and dropped my head; my arms wrapped around my body like a protective shield. My teeth sunk into my lips as another tear slid down my cheek.

I pivoted at the sound of a deep sigh. Jax's eyes showed no remorse, only irritation.

He tossed up a hand. "Are we done here?"

My face fell. *No.* I stood tall and rolled my shoulders back. *Tears will have to wait.*

Elara, don't let him treat you this way. I flinched at the voice in my head. *Go on, get angry. You have every right to unleash hell on him.*

I tossed the masked figure a coin, then stormed toward Jax and said, "I don't know what's worse, thinking you were dead or looking at you now. Because this ghost of a person is just a haunting reminder of who you once were."

Jax rubbed his hands together while shaking his head at me. The wicked smirk returned, his lips twitching with angst. "Well, you know what they say?" His warm breath grazed my face when he added, "Life's full of surprises, isn't it? Sorry to disappoint."

Every fiber in my body ignited with rage. I grabbed his arm when he tried to walk away, and when he turned, I said, "*Fuck you*, Jax. You have no idea what I've been through—"

His voice exploded with malice as he got in my face. "What you've been through?"

"Yes!" I yelled. "What I've been—"

I stumbled backward when he moved closer. "No, go ahead. What were you going to say?"

"You don't know what I've been through—you weren't here Jax. We—"

"I was tortured, for every second, of every day, for three weeks."

"We didn't know!" I hollered. "Archer—"

The whites of Jax's eyes turned a bright shade of red. "No. You're not hearing me." His hand trembled when he held up three fingers. "Three weeks, Elara. One, two, three. You can count, right? Had I the chance, I would have ended my own life."

I swallowed a painful lump and looked away. Jax ran a hand over his beard before continuing.

"So, I'm sorry that *you*, Elara, got caught in the middle of it all, but the person you once knew is dead."

"No," I cried, touching his arm. "I don't believe that. I can't."

Jax knocked my hand away. He took a step closer, his eyes never leaving mine. I stilled, and when he spoke those final words, my heart fractured under the tension of the heavy chains. "Well, you better start believing it, so take my advice and stay the hell away from me."

My numb body swayed back and forth in the breeze. Once again, I had lost Jax, but this time for good. The man I loved had vanished into a dark, tangible void—a pit of despair without a rope of hope to save him.

It's over. It's all over.

My vision blurred with defeat as I looked at the Lunin. As if we had chatted about the weather, he pulled his gray knife from his back pocket and circled his arm, warming up for another round of target practice.

With nothing left to say, I stormed past him and jogged toward the house.

Cyrus scrambled to his feet when I pushed open the door.

"Sis?"

The sight of my brother pressed play on my emotions. Tears streamed down my face as I cried, "I'm done. I'm done with everything."

"What are you talking about?" he asked, rushing to my side.

I sobbed into my hands. "I can't do this anymore. I'm not strong enough. I want to go home."

Cyrus pulled me into his arms. "I know you're tired, sis. I am too, but we can't quit now. We need to wait until Jax has—"

"No." I pushed him away. Hearing the Lunin's name pulled the chains tighter. "We can't depend on Jax anymore."

"Elara, listen to me. We can't defeat Zenith without Jax's help. You have to be patient. You have to give him more time."

"Time? He's not willing to give it any more time, Cyrus. He told me to stay the hell away from him."

The Solin's lips paused when the front door opened. In walked Jax. Without acknowledging us, he tossed the spare knives onto the coffee table. They spun like oversized hands of a stopwatch, a harsh reminder of my previous words. Indifferent, Jax watched them spin, then shifted his gaze between the two of us.

"I'm leaving."

Cyrus took a cautious step forward. "Where are you going?"

"Does it matter?"

"Yeah, it does. The Collectors are looking everywhere for you, Jax." He pointed at the fresh scars that decorated the

Lunin's face. "And you're not fully recovered. Iah still needs to—"

"None of that matters anymore."

My skin radiated with heat. "So you don't care if they capture you again? You don't care if Pollux takes you back to Zenith?"

With zero hesitation, Jax said, "No. I sure don't."

I flashed Cyrus a pleading look, hoping he would intervene on the madness.

"Jax, you're not thinking straight. Why don't you—"

Laughter—unstable laughter moved the Lunin's shoulders up and down. He tapped the scar where the drill had entered his head and said, "My mind is crystal clear, Cyrus."

I held my breath. The eerie calmness in his voice sucked the life out of me. My brother shifted his weight.

"I can no longer assist you with this mission." He glanced at the knives on the table. They had stopped spinning. "My time is up."

I clenched my teeth. "You told us you would never abandon us on this mission." He shrugged. "It was all a bunch of lies, wasn't it?" Another shrug. I glared, taking a step forward. "You are a nothing more than a liar and a coward."

"Yeah." His eyes locked onto mine. "Maybe I am."

Cyrus paled, stunned by Jax's confession. A tear fell onto the floor as I watched Jax turn and walk out of the house. Another dropped slid off my cheek when he never looked back.

We stood speechless; the only sound came from the crackling logs in the fireplace behind us. Cyrus reached for my hand. I held it tight, accepting our new mission together.

Jax left me in more ways than one that day. He left me with a broken promise along with a broken heart. The Lunin had a choice—and he chose to leave—he *chose* to leave me.

I shut my eyes and thought of my adoptive parents. *We're officially stuck on Aroonyx for the rest of our damn lives.*

As if hearing my internal dialogue, Cyrus said, "Then we go back to the old plan and move forward with defeating Zenith." I nodded, unable to speak. "We'll stay here at Iah's, train our asses off, and take our chances in the villages."

Cyrus spoke in a voice that emanated authority and determination. Something inside of him had changed. My brother was ready—he had risen to the challenge.

My head turned when Orion stepped into the hallway.

"I'll stand with you," he said, walking toward us. "I'll help you defeat Zenith."

Cyrus extended his hand, welcoming the Lunin to our elite club. "I'll train you and make sure you're prepared for what lies ahead."

"I accept the challenge."

I stood beside the two men, lost in thought, reflecting on everything we'd been through over the past year. I wiped away a tear. Jax had sealed our fate. We would defeat Zenith without him by our side.

I touched my chest, searching for the warm light in my heart. It flickered—only a speck remained. *You must stay strong. Not for yourself, but for the two courageous men who stand beside you.*

The next part of our journey would be long and challenging, but somewhere inside a bit of hope surfaced. Faith: the evidence of things not seen.

I had to believe that the good in life always prevailed. I had to believe that in the end, the truth would triumph.

Orion smiled as he reached for my hand. He gave it a gentle squeeze, acknowledging his commitment and dedication to our future.

A comforting peace washed over me—acceptance. I would always love the man with the piercing blue eyes, but moving forward meant letting him go. *Jax might be the person I want in my life, but maybe*— my breath hitched when the Lunin beside me locked his eyes with mine—*Orion is the person I need.*

Acknowledgments

At times, the life of an author can be a lonely road. I'm grateful to the following people, for they keep me moving forward when I want to give up.

God—the first one to thank on my list. If that name offends you, then move on. These books would not be possible without His love and guidance.

Justin, you are my rock—the one person in my life who never falters, never gives up. I love you more than you'll ever know. Thank you for keeping me fed with smoothies and tasty treats while I spend countless hours at the computer. Thank you for making me laugh, loving every part of me, and THANK YOU for loving my characters with an open heart and an open mind.

Emerson, you are the brightest light in my life and my biggest fan. Watching you on this journey has made me a stronger person—a better mother. I'm grateful.

C.L. Ashton, words can't express the love and gratitude that fills my heart when I think of you and our friendship. You are my soul sister, my best friend, the sunshine in my life—my Idalia. Thank you for being the world's best beta reader and advisor. I love you, girl.

Mom, your constant generosity overwhelms me. Having you in my life is something I never take for granted. I don't tell you enough, so I'm going to write it down—I love you.

Dad, thank you for always believing in me and being a hard ass when needed. You are the Samson in my life. I love you to the moon and back.

To the rest of my family and friends, thank you from the bottom of my heart for your love and support.

Captain Von Trapp, I appreciate your guidance with medical terminology and combative maneuvers. You are the biggest badass I know. Thank you for your selfless service to our country.

Jay Kristoff, thank you for showing me the beauty behind the dark and twisted, and giving me the courage to tap into my hidden potential.

Tiffany White, thank you for polishing these books to perfection.

The following people have watched my journey from the beginning and have showed me a lifetime of encouragement and support.

Lucy Castro, Derek Buckler, Ashley Rafiner, April Woodard—we'll always have Vegas baby—Allen Cheesman—my book angel—Jessica Snelson, Josh Langlois, C.N. Jannain, and Carol Beth Anderson.

A huge shout out to the IAC team. Why? Because indie authors are worth it.

Once again, a very special thanks to Dan Smith of Bastille, Ryan O'Neal of Sleeping at Last, and the other talented musicians that create the magic that inspires me. Your music holds my hand through this journey, and your lyrics have shaped my characters and themes more than you'll ever know. Thank you from the bottom of my heart for your gift of storytelling.

To my beautiful readers: you are the reason I keep moving forward. Your kind messages and uplifting words dissolve the self-doubt that weighs on my shoulders. Thank you . . . for loving the characters and world I created.